KILLING TIME WITH STRANGERS

KILLING TIME WITH STRANGERS

W. S. PENN

The University of Arizona Press

Tucson

The University of Arizona Press
© 2000 W. S. Penn
First Printing

∞ This book is printed on acid-free, archival-quality paper.
Manufactured in the United States of America

05 04 03 02 01 00   6 5 4 3 2 1

Library of Congress Cataloging-in-Publication Data
Penn, W. S., 1949–
    Killing time with strangers / W. S. Penn.
        p. cm.
— (Sun tracks ; v. 45)
    ISBN 0-8165-2052-6 (alk. paper)
    1. Indians of North America—Mixed descent—Fiction. I. Title. II. Series.
PS501 .S85 vol. 45
[PS3566.E476]
810.8′0054 s—dc21
[813/.
                        99-050962

British Library Cataloguing-in-Publication Data
A catalogue record for this book is available from the British Library.

Publication of this book was made possible in part by a grant from the National
Endowment for the Arts.

For Jennifer, mi amigueta

KILLING TIME WITH STRANGERS

Chapter One

I.

Life may be a record of failure.

Take Palimony Blue, for instance. Or his father, La Vent. Their failures have been mostly failures of the heart. Both mistrust their own worth. That's a fact. And even if it is a fact that doesn't shake the foundations of the world, it sure does keep me busy. I am a spirit guide. A *weyekin*, the Nez Perce Dreamers call us. I am here in this story only to help Mary Blue bring into the world the one lasting love Pal needs to overcome the diffident shyness that runs so deep in his blood. Make her exist in words, in Pal's words, so he can refuse the consternation caused by the conquerors and passed down to Pal from his grandfathers. For La Vent, it's too late. But not for Pal. Not yet.

" 'Course you keep dropping the ball, it will be," Mary Blue says.

She has her back to me. She is kneading bread dough on the countertop by the sink. The morning light enters at the angle of dawn. It divides the plants in the bay window over the sink and illuminates the dusty air around her bent-over body, making her larger than she is. She's not a large person. She's average height. And the fact of the matter is that she is rather thin. Not skinny thin, but definitely not the size of the people who sneak handfuls of food from the bulk bins at the market.

I keep my own counsel, turning the mug of hot coffee between my cupped hands with my thumbs, and grinning, remembering how Mary Blue looked yesterday. Colorful would be the nice way to describe it. Everything about her is conservative, except for color. She wears her hair long and tied at her shoulders by a simple strand of leather or cut of yarn. Indeed, her hair is a deep brown color that reveals its secrets of dark red only in certain angles of bright light, and with her green eyes and straight nose that is only now growing wider with age, you might think she does not look the way Indians should look. Except for her dress, maybe. She most always wears long skirts that wrap around and tie at her waist and simple blouses or shirts, some of which have an open hand beaded over the left breast or some small circular design stitched into the fabric on the back. When she goes out, she often wears a serape to cover her shoulders or, if it's raining, a long scarf to cover her head like the rebozos her Mexican neighbors wear to Mass on Sundays. But colors. Mary Blue likes colors. High colors, an adaptation to the Mexican culture around her, a culture that despite all the attempts by Anglos lurks everywhere just below the surface of California, where Mary Blue lives. And yesterday, she went down to the local market wearing a bright purple skirt with a red blouse beaded on the back in white. From behind, she looked like a fuchsia, a bed of fuchsias in full bloom.

"What're you grinnin' at?" Mary Blue asks, folding the dough into a ball and pounding it with her fist to drive out the air bubbles.

That's the thing about a Dreamer. She can see things because she has foreseen them. She's made them be. Or not made them be, but made the context in which they can and will come to be. Even my grinning. Even, of course, me. I mean, as her *weyekin*, her spirit guide, I wouldn't even be in her kitchen at dawn if she had not summoned me. And without the context for it which she has envisioned, I could not be here for you, either, telling you the story until Pal learns to tell it to you for himself, teaching him the whole time to tell it and retell it until he gets it right.

"And this time, the right way," Mary Blue says darkly.

She may not be physically imposing, but she has presence, let me tell you. And I'm not grinning now. I know what she means and what she means is that so far I have screwed up royally. I have paid for my mistakes, though. That's the thing about this *weyekin* business, you screw up when you're in the shape of Pal's friend or brother, and the next time you are given form you might show up as a seagull or a corpse, a squirrel or a coastguardsman with an excess of melanin in your skin.

As you people like to say, I've been there.

2.

Wait a minute, you say? This is supposed to be a story about Amanda; now the person telling it says that he doesn't exist in my kind of time where I have to constantly juggle e-mail, beepers, and cell phone calls while driving the kids to and from day care and day-trading by laptop trying to outwit the wits of Wall Street so someday I can just do it or have it all (or both)? I'm supposed to believe that he's even been a seagull? As in *bird*? you ask.

Yep. It isn't my fault that I was never alive the way you think you are. I have never been a human being in the sense of "He was born, drank coffee, and died, may he rest in peace." But I have been imagined as existing in your world by a real human being. As hard as it might be for you to believe, that makes me more alive than a whole lot of folks. Not you, of course. You're not among the people made deaf and blinded by their unexamined lives. The walking dead don't tell stories and they definitely don't read them.

Anyway, if you ever imagined yourself as a seagull, even just for a moment, you'd understand how much fun that is. Imagine the screech and cry that come from eating all that garbage and all those washed-up scraps of fish. Imagine following the *Q.E. II* back and forth and back again waiting for the stewards to dump tons of waste into the ocean, waste you have to pick through quickly before it sinks, just so you can eat. It's boring, if nothing else. Communicating with people is nearly impossible. And you live with perpetual diarrhea and heartburn. Your only real joy comes from the dark suits or fancy hats people wear on deck which with a life of practice you can smear with seagull glop, and even that is joy that you can't enjoy fully because all you can do about it is screech and cry. You can't share it with other seagulls the way human beings can share it with others of their kind. Although given the way some people speak, I sometimes wonder. But perhaps I am too harsh.

Seagull isn't the worst of shapes, though, and I have taken many shapes and been many things. When Mary Blue first dreamed me into the world, I was only a way of knowing, and what she knew was that the shy but basically good-hearted La Vent would ask her to marry him. It wasn't until things had changed in unforeseen ways that she saw what she should have expected and, pregnant with Pal, that she began to get the idea that I could be more than a way of knowing and not until Pal was in grade school that I found myself holding down the job of a schoolboy companion or brother to the lonely Palimony Blue. Sometimes my name was Chingaro, like at the birthday party of La Vent's boss's son. Sometimes it was Parker, and finally it was Hinmot. In between, each time I failed to get Pal to dream a world in which he could properly live, were the animals, the nameless and speechless seagulls and squirrels, or the corpses—of math professors, no less—and ghostly disappearances.

It begins on the afternoon I came within moments of succeeding. I'd been playing "Uno" with Tom Yellowtail, my fellow *weyekin*, when I was dreamed into existence by Mary Blue, called by her again as a *weyekin* for Pal and given human form. It wasn't my fault, really, that I failed. If Mary had called me sooner. Maybe if I hadn't just shouted "uno," and waited to play one last card if I could. Or maybe if there were less garbage floating around in space making the journey as slow as a cautionary tale. But she didn't. And I did. And there isn't. So I arrived unprepared, only minutes before Amanda—the very Amanda I'd been teaching Pal to dream of for what seemed like forever—pulled her car back out onto the highway and drove away.

Listen.

3.

Pal was on his way home from spending the night with Tara Dunnahowe. Tara was his former girlfriend. At least, she was the girl he had imagined to be his girlfriend. I never did quite convince Pal that a girl like Tara, raised with all the Dunnahowe privilege and possession, could never live up to the image of steadfastness that Mary Blue tried to ingrain in him by means of the stories she told him as he was growing up.

Tara was not entirely to blame for the fact that she could not be true to Pal—or anyone else, for that matter, but which was not my concern. After all, someone who has everything given to her has to keep an eye out for the things she does not have or has yet to get. In Tara's case, it was cars. And clothes. And, well, yes, men. Smooth men. Ridge-bellied Roundheads, my friend Tom Yellowtail calls them. Suits is what Henny Penny calls 'em. (Oh, yes, Henny Penny, like Chicken Licken, is one of us, though she's one of us who services Anglos and other white folks. In fact, Henny was one of the original angels dreamed up by Dante Alighieri to hang around singing hosanna, stuck like a bee to flypaper on the multifoliate rose until the day God died. Chicken Licken, well, you know who Chicken Licken is. His spirit is small and afraid.)

"Suits" would be an accurate synecdoche in most cases. But with Tara's flirtations being déclassé, the men were more often cotton Dockers with corduroy jackets (in the most extreme cases, with suede patches on the elbows). Men with beards. Well-trimmed beards. Or mustaches. Or long faces grayed by serious investigation and the lost ability to talk to human beings without sucking air in through their pursed lips. Hands and lips palsied by frustration at trying to teach a sea of youngsters immunized against thought or feeling by rock and roll. In plain language, college professors. Though again, in Tara's case, they were community-college professors, men who are overworked and therefore pride themselves on teaching.

Pal, neither a suit nor a ridge-bellied Roundhead, was Tara's first and only experiment with the racial déclassé. In fact, she wanted a black man, but none of them was interested, so she settled for Pal's

Indian umber tan. To be blunt, Pal was nothing more than an interlude to Tara between an assistant and an associate professor, and the idea that she would give up fucking her teachers to remain steadfast and true to Pal was as absurd as him imagining that she would give up her high grades or her convertible sports car that looked like a bright red bar of soap. Pal, however, had been raised on stories, and when he imagined Tara, he made her steadfastness part of the story. To convince him otherwise was simply impossible, even for the best of *weyekin* in the best of Dreamer dreams.

Now it was over—at long last he recognized a certain chill in Tara's attitude—but nonetheless again true to his own naming, he remained her pal. Which meant that when she needed him, she called him. He even spent nights with her when she wanted, sleeping beside her, holding her, his erection squeezed between his thighs so as not to give offense or seem too pushy or male, comforting her and calming her worries.

At present, she was consumed by her fear that her newest lover, an associate professor of Immediate Thought and Events at Ohlone Community College, might cheat on her. Joe Manifest had gone off for the weekend to elbow others of his species at a convention on the Romance of the West and the Future of Frontiers. He presented his paper, "Whose Only Son Will Be Given Now?" at 8 A.M. on the opening day, and then stayed around to lounge in hotel bars, flipping through the hundred-page directory of papers and sessions pretending to be interested while watching women out of the corner of his eye. Tara knew the temptations. She worried that Joe might get a little tipsy and try to ball one of the cocktail waitresses, or some female historian with breasts the size of apricots—a change from Tara's breasts, which were so large as to be not only unmanageable but also the first thing other women noticed about her.

As far as Mary Blue was concerned, Tara deserved to worry these worries. Her fears that Joe Manifest would cheat on her were based on her willingness to cheat on him.

"Including you, Pal," I whispered in his ear.

The mere fact that Pal hadn't come down with crabs or worse in this age of AIDS was largely a miracle, given the number of men Tara had slept with. Indeed, for some months she had starved herself into youthful though mottled thinness so she could pick up high school boys and fuck them two and even three at a time, performing like acrobats in the seats of her red convertible.

For those things alone, Tara should spend the rest of this life and the next traveling through the hot places of suspiciousness. For the way Pal felt when he finally decided, as he was programmed by history to do, that it was he who was unworthy of her, that of course it was he who was insufficient as a friend or lover for someone as wonderful as Tara Dunnahowe, she deserved far worse. In the end, she dumped him—actually, she never really dumped him, she just forecast the end and then let him realize it. As a *weyekin*, I tried to tell him all this in whatever way I could. But Pal didn't want to hear it. He doesn't have a mean beam in his floor plan. He lacks the heart to tell Tara the story of the vision I provided him of Joe Manifest, naked and perverse, walking from hotel room to hotel room, waitress to historian, apples to apricots, his banana out and admiring himself among his permutations in the highly polished mirrors of the Banff Springs Hotel. Instead of laughing at the sight, Pal whispered, "Ssshhh. Sleep now." Instead of telling her that her kindness to strangers had set his heart back two generations, he put his arm around her like a cliché, tucked her head into his shoulder, and squeezed her gently.

"You're being silly," he said softly. "You're worrying too much. I'm sure he misses you as much as you miss him."

"You're so sweet," Tara said. "Sometimes I think I should never have let go of you." She yawned. A big yawn. A gaping yawn. "Goodnight," she whispered. And then she was gone into the land of what she called dreams.

"Let me go?" Pal wondered. He lay there in the darkness holding her, trying hard not to want to make love to her even though the press of her buttocks against his genitals made him want to howl like Coyote. "Let me go?"

He stared at the ceiling. He could not help but admire the way that, as worried as she had been not fifteen minutes ago, she could sleep so soundly so quickly. He wished Joe Manifest had kept to his professorial office and that he had not stepped out of his history and into Pal's. His arm went to sleep. His shoulder began to ache. But he didn't move. Not until the dullness became painful did he even consider moving for fear of waking Tara and making her angry at him for having disturbed her. Finally the pain was too great even for him, and he risked slipping his arm out from beneath her neck. Her head bounced on the pillow heavily and he held his breath while the feeling returned to his arm. As soon as the circulation was enough to let him, he edged his legs out of bed and got up, dressed in the dark, and let himself out of her apartment, locking it behind him. He paused to watch the moon, which he could feel was almost but not quite full, slide through the outreaching branches of the black walnut in the courtyard. The water rising to its rest and falling into the well of the fountain was the only sound he could hear. "Safe swimming," he said to the goldfish that paused and then flickered in the water. He opened the wrought-iron gate of the mock-Spanish villa and let it close slowly and quietly behind him.

4.

Old Paint waited patiently for him in the parking lot. The driver's door to the army-green Volkswagen microbus creaked loudly as he opened it and climbed in. He failed to take notice of the engine's complaints as he left Los Gatos and began driving Highway 17 up the east slope of the Santa Cruz Mountains. He felt a complete failure and the feeling made him deaf to the sound of Old Paint's Corvair engine struggling to fire on all four cylinders. As the upgrade stiffened, Old Paint lost power and slowed and Pal downshifted. For a mile or so, Paint seemed fine. After all, Paint was complaining more often lately, not like an old man who needs your attention and fears losing it so he complains to make sure he knows why he's lost it, but more under his breath like that old man's more cheerful friend who is living with pains he'd rather conceal. Wherever he could, Pal took Paint out of gear. Sort of gave him his head and let him coast, trying hard not to imagine rockets and sprockets shooting out of the engine block to light up the pre-dawn sky with the fireworks of yet another failure.

Pal wondered if he could have been more help to Tara. He hoped when she woke up in the morning—this morning, not long from now, given the absence of owls and night-hunting mammals from the hills around him—she'd feel better. He wished he could do something for her, and yet somewhere deep down inside himself he resented wishing it. But anger and resentment were not the way of a Dreamer. He knew that much. Anger only got in the way of thought and feeling, like violence gets in the way of significant action.

Abruptly, the engine lost power again. Pal let Paint slow to a crawl, double-clutched, and downshifted to second gear. When two hundred yards later he had to stop to shift into low gear, he began to realize the meaning of the noises Old Paint was making. At last, trusty Old Paint could barely lift his head high enough to limp to the roadside.

I would have known what the problem was. I've been around, after all, since the Model T—in fact, since long before the internal combustion engine. I go back before even the invention of the wheel. I know enough about cars and trucks and have such good relations with them that I can hear even a faint noise, cock my ear and identify the problem, pull off the road with you, and help you fix it without even the risk of getting your shirt dirty.

But for Pal, lamebrained as he was, to fix was to cure. And so, when Paint pulled up lame and refused to go on, although in the thinning darkness he looked into the engine compartment with a medicinely air of authority, about all he could do was to jiggle the spark plug and distributor wires, stroke Paint's fender like the haunch of his horse, and stick out his thumb, depressed by the thought that before the sun again reached where it now stood, his dear companion would be stripped and his carcass burned by the night-riding younger brothers of former amigos.

The sun rose and traffic over the mountains picked up. Pal adopted what he imagined looked like a nonthreatening pose beside the road. He hoped that one of the urban explorers crossing to the coast might actually stop and give him a lift, and he followed car after car with the arc of his thumb as they passed.

The warmth of the sun lagged a good hour behind the light of its rays and it was still cold. Pal was forced to lift his feet to encourage the circulation of blood, first one foot, then the other. His head bobbed. It became a dance in the crystal morning, something he hadn't done much of since he was a kid and La Vent took him over to the Indian Center on Saturday afternoons.

It began to feel good. Typical for him, it made him happy in his failure. It made the cars that passed him more frequently seem all the same car, passing him over and over again, circling the mountain afraid to stop or park in his neighborhood. All of them driven by the same Mr. Plaid talking sideways to his missus, both of them riveting their eyes to the road before them as though in his steering and her riding concentration neither noticed Pal standing there beside the road waving his thumb at them. He felt as though he were becoming invisible.

The morning passed into afternoon. Still he danced, pausing to rest against the capless hubs of Old Paint's wheels. His feet felt lighter, his knees lifted higher, and he began to circle and turn.

Mr. Plaid, goaded on by Mrs. Plaid, began to accelerate when Pal came into view. He no longer riveted his eyes to the road, staring down the distance, but straight at Pal as though his thumb were an insult, an outrage, a glaring immorality that made him angry that this crazy man would ask such a thing of him, Mr. Plaid, of all people. Mrs. Plaid, equally offended, began to point Pal out to her children: "Lookit, Baby Check. Look, Tartan. Look, Kilt."

Checklet, Tartan, and Kilt stared out the window at him as though he were an exhibit of old bones they were passing by on the monorail at Disneyland, or a crocodile at Steinhardt Aquarium at which they wanted to throw quarters, aiming for the eyes and nostrils.

By the time I finished my game of Uno and managed to get down there, Pal looked dejected. He had this ridiculous look of hopeful disappointment on his face. It was a look most people would have called blank and unemotional. A look that was motionless because it contained all the failure as well as all the future success that was yet to come after generations of belief that patience and humor would eventually, one day, win out over the actions of history. A look that seemed placid because it was stirred by conflicting emotions that, once spilled, would flood out and drown one's identity in the turbulence of them. It was a look akin to Mary Blue's face when she was dreaming, though in Pal's case a look still stupid with fantasy. A look more like his father La Vent took on when he began to sermonize innocent passersby from the back deck of his old taxi and the people pointedly ignored the neediness of his preachments.

I stood to the side and watched him for a few minutes. Dizzied by the sun's light beating relentlessly down on his dancing, he lost himself in fancies which I offered him, fancies of hot-wiring urinals so Mr. Plaid and Tartan would get 220 volts up their floor plans the next time they peed. As time passed, he cared less and less. He began to hear voices. La Vent's, telling him to repent. Mary Blue's. Mine.

"They're afraid of you," I told him. "Remember that the Plaid family needs to make you a dinosaur of deficiency in order to moralize their love of rape and pillage and plunderous pollution."

"I know," he replied. His face momentarily stirred with emotion. "On top of that, there're those murders."

There had been several ritual killings around Santa Cruz in the past few months. Grunged teenagers with metal studs in their tongues driving their daddies' four-by-fours out into the hills to sacrifice the little brothers and sisters they picked up after school.

It annoyed me. He was excusing the Plaids for their lack of human kindness, as though he might ever have been a murderer or rapist. Jesus, with his diffidence, he was so far from being a rapist that even his girlfriends could not always be sure if he wanted to have sex. He never wanted to impose on them, ask them to do something for him, after all.

"You asshole," I said. "When was the last time someone like you was a serial killer?"

"True enough," he said. He laughed. He was used to my calling him an asshole. "Nevertheless," he began.

"No 'nevertheless' about it," I said. "It's usually some well-to-do white guy who likes to cut up thirteen-year-old boys and eat them after sodomizing and torturing them."

"I know." He paused, taking a breather from his dancing. "You think it's in their blood," he said.

"It's in their stories," I said. "Maybe their religion, too. People like you just kill themselves."

"That's in the blood," he said.

"Nah. It's in your desire. Like La Vent."

Pal began to dance again, slowly, thoughtfully, cautiously. Suddenly, there she was. Amanda. His Amanda. The very Amanda that Mary Blue had been trying to help him dream since he had been but a boy. The Amanda he was so close to dreaming last night as he comforted Tara. Amanda. All those other women, all those failed attempts at dreaming Amanda into this world. And there she was.

She pulled her car up on the shoulder of the road. The passenger window rolled down. She leaned across her passenger in the front seat to ask Pal where he needed to go and from the first hint of her smile I knew it was she. Her smile was wide and generous, her brown eyes soft and kind as love itself. I was certain. So certain that I closed my eyes and began to think of taking a long vacation, maybe spend some time with Henny Penny or Tom Yellowtail, do some fishing out beyond Arcturus.

I heard her car start back up, and I began to wave even before I opened my eyes.

"What are you waving at?" Pal asked.

"What are you doing here? Why aren't you in that car?" I pointed frantically at the disappearing car as though I could draw it back, my visions of fishing gone to images of seagulls or worse. "What happened?"

"Headed to Watsonville," he said. "I need to go north."

"She would have taken you north. She would have driven you home. She would have taken you anywhere you want to go."

"Maybe. Except for her boyfriend. He didn't look too happy about her stopping."

"Fuck her boyfriend," I shouted. "The hell with her boyfriend. That was Amanda. Don't you know that? That was not just any Amanda. That was *the* Amanda! You freaking idiot." I began to jump up and down. "You know what this means?"

Pal ignored me shouting. He turned and looked up the road to the spot where her car passed over the rise and out of sight beyond the red- woods and spruce that lined the shale cliffs, out of which the mountain pass had been blasted.

"Maybe you're right," he said. Then Pal hung his head in frustra- tion and failure and, hearing the growl of a logging truck downshifting for a grade in the distance, tried not to cry.

Chapter Two

I.

Normally, spirit guides are not something you pass on like accumulated wealth or property in a capitalist economy, but something for which you constantly prepare your mind and heart by dreaming. By dreaming, I do not mean those nightly terrors most folks call their rapid eye movements. I mean reentering a state of mind that patiently but actively creates the circumstances in which the dreaming may take effect and become real. And the success of this reality is not measured immediately or even tangibly, but generationally, over longer periods of that unreality people call "time." To a Dreamer, time is but a construct to avoid the very kind of activity Mary Blue calls dreaming. Time is a fabrication that allows people to wear the straitjacket of being constantly out of it, in a constant hurry like the White Rabbit in Lewis Carroll's book and always late to what is always called an "important date."

Time is taught to Anglos by schooling. By going to school, they learn how to rise in the morning, salivate, eat (almost anything will do, it seems); go to school or work, salivate at midday, eat (things worse than breakfast); hurry back to school or work, salivate in the evening, leave to eat (a few workaday throwbacks even go home to eat with their spouses and children); do some homework while watching 3.4 hours of television to kill off any real dreams lurking around the bushes of the brain and thus prepare the mind for the morrow; and sleep until it is time to salivate once again. That is why school, in the West, is compulsory.

But every now and then someone wakes up enough to say, "Wait a minute, I don't want my life to be my epitaph: *'He was born, drank coffee, and died.'* " He resists the tick of the clock, looks out the sealed window of his (or her) office building like Mary Blue once meditatively looked out the kitchen window of Arturo's Mexican Cafe in which she worked, and loses himself in untimely imaginings. The difference is that the man in the building with his mind prepared by television and his life prepared by schooling imagines the things given to him to imagine, pictures, not images: sex, drugs, and rock and roll, the ownership of boats and cars and girls, journeys of escape and delusions of James Dean freedom, things which may be dismissed as daydreams or fantasies, having no basis in the past and thus no possibility in the future.

Mary Blue does not watch television because it would only serve to remind her how colorful technology was making the world of human beings colorless. Instead, when she looks out the window, she first clears her mind of things. The images that then are free to enter her mind are not pictures of things to have or get. They are images from the past and of the future that find the door of her mind open, enter, and then with her active help take shape to become a way of living in the world. With continued imagining, this way of living slowly creates the context for what is envisioned by guiding her choices as they occur, one at a time. Even little choices—actions such as answering the phone or quickening her pace so as not to be late to the cafe—are guided by this context. Phones are answered only if the solidity of her solitude is not interrupted by the ringing. And if she finds herself starting to rush too much, she stops. She knows the value of minutes. She knows that there is no such thing as "saving" time and as much as people talk about doing it, it is only a delusion invented to get them to try to lose even more time doing potentially meaningless things.

By the way, just to be clear about Mary, "meaningless" does not include sharing stories with a friend. Nor does it include playing games with children. The times she has played Candy Land or drawn Magna

Doodle with the Rota or Wasageshik children are as unnumbered as the sands of the sea. When the choices are bigger (not more "important"), she can call on her *weyekin*.

A hundred years ago, *weyekin* were mostly animal spirits. But now they include spirits like Tom Yellowtail, who once lived on the earth as a storyteller, highly honored by his people, the Coeur d'Alene. They give Mary someone to talk to. *Weyekin* can be something like what folks call a conscience, except it's way beyond simple concepts of good and bad, way past normal judgments. And they can also be agents to carry her dreaming out into the world, the way earlier people placed their sins on the back of a goat and sent it wandering into the wilderness. If the choices are huge, well, then the *weyekin* might resist her dreaming and she has to actively enter a frame of mind and heart that creates a kind of vacuum and sucks the *weyekin* out of the ozone. Mary Blue creates this vacuum by rocking rhythmically while singing or chanting to herself in solitude. By now she has practiced it so long that she can also achieve the vacuum by losing herself in repetitive tasks like making tortillas or walking for the sake of walking or by concentrating her will out of existence by complex tasks such as beading. She is so good at it that even though I never resisted much—the fact is, I liked Mary Blue with her colorful presence almost immediately—I don't resist at all, anymore. Neither does Tom Yellowtail nor, for that matter, Henny Penny, though she does get a little peckish about it, now and then. Chicken Licken is the one who complains all the time. He works with Anglos from northern Europe. "Gotta go hear them run around saying 'The sky is falling, the sky is falling' again," he complains. But that's because Licken takes it personally. His feelings are hurt by the unwelcoming accusation.

2.

The first time Mary Blue imagined me into her life it was almost an accident. I say "almost" because dreaming is not accidental, though the dream might well be. She was prepared to dream by the stories her grandmother had told her as well as by her own observations of the efficacy of actively dreaming as she watched her grandparents and parents, her cousins and brothers, move through the world.

She was working in the kitchen of Arturo's Mexican Cafe, singing a song her grandmother had taught her as her hands shaped tortillas for the customers. *"So we'll be together / So we'll be together / When human beings come together / When you find my song / When you know my song— ina / When you find your heart again / Here at the center of the earth—ina, ina / So we'll be together."* As she sang this over and over, an image took shape in her head much the way the image of the crucified Christ once took shape on a tortilla. It was an image of a young man who had lost his heart as well as lost his way in life. He was very close to deciding that he was a failure. He was not a particularly handsome young man. He had an oval face, a straight nose and straight eyes, the clearwater blue-green of which was darkened with the memory of good humor. His father had died recently. The young man was driving into the desert where his father's bungalow sat like a sentinel, out beyond the reach of county sewer and water projects, with a windmill-driven well pump and hurricane lamps for light at night. The young man was not sad. He would miss seeing his father. But it was the way of things and he thought he would never give up talking with his father, invoking his father as a kind of afterworld spirit with whom he could converse and from whom he could even seek advice. In fact, the young man was in part angry: Given his own sense of failure, his father's dying seemed to him to represent a failure of the will or heart, a large part of the failure the son had to inherit, certified by one lonely word on his father's boarding school transcripts.

The son's name—though Mary did not dream that, yet—was La Vent, La Vent Larue. He was an Osage breed, a mixblood made urban by the migration of Osage out of Indian Territory to the Southwest, as far as Los Angeles. A crossblood caught in the same tendency of contradictory feelings as Mary Blue, herself, whose mother was Nez Perce but whose father was Scots-Irish. A trapper even after there was little left to trap, he tried to transmit to his daughter his own willingness to see failure instead of future success, to feel hopeless when hope was one of the few things the Nez Perce had left, to see the glass half empty when it was half full and waiting for rain. This propensity to believe in failure, however, was not all the fault of her white father. No, failure in Mary Blue's family had been around longer than in La Vent's, for hundreds of years—from long before that sniveling Sacajawea led Lewis and Clark west, clear to the ocean. After Sacajawea came the inevitable incursions of the Methodistic missionaries who taught the Nez Perce to see even things as natural as death as additional examples of failure. That was why the Nez Perce had struck the seven drums, turned away from the half empty visions of the Methodists, and danced their way back to their old ways, the ways of dreaming.

3.

With the perspective of her own past, it is no wonder Mary Blue watched La Vent Larue sort through his father's effects with a feeling of compassion so strong that it resembled love. She saw him arrive at his father's bungalow and park. He went inside to the bedroom. From a top shelf in the closet, he took down the cardboard carton in which his father had kept his important and private papers. He sat cross-legged in the center of the floor and in the indirect light that came through the glass door, which looked east from Daggett to the Cady Mountains, the Devil's Playground, and the Providence Mountains beyond. It was a desolate place. His father had moved out there from East L.A. as a compromise between the geography of urban life and its increasing violence and the geography of the hot places of his past in Oklahoma, balancing the feeling of missing his Indian and Mexican friends against the sentimental attachment to the place he still called home. Though the place was desolate, the light was not and, as his father always joked, he had Harvard as near as Coyote Lake. And both were dry.

In that light, though without his father's innate sense of humor, La Vent took papers from the box, unfolded them, read them, and sorted them into the pile of papers to keep and the pile to discard, which remained small. He found a first-class envelope embossed with "Bureau of Indian Affairs" that warned of the federal penalties and fines that could come from unofficial use. It had no postmark. But then it had no addressee. Slipping out a single, clay-based sheet of photocopy paper, he unfolded it gently. It was from the Haskell Indian School. The date was smeared and blackened but it looked to be 1903. Expecting to find grades or marks that evaluated his father's skills in the Industrial Department where he had been trained as a welder for three years, he found only one word, printed in capitals, a word that would hang like a perception over La Vent for the remainder of his life: DESERTED. A failure, for sure, he thought, and one that could never be rectified. No grades, no record of satisfactory or unsatisfactory performance (though desertion seemed to imply dissatisfaction on the part of the authorities). No citizenship grades (he didn't stop to recall that Indians were not American citizens until the middle of his father's life). No evaluations at all, outside of those three syllables of failure.

Here, La Vent thought, here was the root and cause of what lately he felt to be happening around him, a personal sense of failure that could be phrased for lack of a better explanation as "history repeats itself." His father had failed in school. He, himself, was not failing, but he was having great difficulty being proud of his work in school and now, with the difficulty of pride, here was this inherited shame. Desertion.

La Vent never stopped to ask himself why his father had kept the transcript all those years as though he were proud of desertion.

"Isn't that his failure and not his father's?" Mary Blue wondered.

"Could be," I said, entering the cafe's kitchen a little breathless from the suddenness of my journey.

"He should see the cycle. He should know how his father went from a boy who tried to please, who wanted nothing more than to be appreciated, to a young man who discovered that Anglos would never appreciate him and so he left, to an adult who still wanted to be appreciated and who was willing to travel anywhere and weld anything for the companies he worked for, to an elder who remembered that the harder you tried, the more you desired their respect and appreciation, the less the Anglos gave of it and thus the only true course was to desert."

"*Escape* would be a better word," I said.

"Uh," Mary Blue said. "Yes. Can we help this young man understand that?"

"La Vent? I'll try," I promised, just as Arturo came into the kitchen. He was the owner and cashier of the diner.

"*Chingado!*" he said, the moment he saw the huge stacks of tortillas Mary had made. It was enough to last at least a month, if he could find freezer space. "I'll be *chingado*," he muttered, the softness of the dee making it sound like "chingaro" with a rolled "r" to Mary's ears.

And that's how I got my name as a *weyekin* in human form. Chingaro. Chingito, in the affectionate diminutive.

Chapter Three

I.

"Easy, huh?" laughs Tom Yellowtail. His baggy face tries to rise to a smile and his narrow prankster's eyes protrude outward from the eye sockets, shining with a humor so old it could be called wisdom or survival. Tom's not Nez Perce. He's Coeur d'Alene. Close enough to Nez Perce, though, for him to know full well how it's impossible to tell the success and failure of the son without telling about the mother and father. How things in their endless relationship keep circling backwards. How in its connection to the past, the present cannot be told by itself without losing both its tense and tenor.

Tom likes to remember for me how at first I thought being Pal's *weyekin* would be easier than being Mary Blue's. "I've served the mother," I once said to him. "This is only the son."

"You've been hanging around Chicken Licken too much," Tom laughed. "You're forgetting he thinks different."

"Licken's not so bad," I said.

"I didn't say he was bad. I said that he thinks different. It's understandable, given the people he works for. It's only natural that given the way they see their children as lesser in everything they think and do that he would, too. But what's natural for Licken and his people is unnatural for the human beings we work for. They see . . . Mary Blue sees . . . children as extensions of community. Each generation has an even longer past to be understood and told about. The stories get more complicated. Not less. Longer. Not shorter. Licken's people want nothing more than for the story to shorten down to a description of the present. What Mary Blue sees as a sort of emotionally charged set of grunting sounds."

"They do seem to wish that less really was more," I said.

"And what they wish, they make, right? They want a frontier, they make it with napalm. Just ask Licken. Remember that pompous old fart who passed through here a while ago, name of Johnson?"

"The old windbag who kept insisting we call him *Doctor*? *Weyekin* like a pork chop. As you said, he wanted to be called *Doctor* because he had no Johnson."

"Gotta hand it to him. Had a pretty big career out of so little work."

"Yeah, but his whole frigging life was nothing more than one long complaint and promise."

Tom grinned. Though with the bagginess of his cheeks, you wouldn't have known it was a grin if you weren't watching the way his eyes narrowed and his jaw set behind closed lips. "Wonder how he felt when Sammy Coleridge sneaked up behind him with his pants down? *His* life was about to be examined."

"Guess he had to suspend his disbelief a little," I laughed.

"Odd how they don't want their listeners to take part in how their stories make the world, though, isn't it?"

"What else you gonna do with someone like Chicken Licken and all that running around saying the sky is falling? Must make them pretty sad."

"I don't know. Last time I saw Coleridge docked like a shuttle with Johnson's space station, he didn't look like he was so unhappy."

"Till Johnson farts."

"Chingito, my friend, just when will you learn? Old Johnson farts out his mouth."

Forgive me, I know in a less-is-more world all that looks like yet another digression and that even some would-be Indians can't stand digression. We don't call it digression, though. We call it supplementation and for us it's part of the fun of a story. Indeed, it is the story. It adds richness and texture into the process of me, the storyteller, trying to connect with you, the participator in my telling. Slowly and by means of these supplementations, I can find out what you like and what you don't like. What you are willing or unwilling to see.

That conversation with Tom Yellowtail went on for a long time. We joked about a good deal of the history of aesthetic theory. We made jokes because we find making up theories about telling stories is amusing, not because the way different people tell stories isn't interesting. It is. In fact, as far as we're concerned, without storytelling human beings don't exist.

But anyway, I remember our conversation because that was the day I was finally beating Tom at Uno and Mary Blue interrupted by dreaming me down to watch her make those stacks of tortillas. That was the day she gave me my name, a name I try to keep polished so that when it passes on from me to another *weyekin*, it will still be a good one, one worth having and taking care of.

"Be right back," I said to Tom when the rhythmic pull from Mary Blue felt as strong as the receding tide. "Right back" means anything in the relative time of a timeless existence.

I did come right back. But after La Vent Larue discovered the greasy diner in which Mary Blue worked, especially after he saw Mary for the first time and began inhabiting the same booth like a mussel waits in its shell, I began getting recalled like a Chrysler car—except by Mary Blue and not the National Transportation Safety Commission. And now what with Palimony Blue Larue, I'm going to be telling Tom "Be right back" more often as I go off to play minor and major roles in Pal's life until he finally learns how to dream into living words the love of his life. Her name, Amanda, you already know.

But first things first. To understand Pal, you have to know something about La Vent. Hopefully then you can begin to understand how his need to be liked could begin to be slowly poisoned by his ingrained suspicion that he was never fully or completely likable.

2.

Therefore, the father.

When he was young, La Vent Larue thought he was just like any of the other kids around him in southern California. He wanted to believe he was just like them, anyway. The only difference, he decided, was that his year-round tan was a slightly different hue, a sort of dark reddish-brown color like cut earth and not the light walnut stain of his Coppertone friends.

True, he sometimes danced the Mexican Hat Dance a little more enthusiastically than most of his classmates, the ones who were neither Mexican nor mixblood. And he behaved in strange ways that were so slightly strange—smiling secretly when the Coppertone kids assiduously wrote down dates and their meanings. His teachers had difficulty understanding that the difference between La Vent and their other pupils was a difference of blood, and not a problem of attitude. In his blood were stories and the secret intuition that how you told your stories made all the difference in the world. In his blood was the ability to listen to the teachers tell their stories and be able to repeat them without writing them down. You might imagine then that when what his teachers said were not stories but facts he would have to scribble it down. But at those times—which became more frequent, the older he got—they seemed to him to be unimportant for the very reason that without a story to give them context, facts are meaningless to human beings.

All in all, as a boy, La Vent kept his smiles to himself. His early schooling amounted to little more than his secret wonderings that his friends and teachers seemed to take their historical fabrications like Betsy Ross or that hopelessly lost but courageous sailor, Christopher Columbus, so seriously. La Vent just wanted to be liked.

It was this wanting to be liked that made him smile more when his friends took the liberty to test his sense of humor—which back then he had. They told him harmless little jokes, like the one about the Indian girl who questions where her name came from and finally in frustration her mother replies, "Why do you ask, Broken Rubber?" Although when Alvin Grulling, the shortest boy in his grade, asked him where his turban was, he grew a little huffy and said that was Eastern Indian, not his kind of Indian. Alvin, however, was as slow as he was short, able to remember only one joke at a time, which he would repeat for most of a year as though once it had been funny. When Alvin modified his favorite joke from ragheads to bonnet brains and asked, "How many bonnet brains does it take to screw in a light bulb?" La Vent jumped him, knocked him to the ground, and pinned his arms to the asphalt with his knees. Alvin began to snuffle with fear. He later told the principal La Vent's attack was wholly unprovoked. Nonetheless, La Vent made him admit that the Indians Alvin saw in the movies didn't have light bulbs, and that it was Poles, not Indians, who went with the joke. Alvin became his friend, shadowing him around school with a beatified grin on his face.

After that, La Vent decided not to let the jokes bother him. When his friends called him "Chief" or laughed at the colors of his clothes, which, though secondhand, were very colorful, purchased from the Salvation Army store in the increasingly Mexican East L.A., La Vent tried to take the teasing in the right spirit. He smiled, as best he could.

True, he rooted instinctively against the Dallas Cowboys. And when his teachers preached about the importance of the rights of private property, his head swelled and ached with questions.

They were questions that his father knew by heart, but which he rarely mentioned except when overcome with emotion. Sometimes, he let slip some comment about white people. But he quickly added that he, too, was part white, though he'd never been able to figure out which part, laughing away the directness of his comment about whites and its hint of bitterness. He wanted his son, La Vent, to inherit the good and not the bitter. So he never sat him down and told him stories about oil leases and Osage people who were murdered for them. He never told him how the Osage bought their land back from the federal government only to have the government take it away a second time. Instead, when he told La Vent stories of home, he stuck to stories like Buffalo

Man, who gains the power to transform things, including himself, by drinking from one particular pool. Warned by the pool never to drink from any other, Buffalo Man finds himself a long way from home. He feels thirsty. So thirsty that he forgets the pool's warnings, and drinks from another one. At that moment, he loses all his power, forever.

It was a story meant to tell La Vent about the importance of finding his source of power and sticking to it, no matter how thirsty for other sources or other powers he might become. But his father miscalculated how much La Vent wanted to be liked in his mostly white school. For La Vent, it became a story about how far from the source he and his father were, living as they were in L.A. It became a story not of confidence and focus, but of hopelessness and wandering. And every time he heard it, the story left La Vent feeling lost and alone, more determined to ingratiate himself to his teachers and friends.

So with an Indian determination—and please remember that we're talking about human beings who survive even the romanticism of Hollywood—La Vent tried to take after his father. He judged his own secret feelings and questions to be minor or unimportant. He corrected and guided his own judgments with the same skill he demonstrated years later when he served on the zoning commission for the city of Gilroy and allowed developers to bulldoze Costano burial sites as a way to pave over questions about property, private or otherwise. He avoided being bitter or cynical, never confronting his friends and acquaintances with anything resembling the truth. And so he continued to get along reasonably well at school. In outward appearance, he was at peace, and like his father, or like he imagined his father (his mother, Mary Liptrapp, had died in childbirth, so he had no help from her in this process), he would rather desert than risk losing the friendly approval of the trader whites.

His real success came as an athlete. It was a vegetable man, the manager of the produce department at the local Alpha-Beta grocery store by the name of Don "the Cuke" Gutierrez, who spotted La Vent pushing a supermarket cart past the display of beans and recognized the potential in the sheer length of La Vent's legs. "The Cuke" coached on weekends for the Police Athletic League and instantly, as if in a dream-vision, he saw La Vent passing swiftly over the boards of high hurdles without so much as a hop. With the Cuke's private coaching every Saturday and Sunday afternoon, it did not take long for La Vent to become a countywide contender and eventually an all-state high hurdler, making up what he gave away to the sheer, fleet-footed speed of his opponents with the half-seconds he gained crossing the hurdles.

As a champion hurdler, La Vent achieved a sort of popularity in high school. He enhanced this popularity by making himself more likable. Good-humored and easygoing. Willing to laugh. To prove that he was not uptight, he told jokes about Tonto turning to the Lone Ranger when they were surrounded by hostile Apache and replying to the Lone Ranger's "What do we do now, Tonto?" with "Whaddaya mean *we*, kemosabe?"

When he told these jokes, La Vent gently elbowed his classmates and winked. He laughed heartily to make sure that they understood that he was only joking and that he believed that any difference between them and him was only on the surface, an accident of birth. He showed off his "Injun-uity" cards gleaned from the depths of shredded wheat boxes and laughed at the way the Indian hand signal for "enemy" was a head-to-ground chopping motion with the hand, as though trying to split cherrywood with a stone tomahawk. Alvin failed to see the humor. Alvin went around making the chopping motion whenever they crossed paths with someone he disliked, which forced La Vent to bore people by repeating this anecdotal item in the repertoire of his good nature and then explaining it.

Little wonder that La Vent began to envision himself like his favorite comic book hero, "Straight Arrow." Straight Arrow was the good and honest cowboy who believed in private property and justice, who transformed himself, much like Clark Kent, into a pale-skinned Indian hero whenever injustice or the intentions of evil demanded his services.

And little wonder that in the visions of this newfound popularity, when track season was finished and basketball season began, he gave up his post as class treasurer to become the school mascot. He even beat the captain of the football team in a runoff election so he could dress up in buckskin and beads to tumble his way into the center of the court at halftime and lead the crowd in cheers he, himself, invented.

La Vent did not desert. Although late at night during the summers, when he'd be sleeping in a bedroll beneath the stars beside his father, camping out and fishing the lower reaches of the Yosemite River, he sometimes felt tempted. He lay there on the bed of pine needles placed over the moist packed ground, staring up between the tree branches at the Milky Pathway of departed spirits, breathing the air that was full of the odor and dust of pine and oak mixed with manzanita and fir. Nearby, the small creek fell among ferns into a shallow pool. Its song seemed to voice his questions. But he was too embarrassed to ask his father why all his popularity and all his good-natured cheers felt dim-witted and dull. Why they left him feeling as though he were hungry without fasting, or sweaty without exertion or ceremony. As yet, he did not know that was exactly what his own father had done, deserted from alien notions of success. La Vent would not know that until his father closed one of the circles of life and he found his old Indian school transcript. Simultaneous with his beginning to square the circle of his own, La Vent never did understand what that transcript meant.

3.

La Vent graduated high school, which made his father truly proud. He had done well. Fearing the loss of the kind of limited world in which he could be popular, however, with his good grades and the testimony of the high school's guidance counselor as to his general good-naturedness, La Vent soon found himself attending college, working all night in a gas station to finance the gap between his scholarships and his expenses. He was grateful for the job and his gratitude made him willing to serve. He never refused to check a person's oil or clean a windshield, even if he was treated with inbred disdain. And if he could, if it did not conflict with important lectures or seminar sessions, he worked any shift, double shifts, and, when there was overtime to be had, the owner of the gas station could count on him. "La Vent," the owner would say, "you think you could . . . ?"

"No problem," La Vent would reply, even before his question was articulated. "Just let me check my classes."

Perhaps it was not college but his work, the way people treated gas jockeys in those days like barely civilized Mexican migrant laborers or parolees from prison, sitting in their cars and ordering him about as though he were not human, that began to wear on La Vent and make him feel a little lonely for some other kind of people.

Perhaps it was his two-week stint in a college fraternity, which originated as a way to save on his living expenses. Watching Alvin stand on the dining room table and put his finger in a jar of jam and then into his right ear, as he was told to by the hazing brothers of the fraternity, disturbed La Vent. He quit the fraternity. He also abandoned Alvin.

Whatever the reason, whenever he wasn't working, he drove out into the desert to visit his father, sitting with him silently for hours watching sun and shadow above Soda Lake to the east. He felt as though all this college and work had obscured his path, that he had lost his way. Driving back to L.A., he began to circle the desert as though his heart were there, driving north, south, or east, looping in toward Los Angeles unwillingly. One Sunday, he stopped in Adelanto at a greasy Mexican diner to eat and watch planes from the air force base take off, circle, touch down, and take off again. The food was so good that he began to frequent the diner. It was patronized by slow, peaceful people and that made him feel, well, kind of at home. Not to mention the fact that the food was to his liking, untainted by government regulations and which you could eat unworried by the cholesterol police. He felt happy there, and when the diner's owner shouted "*Chingado!*"—as he was wont to do at any provocation—La Vent laughed for the first time in ages with true good-naturedness, and with no reason at all. The other regulars, who had come to accept his presence, smiled and nodded at his laughter.

He felt as though he was drawn to the diner. One Saturday, he found out why when he overstayed the diner's closing, and he saw for the first time the shy and modest girl who made the flour and corn tortillas that he and the other customers came to the diner to eat like bread. He couldn't tell how thin she was because of her loose clothing, but she seemed somehow plenty big enough for him. Her reddish brown hair was braided neatly and coiled at the back of her head. And he laughed at the fact that she seemed to like bright desert colors more than he.

Mary Blue was a mixblood like him who, as he eventually found out, was happy just to have work in a state like California. The first time she looked at him and seemed to nod, he tried to smile. But facing her, suddenly he felt overwhelmed by timidity. He turned his eyes down toward his plate of refried beans. After that, he was sure that by not returning her faint smile he had offended her. She hardly looked at him. If she smiled, she smiled privately as though smiling over a joke only she knew the punch line of, and not at him. He certainly could not coax her into conversation with him. Indeed, she skirted any chance he created of having a conversation, however brief it might be.

For the next year and a half, La Vent drove out to Adelanto to sit in what came to be known to Arturo and the other regular customers as "his" booth. He ordered food, talked to the other people who stopped by to drink the thick black coffee, and waited for the diner to close. When she emerged from the kitchen, he again tried to create an opportunity to converse with her. He became as familiar as the green vinyl upholstery, though sometimes she stopped the rhythm of her hands as they deftly cut and sliced or pressed flour into the mold for tortillas and went to the order window where, unknown to La Vent, she watched him eat his food.

One rainy night, as she put her hand on the door handle to leave, he summoned all his courage. He asked her if she'd like a ride. The words seemed huge in his mouth. They stuck like a hairball in his dry throat. But enough sound came out to cause her to turn and say, "What?"

"I said would you like a ride? Home. You know, in this rain, so you don't have to wait for the bus, I'd be happy to, I mean, if you would like. . . ."

"A ride would be nice," she replied, modestly.

"Really?" he said.

"It would be nice not to have to wait for the bus in the rain," she replied.

"I . . . uh, let me grab my jacket," La Vent said. He left a tip. In his hurry, he forgot to pay.

Arturo just watched them leave. He watched La Vent hold the door open for her as though she were the queen of England. He watched out the windows as La Vent repeated the gesture at the passenger door of his car and drove away in the rain-swept lights from the diner's sign, which had not yet been turned off. He watched them and shook his head with a grin on his brown face, muttering, *Chingado.* It was not a curse, but more like a cheer.

From that night on, it felt to La Vent almost like fate. Much to the consternation of his boss at the gas station, La Vent began to refuse overtime. When asked if he might be able to . . . , La Vent spurted, "No." He skipped every class he could. He borrowed notes from former fraternity friends like Alvin. These days, Alvin wore only Stay-Prest canary yellow slacks with knit polo shirts and black loafers without socks. Still, he seemed to want to be La Vent's friend again. Using Alvin's notes meant getting lower grades. Alvin had no sense of focus or of the relative importance of different pieces of information. And La Vent did not assimilate the information he read as well as he would have done if he had listened to the lectures.

All this newly created free time he spent at Arturo's Mexican Cafe in Adelanto. Indeed, the sheriff's department did not consider the diner closed until La Vent's purple Edsel had left the parking lot. Only after it was gone did they bother shining a spotlight across the grounds as a deterrent to burglars, Pinkertons employed by local farmers to drive Mexicans out of business, and the Ku Klux Klan.

Much to his surprise but not without a kind of pleasure, La Vent discovered that the girl who made tortillas might be shy, but it was a shyness that came not from timidity but from modesty. Indeed, she was as tough as an old tortilla in her way. It would take La Vent nearly another full year of talking rapidly on the way from the cafe to her apartment above the hardware store, filling the air with such a web of words, to make her dizzy enough to accept a proposal of marriage. His proposal of marriage.

One night, he turned left out into the desert and drove her up to Four Corners. There, he pulled off the road onto the shoulder near the one intersection marked by four stop signs. He turned off the engine. Without looking at her, for fear a look from her would stop him from speaking, he began, "I waited nearly a year and a half just for you to speak to me."

Mary Blue turned. She touched her braided hair lightly with her right hand. With her face calm and expressionless, she corrected him. "Five hundred days," she said.

"A long time," La Vent replied. He did not stop long enough to wonder how she knew the precise number of days. "Long enough to show you that if nothing else, I am steadfast. I would always be steadfast. I'm a good worker. I can earn money enough so that you wouldn't have to work at the cafe if you didn't want to. I have the chance at a good job up north, up in Gilroy. . . ."

Mary Blue felt a strand of hair fall loose and she reached up with her other hand and brushed it back, tucking it behind her ear. She fingered the beading over the pocket of her blouse. "What," she said, "are you trying to say?"

La Vent almost lost his nerve. "Here," he blurted, reaching into the back seat for a gift-wrapped box of cactus candy, "I bought this for you." As Mary slowly unwrapped the box—her hands were powerful but at the same time thin and delicate, precise—he took a firm grip with both hands on the steering wheel and, staring straight out the windshield at the desert night, said, "I want you to marry me. I won't take you home until you say yes."

Mary Blue turned her head and looked back down the road as if she were considering the distance she would have to walk at that late hour. Then she turned back to look at him, his stern profile lit only by the half-moon's light. She knew that if she told him to take her home, he would. She knew that she was stronger than he was. She saw that it was this strength that he thought he loved and that instinctively, he knew he needed. She smiled. "Well, then," she said slowly, "what choice do I have?"

"You'll do it? You're saying yes?"

"I've gotten used to not having to walk," she replied.

4.

"You should have warned her," Tom Yellowtail interrupts.

"About what?"

"About the way he wanted with all his heart to be needed. To do things so that people would appreciate him."

"She knew that. She didn't need me to tell her that."

"Maybe," Tom says. "But you could have told her how much he wanted to be needed."

"I didn't know."

"You should have."

"Come on, Tom. How was I supposed to know? I'm a frigging *weyekin*. A spirit guide, not a private detective. Besides, who could have imagined that once he was married to Mary Blue, La Vent would get worse, not better?"

"You should have, is all I'm saying," Tom replies.

Mary did not want to miss her own wedding. So instead of a formal ceremony at a church, they married in his father's house. The ceremony was small, but well attended. Enough of the people from Adelanto attended to make the young fraternity men in yellow slacks seem out of place in all but the brightness of their clothes. Arturo came, all dressed up in a bright pink tuxedo, with all seven of his kids. His wife wore a mantilla. She made the five-tiered cake herself, as a gift to the bride and groom. La Vent's father carried around bottles of bourbon, pouring out tumblers of it for those who did not want champagne, spilling a good deal on his own jacket and slacks as the day grew longer. Everyone drank and ate. Arturo catered the event and other people brought dishes—casseroles of chorizo and rice; salads of artichoke, avocado, chicken, and cheese on beds of lettuce and home-fried tortilla chips; fruits and vegetables grown in victory gardens behind modest houses. The feast lasted three days. People went home to sleep and came back in the early afternoon. For the first time in decades, everyone in Daggett could say all at the same time that they were full with food. Stuffed to breathlessness and, for the time being, content.

Two months later, La Vent graduated from college. His grades were low because of the number of classes he had skipped. But they were still good enough for several counties and cities to rank him among their top three applicants for zoning and ordinances in their city (or county) planning commissions. César Chávez had organized migrant labor in the San Fernando Valley, and white people of compassion were refusing to eat grapes anywhere but in the supermarket, unwashed (a sign of solidarity with the farmworkers who were sprayed weekly with pesticides) and unpaid for (a blow against the profit margins of the markets who did not buy union produce). Ahead of the rest of the nation, the mood of California was egalitarian. Increasingly, what people conceived of as just and fair was being made into state and local legislation. And even though the interviewers knew next to nothing about the Osage—one personnel official confused Osage with a dime novel titled *Riders of the Purple Sage*—they knew at least as much about Osage as they did Chicano or black. And La Vent impressed them all as someone who would add to their workforce as well as to their statistical profile of employees.

He came home one evening, having flown into LAX from San Jose, to happily announce to Mary Blue that they could begin packing. In a month, they were moving north. He had accepted the offer of a job as a consultant for zoning in the city of Gilroy, less than an hour's drive south of San Jose.

"The mayor of Gilroy is a man of vision," La Vent said, proudly. "He really wants me. In fact, before I left he put his arm around my shoulders and told me that I was exactly what he wanted. I took the job on the spot." He added sheepishly, seeing the look on Mary's face, "I took it before I even asked what the starting salary would be. But it's a good one, anyway. They really do want me, see."

"I'm beginning to," was all Mary Blue said.

"Guess I'll go down to the market tomorrow and look for boxes," La Vent thought out loud.

"I'll begin cleaning and wrapping," Mary replied. She was not unhappy. Neither was she as excited as her husband. She would wait, watch, and see how it all came out. She would not dream any of it into existence, but let things happen as they might.

Jane Kirkland, the mayor's administrative assistant and personal secretary, met them outside the mayor's office after their slow but uneventful drive north in the old Edsel. They had towed a U-Haul trailer full of the possessions they valued enough to pack and move. Mary had spent an entire day carefully disassembling her loom. She made La Vent twice return to the U-Haul outlet to rent extra pads to protect the wood plank table on which she did her beading. She had made the table herself, and every knothole, every scratch, every ring-shaped stain of coffee was important to her. She knew them all by heart.

"What do you care?" La Vent asked, frustrated and tired. She was sending him back again to the U-Haul station. "It's only an old table. Leave it. We can afford to buy you a new one."

Mary straightened up. Although she wasn't tall, average height at best, she looked tall at that moment. She rested her palms on her buttocks and arched her back, stretching the muscles stiff from bending and packing. Then she looked at her husband. Her green eyes were dark. She started to explain. Then she stopped. "I care," she said simply.

She bent back over the box of dishes she was packing. La Vent sighed a martyr's sigh, grabbed his car keys, and left.

Jane Kirkland stared open-mouthed at the Edsel as the new consultant and his wife drove up. As Mary Blue got out, Jane raised her hand and shielded her eyes from the bright mint green of Mary Blue's shirt. Mary Blue took notice of the immodest hemline of Jane's summer dress.

Jane pulled herself together and had them follow her in her car out to the house which the mayor had leased for them on the edge of town. It was a small two-bedroom adobe house fronted by a low whitewashed adobe wall and an iron gate, and backed by a ring of cactus. The yard was hard and flat, almost as white as the adobe in the hot sunlight. But the earth was dark. Mary could see that with tilling and turning, the earth was rich enough to grow whatever flowers and vegetables she might want. All in all, Mary liked the house, even though she frowned a little when Jane explained why the mayor had leased this house, isolated from a new development of faux-Spanish houses just like it by half a mile.

"Buzz thought you might like your privacy."

"Buzz?" Mary whispered to La Vent.

"The mayor," he hissed.

"Your children, though, will go to the same school with the kids in those houses over there." Jane pointed, as if the development weren't the only set of houses to be seen. The rest of the view was scrub not unlike the desert around Adelanto. Brown hills rose behind the scrub and brush and fields—hills that would surprise Mary when they turned emerald green with fall rains. The low treelike vines of a winery sloped away and up to the south. "I expect you'll have children?" Jane asked.

"I expect," La Vent replied cheerfully.

"You people always do, don't you?" Jane said mildly. "Well, here are two sets of keys. I'll let you unpack and start settling in. Here's my number, in case you need something, and . . . and we'll see you bright and early Monday morning?"

La Vent smiled and nodded.

"Nice meeting you," Jane said to Mary Blue.

"It was good to meet you, too," Mary replied without emotion.

"Bye, Jane. Thank Buzz for me, will you?" La Vent said.

Jane had started for the gate. She stopped. "The mayor, you mean? Certainly. I'll thank the mayor for you," she said icily.

After Jane was gone, La Vent and Mary Blue walked through the house, admiring the red tile floor in the kitchen and bathroom. Wall-to-wall carpet covered the rest of the floor, a neutral color that took all of their possessions, and then some, to add color and give it life. But Mary was good at it. She used her small loom to make wall hangings in reds and blues. While she waited for the house to take on her character and life, she wore the brightest-colored clothing she could find in her trunk. Not heavy, but with a substantial presence, customers at the pharmacy or the food market seemed to make way for her as she pushed her cart down the aisles, pausing to stare at the peacock-colored woman who, it was generally known, was new to town. The Mexican women at the discount warehouse liked her almost immediately.

La Vent flourished. His pride and his great joy at being wanted and appreciated made him seem as though when he walked he walked on his toes, lightly, quickly, in a kind of straight-line dance. In his first month, he developed a pride in his work that was unmatched by any of the other consultants in the zoning department. Often, he brought that pride home. Sitting before a plate of tortillas and stew meat, he told the increasingly quiet Mary Blue how the mayor had once again called him in on a highly sensitive, special consultation.

"He calls me Straight Arrow," La Vent told her. "His straight arrow. Says he can always trust me to do the job and do it right. Right now, we've got this problem with eminent domain that I'm working on. He wants me to find a way to reclassify the vineyard south of here. Get rid of those ugly eyesores the migrant laborers live in. Upgrade it to a zoning status that will allow Bill Diggum to build a condo complex on a lake, and put in a golf course as well as a shopping mall."

"What about the families?" Mary asked.

"What families?"

"The migrant families."

"Oh. Who knows just how much migrant housing we will need locally, what with the vineyard gone. But of course he's committed to using some of the tax revenue to build whatever we need for those people."

"Those people?" Mary Blue asked. Her voice lacked heat, but her heart was pounding. "Arturo, his wife, all the people at our wedding who weren't in canary yellow pants are *those people*," she said.

"Oh. Yeah. Well, they're not the same, really, as migrant laborers. Arturo's a citizen, after all. Those people who live in shacks like the vineyard runs are Mexicans. Most of them are illegals. They sneak up here. They can earn picking ten times what they'd earn in Mexico working all year long and then they take the money back to Mexico. Our money," he added. "Money that should be spent right here in Gilroy."

"He understands perfectly," the mayor said to Jane Kirkland two days later, after he recovered his breath from watching her bend over in the cotton-blend skirt she was wearing. She had peeked into his office while La Vent was giving his report on the vineyard to the mayor. She raised her eyebrows, keeping them raised until La Vent noticed and excused himself. The mayor apologized, telling him he was sorry, that he'd like to spend all afternoon chatting. But he had to meet with the planning commission head and later go to a dull dinner with Bill Diggum and Henry Pavum, the owners of Diggum and Pavum Development, Inc.

"Let's get together tomorrow," he said to La Vent. He winked at Jane.

"Gee, he seems to be all booked tomorrow," Jane told La Vent. Flipping through the appointment calendar on her desk, she noticed that Buzz's wife's birthday was coming up. She jotted a note to buy her something expensive but not too personal for Buzz to give her, like a Kirby vacuum or maybe a Peter Max poster. She told La Vent that he should check with her next week, and she'd schedule him in for a meet.

"He's a busy man," La Vent said to Mary. "You can't imagine what it takes to be a mayor, even of a town only the size of Gilroy. Especially of a town the size of Gilroy," he added, "what with trying to compete with cities like San Jose."

"I wouldn't want to," Mary said.

"What do you mean by that?" La Vent asked.

Mary's face remained as calm as sunrise. He couldn't tell if she meant it positively or negatively. "Nothing," she answered.

La Vent accepted her at her word.

Two days later, Jane Kirkland sent over the glossy pamphlet the mayor's office produced on the basis of the report La Vent had filed. It was seven pages, complete with three-color pie and bar charts. It proved beyond a doubt the need to develop the gently rolling hills owned by the vineyard in order to attract tax revenue southward from San Jose. As if that were not enough to make La Vent Larue a happy man, when Bill Diggum saw him downtown at lunchtime, he called out to him across the street and jaywalked just to tell La Vent how beautiful the brochure looked. What a good job he had done.

"You, my friend," Bill said, "are just what this city has always needed. You are a credit to this town, to your people. In fact, it's people like you who have helped make this country great. If only all your people were like you," Bill said, slapping La Vent on the shoulder.

Indeed, there were people who hardly seemed to know that La Vent was a minority. And as he worked his way up from junior to senior consultant in the zoning commission, if someone asked La Vent if he was Mexican or something, you might hear him reply modestly, "A little Osage, maybe." You could almost hear the palpable sighs as a relaxed, relieved sort of expression washed over the interrogator's face like the seawash over sand as he thought, "Thank God, a civilized one, one you can work with and not have to tippy-toe around all the time feeling guilty."

La Vent did not make a public point of his mixed blood. He did not want to make a point of it. It wasn't that he was embarrassed about it. Rather, it was that other people seemed to get embarrassed when and if they found out. And La Vent did not want to make other people feel uncomfortable. In his short-sleeved white shirt and bolo tie the mayor bought him for his birthday, out of what he dreamed was compassion, he prided himself on making it a point to help those who discovered his background find him one they could work with.

CHAPTER FOUR

I.

La Vent was full of himself, and it wasn't long before Mary Blue found herself with child.

"Here we go," Henny Penny says. "At last. Jeez. I thought you'd never begin." Henny waddles over behind me. Her high voice sounds high and nasal as though she's been pecking around Michigan too much and the midwestern twang has worn off on her.

Tom Yellowtail smiles. He knows as well as I do that there is no beginning. There is no moment at which you can point your finger and say, there, there is where it all begins. He smiles because he understands that if there is no beginning, then there is no end. The stories get told. The stories get retold. And even if they get retold in different words, they are the same stories. There is no such thing as unemployment for *weyekin*.

Tom's smile turns to broad laughter when Chicken Licken, just come back from Bosnia, bursts in and adds, "He's always doing this. He's always out of order. You're out of order," Licken says to me.

Tom's jowls lift as though pulled up by puppet strings attached to his eyes, which open wide, and he laughs out loud, a "Hah!" that will be recorded by NASA as space noise. "He's out of order?" Tom laughs. "You're out of order."

In her third term, I sat with her and kept her company while La Vent snored in the other room. She sat up late at night with the radio on but with the sound low so as not to disturb the baby inside her, rocking herself into a state of quiet, if not sleep. Sleep seemed impossible, even to a Dreamer. When she lay down, she felt like a 747 was parked on top of her, one wheel on her bladder and the other wheels on other internal organs like her kidneys or liver. As Tom and I know, the entire argument over whether Nature is more powerful than Nurture is a false argument invented and propagated by people who are, in a word, un-Natural. Nature, like the action of a story that's been told so many times as to become legend, is predestination. Nurture, like the words and context of the story, is like free will. The story always comes out the same, though how it comes out the same can differ. So knowing La Vent as I did, I sat there with Mary.

She was concerned. Curious. She foresaw that her son, Palomino, might be swift of foot and light of hair. Perhaps long of face.

"It's no accident that children grow up to resemble their names as though those names were fate, regardless of good or bad. Or whether their parents had any idea what the given names might mean, and thus foretell," I said.

She did not look comforted. She rolled her green eyes over at me, her hair loose and fanned out against the back of the recliner. She had a strong premonition of troubles with love. Yet she had been unable to figure out where that premonition came from. Even though she now could see how her life with La Vent was not going to be the model it should. Even though she understood that, after generations of being told you aren't good enough no matter what you do, diffidence and insecurity could enter your genes, it still did not seem to account for the vision she got when she dreamed of her son. She saw him always trying to please, and she was not unhappy for it. But she also saw him picking the wrong kind of girl to love, saw him as backbendingly kind to girls who simply didn't care a whit about him. It seemed too extreme, this vision. So you can hardly blame her for discounting it like the echo of voices over crossed telephone wires, if only because she did not envision herself giving birth in a place where some clerk could take it upon herself to arrogate the naming of her son and change "Palomino" to "Palimony."

"The naming is everything," I said.

"But if I'm midwifed at home, the naming will be at home," she said.

"Things happen," I said. "Things change on you."

"But what?" Mary Blue wondered. What could change things so much that her son would be given the wrong name?

"Of course, as much as they change, they remain the same," I added, trying to get her to remember the farmworkers. They came to La Vent's home to plead with him, to get him to point out to the mayor that those shacks he called unsightly, with all their red tags from county inspectors, were what they called home. To remind La Vent that he had glibly promised them that they would be taken care of. That they wouldn't be forgotten in the processes of bureaucracy. That they would have new and better lives. After the son of one of them—a son who was as nameless to the mayor as his father—was shot and then beaten to death by a former prison guard working night shift security at the power station, La Vent panicked. He didn't know what to do, so he flew off to San Francisco on business.

The farmworkers returned, seeking La Vent's help. They imagined from the tenor of his complexion that he was one of them. Mary Blue opened her house and yard up. She fed them, gave woven blankets to their babies, and let them use tar paper, cardboard, and tin to build shelters in her yard.

When La Vent returned, he was furious. He, himself, handed the farmworkers the order to vacate, while seven county sheriff's deputies in riot gear stood restlessly and anxiously behind him. The farmworkers left peacefully, sorrowfully, and the sheriff's deputies moved in to dismantle the small village of tin.

And still the farmworkers believed, until the day the same deputies stood behind the sheriff who evicted them from the vineyard in which they and their grandparents and children had toiled, that La Vent was one of them. That they could bring their problems with the city to him and that he would try to do what he could. He had, after all, given his word.

2.

As Tom likes to put it, what happened was that Mary's baby failed to prepare properly for landing.

Whether from inattention or inability, Pal failed to turn and face the back of her womb. La Vent, being La Vent, panicked. Fortunately, the midwife convinced him to gather up Mary Blue, skip packing clothes and toothbrushes, load her gently into the new station wagon, and split for the hospital with his struggling wife, rather than take any chances.

A good thing, too. Instead of squeezing out to begin describing his dry new world with angry cries, Pal's block head got stuck in the birth canal and the doctors were forced to perform an emergency C-section, reversing the direction of his birth. Pulling him back into the womb and then lifting him out, they handed him off like a football in a delayed draw play to a pack of technicians who rushed him out of the room to surgery. There they rammed tubes down his nose to vacuum out the excess amniotic fluid he had swallowed. They massaged his heart and lungs, and at last he gave out with his first tentative and extemely grateful, muted wail. At last they brought him back into the maternity ward. Gratefully, almost tearfully, Mary lay there, exhausted, holding her son, for the time being unconcerned with what was to become of him.

Given what Pal had put her through, Mary slept on the second day. She woke only to breast-feed Pal. She pulled her stitches laughing at the expression on La Vent's face as he gallantly did his duty and changed Pal's first diaper filled with the meconium that looks and smells like an oil spill.

It was on the third day that La Vent poked his head through the pneumatic door of her room to tell her that things had changed in just the way I had predicted. The clerk in charge of filling in the forms assumed that Pal's name was a mistake. She took it upon herself to correct the mistake, before it became infused on a certificate of live birth.

"Hey," he said, trying to smile as he poked his head around the edge of the curtains that were drawn around her bed for privacy. "How're you doing? Really put you through your paces, didn't he?"

His proto-laughter and sheepish whisper, combined with the worried expectant look on his face, told Mary that something was wrong.

"What is it?" she said. "What's gone wrong?"

"Wrong? Uh, nothing. That is, well, you see, the clerk who recorded Pal's name? She, well, she said she didn't think anyone would name their son like a horse."

"My baby's all right?" Mary asked, already beginning to correct her vision of the birth of her son.

"Yeah. Sure. He's fine."

"Then what?"

"Well, the clerk recorded his name *Palimony*. Not Palomino."

"Palimony? What does that mean?" Mary asked.

"Don't know," La Vent replied.

Mary Blue should have been angry. She would have felt angry at La Vent if she hadn't realized that this was what I'd been trying to warn her about all along. The failure was hers, more than her husband's. She had dreamed. But she had not seen the dreaming. Partly, she was addled by sleeplessness and the need for dream sleep had intertwined with dreaming like the double helix of DNA and confused the appearance with the substance. The failure was his. But it was hers, too. And hers was all the greater because she was the Dreamer. And because she knew so well La Vent's tendency to fail in ways only she would call failure. Others might call them success.

"The good news is that we can still call him Pal," La Vent said. "Can't we?"

Mary stared out the window at the exhaust trails of jets racing no-where in their tests of speed over the central plains of California and shook her head.

"Funny," La Vent went on. "I never *dreamed* someone would change 'Palomino.' "

"You never dreamed at all," Mary replied, turning from the window to her husband. " 'Palimony,' " she muttered, repeating the name to her-self. She had to get used to it, and fast, before something else happened.

Already several steps along his way to becoming a five-star bureau-crat on his journey of denial, La Vent tried in his own unamused way to see the whole thing as funny. People had not yet invented the concept of paying women to move out of men's apartments and houses, so he saw no real harm in the fact that Pal was now named after an as yet un-believable idea.

"Funny," he said, "isn't it?"

Mary groaned. " 'Palimony'?" she said. "That's funny?"

La Vent continued nervously, "It's still Pal. We can go right on and call him Pal. We probably would have done that anyway. Even if it did say Palomino." He smiled and shuffled his feet.

Mary was not amused.

La Vent feared that she was angry at him. Not a Dreamer, and as someone who these days wanted to emulate Diggum and Pavum, he had no way of knowing that she was angry only with herself for letting La Vent talk her into naming a boy Palomino in the first place and then not taking proper care to watch over the filling out of forms. He forgot that she was the daughter of a Nez Perce chief that dime novels and government apologists made up, and then made famous. She had grown up with the frustration of dealing with bureaucrats. Washington bureaucrats were bad enough. Indian bureaucrats like Lawyer and the rest, in their desire to fit in, were worse. They were more thick-tongued and full of logical arguments sculpted out of the air behind their teeth than the cruel Indian agents and army officers who had kept her father, even in his last years, from returning to the valley where his father's bones were buried. La Vent had no way of knowing that when he laughed that weak "Heh-heh" of the proto-bureaucrat, a laugh that looked more like a body burp from an asshole than a real and honest wide-mouthed laugh, Mary felt the bitterness rise in herself. He should have taken care to watch over the filling out of forms. As an aspirer to triplicate himself, he should have known that replication was the most important event in American life.

Mary shook her head slowly. "They take their forms seriously," Mary said. "It is ceremony to them. The only ceremony they have left," she added with a peculiar obsidian gleam in her eye. She should have known the possibility of some officious nurse taking it upon herself to alter the spelling of the name on Pal's birth certificate. Her cousin Lionel Lighters' name had been changed from Light Horse (there was no "Lionel" about it, ever). After most of the Indian had been killed and much of the man saved by Christian educators, he was adopted out from the Goodwin Mission Boarding School, which was like being an indentured servant until he was old enough to run away and disguise himself in the cities.

She also knew many people who had lost touch with the meaning of names, people who no longer discovered names in dreams or in their own histories but called their children anything from Aspen to Zither without a second's thought as to where the kid might be coming from. Some of them went several steps farther, complicating the process by naming their kids after cough medicines and laxatives, or giving them the misspelled appellations of Christian or Islamic heroes like "Isiah" or "Muhmed." Working at her loom, she watched these kids grow up misspelled, if you will, askew, askance, aslope, awry, Isiah growing up not to be a helper but one who needed a lot of help, Muhmed developing a penchant for the quiet quotidian rather than the prophetic.

She jettisoned as much bitterness as she could and, nodding her head at her husband's apologetic whisperings, took his hand and said, "You're right. We can go ahead and call him Pal. We'll have to see what happens."

So Pal he was.

3.

She had wanted to name him Hinmot. But for her premonitions, she would have. But she foresaw Hinmot's slipping out of the birth canal quick and early, his brow furrowed and his fists clenched. She saw how that could lead to his scratching and clawing his way through school trying to convince the other kids and his teachers, too, that his name was not Thunder Rising to a Higher Place but Hinmot, that he did not want his name translated as though it were more foreign than the deaf German who wrote Beet Patch's Ninth Symphony. She could predict ahead of time how often she would be called upon to draw her shawl over her denim-blue shirt with the open hand beaded on it and ride the city bus to the school to listen to Hinmot's teachers classify and categorize their own ignorance as they detailed the ways in which Hinmot fought fitting in nicely.

Pal, on the other hand, was a tractable and quiet baby. He ate when she fed him. He suckled at her breast heartily but not greedily, rolling his unfocused, grateful eyes up at her apologetically almost as though he felt bad for the soreness of her nipples. He went down for naps. Even when he wasn't sleepy, he would lie in his crib gurgling and cooing and trying to bat the padded bears on the mobile that Arturo's wife, Esperanza, brought as a gift when she came to see him. When you changed his diaper, even if he had a rash, he would lie there grinning up at you as though he knew the soreness was only temporary and that soon enough things would be better. And when it became time to toilet-train him, he would sit patiently on the padded child's seat, his pudgy feet on the stool Mary put in front of the toilet, waiting as much as twenty minutes for something to happen. When it did, he would get down with the same pleasant smile that he wore while he waited. In short, Mary began to believe that her son was an incorrigible optimist.

It was in kindergarten that she discovered the other side of him. The teacher complained that Pal built sturdy forts out of wooden blocks and then made his classmates defend them, huddling inside as he ran circles around them whooping and shouting and slapping his thighs with his hand like a horse's gallop. Now and then, he dashed up to the edifice and reached over to tap one of them on the head with a stick before he raced away, out of range of the blocks they threw at him tentatively, fearfully, until the teacher broke up the dangerous game. Afterwards, though, when the blond-haired little girl brought her rush mat over and laid it down beside his at nap time, he lay as still as yucca until she was asleep. Then he picked up his mat and stole quietly off to a corner of the room where he lay down alone, furrowing his brows and growling at anyone who ventured to come close.

As much as they hated to pigeonhole any child, in first grade the authorities were forced to inform Mary of the things he sometimes did, the history in his blood boiling over as he stomped the sombreros for their Mexican Hat Dance.

"Sombreros," the guidance counselor said angrily, "that we've used for a decade. Authentic sombreros Mr. Ross brought back from Mexicali. Sombreros that can never be replaced."

Once, he gave his entire lunch to a black girl who had forgotten hers. And yet not an hour after that kindness, he leapt from his desk and rushed forward to try to choke Mickey G. Wills as he gave an oral report on Captain John Smith.

"He's kind," Mrs. Robinson told Mary Blue. "Very generous and very patient with kids who need help. Especially the colored kids, come to think of it. The Mexicans and Negroes. Yet for no reason, he becomes as mad as a hatter."

In second and third grades, his teachers saw him as nothing more than an irritating interruption. He made them admit where 80 percent of the world's gold came from and how in the Potosí silver mines eight million Indios died for their currency. When he insisted that it was Castile that began the slave trade, they tried to view his behaviors as a kind of liveliness.

"I have not got a clue as to where he gets these things," Mrs. White told the vice-principal, as Mary Blue sat quietly in his office. The yellow-and-blue serape she wore filled the armchair in which she sat and made her look thick and heavy. Her eyes were narrowed as though she was squinting or laughing. Beneath her serape, she folded her strong hands into her woven skirt. She curled the fingers of each hand against each other, hiding her fingerprints like her identity in a grip of yin and yang.

"It's like he makes things up out of the blue," the vice-principal told Mary.

"As though," Mrs. White whispered, correcting the vice-principal.

"As though he just imagines these things." The vice-principal smiled, making a mental note to seek Mrs. White's early retirement as soon as the opportunity arose.

Mary Blue knew that all along Pal thought that he was helping (except when he tried to strangle Mickey G.). He was only correcting information that his teachers, being teachers, would want to correct. He, himself, had no idea how he knew these things. He didn't understand, at first, that his helping was only an annoyance. How could he know that like anyone else, his teachers just wanted to get through the day with what they knew intact? And here came this mixed-up kid who seemed determined to make them look bad.

By fourth grade, they grew weary of him. They began to act like they hated him, and not so secretly. They agreed to set him easy tasks and they refused to worry if he didn't do them. Whatever he did, despite the protests of the fifth-grade teachers, they gave him passing grades, fully intending to pass him on to someone else.

4.

"I don't get it, Mom," Pal said one afternoon. Mary Blue sat beading a pair of leather moccasins for Arturo and Esperanza's baby-to-be. "I thought I was helping."

"So did Sacajawea," she replied.

That night Mary Blue sat up alone after the house was dark, a fringed shawl around her shoulders to keep off the chill of the central valley nights. The single high-intensity lamp gave off a glare, but no heat. She picked up beads on the tip of her needle with impossible ease and then stitched them one at a time into the sunrise pattern that would have a sky blue background. As she pulled the thread tight, locking each bead into its place, she rocked slightly but regularly.

I ask you to imagine how chagrined and embarrassed I was, a *weyekin*, a spirit guide for Mary Blue, to be summoned and then the following day to find myself reduced to a grammar school child being led by the hand by the principal down the corridor to a cinder block school classroom in the town of Gilroy, California. As a new boy, an unknown quantity in a tired teacher's classroom, I was seated at a desk at the back of the room beside the crack babies, the children of illegal immigrants, and Palimony Blue.

We became like brothers, Pal and I. I was just as wild as Pal on the playground at recess and after school. But in class I showed him how to keep his emotions in check. I taught him to cultivate a lack of reputation. Whereas he wanted to burst out and ask how anyone could believe in private property as a right when it was based entirely on theft, I knew that deep down inside he wanted nothing more than to have the teachers and his classmates like him. He began to say less and less in class, eventually not saying anything at all, even when they asked him questions. Shorter now than kids two grades behind him, his growth stunted by caffeine or the magazines his father left in the bathroom, Mickey G. Wills presented a report titled "One Nation Under God." Pal sat through it all without moving, the grin on his face causing Mickey to sputter and stammer more than if Pal had put his fingers around his throat and squeezed. There were times, now, that the teachers gathered in the teacher's prep room and wondered if Pal was not retarded, slowed down by his block head sticking in the birth canal, the retardation just now beginning to reveal itself.

Pal's brow became furrowed with worry and anxiety instead of anger. After several months of his patient solicitousness, the teacher began cautiously moving him like a chess pawn, one square at a time, forward, integrating him into the mainstream of the class. Mr. Aguire even decided that he sort of liked Pal. He was a pal, always the pal, wanting, desiring, doing anything to be the pal, trying to disarm the hurt he might feel at what others said by joking. For example, he called Beethoven's Ninth "Beet Patch's Ode to Hey-Yea-Yea." Even if they did not get his jokes, which they did not, his classmates were glad to find him calmer, quieter. He kept more to himself and he was less apt to question or challenge.

Imagine his (let alone, my) surprise when in the face of his transigence and tractability his teachers began to feel sentimental and forgiving. They now remembered him as having an enchanting fierceness that they had, all things considered, liked. Appreciated. Imagine how he felt when he overheard his third-grade teacher say to his fifth, "At least he was alive."

His second-grade teacher couldn't have agreed more. "That he was," she said wistfully.

He wondered if, by their saying that in his outspokenness he had seemed *alive*, it meant that he, now, as well as the other students (and maybe even the teachers themselves) were what you could call *dead*? It seemed odd that they could say that but then overlook the meaning of what they said, like a colonial soldier looks out over the shaved points of the stockade wall and thinks how good it is that the wall is there, but never once wonders that in order to keep *them* out there he has to keep himself in here, essentially putting himself and his friends in prison.

"Yes," the fifth-grade teacher agreed. "Alive." Even he had to admit that he missed the original Pal. It would be better to have him interrupt, to disagree, to question, even to argue. Anything was better than the class of day-care dullness raised on quality time in front of their televisions that now filed in every morning.

Chapter Five

I.

As any forty-year-old realizes when he speaks and he not only sounds like his father in inflection and pitch but also uses the exact words his father would have used, the problem with nurture, what of it that has effect, is that it is all there in nature. All a *weyeķin* can do is try to highlight portions of what is already all there. That is, the plot is there. This plot is little more than a story of Pal's learning to dream for himself, and there is nothing for you to learn from it if you're not interested in dreaming. The way in which the plot occurs, the process by which the threads are traced, can change. But it cannot change much, defined and contained as it is by the predetermined plot, which, in this case, is genetics. Pal was going to be either like Mary Blue or like La Vent. Or, if I was successful, he would be a Dreamer faithful to himself and content with how he was like Mary Blue, perhaps with a little of La Vent's ambition thrown in if for no other reason than to create the illusion of progressive change.

Teaching Pal in grammar school was a successful failure. I had taught him how to restrain his feelings but not his overwhelming need to be liked. And I had not come close to teaching him why, which was, of course, Amanda. Love itself.

"Good going," Mary Blue said as she stood with her back to me at the kitchen counter dicing chicken and bell peppers. On the stove top was a pan of chocolate sauce for the mole. Once she was finished dicing them, she would tilt the cutting board and slide them into the spicy-sweet sauce and simmer them in it. When it was done, it would all be ladled over a plate of brown rice. "You are supposed to show him how to get along. You aren't supposed to make him into *that*."

She raised her knife and pointed at the man in a polyester suit getting out of the car in the driveway. You could see him exercise the muscles of his face, contorting it as he dropped the smiling slave face he wore during the day and donned the Lord of the Castle face he wore at dinner.

"Sorry," I said. "But you're the one who gave me the raw material. *That*, as you call your husband, is the warp or woof on the genetic loom. How can I teach him what good relations are when the only example I have is Pal's relation to you?" I was a little annoyed at the way I was being put on the spot for doing my best. I thought she owed me an apology. For a moment, I even expected her to speak words of apology.

She turned and pointed the knife at me, tapping it in the air to punctuate her words as though she were tapping a drum. "Let me remind you that I can send you packing any time and you can spend the rest of eternity with Tom Yellowtail wishing you had something to do."

"I wouldn't mind," I said. I was bluffing. I loved Tom like a brother, but a *weyekin* with nothing to do is like a human being with no imagination. "I like Tom. And Henny Penny."

"There's always Chicken Licken." She grinned, threateningly.

"How do you know about all these *weyekin*? Where did you learn about Licken?"

"You forget that I know the mayor."

Licken would be his, all right. As Anglo as they come. A little frightened guide for a little frightened spirit that protected itself with the power gained by spreading more fear. The power of the field boss who keeps illegals in check with the threat of the INS and deportation.

"I've gotten used to Licken," I said. "He's not so bad, as long as you don't pay attention to him."

Mary stopped ticking the knife in the air. She pushed her lips together in thought. Her dark eyebrows frowned. Then she laughed. "I'll give you to someone."

"Yeah? Who?" It'd be something to do, at least.

"How about . . . ?"

She named a living writer. A nationalist writer from a country with a lot of permafrost. I stifled a groan.

"Better yet," Mary laughed loudly. The beadwork on her shirt seemed to dance. "Sylvia Plath. That's who I'll send you off to."

"Okay, okay," I said. "You win. Anything but Sylvia Plath. Jesus, she's already dead and she still keeps sticking her head in the oven. Talk about self-pity. I couldn't take it."

"I know," Mary Blue said.

Lord of the Castle La Vent crossed the entry hall, set down his briefcase, and entered the kitchen. He waved an envelope in the air. It was square like a birthday card.

"Our only son has been sent this from the mayor," La Vent said, officiously. He handed the envelope to Mary with a small looping flourish.

I withdrew to the corner where she hung her tortilla press, her grater and food strainers. Mary took the envelope, peeled it open with her forefinger, and drew out the folded card inside. Opening the card, she read it. Then she folded it closed. Closed her eyes and looked out the window, swaying back and forth. Turned her back on La Vent, who stood there smiling. After several minutes, she opened her eyes, reopened the card, and read it a second time.

"You can read it a hundred times," I whispered from my corner. "You can't change the words."

La Vent stopped smiling and looked toward the sink beside which I sat, now, on the cutting board built into the counter. "You hear that?" he said. "Sounds like wind in the trees. It seems like this house is haunted, almost."

"It is," Mary Blue said. She squared her shoulders and stood up straight, pulling herself together. "But not how you think. So?" she said, handing the card to La Vent.

"So, what?" La Vent said.

"So does Pal have to go?"

"It's the mayor's son's birthday."

"I see that. I didn't say, Whose party is it? I asked if Pal had to go to it."

"Why wouldn't he?"

"Maybe because he doesn't even own a pair of yellow slacks," Mary Blue muttered.

"Goddamn it, Mary. I liked those guys. Those guys at our wedding in the yellow slacks you disdain so much helped get me through college. Without them, I wouldn't have had the time to be in Adelanto at that stupid beaner cafe eating that crummy food waiting for you to bother talking to me."

"Ummm," she said. Her anger made her rock back and forth on her feet slowly, slightly. Her strong weaver's hands tightened into fists. She tucked then into her armpits, crossing her arms beneath her breasts, hugging herself and holding herself in check.

"Like it or not, this boy's father is who feeds us."

"I hope Pal has been invited as a guest? Not as an extra servant?" Mary said. Each word was distinct and cool.

"He'll go. I've already accepted for him," La Vent said. "It's already done. It can't be changed now."

"We'll see," Mary said. But she was speaking to me, not to La Vent, who stormed out of the room shouting, "Pal? Pal? Get your butt in here."

He attempted to sound angry. But he only sounded hurt and annoyed. He had come home with the invitation, expecting his wife to see its having been proffered as another milestone in his career, a small but very pointed and significant success. To be invited to the mayor's house for a formal event was, well, to be both accepted and appreciated. To have your child invited meant that the appreciation and value were so great as to be transferable.

2.

She stayed up all that Friday night, chanting, talking to herself and then to me, adding details to her picture of the party, modifying them, dreaming how the event would generally go, over and over, until she was calm and content with the outlines of the vision. On Saturday morning, she watched calmly with silent objection as outside the window she saw La Vent put his hand on Pal's shoulder and steer him into the station wagon as though at any second Pal might bolt, dashing off into the new construction in the hills to hide from his fate behind stacks of lumber and brick or inside the cab of dormant bulldozers until dark. La Vent had purchased Pal new cotton slacks, yellow-brown, the color of the upturned hills in the distance. His mother had seen to it that the shirt he wore was bright and patterned with the small shapes of dinosaurs, brightly colored triceratopses and stegosaurs among black and threatening *T. rexes*. From a distance, as La Vent pushed him down into the seat of the car, the dinosaurs looked like bright polka dots widely spaced across a white shirt.

Mary smiled. She watched La Vent start the station wagon. His face turned toward Pal as though he wanted to say something. He didn't.

She watched as La Vent drove out past the developments and across Gilroy, up into the hills north of the city into a neighborhood where none of the streets ran straight. Some of the streets were crossed by speed bumps, low ridges of asphalt that if you went too far over the speed limit threw the driver and passengers up from the bench of their seats, threatening to bonk their heads on the roof and causing the car to swerve and shudder. Pal took these bounces quietly, silently. He was curious about the party he was being taken to.

His father could not stop marveling at the neighborhood and houses. "My," La Vent uttered. "My, my. I didn't know houses like these even existed in Gilroy."

He drove more slowly, turning his head this way and that. He braked lightly and ducked his head up into the arch of the windshield to better peer out at a house that towered above the road like a fort. La Vent's vision of a better life for Pal and Mary took on the image and shading of these houses, of this reality. He stopped and backed up.

"Would you look at that," he said. "Look, Pal. Can you imagine how happy you'd be living in a house like that one?"

It was a mock-Spanish villa, whitewashed and shining behind wrought-iron rococo gates. The shrubs that lined the driveway leading up to the entrance portico were trimmed into geometries of square and diamond. The lawn that curved down toward the street like an open palm was large enough to carpet the Wallowa Valley that Mary Blue came from.

Pal dutifully looked. "No," he said. Then to temper his words for La Vent's sake, he added, "Not really."

Every corner had a stop sign. There was no racing through this neighborhood. You were meant to stop and look and admire and if you didn't, if you rolled your low-riding Chevy through stop signs as you cased the neighborhood, the police had reason enough to pull you over and question and ticket you.

There were no curbs. No center lines on the asphalt roads, which were dark and fresh as though they'd been washed. Every kind of tree lined the curving streets—mulberry, maple, ginkgo, oak, black walnut—all of a size and a greenness that made the tiny sprig of spruce Pal had planted with his school in Coronado Park seem hopeless, pointless, insignificant.

Pal squirmed in his seat. "These pants itch," he said.

"Don't be silly," La Vent replied. He was still staring out the window at his favorite villa, lost in a transubstantial housing dream.

"They do, Dad," Pal protested.

"Where?" La Vent said, taking his foot off the brake and letting the station wagon start to roll forward again. Slowly. "Where do your brand-new slacks itch?"

"Here," Pal said, pointing at his thigh just below his buttock. "And here." He touched the insides of his thighs near his genitals.

"Well, you'll just have to live with it. Whatever you do, don't go scratching your unmentionables or pulling at your pants on the behind. These people are well-to-do. They're refined. They won't look kindly on your reminding them of such things."

"Okay, Dad," Pal sighed.

"Speaking of which, where is your bow tie?"

Pal patted his shirt pocket. "Here," he said.

"Why aren't you wearing it?"

"You said I could wait," Pal replied. "I'm waiting."

"You will put it on."

A flight of bald-faced hornets hovered near the passenger window for a moment. Pal felt tempted to stick his face out the window and try to catch one in his teeth. Getting stung by a bald-faced hornet would end this journey, reverse it swiftly, as he was rushed to the clinic for care. But he wasn't brave enough and the hornets buzzed off. The tie was a clip-on that Pal knew would fool neither the visually impaired nor the blind.

"You may take the tie off if no one else is wearing one."

"What if one kid is wearing one but nobody else is?"

"You can take it off then, too."

"How 'bout two kids?"

"I guess then, too."

Pal hoped there wouldn't be more than five boys at the party. He didn't push for three kids with ties. He knew that if he pushed La Vent too far he'd say something like if Pryce Packard, the mayor's son, was wearing a tie then Pal would have to, too, regardless of what the other children did.

"This must be it," La Vent commented, reading the bright brass numerals on the gate pillar. He pulled through the gate and slowly edged up the crushed-lava drive, the big wheels of the station wagon making the headlights and grilles of the sedans and four-by-fours turn and stare at the noisy intrusion of the vehicle.

The Packard estate was a tri-level of storied adobe with lacy iron-work on the upstairs balconies. A red tile roof and four chimneys; shrubs trimmed into the shapes of birds and animals, outdoing the gardeners of the houses farther down the hill; and what will always define what people would mean by a "riot" of wildflowers. Except the riot was of color and not movement and location. An arched oak door, the planks strapped with black iron and bolts resembling a medieval jail. The litany of proper behavior La Vent had put Pal through did not prepare him for this. He nervously and dejectedly stood on the stoop waiting for the door chimes to quit playing "Be All That You Can Be"—a musical tribute to the defense contracts from which, before running for mayor, Pryce's father had made his fortune.

Pal stood beside his father with his eyes closed, rocking slightly, starting to feel good in his rocking. He tried to imagine Mary Blue. What would his mom be doing at this moment? (Mary Blue smiled. The answer was that she was dreaming and in her dreaming she was watching Pal trying to imagine her. She was dreaming and trying to make sure that at the end of the day, when the party was over, she could call him back, back to her, back to home, back to himself—what self, at his age, he could be sure he had.)

A man clothed stiffly in black and white answered the door chimes. Pal opened his eyes. La Vent pushed him forward, told the butler who this child was, and then abandoned him like a child abandoned to Christian missionaries and drove away.

3.

Perhaps Pal felt like a child who is collected by a well-intentioned official and driven on a wagon to the nearest railway station where he waits with several other overdressed, dark-skinned children for a steam locomotive to pull up and stop, shyly looking at all these other scared and frightened children who are then loaded onto the train and railroaded off to boarding school where they will be made to exchange their own language for English, with the concurrent general improvement in civility and manners. Perhaps Pal stood in the entry hall to the Packard estate feeling not unlike Christine Quintasket felt when, needing to speak Salish—the only language she knew at her young age—she knew that if she did she would be beaten or locked for days in a dark closet.

"Mr. Packard?" Pal says hopefully, politely, obsequiously, fearfully. The front door thunks closed, solid and muffled, behind him.

The man in stiff black and white smiles down indulgently at his

upturned face. His smile makes Pal feel like an idiot. The man raises
one finger toward his god like a candle held up to light the way and
leads him down a corridor. He opens an interior door.

"Mrs. Packard?" Pal asks, again as deferentially as he knows how.

The woman is young and plainly dressed. She smiles kindly. "No,"
she says, coming over to him and lifting his little gift out of his hands.
The small box in which he has wrapped Mary's carefully hand-netted
spirit dreamcatcher with a peacock's feather hanging on a beaded stem
seems to shrink like a sprig of spruce beside the other large wrapped
boxes spread out across the back lid of a black baby grand. Pal wishes
that his own father had not forsaken him to this humiliation. Politely,
he follows the woman through large French doors that open out onto a
slate patio.

"Palimony Blue Larue," she announces out loud and, as far as Pal
can tell, to no one in particular. He forgives the giggle she stifles behind
her hand, which she cups over her mouth, her eyes flashing above her
high cheekbones and contained by her dark eyebrows. She gives him a
peculiar look, apologetic and friendly at the same time. Then she with-
draws, walking backwards, pulling the French doors closed as she goes.
Pal stands alone on the slate blinking like a prairie dog in the bright
afternoon light.

What seems to be minutes pass.

Finally a woman in tennis whites rises from a clutch of women
gathered beneath the ample shade of a huge red-and-white striped patio umbrella. She slides her chair back on the slate without a sound and
strolls across the patio to Pal. She reaches out three fingers to shake his
hand. You can see by the way he wavers like a sapling in wind that he
feels a huge desire to dodge her handshake as if she had a joy-buzzer
hidden in her palm. He manages to stand his ground and take her
greeting like a man.

"Hello," she says. "You must be . . . ?"

"Pal," he says.

"Pal?"

"Palimony Larue."

"Ah, yes, the little. . . . His honor said you'd show up. Weren't there supposed to be two of you? A twin brother? Blue or something? Well, no matter. Pal. That is certainly an interesting name, is it not? You people are so clever, aren't you? With names." Straightening up and looking around as though she expects his mother Mary to be hiding in the topiary, she asks, "Did your ma-*ma* come in?"

Pal wants to tell her nice and politely that his ma-*ma* never would have given him up to the discomfort he feels, that it was La Vent, his pa-*pa*, who abandoned him here. But all he manages to do is shake his head, no.

"No? Well, too bad. We were looking forward to meeting someone like her. Her being a real . . . well, you know. Another time, perhaps. Maybe she can advise me on some Jemez artifacts I'm thinking of buying. As an investment, of course. So tell me, how did you get such an interesting name?"

"It's a long story," Pal mumbles as politely as he can. The shyness he feels in talking about himself is exacerbated by the sheer comfort of Mrs. Packard.

"Ummm. Why don't we go introduce you to the other children," Mrs. Packard says, obviously uninterested in just how long a story it is.

The other children are gathered in a semicircle before a Fauntleroyed boy who is giving them orders on how to play croquet.

"So far, let's see, we have Patty." She points out each child and describes them by telling Pal what their fathers do. "Her papa is in publishing. Next to her is Leland, development, then Edsel, automotive, as you might gather. Corliss, she's a little like you. She's another little . . . Corliss is new to our group," she adds brightly, as though this will make him feel less out of place. "Her father does diamonds. Lots and lots of diamonds," she adds with a quick intake of breath that sounds like a gasp. "Uh, then Mark, whose daddy does hotels. Go on, now, they're just starting a new game."

Pal staggers down the stone steps to the acre of putting green the Packards call the back lawn like a boy entering a dream-vision of alienation. "Hi," he says to Pryce Packard. "I'm Pal."

Pryce turns on him with an angry look of frustration. Pal is interrupting his orders about how to play croquet his way. He drops his mallet in disgust. "Wait your turn, will you, Chief?"

"Pal," he says. "Sure." He moves over to the end of the semicircle.

The other children, when Pryce is finished, line up to begin the game. There are not enough mallets to go around so Pal doesn't take one. Not knowing what else to do, he tags along after Patty.

"My father does zoning for the city," he tells her, imitating Mrs. Packard and hoping that this will break the ice. "He's on the zoning commission. That's why the Packards invited me to the party."

Patty gives him a blasting, explosive look. "Probably zones out," she replies, acidly, "from the looks of you."

Pal figures he and Patty aren't going to be close friends. He ignores her and tries to laugh like La Vent, "Heh-heh." It sounds like a burp and tastes like indigestion.

Patty bends over to place her ball on the turf and her skirt rises to reveal panties that are multicolored, swirled with bright yellows and reds and blues as though she's sat in varicolored pots of paint. Letters are painted over the bright colors, but Pal cannot make out if the letters spell words or what words they spell.

"Did you know you had graffiti on your undies?" he asks.

"That's not graffiti," she says haughtily, predicting the future of underwear. "That's art." She moves away from him.

He closes his eyes tight and wishes with all his might that a friend, some kid like him from the old neighborhood, would show up suddenly. He forgets that La Vent, his own father, is in part responsible for the fact that there are no longer any old neighborhoods in Gilroy, none older than the one he is in at the moment.

Giving up on Patty, he decides to give Mark a go.

"Hey, Mark," he says, crossing the croquet court.

Mark gives him an indeterminate look. "Are you addressing me?" Mark says.

"Yes. I. . . ."

"Excuse me," he says, "but what makes you think you can just walk up to me and act like you're my friend?"

"I'm sorry," Pal says. "I didn't mean. . . ."

"Where I come from we don't make friends with Wagon Burners."

Edsel isn't much friendlier, although with a front end like he was pushing, Pal forgives him out of compassion. Pal had always kind of liked the photos Mary showed him of La Vent's old Edsel car because the toilet seat designed into its grille seemed so unusual, so out of place in the finned world of Detroit cars, and Pal liked odd things. But that was on a car. On a person, well, even though he sees where the design comes from, an industrial replication of reality, it isn't so attractive. It's kind of like a hair lip and leaves Edsel seeming to grin when he is concentrating on making his mallet strike the round colored croquet ball with deadly seriousness.

And Leland? Poor Leland seems retarded. He keeps shaking his head as though there's sand in it that keeps shifting on him and he's trying to get it to shake out flat and smooth.

Only Corliss is nice to him. "Hi," she says.

"Hi back," Pal replies. He feels as though he's fallen in love, but as he follows her about the croquet grounds she stops.

"Would you mind?" she whispers sweetly. "It's hard enough for me to make friends without you breathing down my neck."

"Sorry," Pal whispers back.

4.

He was just about ready to cross the brook at the back of the lawn and strike out for home on his own when, according to Mary Blue's dreaming, I came jogging up out of nowhere, another brown-skinned boy at the party, like Pal.

"Yo," I said, "how's it hanging, Pal?"

"How . . . ?" A wave of relief washed over him. His wish for a kid from the old neighborhood had come as true as Mary could make it.

"Chingaro," I said. "My name. Remember me? School, a couple of years ago?"

"Chingaro. How are you . . . how did you . . . ?"

I waved his questions away. A spirit guide does not explain. "No never mind," I say. "I'm here, now."

"Chingaro," he says again. "Man, is it good to see you."

"I know, man. I can tell. Chingito, though, okay? Like old times, hey?"

I took a look around. Scoped out the company. Patty bent over to move her ball so she would have a better angle on a croquet hoop. I said loud and clear, "They call that art? Looks like graffiti to me."

I nudged Pal with my elbow and winked.

"Old art's been coming to that for a long time," I said.

Pal laughed.

I snapped to attention. "Yo!" I shouted. "All you Chicken Licken sky-is-falling fans listen up. My name's Chingaro. My pa-*pa* does pro-phyl-ac-tics."

The other kids just stood there staring.

"Rubbers," I said as loud as before. "You know, they go on your dick?" I cupped my unmentionables with both hands and gyrated, slowly. "If you got one," I added, looking around. Leland was drooling. I couldn't help but feel sorry for him and I had to remind myself that these were the offspring of *wétiko*. That's a Cree word. Means someone who consumes other human beings for profit. In other words, fucking cannibal kids. No feeling sorry for cannibal kids, I told myself.

The other cannibal kids stood stolid, looking at me and Pal. You could see them thinking that just because Pal and I arrived at the party already tanned, because we were already colored in, so to speak, we were about as likable or as interesting as figures in a used coloring book.

Pryce moved first, throwing down his mallet in disgust and marching over to the patio where he complained to his mother loudly about how those goddamned colored kids were going to ruin everything.

I ignored the words Pryce used about Pal and me. Grinning, I picked up Pryce's mallet, strolled over to Leland's ball by the first wicket, and gave the ball such a blow that it disappeared into the woods. Patty laughed. She took her mallet and started swinging, striking randomly at anything that stood still—balls, other kids, the wickets, the unlit tiki torches that outlined the path to the lawn. She hit the flat disk of a built-in lawn sprinkler, causing the sprinkler to pop up and begin spraying erratically. Within minutes the croquet game degenerated into a turnless random striking of balls. Everyone but Pryce was laughing and having fun chasing their balls this way and that as Pal and I knocked them off the court. Pal gave Edsel's ball such a blow that it ended up on the other side of the brook below the lawn. Corliss's ball went hop-skipping across the tennis court, skipping and spinning, seeming to gather momentum on its way. She watched it, shrugging.

Pal offered to go get it for her.

"Don't bother," she said. "It's too much trouble." She sighed.

After croquet, which sort of ended by default because the balls were all gone and several of the hoops had been fashioned into objects as arty as Patty's panties, Mrs. Packard called the children up to the patio for lunch. It was served on gaily decorated lap trays by the young woman who had led Pal through the house when he arrived.

Pal and I made a game of figuring out what it was we were eating. But after Leland said they were Rocky Mountain oysters and Corliss circumspectly explained what those were, Pal decided to settle for not knowing. He concentrated on the colors and tastes and textures without asking whether they were eating bull balls or dolphin eyes.

The melon that fell into his lap, of course, he recognized, despite Mark's pronouncing its name with a Castilian "th"—cathaba.

No matter what Mark called it, the casaba slipped into his lap, leaving small sweet patches of wetness on his trousers. Patty stared angrily at the stains as though she wanted to blow them up real good.

All Pal hoped for was that the wet spots would dry out before the clown arrived, or before the inevitable resumption of fun and games and he had to stand up and parade around, the stain in his crotch as conspicuous as Patty's panties.

"Hey, man, just call it art and let it show," I said. I refused the offer of fruit for the third time. I wouldn't eat any of it; I knew what field workers do to melons when they're picking and, frankly, I'd rather eat the balls of bulls.

"I know why we work for them," I commented as Mrs. Packard handed out door prizes to every child but me and Pal after the completion of another game. We'd been removed from participating because we pretended not to understand the trick, which was to let Pryce win at ring toss and lawn darts and the treasure hunt for prizes concealed in the yard, during which Pal found Corliss's croquet ball and buried it.

The butler brought out a board with a donkey painted on it. Pryce, going last, tilted his head and peeked beneath the blindfold and put his tail right on the old donkey. I went a bit nuts and started shouting.

Pal knew better than to do what he did to the piñata. Failure sometimes has difficulty tolerating failure in others, and besides, sweet Jesus, it was going to take a week for Pryce Packard to hit it hard enough to break it. Even without a blindfold, he kept missing it or just grazing it, the stick glancing off it as though it were stone.

Pal kept the maid company in the kitchen. He told himself that it was misery to live like that because it was just too easy.

When five-thirty rolled around and La Vent arrived to pick him up, the maid led him out from the kitchen by the hand and, before parting, gave her little pal a little hug.

Pal was glad to see La Vent.

He said to Mrs. Packard and her friends having sherry in the sitting room that he was so very grateful that his son had gotten to have such a good time. He made Pal say two or three times how nice a time it was (Pal wondered where I'd gone). Pal felt ashamed, embarrassed not by his father's civility, but by his eagerness under the scrutiny of the women, who were so comfortable they may as well have been in their own homes.

The drive home remained like a dream as Pal went over the events of the birthday party (what became of Chingito?). By the time that La Vent and he had driven back into reality, he had reduced the afternoon to a set of events that he could tell Mary Blue. He knew she had given him Chingito. He did not know as yet that the entire dream of the party was Mary Blue's anymore than he realized that the nightmare of its reality was La Vent's. By the time dinner was over, the party had become like the shadows of memories for Pal, shadows which seemed to lurk just out of reach.

Pal finished clearing the table and doing the dishes. He went in to thank Mary for the gift of Chingito.

"You're welcome," she said.

Pal stood in front of her, shifting from one foot to the other. "Mom," he said at last. "Can I ask you something?"

"Yes."

"What's a minority?"

"I wouldn't get caught up in that, if I were you," La Vent said, coming into the kitchen after wiping off the dining table with a damp sponge.

Mary held up her hand to silence him. Thinking carefully, she frowned, her eyebrows casting her eyes in shadow. Then she smiled. Nodding, she said, "It's what we are in this city." Happily, she added, "It's what they are in the world."

La Vent stood there staring at her. "Excuse me," he said. "I've got work to do."

La Vent didn't agree with Mary Blue. And he didn't want her teaching his son that kind of crap. But he knew better than to argue with her. Especially when she was as angry as he could see that she was.

And was she ever. Not with La Vent. Or Pal. With me. Can you imagine that?

Later that night after La Vent had fallen asleep over the paperwork on his desk and Pal should have been asleep in his bed, Mary Blue sat, her face hidden by the darkness of the night with only her hands illuminated in the halo of light cast by her high-intensity lamp on her beading table. She decided then to begin working on a new project, a beaded cradle board that would be a history of Pal's family. She began by drawing with a fine-point marker, outlining the shape of events she already knew at the bottom of a sheet of deerskin. Later, as she dreamed them and they came to be—which was not always exactly like she envisioned them in her dreaming—she would use the marker again to draw them in around a U-shaped border. At the center, when *she* came to be (if she came to be—that was up to Pal), she would put in the signs and shapes that represented love itself, Amanda by name, and the children created by that love.

But for now, she was angry. "Congratulations," she said, when I arrived.

"What now? I did my best. I didn't fail Pal."

"No," she said angrily. "You didn't fail Pal. You failed me."

"How's that? How can I succeed with Pal and not with you?"

"I did not say you succeeded. I said you didn't fail. There's a difference."

"All right. So?"

"So what you did by disrupting the birthday party helped my son decide whether or not he wanted to be liked by that kind of child. He doesn't. That's right."

"So I succeeded."

"You made them look like fools. I should not have to remind you that they are not fools. Those kids know from birth, if not from conception, almost by instinct, how their world works. To make them look foolish, you have to enter their world. That's what you have taught my son. Not only to enter their world but that by making them look foolish, he can disregard them. Like Hamlet he can go around saying, 'Seems, madam? Nay, I know not seems.' But I don't want him in their world. I want him to envision and make a world of his own in which they are not foolish but all their knowledge and instinct don't matter because they don't have any effect."

"Sorry," I said, seeing that she was right. I'd forgotten, maybe because of getting to like Chicken Licken.

"Sorry isn't good enough," Mary Blue replied. "I want my son to learn how to dream. You are going to help him do that."

"I'll do better."

"You will," she said. She did not have to add, "Or else."

Chapter Six

1.

Tom was on tour when I got back, off telling creation stories to Coeur d'Alene children. I missed him. Creation stories are fun to tell and I wished I could have gone along with him to watch him adopt the formal attire of a railroad engineer and listen to the minor differences between the way the Nez Perce and the Coeur d'Alene worlds come to be. I needed to talk over what I should do next about Palimony, if I didn't want Mary Blue to give me away to Sylvia Plath or worse (or perhaps not actually worse, a *weyekin* can't be sure) dream me into the shape of a small rodent like a rat or a bushy-tailed fox squirrel.

"Wow!" Henny Penny said when she saw me. "You look bad. Real bad."

"Looks to me like everything is falling down on you," Chicken Licken said. "Like a few of the falling things have clipped you on the chin. Like your world is coming to an end. Like the sky is falling. That's it, isn't it? The sky is falling. The sky is falling. I'm right. The sky is falling."

"Chill, Licken," I said.

"I feel bad," I said to Henny. "Nothing seems worse than to put in all this time and then get criticized for the results."

"What's up?" she asked. Henny was kind. Which was one reason I liked her. Although it was out of kindness that things so often went wrong.

I told Henny about the party. She thought it was pretty funny. She liked the bit about Patty's undies with graffiti scribbled on them. "So what's the problem? Sounds like Palimony got home intact."

"I made the other kids look like fools," I said.

"So? They are. Lots of them are. Believe me. I know. That's why I'm usually sitting around here with nothing to do instead of being there, helping them."

"Mary Blue says no. They're not. And the more I think about it, the more I think she's right. I keep seeing little Pryce Packard go at the piñata. While the way he swings at it and keeps missing makes me want to laugh, at the same time I see all the other kids, except Pal, stand back and watch. In my vision they're almost bored. Pal went bonkers. But the rest of the kids look bored as though this is the way things ought to be. The way they have always been. The way they will always be repeated. Pal's bonkers and they're yawning. Pal thinks it's unjust and unfair. They don't even care about fair."

"Hmmm," Henny said thoughtfully.

"Mary Blue brought up Hamlet," I said. "How she knows about him, I sure as hell don't know."

"What's that?"

"Promise you won't tell Tom?"

"I swear," Henny Penny said solemnly.

"I played the part of a ghost a long time ago. I was young. Just messing around. I happened to be in northern Europe and there was this stuff going on with Little Ham's mother bonking her husband's brother. Wouldn't have made a bit of diff if it weren't that these guys were in charge of the whole country. Hamlet suspected. I figured a good ghosting would get him moving. And it did."

"So? You did what you set out to do."

"Yeah. But by pretending to be Hamlet's dad in a sheet I ended up making Hamlet dead. Mary's right. I got Hamlet to take seriously a world that with counseling or psychotherapy he could have learned to ignore. I just did it again with Pal. Although psychotherapy is not an option for a Dreamer's kid." I sighed. "Oh, well, at least I didn't give him a lot of pompous advice like that Polonius telling his son to stay within himself, stuff I'll have to take back."

"Where are you going?" Henny said, as I turned to leave.

"I figure I better go work over the father, again."

2.

While I was gone—what Mary would call for a long time, whereas for me and Henny it was almost no time at all—Mayor Packard had ordered La Vent to find a way for the city of Gilroy to bulldoze a site sacred to the local Costano Indians.

"Do what?" Mary asked. She was sitting in the front yard beside a fountain La Vent had installed, a pineapple daiquiri in her hand. The capped blender stood upright in the fountain's pool nearby, keeping her refills cool. She sat, letting the sound of the splashing fountain sink into her, watching the rainbow-making fans of water rise, arc, and fall, and staring west over the low adobe wall that fenced the yard. The clouds over the mountains looked heavy and dark, their bellies lightened only by the angling light from the sun. She knew that as heavy as they looked, they would not bring rain. Not to Gilroy. It was hot and dry, and even the fountain seemed a luxury to her.

La Vent came through the gate—iron, wrought, with sharp lance-like tips, a combined expression of envy of the mayor's neighborhood and fear that the Chicanos might try to return. Though even a child could crawl over the low adobe wall, the gate made La Vent feel secure. He walked heavily, slowly, as though he bore a heavy rucksack on his back. He looked at the ground as he walked, as though he feared the "Click!" of a field mine beneath his patent leather loafers.

Now he stood at her shoulder watching her drink slowly. He thought for a moment that he should criticize her drinking. He wasn't sure he liked her sitting outside. Everyone could see her drinking. How many times had he heard comments about Mrs. Packard and the habits she indulged herself in while the mayor was off campaigning for the city. But he also wanted to tell her about the Costano burial sites and he did not want her to criticize him. So, in his own mind at least, he traded his criticism of her with the criticism he knew she'd want to produce the minute he told her. Besides, she really didn't drink that much and never during the morning or the afternoons. Not like Buzz's wife.

"You're going to do what?" Mary asked again. The tone in her voice was not critical. It was astonished.

"Buzz, the mayor, wants to remove the bodies from a site along the road to Freedom. Build a new mall."

"The site belongs to the Costanos, though. That it?"

"The twenty of them who can still claim blood enough to be Costano. Yeah."

"Their ancestors are buried there. Their grandmothers. Their grandfathers."

"I know. Buzz agreed we'd get some archaeologists and anthropologists over from the campus at Santa Cruz to help us dig them up and then rebury them. Somewhere out of the way of future development. And with all the proper ceremonies. He's even offered to kick in some funds to improve the site, make the new grounds pretty, like a park."

"Just what I'd like. My kids playing softball on my bones. Having a picnic."

"Not like that. But a pretty place to walk. A peaceful place."

"Do the Costanos want this?"

"Well. . . ."

"I didn't think so." Mary took a sip of her daiquiri. She shook her head. Looking up at the clouds, which had blown in closer but still without rain, and then at her husband, she asked, "The words 'Lovely's Purchase' mean anything to you these days? Pierre Choutou?"

La Vent frowned, his lips locked tight. He looked at the ground, which he stirred with his feet. His father had told him stories of how Osage land was taken from the Osage. How the Osage people bought it back from the government, only to have it taken from them a second time with the help of Pierre Choutou. How could he forget? Back in their courtship days, he, himself, had been the one to tell the story to Mary.

"I suppose now you think Lovely's Purchase wasn't theft, like you used to, but something like a cultural misunderstanding. Am I right?"

"Look," La Vent said, getting angry. "I don't have to stand here and listen to this. Let's be honest, okay? You sit around all day beading or drinking daiquiris or just doing whatever. I go to work."

"Dreaming is work," Mary said. "So is beading."

"Maybe," La Vent said, determined not to let her win this one. "But you get to do it alone. When you feel like doing it. I go to work with people I don't always like and I have to do things I don't always like to do. But I do them because I have a family to support. You and Pal want a house, a car, food and clothing? I have to keep the mayor happy."

"Buzz?" Mary asked. "Happy? You?" The irony in her voice was as heavy as the rainless clouds.

"Buzz," La Vent said. "He's gonna bulldoze that site. Do you understand? He's going to do it with me or without me. But he's going to do it. I've got a chance to get him to show some consideration to the Costano people. Elsewise he's just going to ignore them. There aren't exactly enough of them to vote him out of office."

Mary Blue closed her eyes. She'd heard it all before. She'd heard stories about it from her own mother. She still could hear the old stories about Lawyer and the rest of "them Indans" that her mother had given her, the same stories that, time and again, her grandmother told her mother, trying to rinse the bitterness from her voice like the grit from the garments she washed. Stories about how the Nez Perce had taken up the Book and its ways because the ways of the missionaries and the Nu Mi-Pu seemed so similar. The book itself and the God the missionaries talked about seemed so powerful, a better way to the afterworld. Slowly, over time, Mary's grandmother's band had turned away from Christianity, away from the promises that seemed convenient only for the ones who made the promises. The other bands and the other Indians like the one called—in that predictive futurity the Human Beings had—Lawyer went right on calling themselves Christian while in their hearts they became less Nu-Mi-Pu.

Mary's grandmother told other stories. How their band was loaded on flatboats and taken down the Yellowstone to the Missouri and on to Eeikish Pah, the Hot Place, the place that for the no-longer-Christian Human Beings seemed so much like the hell the missionaries had promised. In her heart she had hated the missionaries, the Indian agents, and most of all the Christian Nez Perce who sold off the bones of her fathers and mothers, the Wallowa Valley, even the camas roots at the end of the Lolo Trail. Mary's grandmother had died of bitterness, her sharp tongue raking her spirit like the talons of an eagle until it bled to death. As a girl, Mary Blue had sat beside the old woman's bed and listened and watched and it was the sound of her dying that had determined Mary not to tell these stories to her own children after they were old enough to listen. Carefully, she avoided telling them to Pal. She resisted the bitterness in that way—which explained her silence, the endless silence that was like a cathedral before Mass or the last sigh of history. Those stories were all she knew besides dreaming (which was also story, which was also dreaming, which was . . . and so on to the beginning). She did not want Pal to inherit the bitterness, the sour feeling that came from being betrayed by one's own people, by the other bands made up of one's own cousins, brothers, and sisters.

Still she waited now, beading quietly at her table, and dreamed, disturbed at the way her mind ran ahead to see things she did not want to see, or things that had not yet happened. It took time. And it was hard. It's easier in novels. Especially in the mystery novels *Amanda* would read (Mary was just beginning to imagine *love* for Pal) where things happen day by day, while the keystone to the arch of clues is withheld until the end. Those day-by-day things have an order, a plot that is so unlike life as to be entertaining as well as relaxing, alleviating the worries the reader would have if he sat down to piece the story together. The end of a mystery is the solution to a problem. But there is no end to the problem of living. There is no end to the need for love. There is no end to dreaming.

In the end, she could not overcome Pal's shyness, his inherited sense of not being worthy, a sense instilled and honed by history. Not alone. She had to leave a lot of it to Pal and me.

It would take time. Remembering the stories without ending up bitter was something that Pal had to come to himself. All she could do was dream and, by dreaming, offer choices for him to make.

So Mary Blue sat beading, rocking slowly, almost unnoticeably, and dreamed, dreaming and thinking, envisioning her son. She saw some of the false steps he would make as he began dreaming his own Amanda. She saw him try to get used to the smell of old white people who shouted "Amen!" to fight off their fear of death as well as to get God's attention, an expression of hope that after all the things they've done in their lives, He really will forgive them and not just leave their frail bodies lying where they fall, sardonic grins or grimaces exposing their yellowed teeth, the dried-up whiteness of their spittle drooled and dried on their chins.

She saw a girl (that's not her, Mary thought—she's not the one) drag Pal into the shrubbery behind a church building. The girl's blouse popped open and her breasts fell into Pal's timid hands. Mary closed her eyes to give them their privacy, while she grimaced (or did she grin? I confess I can't always tell, in my condition of *weyekin*). Pal imagined that he felt God watching them the way He was supposed to watch the sparrow. It made him nervous. He wondered if the sparrow felt the same and if that was why the sparrow twittered.

Mary Blue shook her head. Right now, she had La Vent and the Costanos on her mind. She had to concentrate on them. She opened her eyes, got up slowly, went to the stove, and picked up the tea kettle, which she filled at the sink and then returned to the stove. She turned the biggest burner to "High," and waited for the water to boil. Warming the cup with a shot of hot water that she swished around in it first, she dropped in a tea bag and, holding the string on the bag with her thumb against the cup's handle, carefully poured hot water over it. She added three teaspoons of sugar (no milk) and then returned to her beading table.

She closed her eyes again, closing out everything around her the way white beads on Comanche moccasins hide the designs, and began to rock so slowly that she did not spill her tea or even burn her lips when she sipped at it.

3.

In the same month that the mayor's teenage son was acquitted of raping and then attempting to immolate a fourteen-year-old Chicana from the shantytown out beyond the old vineyard, La Vent was visited in his office by three Indians. Whether they were Costano or not, they did not say. They entered quietly. They were well dressed in business suits in spite of the hot summer day, and their longish hair was neatly trimmed or pulled back and held tight by feathered thongs. Two carried briefcases. The third carried architect's tubes beneath his arm.

What those Indians said to La Vent, what they showed him or what story they told him, he never said, not even to Mary. But that night, as he sat pushing chunks of lamb around his dinner plate with hunks of fried bread, he did not mention the mayor. And thereafter, he rarely mentioned again how proud the mayor was to have someone like him on his staff. When he did, he finished the statement with a small, timid, but very audible laugh. For the first time in the years that Gilroy was growing into an unwieldy canker on the leg of what would be called the Silicon Valley, Buzz Packard let it be known that he thought La Vent's reports on zoning and development less than useful. He even stopped by the house one afternoon while La Vent was out to talk to Mary Blue, but he came away shaking his head out of pity for La Vent. Mary had offered him coffee and some cookies from the batch she was making for Pal when he got home from school. She had listened politely as he tried to find a way to bring up the subject of her husband's job performance. But she had not helped. He could tell she knew what he wanted to say and that he wished to enlist her support. But she sat there with a look on her face that was blanker and less readable than an empty page. Whenever Buzz led into the subject and then paused, all

she did was utter "Ummm" or, toward the end of his visit, say "Go on."
No wonder it was hard for La Vent to focus on his work, the mayor decided, having to come home to this strange woman every night. She
looked like a parrot. But she behaved like a witch. The mayor decided
to be La Vent's friend.

He called La Vent into his office, giving his new, young administrative assistant, Nancy, careful instructions to listen in on the office intercom and interrupt his meeting with Tonto when she heard him clear
his throat three times in succession.

"Listen, my friend," the mayor said. "What we need here is perspective. Agreed?"

La Vent shrugged diffidently.

"You have always understood that I am a man of vision, right?"

La Vent shrugged again.

"I had the wherewithal to bring you on board, didn't I? And look
where we've gotten. In just four short terms in office. Gilroy is a city to
be reckoned with. A city we can be proud of where people from all
backgrounds and all kinds of experience can come together and take
pride in our joint accomplishments. Yes?"

La Vent shrugged and gave a little smile.

"Yes? Say yes," the mayor said.

"Ummm," La Vent agreed.

"I believed in you. I trusted you to do the right thing. I always overlooked small details like the mistakes you made early on, like inviting
that bunch of Mexicans to camp in your yard. I forgot completely what
happened with your kid at my son's birthday party years ago."

The mayor cleared his throat and coughed. Nancy jumped, startled
out of her lonely fantasy. Buzz had hinted that she would accompany
him on his next fact-finding trip to Maui, suggesting that to economize
they could share a suite. Had he cleared his throat three times? She began to fret. But then she heard the mayor go on. His stentorian voice
seemed amplified by the intercom.

"Anyway," the mayor went on. "Let's talk about these Indians who
keep coming to see you. I don't know how to say it other than bluntly.

You know me, a straight shooter to the end. My one failing." He chuckled. "Bluntly, these Indians are stupid. They can't see the future."

"But . . . ," La Vent began, clearing his own throat and causing poor Nancy kitty fits. She suddenly realized that she could not tell who was clearing whose throat.

Buzz held up his hand. "Let me finish," he said. "These Indians are clinging to things that have vanished. Things that are dead and gone. Their world went kaput a long time ago but for some reason or other they think they can make it come back. Like they're going to own California again?" The mayor laughed sarcastically.

"But they didn't. . . ."

"Let me finish. They, or you, for that matter," Buzz interjected darkly, "would be making a big mistake trying to stop this project. A big mistake. To try and stop progress is not a smart thing to do, is it? And a shopping mall is progress. If they weren't so shortsighted, they would see that this mall can help them as well as everyone else. That the income from it will let us build schools for their kids. Give them jobs. Good-paying jobs in construction while the mall goes up. Good-paying jobs in the stores and restaurants once the mall is built. It'll give their kids a future, I'm telling you. And for the future, who cares if a few old bones have to get moved. Why, I'd dig up and move my own mother if it meant that thousands of people would benefit by it."

La Vent felt tired. Weary. He did not protest.

"But no," the mayor said, stumbling slightly in his speech. He had been about to say "Let me finish" for a third time before he realized that La Vent had not tried to interrupt. "No." He shook his head with compassion and pity, a gesture he knew from studying videotapes of himself that said, *What can you do, these poor people just are not up to the mark and don't understand that we're only trying to help.*

"No. These Indians come into your office and ask you to help them stop progress. They just want everything to remain backwards. To go backwards. If they had their way, we'd all be walking wooden sidewalks and trying not to step in horseshit. They are failures, my friend.

They don't know how to live in the modern world and they don't want us to live in it either. That's failure. They are failures in everything."

Buzz cleared his throat carefully three times.

4.

"In everything but being Indian," Mary thought when La Vent told her about his meeting with the mayor. She kept it to herself. Just as she kept to herself other comments like, *Yeah, Gilroy is a city where people from different backgrounds can come over and clean your house or sweep your pool.* And, *If he's forgotten completely Pal's behavior at his son's birthday party, then why is he still mentioning it? And why has Pal never been invited to another one?*

She kept these comments to herself, however. Out of love for the increasingly sad man who sat at the kitchen table having come home early just to tell her these things. Out of love and understanding for the fact that he felt himself a double failure. Primarily, he was feeling as though he was failing her and Pal, like a hunter who cannot shoot straight and whose family might starve. She didn't want him to feel that. Secondarily, he was feeling as though he had tried to rearrange his insides for the mayor and failed. That he had tried to change, adapt, become a person who could succeed in the world of the mayor. The more he'd changed, the more the mayor's world changed. It always seemed to stay two steps ahead of La Vent's adaptive abilities. Now all he felt instead of a desire to adapt was a desire to go to sleep. To rest. To give up. His own son had once accused him of being an "apple." Though Pal had apologized immediately, saying he didn't mean it, in essence it was becoming true. La Vent was becoming like the Nez Perce called Lawyer who sided with the whites so much that he taunted and abused Chief Joseph for having resisted removal. But La Vent suddenly had taken one more step than Lawyer, one step that made him able, if not to envision the future, to see the past clearly. See his part in the past. The things he had helped the mayor do.

It was this that made La Vent begin to talk to you regardless of whether or not you were listening. He began to confess in detail the things the mayor had used him for, all these years.

Pal was shocked, when he heard it.

Mary was not. She understood that in the end it was her husband's trying to change that got him. And it was the mayor's making him want to try to change that made the mayor the conqueror and La Vent the conquered. It's as though you have two trains of thought and even though you come up with the correct answer they make you feel inadequate for the way in which you do it. People like the mayor have years and years of experience doing this. Because they seem to do it gently, with as much love as any Christian missionary or history teacher, you find yourself feeling a little ashamed, which is why, when they tease you for being unable to solve the problem in the right way, you sink into a silence as still as a potted plant. It is also why, when you find out they are criticizing you for not knowing the true parameters of the problem—because you can't even imagine them—you take up talking from your teeth.

Which is what he did. He took up talking through his teeth. For some time, La Vent attempted to straighten out his story as though one thing led irrevocably to another.

The Indians came back not long after the young Chicana girl at long last died from her burns and the mayor and his son held a special memorial service filled with flowers thicker than a field of migrating monarch butterflies.

Then La Vent began to suspect his buddy the mayor of his own transformations and that he was being used to accomplish them.

To ignore the feeling that began to nag him like the unremitting itch of mosquito bites, he took up skydiving, both to relax and to forget about the office. Skydiving. Jumping out of teeny planes over the central California valley and swallowing his stomach as he fell freely toward earth until he pulled a small cord that released a parachute which clawed at the air and jerked his shoulders nearly out of their sockets.

But free-falling at mother earth reminded him too much of something. What, neither I nor even Mary in her dreaming ever knew. Toward the end—or toward that end which was only the beginning of yet another phase of life—La Vent took up soaring, or gliding as some people call the silent wind-rush flight of those engineless planes. Soaring was a good deal more expensive than skydiving. There was the glider, the lessons, the pilots and planes to lift the glider up into the current sufficiency of air.

Mary refused to do anything to stop him. Instead, with steadfast love and faith she encouraged La Vent in these hobbies. She even invited him with her natural silence to talk about them endlessly, encouraging him more and more as his former, compliant, agreeable nature began to harden into something that resembled bitterness.

He found himself caught as much between the earth and sky as between those three Indians and the mayor. Like Armstrong Custer's Osage scouts who worried more about other Indians settling on Osage land than about white people, La Vent at first nursed a bitter feeling against the three Indians, expecting his boss, the mayor, whom he had served willingly like Straight Arrow, to defend and protect his position.

Yet it began to seem as though every day the mayor had a new quibble, some petty challenge to what La Vent had done for him the day before. More and more often, La Vent found himself explaining his words and what they meant in a way that felt uncomfortable, editing and modifying his very sentences right there in the mayor's office until the mayor nodded, perhaps not with approval, but at least acceptance.

As his day-to-day need to explain himself and what he had done or said, or not done or said, grew, he was forced more and more often to think in such logical ways that he began to go mad.

Chapter Seven

Bringing in those three Indians for Mary Blue was no easy task. First I had to find them. And you can just imagine how tough it is to find real Indians in a city the size of Gilroy. Then I had to visit with them, sit with them until they decided that I was okay. The fry bread alone would have put ten pounds on my frame but for the fact that I was literally run off my feet trying to do it all.

Pal was in his teens, at a time in life when most boys and girls act a lot like squirrels learning how to mate. Moreover, he was removed by time and geography from communal examples of love and courtship. Not to mention La Vent's stalemate with Mary Blue. Perhaps stalemate is not quite accurate. It was not troubled by argument or anger; better if it had been. But it was troubled, and in a way that left La Vent outside the center of Mary Blue's dreaming as she turned that energy evermore toward her son. She was young and thus not very good at managing the details of dreaming when La Vent drove her out to Four Corners and refused to take her home until she agreed to marry him. For Pal, as he first realized the power of dreaming and then made his first false steps at doing it, Mary Blue dedicated me to the management of details, even though she was well aware that the details are exactly that part which cannot always be controlled but find their expression in time and circumstance. The fact that Pal was Nez Perce, however, assured Mary that Pal's diffidence would keep him a watcher and waiter, and not a too eager participant. She told herself that Pal knew squirrels. It was no great leap for him to connect their tail-shaking, chattering behavior with that of his schoolmates.

She did worry momentarily, picking nervously at a loose thread on her rebozo as she closed her eyes and envisioned him standing inside the nave of a Catholic church. She frowned, her broad flat forehead lined with consternation. What was he doing, genuflecting, kneeling, imitating the gestures and movements of the Mexicans around him? She saw him leave the church, hop in the back of an old pickup truck, and ride out to a cemetery south of town, and she realized that she was watching the service for Pal's classmate, the Chicana whom Buzz's boy had raped, doused with gasoline, and burned.

Pal stood back from the grave. Near to it, lining both sides of the rectangular hole, stood the girl's family and close friends. At the foot of it clustered the girl's school friends. Most of them were shaking with tears they were trying to control, some of them summoning up more feeling than any of them had ever before imagined feeling. Pal stood quietly behind them. He stood at a distance, hardly able to see the grieving family, where he could barely make out the edges of the open pit in the ground. The grave. From time to time, he shuddered at the thought of what was about to be done. After the coffin was lowered into the ground, people stepped forward to drop flowers onto it or they picked up a handful of dirt and tossed it into the grave. It took all of Pal's self-control to step forward with them, pick up some dirt, and, with his eyes closed, toss it in the direction of the grave. This was his first burial and the grave scared him. Something deep down inside him caused him to imagine the dead girl's spirit banging on the silk-lined box, scratching at the lid, and calling for help. Slowly, the spirit suffocated, shriveled, and then, like vapor, disappeared into a humidity sealed inside the coffin that would make even the busy worms feel as though their work was unnaturally hot. There should have been a hole, he thought, at the head of the coffin. The coffin should have been set upright, the corpse stood on its feet for at least five days before it was buried. That way the spirit could start its journey through the after-world without all that banging and scratching, and without the poison of panic. As Pal shuffled forward with his eyes closed, he nearly toppled into the grave. But one of his classmates, LeeAnn Vezzani, who'd had her eye on him ever since ninth-grade English, saw him waver in his grief. She stepped forward quickly to grab his arm. When Pal opened his eyes and saw who was holding his arm tightly against her breast, a second kind of fear overtook him and he had to close his eyes and shake his head to clear it, to separate the new fear from the fear of suffocating in a closed coffin.

Mary Blue saw that LeeAnn was short and sturdily built. She raised her eyebrows, seeing how well developed LeeAnn was already. She was blond. And all the other kids knew she was Italian, which made her exotic; until she began attending their school they had never seen a real live Italian before. Her favorite kind of clothing seemed to be angora sweaters and loose mid-thigh skirts that swayed against her thighs as she walked. Her hair was long and straight, except for a modest flip at her shoulders. Her eyebrows were dark and foreboding. LeeAnn made Pal aware of her, too, though not because her breasts were visibly more developed than other girls or her legs, though shapely, were strong with muscles that rippled her calves when she reached up on tiptoe to wipe the blackboard with an eraser or, out on the playground, when she jumped slightly to hit a tetherball. That was why other boys drooled and tittered. But what Pal noticed was her self-assurance. In eighth grade, the hoodlums hid in the storage closet in the back of the room and when LeeAnn strolled in from lunch to her desk, crossing the front of the room, they threw whole pieces of blackboard chalk, arcing them just in front of her, high enough to make them shatter against the blackboard. Other girls ducked and giggled as the chalk scattered at their feet. But LeeAnn walked at an even pace, her posture erect, her shoulders back, her skirt swinging ever so slightly with the roll of her hips, as though she was not aware of the splattering chalk sticks or, if she was aware, as though she was not willing to duck and twitter and give the boys—all the boys, even the wimps who sat in their desks admiring the brashness of the hoods—what they wanted.

Pal thought her self-assurance and containment wonderful. He wished that he could have something like it, himself, especially when LeeAnn singled him out at the funeral. LeeAnn took him over, after that, advising him on how to dress, telling him he'd look good in a light yellow shirt with a button-down collar and not that pink-and-black T-shirt he usually wore. She smiled sweetly at him when, a week or two later, she found him at his desk in button-down yellow. She laughed when she told him he should cut his hair and he showed up at school with a butch.

"A little longer than this," LeeAnn said, running her palm lightly across the tip of his buzz-cut hair.

After that, the hoodlums began to lay in wait for him outside the playground and the wimps joined them in the chants about Pal and LeeAnn that were supposed to embarrass him. They confused him and made him feel bad for LeeAnn. Couldn't they tell that she was just being kind? Although he could not quite articulate her reasons for these kindnesses. Nonetheless, he understood plainly from the beginning that a girl like her would never like a strange boy like him in the way the chanting boys suggested. That didn't stop her from increasing her kindnesses. She sat with him at lunch, when normally he sat alone. And she even refused to laugh when he finished lunch by drinking a small bottle of white chalky medicine to alleviate the pains in his stomach that the doctor diagnosed as ulcers, but that Mary diagnosed as incapability. "He wants so much to be liked," she thought, pursing her lips. "Like his father. But he has no idea how to let people know that he wants it." The ulcer was caused by the inability, Mary believed. And it was without medical cure, though possibly there was a spiritual one.

"That's what you're supposed to be for," Mary Blue told me, peering at me over her game board. Mary and I were playing Little Big Horn. Actually, it was Battleship, the game in which you call out columns and rows and try to sink your opponent's five ships with red and white pegs. We had modified it. Instead of sinking ships, it was men.

She got up, scraping her chair across the linoleum. "So how 'bout it?" she said.

She was getting bossy, I thought.

"What?" she asked. "What was that you were thinking?"

"Nothing," I muttered. "C-5."

"Miss," she said.

Once, even, LeeAnn invited him to walk her home and when they got to her house, which poised on the outer edge of a wall-enclosed development, she insisted that he come inside to talk. LeeAnn served him cannoli and homemade lemonade, the glasses and sweet treats prettily arranged on a silver serving platter. Every time he took a bite or sipped from his glass of lemonade, as though she wanted to see him splutter or choke, trying to swallow so he could reply, she asked him questions about himself. The room was carpeted wall-to-wall and the furniture was dark cherry and fine. The brick fireplace looked as though it got scrubbed weekly, inside and out. The curio cabinet was solid glass. And the sofa was so soft and deep that he imagined he would have trouble getting up. Then, she did laugh, but not at him as much as with him. And when he decided that he had overstayed his welcome and left, she seemed sincere in her wish that he would stay.

The fact was that LeeAnn Vezzani, Italian and feeling as out of place in Gilroy as Palimony Larue, would very much have liked to go steady with Pal. But he had no way to imagine that. He did not know that she was happy when the hoodlums and wimps teased Pal about being her boyfriend. She would have been happier if Pal had blushed instead of apologizing to her for the way the other boys insulted her. At first, LeeAnn believed Pal was only shy and that with time he'd come around. But she had never encountered someone who believed clear down to his toes that he was not worthy of someone like her, that any kindness or affection she showed could only be friendship and nothing more. Eventually she was forced to give up her project of transforming Pal.

Still, almost two years later, she could not help but watch him as he stepped forward toward the grave, grabbing his arm to steady him from what she assumed was overpowering grief. Sally Pedon, however, who saw how quickly LeeAnn moved when Pal started to sway, turned around in her seat the next day and, peering at Pal through her plain horn-rimmed glasses, said, "I bet you would give anything to sin with her," pointing a sharp finger across the room toward LeeAnn, whose bright clothes made her exude a cool desirability, like ice cream.

2.

Sally made sure Pal knew that he was worthy of her, and almost the first thing she admitted to him was that the horn-rimmed glasses she wore were fake, flat prescription glass that had no corrective power at all. She wore them for humility and to avoid the temptations of vanity. To Pal, the visible results of self-conscious humility seemed attractive, as though it was a modest shyness.

Two years older than he was, she had been put in the same grade with him because the home schooling her mother and father had provided her had taught her everything she needed to know about the Good News Bible but very little about algebra, French, or world history. Indeed, Sally's sense of history at first seemed to Pal reminiscent of his own. History was deep and endless and beyond one's individual control, despite the seriousness of one's connection to it. The major difference was that history, to Sally, was a problem that could be solved by God and whenever the solution seemed, well, slightly irrational or unjust, that was because God was inscrutable. Thus, the ways of God maybe could not be justified to Man in Pal's mind; the ways of God did not need to be justified to anyone in Sally's. Her certainty about this, the easy way in which she seemed to anticipate his questions about history and God, attracted Pal so much that he gave in to her wishes and began attending the Church of the Rock with her. Her father was the pastor of the Church of the Rock and he welcomed Pal, both into his church and into his modest home furnished primarily in Renaissance British paisley with dark golds and dulled reds that refused to clash with the Formica and veneer of the tables and chairs. The church Pastor Pedon served had been tiny and poorly attended when they moved to Gilroy.

But by knocking out a side wall to the sanctuary, installing clear thermal glass, and wiring drive-in theater speakers to posts in the parking lot, the congregation had grown to a size that rivaled the Catholic cathedral out in the valley. What with La Vent talking mostly to himself these days, Pastor Pedon seemed rational to Pal and, as I've said, he felt very, very welcome.

It was a wonderful change from the way he felt everywhere he went. Even at the local pharmacy, even though the pharmacist knew his father, Pal felt as though he was watched with as much suspicion as the Chicanos, who came to the pharmacy to research new ideas for their low-riders in *Hot Rod* or *Road and Track*.

And do not imagine that Sally Pedon was some wispy preacher's kid who could not enjoy life or who did not know how to handle boys, especially shy Indian boys two years her junior. Why, one time I was walking through downtown Gilroy on the way to La Vent's office and I happened to look through the plate-glass window of the pharmacy. There was Sally, a *Penthouse* disguised inside the vee of *Sunset* magazine. She had removed her glasses so she could see better and the effect was stunning. She about took my breath away. Had I not been on my way to listen to La Vent talk crazy at me, her simple, un-made-up beauty and her dark brown hair freed from its usual bun would have made me stumble and start.

The weekend Pal fell in love with her, she drove him in her Dodge Aries "K" car up into the hot hills. They crossed a high bridge arching the sandy mouth of Lime Kiln Creek's confluence with the tides of the Pacific, and turned left in a full U-turn, down past the boarded-up kiosk of an abandoned camping ground. A buzzer's trip wire ran into the kiosk, and a telephone line ran from the kiosk to a house trailer, which tilted at one corner as though it longed to enter the creek and be flushed to the ocean. The individual campsites were marked by oiled logs chained together in the shape of U's and, parking her car in one, they hiked up past a cinder block building with no roof. Shower pipes, without heads, stuck out from the walls.

At the back of the campground was a steep rock wall beside Lime

Kiln's waterfall. A switchback path of rock steps led them up to the top where, for a moment, they stood blinded by the sunlight on the edge of a shallow bowl of a flat plain that was hidden, tucked between the coastal mountains. Half a mile away was a mission of buildings, huddled together in a compound, complete with a rust-red barn and adobe pillars with an arch of iron filigree.

"This is it," Sally said. Her excitement made her breathless.

"What is it?" he asked, following her down the path packed flat through the wheat grass that was beginning to take hold on the field around the compound.

Sally stopped and turned. Her eyes were bright with anticipation. "It's a convent."

Despite growing up with Chicanos whose Catholicism seemed bred in the bone, and despite being as familiar with the names of their churches and monasteries as with the reliquaries they planted on lawns and parking strips, the same way poor white people planted pink flamingos, plastic deer, rabbits, and squirrels in front of their mobile homes, he had never heard of this convent or of the order of nuns which it housed. His friend Maleta and her *vieja*, Mercedes Rota, had always led him to think that Catholics liked a lot of heart in their orders—as in Our Lady of the Sacred or Our Lady of the Bleeding or the Immaculate Pumping or whatever. The name of this one seemed to him, then, peculiarly heartless, and when he mentioned this to Sally, she replied, "It's not Catholic. It's an independent."

"So it's of no real order at all?" Pal said. It seemed a reasonable question.

Sally stopped and turned to look at him. The anticipation in her eyes turned yellow, briefly, as she squinted. "My sister lives here," she said. "Let me ask you beforehand that you not say anything that might make fun of my sister."

"Sorry," Pal said. She began walking down the path again and after a few minutes he chanced saying, "Your sister?"

"What did you think?" Sally called back over her shoulder. "Who else do you think lives here?"

I don't know, Pal thought, maybe Richard Speck? He frowned, but he kept his mouth shut.

No one answered Sally's knock on any of the oak doors along the cloister walk. Nor was there any response when she knocked on the chapel door. When he peeked inside behind her, a puff of musty damp air struck him in the face like a blow.

Beyond the barn, he saw a dark-colored man wheeling a wheelbarrow away from the compound. He called out to the man, who quickly disappeared, seeming almost to rise into thin air. There was a scream, like a peacock's display or an infant burned by a cigarette butt. A minute later, a stuck pig came crashing out of the barn, blood streaming from its throat. It slowed before it reached the filigreed gate, sank to its knees with a groan, and fell over on its side where it lay panting less and less, and less, and less. A woman in a black nun's habit and a neoprene apron and heavy gloves came out of the barn behind it to watch it die, just before a soft and slightly lisping voice demanded, "May I help you?" startling Pal.

"Ah," the habited woman said when she recognized Sally. "It's you."

"Hi," said Sally. "This is Rachna, Sister Belinda," she said to Pal. "She's the abbess," she explained.

"Abbeychief or abbeyhead, please," said Sister Belinda.

"She's the abbeychief," Sally corrected herself. "Sister Belinda, this is...."

"Ah-ah-ah!" Belinda said, stopping her. "We don't allow men's names here. As you might remember."

"What do you call him?" Pal asked, jerking his thumb irreverently at the dark shadow of the vanished man that lingered just beyond the barn.

"Who?" Rachna asked.

"The guy with the wheelbarrow," Pal replied. "He went around there." He pointed, insistent. Sister Belinda would not look at his face or eyes. It made him behave in a way he didn't like.

"There is no guy with a wheelbarrow," she replied, her smooth liquid voice barely mocking his words. "We have no men here. Your sister," she went on to Sally, before Pal could respond, "is not available. She tried to call you-know-who. She's being disciplined," Rachna said. For the first time, it seemed to Pal, her voice sounded pleased and not hateful or angry. "Now, please, before I am forced to summon Sister Adele from the barn, go."

Another infant's scream echoed inside the barn. The echo followed them like a vulture as they hiked up the path through the grasses that seemed to have grown higher during their visit.

Sally was disappointed. Her lips quivered and she bit them until they turned red and threatened to bleed. They climbed back down the steep switchback path beside the waterfall and got into her car.

"You drive," she said, handing him the keys.

"I don't have my license with me," Pal protested.

"God will provide, if we get stopped," she said.

Pal felt inadequate to her pain. He did not know what to do except continue to keep his mouth shut and to drive. Fortunately, he had a superb sense of direction so, even though he had not paid close attention to the turns they had taken coming over the hills, he made the right turns out of instinct and a visual sense of where Gilroy lay in the invisible distance. He drove cautiously, well within the speed limit yet not slow enough to attract the highway patrol's attention, giving her time, letting her stare out at the rock outcroppings and gullies and trees. It was late, and most of the fauna had gone home to dine on what they'd scavenged up during the day. As he pulled up just beyond La Vent's new Pontiac and parked, he turned to her. He felt bad.

"I'm sorry I didn't get to meet your sister," he said as gently as he could.

Sally turned to look at him. Her once yellow eyes were ringed with red and he realized that she'd been crying all this time. The way they looked at him could only be described as beady, as though they each functioned independently, one by one swimming across his face to capture a distinct image. Then she opened the door, climbed out, and came around to open the driver's door. She let him get out. Gave him a little kiss on the cheek. Got into her car and shifted it into gear and drove away. Without a word of goodbye.

3.

Pal did not know what to do. He thought maybe his relationship with Sally was over. Yet he wanted to comfort her. To do something for her that would make her smile and get over the feelings she was having. But he did not know what those feelings were and he could not imagine what they might be.

That night he dreamed that he was a child running after the colorful back of his mother. He was afraid that he would never catch up to her as she walked down the street, until her hand slipped into the pocket of her sweater and she slowed suddenly, her gait rolling to a stroll no faster than grazing speed, and he realized that he would make it.

Mary Blue loved Corn Nuts. She ate them at any hour with an almost Aztecan sincerity. Where other people found the forgotten five-dollar bill in a pocket and were happy at the unexpected alleviation of poverty or felt excited by the prospect of acquiring the temporary hope of five extra lottery tickets, Mary's great pleasure was finding small stashes of Corn Nuts. Walking down the street, if she happened to jab her hand into a skirt pocket and find some, her walk changed the instant her fingers detected the salty grit of the oversized corn kernels, the rhythm changing from regular to a kind of confident, joyful swagger. As a child running to catch up with her, he could actually see the change in her walk, and it gave him hope. As a young boy, Pal used a tenth of the money from his paper route to buy Corn Nuts, which he left in her coat and pants pockets not so much as a gift or an expression of love but as a way to slow her down.

Thus, Corn Nuts seemed an appropriate gift for any woman who was going the wrong speed. So when he handed his gift to Sally, a slight smile flitted across her face as if the pair of them shared a secret. He could hardly contain himself as she opened the gift-wrap bag decorated with balloons and party hats and streamers and pulled out the two-pound bag of Corn Nuts.

"What, in God's name, is this?" she asked, her anticipation turning to a frown. "Are you making some kind of fun of me? Let me tell you. . . ."

"No," Pal said. "It's a gift. It's. . . ."

He had not intended to cause her this added disappointment. Suddenly, he realized what a weirdo he was and he was ashamed of making such a big deal about the present, smiling and grinning, eager for her to open it, expecting her to laugh and make a joke about being as important to him as his mother Mary. Of course, when she opened the pretty foil bag and found only two pounds of Corn Nuts instead of whatever she may have expected she felt, well, sort of cheated out of what is manifestly hers by right. Pal thinks it's him, not Sally, who doesn't understand, and he blames himself for inventing the oversized meaning Corn Nuts have to a little boy whose mother throws a serape over her shoulders and races out of the house ahead of him in too big a hurry to hear what he has to say.

On the long walk home, Pal concentrates on his feet, listening to their rhythm as he walks at an even pace, left right, left right. In order not to be overcome with regret at the way his gift to Sally turned out, he repeats the giving, imagining the words someone else would say, someone named . . . ? He cannot think of an appropriate name. Despite his willingness to name her, all he is able to do is imagine her having the names of girls he already knows. The Mexican name of Maleta Rota does not feel right. LeeAnn and Sally, or even Mary, definitely seem wrong.

When *she*—the girl he is beginning to imagine—opens the gift-wrapped bag, her only question at the two-pound bag of Corn Nuts is, "How am I going to eat them all before they get stale?"

Without a name, however, the pleasant feeling that her smile gives him seems to evaporate quickly. By the time he reaches his house, she is gone, nothing more than a fantastic memory, and hardly that.

4.

After a week or two of staring at Sally's back as she sat at the desk in front of him at school, he finally worked up the nerve to intrude on her thoughts. He tapped her on the shoulder.

"What!" Sally whispered without turning. Her voice was loud enough to make Mr. Nellis start and LeeAnn turn and look across the room. LeeAnn smiled at Pal, then shook her head as if bemused and turned back to her work, her grin hidden by the fall of her blond hair.

"I need to talk to you," Pal said, catching up to Sally as she walked rapidly home after school. Her walk was stiff but quick. He had to hurry to keep up.

Sally ignored him.

"Listen, Sal, would it help if I joined your church?"

Sally stopped so suddenly that Pal stepped on her heel. She took off her glasses and rubbed the bridge of her nose with her finger and thumb. Then she turned to him, the old yellow anticipation seeming to flicker on the back walls of her eyes.

"You'd do that?"

"I'd think about it. Yes."

"For me?"

Pal nodded.

"Truly? You're not just trying to make me feel good?"

"I'd think about it. Seriously."

"You're so sweet," Sally said, taking his arm. "How did I ever doubt you? Just think," she said, with a breathless kind of amazement, "sharing something that important. And with me. I guess I owe you an apology. I was wrong about you. You're not like Parker. You're the opposite. Completely different. You and Parker hardly seem as though you were related."

Pal wondered who Parker was.

He was still wondering as he turned to leave her at her front door and she grabbed him firmly from behind and, with her left foot jammed against the door to keep it from closing, dragged him inside.

"Uh-uh," she said playfully, that starved kittenish look lighting up her eyes once again. "Now that I've got you, I'm not going to let you go."

She stripped him down and pulled him on top of her on the living room floor before he could begin to formulate his protests. He was completely confused and unsure of himself. He was a virgin. That never seemed to cross Sally's mind as she wrapped her legs around him, her skirt bunching at her waist, and guided him firmly into her. Once inside her, he figured it'd be best to try to satisfy her. He went slowly and gently, hardly moving himself, letting her shift her hips for maximum pleasure and letting her control the pace. She seemed all soft and accommodating. Although when she climaxed she just about bit off his earlobe. He kept up his motion until she subsided and then he tried to roll away, reaching for his underpants hanging from the corner of the coffee table.

"No you don't," Sally whispered in the darkening room. "Nothing doing, you," she added. She tried to sound playful. But she managed only to sound threatening.

"I've got to get home," he said.

"For now, this is home," Sally said.

This time she was on top of him, her head back and the shadow of her breasts quivering just above his lips as she fell inward on herself and timed her rocking to her own rhythms. After she came, after she seemed to return to the same room he was in, he again tried to roll away. He was sweating, exhausted, and the points at which his stomach muscles attached to his rib cage trembled as though they were trying to knot.

"Don't be cute," Sally said. She pulled him away from his underpants again. "Get back in here." Sally sat astride him again, this time with her back turned to him so that instead of her breasts he saw the hourglass of her waist, the fine expanding curve of her hips, and when she was done with that, keeping him sort of stuffed up in her, she managed to roll onto her stomach.

By then, he was too tired not to comply. And he was ever more afraid. Afraid that she would never let him go, never let him rest again.

There in the dark, he remembered, he had his first fleeting vision of the Lolo Trail, of the feeling Mary's grandfather must have had of an utter, bone-crushing weariness as he kept not only the women and children but also himself going—as he had to, if they were to hold on to any hope of freedom.

Finally, she fell off of him. "Whew!" she sighed. "You're a real tiger in disguise, aren't you?"

Tiger? Pal thought. He focused on his heart, making it slow down. Beads of sweat ran off his forearms.

Long silences had never bothered him before. But now it did. He felt like he should say something. Something affectionate. Something suave. But Pal would never be suave. "How's your sister?" he asked.

Sally sat up and buttoned her blouse and slipped her skirt—which sometime during their gymnastics had removed itself—back on. She smoothed it with her hands as she sat on her heels, facing him. She stared at him, half lost in thought.

He, too, began to dress, self-consciously, embarrassed. "I'm interested in how someone becomes a nun," he said.

"Girls," Sally replied.

"What?"

"Only girls become nuns."

"Oh. Right."

"If you must know, our father abused her."

"That's awful," Pal said, embarrassed by her desire for him to know this.

"He didn't rape her or anything."

"Thank God," Pal said. He was relieved. Pastor Pedon seemed no more the rapist than La Vent. It just wasn't in his character.

"Uh-uh. Our father was smart. His abuse was the kind that's hard to prove. I mean, if she took him to court, she'd lose. No one would believe her. That's what Sister Belinda says. It wasn't anything that our father did, you see. It's what he didn't do that traumatized her. He made a wreck out of her life, and then he made her feel guilty for causing the wreck herself. That's why she had to detach from him. Because of the terrible things he did and said."

"Detach?" Pal asked.

"That's what Rachna, Sister Belinda, teaches. Detachment. She hasn't seen or communicated with our father for over two years. She was addicted to him. But then she was addicted to people, in general. That's why she joined Rachna, Sister Belinda. She's got a master's degree in education."

"Your sister?"

"Sister Belinda."

"So what did your father do to make your sister need to disconnect?"

"Detach."

"Whatever."

"He undercut her self-esteem, for one. Like when she wanted to go to graduate school? Instead of encouraging her, he asked if she didn't rather want to be a teacher or secretary. Something practical that girls do."

"That's awful?"

"Don't you see? He asked. He didn't tell her. If he had told her, she could have rejected him outright for his paternalism. No, he asked if she didn't think she'd rather be a secretary. He planted a seed of doubt in the soil of her self-esteem and then kept it watered by asking these things from time to time until finally it germinated and grew and blossomed. He didn't tell her to become a teacher. He didn't forbid her going to graduate school. He just kept asking if she was sure she wanted to go to graduate school instead of doing something girls do."

"Like become a nun," Pal said. The instant he said it, he knew he'd made a mistake.

Sally turned hard and cold. "Men," she spat. "You're as bad as our father."

"How is he taking this disengagement?"

"Detachment. He's fine. You'd hardly think our father even notices. Sometimes, I guess, I've heard him crying late at night. In his bedroom. But when people ask how his daughters are, all he says is that they're fine or that he loves them both with all his heart. He never seems to realize what he's done. He'll find out, though. I'm thinking of detaching myself."

"Why?"

" 'Cause he's doing the same things to me now. Just yesterday he asked me if I wanted to go shopping with him."

"So?"

"Girls shop," Sally said. "Of course if you really are going to commit yourself to Christ, I might just stick around."

5.

Pal sat on the ridge of rock jutting out into the ocean, separating the large public beach to the south completely from the hidden teacup of a cove just north of it. Remembering, rocking, trying to do it the way Mary would do it, which is an act not just of re-creating but also making it your own, in a way you can live with it, as well as in it. Becoming a Christian, committing himself to Christ with all the certainty that seemed to provide, might just be the answer.

A couple—a dark-skinned boy and a girl who looks an awful lot like Sally in a hurry the size of huge—begin the slow descent down the north cliff of the cove. He pauses frequently to help her as her legs reach down to touch another rock and gain another foothold.

I am doing this for him. It's my own performance. Trying to make Pal see. Caught between Mary Blue's dreaming and Pal's initial wishing, which is weaker, less purposeful than dreaming, it's the best I can do.

Pal remains oblivious. Lost in thought. Wandering in regret.

The couple hurriedly strip off clothes. I am playing the role of a boy and like a boy, I fumble with the button on her halter top while she works at the zipper on her shorts. Together, we both tear and pull at my belt until finally I am naked from the waist down and we begin to make love. She climbs on top and guides me into her as I raise my torso to remove my shirt. The white foam of the retreating waves laps at my ankles as she rides, her head back and her eyes clamped shut as though she fears to open them, as though she'll discover that the lover she has imagined is not really there. She works back and forth, faster and faster

toward the promise of release; she slows, delaying the promise; then she
quickens, the forward drop-tilt of her head becoming private and intense. Her glasses slip off her nose, bounce off my forehead, and lodge
in the sand.

My jaw is set. These are the hardest performances, doing it with
someone like her. My head angles back and my back arcs up as I struggle to maintain my strength and the stiffness of my desire, pressing up
and into her, holding myself still and hard and taking a breather as she
works, concentrating on holding myself in check. Control. I grunt with
exertion. My grunts mix with her sharp shrill cries of "Parker! Oh yes,
Parker!" The cries drift up toward Pal on the cliff, disguised or dis-
torted by the constant whirl and screech of a pair of seagulls circling
overhead.

Pal stands suddenly. A large stone comes loose. As if the stone is
alive with purpose it tumbles and clacks down the rock face just missing us. She looks up. I grab her hips, try to hold on to her, and try not to
laugh. I need to keep her attention. I pump into her, hard, deep, as
though trying to skewer her fear. Then I sink back, frustrated, all my
hard work at orgasm spoiled, ruined, the future moment of orgasm I
planned on, expected, predicated the actions and movements of my performance upon, gone. She tears away from my grasp as though she's
late for prayer, annoyed, now, by the way I try to keep her. Fumbling
with blankets and articles of clothing, she hides her nakedness. I can
but lie back and laugh and sigh, my sorry limp penis bobbing flaccid as
I stare up at the figure Pal makes above us on the cliff.

"Shit," Pal thinks. "I've ruined the poor guy's whole year." He
stands meekly at the edge of the cliff.

Does he recognize me as he raises his hand to the sky and calls out,
"Sorry, my brother?" Does he see who, what, Sally really is?

He turns quickly away to follow the path back into the world. The
light angling in through the dusty eucalyptus branches arching the path
that leads away from the private cove lends a shadowy, musty, used-up
feeling. The shade is cool. In places, almost cold, as if small clans of bad

memories linger about in patches. A jackrabbit jumps straight into the air and then vanishes in a crash of bushes and brush. Huge mushrooms the size of small hats tempt him from beneath the green fronds of fern. The silence is large.

He passes a hut built out of scraps of wood and tin, old Folgers and Maxwell House cans cut along the seams and flattened. All in all, it's rather a well-built shelter. It even has a window on the eastern side and a smoke hole in the roof. For now, it seems abandoned, the seasonal shelter of a traveler who will return again and again to live unencumbered by either pain or pleasure.

The path narrows, the brush hunkering up thicker and more impenetrably as with their bay-shaped leaves the eucalyptus bend their heads together to block all but thin, stray shafts of pollen and dust, streaked by light. Dead branches seem to have fallen in clusters. It all looks something like a boneyard after the anthros have left, another world in which one doesn't have to speak, and if he did, his words would be foreign. Not far ahead, Pal sees the trees pull back and the shade blotted out by the brightness of sunlight.

Civilization. The world: San Simeon, a village of five ranch houses from the Hearst ranch, surrounding a parody of a general store. The unstoppable forest of eucalyptus trees: the proliferate result of William Randolph Hearst importing the original parent trees so their heavy oily smell could disguise his own as well as the summertime smell of the panting polar bear he bought and kept in a watery cage on the hill above, near what is now called "Hearst Castle."

Small, fluttering, perishing yellow moths carpet the ground beneath the eucalyptus trees, which still hold the dust among their branches like a light fog. Pal tries to hopscotch around the moths. With each step, several flutter up and then fall, too tired and weary to escape. They'll be dead tomorrow, these moths. They have come here to die. But still Pal tries not to end their lives prematurely.

Purchasing a small silver-plated cross in the general store, he stops outside to use the pay telephone bolted to the wall to call mother Mary collect.

"Butterflies," he tells her.

"Where are you?" Mary asks. Her voice sounds thick and sleepy as though she's just waking up after an unexpected nap. Pal recognizes the distance in her voice. He knows that she's not been napping but dreaming.

"With the butterflies," he says.

"I know," she replies. She's fully aware now. She, too, is back in the unimagined world. As sad as it makes her, she knows that this story will always have in it butterflies, yellow butterflies by the hundreds.

Chapter Eight

I.

Mary Blue was feeling like a juggler who was on stage, smiling, grinning at her audience's audible admiration and wonder, adding yet another bowling pin to the number already in the air, without thinking about the consequences of one too many pins. She knew it was not the final pin that gets dropped, any more than it is the last straw that breaks the camel's back, but all the straws together, in conjunction and simultaneity. It was simply a matter of focus. As she knew, the right kind of vision, when focused, could imagine and dream into existence the necessary contexts for several things at once, especially when those things seemed to overlap, which often happened because of the power of the context dreamed, its breadth and depth.

An example of this overlap was wonder: Pal wondered how he fit into his world, a wonder that was not unlike the wonder of La Vent. These days, La Vent came home to Mary Blue with a sadness the size of a bloodhound's hanging from his face. He seemed almost afraid that he did not belong at home, and he greeted her absently, detached by his fear, but wary and observant. Tentative but needy, he followed her about like an abused puppy as she cleared away her beadwork or sliced zucchini lengthwise to grill together with Vidalia onions, tomatillos, and Portobello mushrooms. These she would salt and pepper, and season with roasted garlic, basil, and hot pepper flakes. Then she mixed them with their juices into a bowl of spaghetti or penne, letting the bowl sit for just a few minutes so that the pasta absorbed some of the color and flavor of the grill before serving it onto plates. The recipe varied. When eggplant was in season, she added it, and she was always on the lookout at the roadside vegetable stands for any variety of fresh squashes which she could also slice and grill and add to the dish. Mary was always searching for new foods to try, and her senses were so experienced that she could taste a dish and come pretty close to telling you what was in it. Indeed, the higher La Vent rose in city government and the stranger he became to her, the more cooking came to be for Mary an activity of bodily rhythm, like beading, or rocking, or walking. And to this day, she still walked out beyond where the vineyard used to be, always with as many leftovers as she could carry, which she distributed to the migrant laborers whose names but not whose needs changed.

The grilled vegetables and pasta was only one among many of La Vent's favorite dishes. She made a tuna with capers, tomatoes, and cilantro in pasta that he couldn't stop eating. Yet these days he seemed hardly to notice the continuous repertoire of dishes he preferred. And instead of talking to her about his work or his ideas, these days he seemed to be so taken with conversations with himself that those who did not love him like Mary did must have thought him toddling mad. His lips often moved of their own accord as if in prayer. At times his replies to his self-examinations were animated. And other times the animation became so sharp that in public places his sharp loud voice would suddenly shatter the ritual privacy of shopping, startling the old ladies stretching carefully upward to reach just the right can of tuna fish in the market or interfering with the pumping illusions of men bent over the filler caps of their cars in gas stations. People in Gilroy were beginning to avoid him—except old Mercedes Rota and her dark beauty of a daughter, Maleta, who seemed to know something of what La Vent was going through.

La Vent still had moments of lucidity, instants when the fog of his words parted like the Red Sea and he could see clearly. It was in these

moments that he began to realize that his good buddy Buzz Packard
was a Lone Ranger. As a Lone Ranger, Buzz was on nobody's side, neither the side of Diggum and Pavum nor the side of the three Indians
and their lawyers who did not want yet another burial site bulldozed
and paved. And if Buzz was the Lone Ranger, then what did that make
La Vent, himself, but Tonto. As he talked to himself in his head, he remembered how his firstborn, his only begotten son (how old was Pal
these days?), used to tell him over and over that "Tonto" meant "stupid" or "idiot." What he couldn't remember was how he forgot what
his son had told him until now when it was almost too late. He had
overlooked his own stupidity. He had fooled himself so often into
thinking the mayor gave a damn about him that it had become habit.
He had to work very hard in this fog of habit to see the truth.

It was a truth that I might express for La Vent by asking, How
much of yourself can you put on hold? How much of yourself can you
give up? And for how long, before there is no longer a connection between the self as it presently behaves in an alien world and the self as it
long ago used to imagine itself? And then how long can it be before
you simply disappear into a kind of uniform fog of sameness?

Back in college, La Vent intuited the answer. He smiled when his
buddy Alvin donned the canary yellow pants of the fraternity, telling
La Vent that it was only temporary, a brief means to end the problem of
collegiate room and board. La Vent knew in his heart that if you stick
your finger into jelly and then stick that into your ear enough times,
you lose contact with the person who felt silly and stupid the first time
he did such a thing. Before long, you actually would be able to order
someone else to do the same thing. He knew that if you sat around bat-
ting the breeze with your fraternity brothers long enough you could
start to make the same assumptions they made—that Mexicans were
lazy, women were pork, and beer was a member of the essential foods
pyramid, the way catsup would be a vegetable for Ronald Reagan.
What La Vent had not realized was that working for the mayor of
Gilroy made him a special, if unimportant, member of what we might

call a fraternity in drag, a fraternity that pretended not to be what it was. It was still a club of like-minded men, and a few women, who assumed that Mexicans were still lazy and unable to control their reproductive numbers, that women could dress and act like men, and that beer was an appetizer to be consumed on the golf course or tennis court before the main course of wine was served.

Talking these things to himself, La Vent began to sense how far he'd come from the hurt young man who had sat night after night in Arturo's Cafe in the tiny town of Adelanto. At night he began tentatively and timidly to take his place in bed beside the listen of his wife. He lay there gripping the bedpost to keep Them—a "Them" that was news to La Vent but not to Mary—from stealing him away, the way they had showed up one day uniformed in charity with epaulets of goodwill and stolen his father, put him on a children's train of windowed boxcars and shipped him off for inspection, redress, and admission and incarceration at Haskell Indian School to have the Indian killed and the man saved.

Somewhere among all these nights and the days that punctuated them, something happened. One day, he trailered his glider down south and went soaring over the Grand Canyon. Maybe he saw something. Maybe he looked down on those magnificent outdoor canvases of Indian art on top of the mesas and hills. Maybe he saw off-road enthusiasts, like his boss's son, spinning their four-wheel-drive vehicles around and around erasing the mesas, or saw the fallacy of his own explanatory thinking. Maybe he just leaned over and lost his cookies.

All I know is that one weekend before Pal woke up, he left the house as his father. When he came home, he had given away his glider to some bone game *viejo*, name of Luther, in Arizona, trading him the whole outfit including the trailer for an antique two-shot derringer, which soon he would use to put himself back on an equal footing with the mayor, momentarily reclaiming his former way of thinking.

Months later, like Jesus in jail, he would give it all up and convert to Christianity with a vengeance that Mary saw coming like a freight train switching onto open track when one night at dinner he calmly and blankly looked across the dinner table and said, "Please pass the Host."

But I'm getting ahead.

2.

After he traded away his glider, he turned his attention to the Pontiac, taping off the headlamps and chrome, lightly sanding the finish, and then spray-painting it first with gray primer and then with canary yellow enamel in an aerosol prediction of what more was to come. He began to treat every day as a birthday. As though he were in a hurry to do something, to make up for something, every day he brought Mary and Pal flowers and presents. These he delivered with an air of unintelligible songs that he chanted with wavering care. Although he had given it up the day Pal was born, he once again began to drink, mostly out of shot glasses, and mostly red wine, which he liked so much. It made him feel so without care, as though his troubles were packed up in an old kit bag, that he could almost understand how Mercedes Rota believed that wine was the blood of Christ. Eventually, in future, he would add to his polite "Please pass the Host" the cabernet phrase "Please pass the transubstantial blood."

Finally, he lost his job. Not because of his drinking, as one might think. Instead, it was the mayor. One day, his friend the mayor called him in. "Listen, my friend, we need to talk," the mayor said. "Things have been kind of stacking up around here. I was hoping against hope that I wouldn't have to do this. But when this last bond issue failed, I realized that as always I have to do the right thing and downsize city government. I'm sorry but I'm afraid that your job is one of the jobs that is going to have to be cut."

La Vent staggered outside the office building, gasping for air. Once there, he poked a picketer named Pablo Morales in the chest. "Grow up," he said to Morales. "Stop hanging around the fort waiting for the fat white father to give you a handout. Even if he does, it'll be so little money, you won't even notice."

Pablo Morales was surprised. He always thought La Vent was on his side. He stood clinging to his picket sign like a life ring, his mouth agape, speechless.

With one sharp laugh, La Vent turned right around in the reddened glow of Catholic Pablo's protestant surprise, reentered city hall, waited calmly for the elevator without saying a single word to himself, rode up to the top floor, and entered the mayor's office without knocking. He interrupted a closed meeting of power brokers, advisers, and Bill Diggum, the contractor, pulled out the antique derringer, which he had cleaned and oiled during his nights of endless waking, and, trying to hit the mayor in his sad little organ, missed. He shot the mayor in the left thigh.

The mayor, who was in the process of selling off more than Costanoan bones and burial sites and banking on the percentages he deposited to numbered accounts in Switzerland, did not want a whole lot of attention or light. He responded, once he was released from the emergency room, disdaining the wheelchair for mere crutches, by acting brave and hearty. To the two reporters who waited for him outside the hospital, he said, "Guess I'm tougher than you thought, eh?" And then he gave a little speech about misperception and the greatest good for the largest number of people. "I forgive my attacker, La Vent Larue. Up till now, he has been a loyal and hardworking employee. I hope it's not misplaced generosity, but I plan to ask for clemency for him. Although, of course, for the good of the future, I have to press charges of some sort, eh? You have to punish these people, after all. Like children."

The mayor cut a deal with the county prosecutor that would send La Vent to jail, but only for several months. After that, he could be paroled for good behavior—which meant, really, for no behavior at all, outside of, perhaps, prayer and Bible study. Out of sympathy for La Vent's dependent family, and to seal his understanding with La Vent, the mayor even wangled a taxi medallion for La Vent's now canary yellow Pontiac so that, having paid his dues to society, properly punished, he had some tangible means of support, driving a cab.

On the opening day of the trial, Mary sat on a hard bench at the back of the room with her hands stringing and sewing beads onto an imaginary strip of leather. As her hands worked the invisible beads into an invisible pattern, she began to see that La Vent's cab was the very one on which before long La Vent would stand at the rail station or the airport or in front of downtown hotels and begin to preach the gospel. She was confused. How had La Vent converted to Christianity and why, she wondered, shifting in her seat, with such a vengeance? Was it an action he took against her? He knew how much she hated Christianity. She didn't mind other people being Christian. Most of her friends were Catholics, like Mercedes Rota, and she admired the ritual and regulation to which Mercedes adhered. But the Rotas were one thing; her family was another. She naturally would do anything to prevent Pal or La Vent from becoming Christian. So why did she envision her husband standing on the trunk of a canary yellow Pontiac outside the adobe mission building that housed the train depot speaking in the aphoristic tongues of Christian fundamentalism?

3.

Though she saw it all as though the events were brush strokes that composed one painting, I'll lay it out in time, make each brush stroke seem as though it is a picture in itself. And I'll do it as much for you as for me. If I piece it together in the right way, you may come to understand the power and the pain of Mary Blue. Only if I piece it together right will I again be dreamed by her or Pal into a shape that is human. That, too, is important to you. As it stands now, I'm a cursed squirrel. An annoying squirrel. After my performance on the beach failed to persuade Pal to see what Sally was, my only pleasures are chatter and nuts.

Mary Blue still was confused on the second and final day of testimony, and when the jury recessed to deliberate on its verdict, she left the courtroom and walked down the wide marble steps to the first floor where for a high price the vending machines dispensed carcinogens. I was standing beside the bank of telephones waiting for her, holding a receiver to my ear and pretending to be making a call while I waited, trying not to look so conspicuous as to invite the suspicions of the security guards running the metal detector gate in the courthouse foyer.

Mary Blue hardly glanced at me as she dropped coins into the machine that dispensed coffee, hot chocolate, and tea. Hot chocolate in hand, she straightened up and looked at me again as though I might be someone she once met at a parent-teacher meeting. She shook her head, and turned toward the marble staircase. Stopped. Turned, frowning.

"Hey," I said, hanging up the phone receiver.

"Chin—?"

"Parker," I interrupted. She had not dreamed me there properly, and given what I had to tell her, I wanted credit for having initiative.

"Parker?"

"Parker in a hurry," I said. I wanted to prepare her with a little lighthearted humor.

"What are you doing here? I was just about to go home and call you."

"I've been around."

"Doing what?"

"Well, this and that. Mostly trying to keep an eye on Pal while . . . you know, while the trial was finishing up and all."

"What's wrong with Pal?" Mary asked.

I could see her heart sink. She knew and she didn't know. She knew immediately that whatever she was about to learn had everything to do with the vision she'd had of La Vent preaching from his taxi. But she'd been so focused on La Vent, on the mayor and getting him to cut the deal with the prosecutor, that she had little energy for her son. A mistake. A chance. But a chance she had been forced to take.

"You got a minute?" I asked.

"I've got two," she said, her face turning dark and foreboding.

I told her as quickly as I could. She listened, participating in the story only by muttering "Umm" or "Uh-huh" as I told her about Sally. I told her about what I tried to do on the beach but how Pal had seemed not to understand that the girl riding the young man on the sand below him was Sally herself. I told her about the yellow butterflies. And finally I came to the point, telling her about Pal's purchasing a small silver-plated cross on a silver-plated chain.

"A Christian!" Mary Blue hissed. "Baptism. My son? You mean in water? With all those good people grinning?"

While Mary was downstairs absorbing the truth of my story, the jury returned its guilty verdict with a recommendation for clemency. The judge asked La Vent to approach the bench. La Vent had sat through the entire trial without speaking once, letting the voices he heard play through his head like squirrels in heat. But the judge—being one who could not resist judging others—wanted La Vent to come forward to face the bench.

Sternly, yet with the charitable voice of the same men who had stolen his father from home and forced him into boarding school, a voice La Vent recognized as though the memory of it were stored in a cleft in his heart, the judge ask La Vent if he felt any contrition or remorse for his actions against the mayor.

La Vent's eyes cleared. The voices in his head stopped. He looked up at the judge and grinned. "No, your honor," he said quietly, deliberately. "I meant to shoot off his dick."

"You feel no regret?"

"I regret only having missed." La Vent looked the judge straight in the eye as he said it, his look an unmistakable challenge to law and order.

The judge was convinced. He saw neither remorse nor contrition in those eyes, but something else, something he would call savagery, a cool savagery as though La Vent felt deeply and calmly that the mayor bore as much blame for the retaliation as the settlers bore for stealing La Vent's grandfather's land. Deal or no deal, jury recommendation aside, the judge could not have that kind of honesty and directness. Not in his court. And so instead of giving La Vent a sentence of six months, he sentenced him to three years in the county jail with no credit for time served. The possibility of parole was to be contingent on La Vent's showing some remorse for wanting to injure a dickhead like the mayor.

4.

Mary Blue rose from her beading table abruptly, knocking the wooden chair over. It fell back against the linoleum with a bang. She went to the stove, picked up her blue ceramic tea kettle, and turned to the sink. The lid seemed to pop off and it slipped from her hand and clattered around on the linoleum. She set the kettle on the drainboard. Sighed. Took five deep breaths. Then she bent and retrieved the kettle's lid, which she rinsed methodically under the running tap before placing it back on the kettle and the kettle on the gas range and fired the burner beneath it. She did not realize that she had not put water into the kettle. She would never have realized it if the kettle hadn't started to smoke and its enamel crack.

She was in a state you would call only half there. She remembered only snippets of the prosecutor's and public defender's arguments over whether La Vent had been justified or right to shoot the mayor or whether the criminal justice system had treated him differently than it would treat a rich man. If Mary paid any attention, it was not to the words as much as it was to the sounds of the voices as though the rhythms and changes in the texture of sound mattered more to her than any of the words that might be uttered.

"It's not all this then that," she muttered.

La Vent's life was over and yet she couldn't even tell where it began. Every time she tried to reconstruct the story, the question "Where did *it* begin?" seemed to front her like a cavalry's charge, while the question "Where did it *begin*?" outflanked her like a pedantic infantry. Her battle to win enough energy to remember the story seemed to leave her head-achey and weary to the marrow of her bones. Whenever she seemed to come to some small conclusion she would remember the stories her

mother told her about General Howard and Yellow Wolf of the Nez
Perce, the way people could turn away from the story's intentions, or interrupt with questions that were not stupid but that were not important,
either. It would cause her to falter, to have to start all over again, once
again summoning the energy to begin, once again finding the echoes in
her heart of the shadowy truths and falsehoods of a story that would
find its expression in words. She was no more comfortable with these
words than you would be with a doctor who calls you into the office
after an examination, invites you to sit down, and then says—gently,
kindly, forebodingly, regretfully (but with a secret pleasure in his belief
that he knows his medicine)—"I'm afraid we've got complications."

She had complications. She didn't have just to dream a place to begin. She also had to dream an audience who knew how to listen. She
had to re-dream Pal.

And then there were the problems of what rules to obey in the telling as well as her worry that she might end up talking to herself like La
Vent. Or worse, like blanket-wearing Indian guides at museums of the
American Indian who proclaim New Age lies, or the mixbloods who
simulate Indian names and travel from college to conference playing
poor videos they've made all about the insult of commodities and sports
teams like Jeep's Cherokee or Washington's Redskins.

In the end, after everything, after all her pain and all her worries,
after her laughter at the way La Vent had replied to the judge, she decided not to complain. She was simply waiting for the future to become
visible the way the desert waited for rain, the way La Vent had waited
to propose marriage. Mary kept her silence. Like her mother's mother
as her band of Nez Perce was removed to Indian Territory, she kept her
own counsel and rode the raft down the river without complaining or
weakening in either spirit or love.

Indeed and in fact, I think that she was actually proud of her husband. If she was sorry at all, it was because she knew what had to come.
Survival was everything. And La Vent would not survive. Stories were
survival. But it was Pal's story and not La Vent's that had room enough
in it still to be properly remembered. La Vent's story had too many

words and someone with too many words eventually comes up dry and without any words at all, at least without any words that matter.

More than a few times, I saw lines radiate out from the large corners of her mouth and blossom into a smile that exaggerated the pronouncement of her slightly flagging cheeks. And then she returned to her waiting. And while she waited, her hands stitched beads onto shirts and moccasins, or onto the sheet of hide for the cradle board in symbols and patterns that only she understood. Only she knew the fuller patterns of history that she beaded onto the cradle board in which Pal and Amanda's baby could be swaddled and carried or rocked and sung to, and at last put down for a nap.

It would take time. But she would devote herself to the task.

Chapter Nine

Let me remind you that messengers get treated badly, especially
messengers bearing what the hearer thinks is bad news. In fact, I will
go so far as to venture to say that if there is a class of true victims in the
world, messengers are the class. Even when we're bearing good news,
the recipients often respond with a "Yes, that's nice" or "This is good."
This is especially true when the recipients are Indian people whose self-
containment impresses others as passive detachment but which is really
a containment that comes from surviving the gifts of civilization and
the awareness that civilization's gifts may be contaminating, like blankets infested with the smallpox virus given to the poor in winter. One
of these days, we spirit messengers are going to organize—Tom Yellowtail, Henny Penny, and of course the already protestant Chicken
Licken—and demand our natural rights to be treated with respect and
care, whether the news we bring is bad or good.

That's what I am thinking, shaking my squirrel's tail and chattering in anger at no one in particular. If it were allowed, I would be angry
at Mary Blue for this . . . this . . . punishing manifestation. But if I let
my anger go, give it free rein and let it run, it comes back home to me. I
am, in large part, to blame for the shape you find me in because I have

failed. I took what I hoped was a brilliant initiative. I got Sally to go with me to that private cove and perform our dumb show for Pal—dumb, anyway, except for her shouting "Parker!" when she came, on the beach. But the entertainment failed to produce the desired effect of making him hate Sally. I guess I should have known it would fail, given that I was not dreamed into that sandy context by Mary Blue. And without a Dreamer to dream the context, the actions within what is therefore a false context have no more power than paint has to throw itself at a blank canvas. On top of that, getting Pal to hate anyone was nigh on impossible.

So here I am, perched on the low branch of a raggedy lilac bush dying in the dooryard of a double-wide house trailer behind the Church of the Rock. The trailer is owned by the Right Reverend Lijah White, Pastor Pedon's new organist. I am waiting for Pal, who at this very moment is inside, placing his name on the list of baptizees for next Sunday's dunking. I am here to offer Pal one name and one name only—Amanda—and encourage him to give her a local habitation in his world by learning how to dream. Dreamed here by Mary Blue, my challenge is to give him Amanda while overcoming my limitations as a squirrel.

A crescendo of Muzak comes from the interior of the church sanctuary. Trailing shouts of "Amen" from the oldest and nearest to God (or to the state of godliness) ricochet out the doors as they open and people begin to emerge. From the other side of the building come the sounds of cars starting. The drivers hang up the drive-in speakers, through which they have heard the sermon, and ease forward over the undulations of asphalt that aim their auto grilles toward the distant mountains if not all the way up to wherever God is supposed to be, as they idle into the line of cars hurrying to exit and get on to Burger Barn and their other Sunday business.

Suddenly, I am grabbed from behind by Lijah White's son, Paulie. His sister, Ruthie, shouts with glee. I am captured.

"Oh, shit!" I say. "Shit, shit, shit." My high-pitched nervous voice

makes it come out sounding like "Chyeh-chyeh-chyeh." I am in for it
now. I know what is coming at the hands of these playful little Christians. Maybe not what, exactly, in detail, but definitely how.

Ruthie has a hammer and a handful of sixteen-penny nails. Being
the children of the Right Reverend Lijah White, who *believes*, she and
Paulie decide to stake out my furry brown body in the shape of a cross,
nailing each paw into the hardpan of dirt. After some debate—Paulie is
young and therefore not into verisimilitude; he favors just cutting it off
with pinking shears—they added a final nail to hold still my bushy
brown tail, which kept flicking into their eyes as they got in close to enjoy the full vision of the pain each nail caused me.

Ruthie procures a knitting needle—a rust red one, if you can believe that I notice at this stage of affairs. She makes an incision in my
side, the way the Romans incised the radical Christ. She is shoving the
needle in under my ribs and then pushing it with her palm to slide it up
toward my beating, squealing heart, when Pal comes out of the church,
towed along by Sally whose other hand is busy unclasping her hair and
letting it fall seductively across her shoulders. She drags him toward the
bushes where, while God's eye is occupied with the sparrow, she lets her
blouse fall open and her breasts fall into his hands.

I chatter as frantically as I can, unable to form the word "Amanda"
so that it sounds human. I'm just barely able to attract Sally and Pal's
attention.

Pal stops when he sees me, staked out and chattering. "What are
you kids doing?" he asks.

"Come on," Sally says. "Leave them be. They're fine."

Pal frowns. "Sounds like the poor thing is trying to say something,"
he says.

"It's only a squirrel," Sally says. "Let it alone. Let's go." She tugs at
his hand.

He shakes loose from her grasp and finds a rock large enough to
use to crush my skull and end my pain. He tries to shove Ruthie aside.
Ruthie refuses to give up her vigilant position beside my cruciform
easily.

Paulie runs off into the trailer as Pal kneels beside me. Tears drop slowly down his cheeks and he shakes his head in a sorrowful silence. Picking herself up out of the dirt and dusting herself off, Ruthie retrieves her knitting needle and lunges at Pal, squirming violently and starting to scream when he grabs her wrists to keep her from stabbing him.

"Holy heavens!" Sally shouts. "Stop! Let her go. Help!"

"Ruthie!" a voice shouts from the trailer's stoop. It is a raspy voice scraped by cigarettes and sanded by bourbon. The owner of the voice, Mrs. Elie White, is short and fat, her face blotched redder than the cotton shirt stretched like canvas over her stolid frame. "C'mere!"

Instantly, Ruthie stops squirming and screaming. Lowering her head, she marches straight to her mother's side. The bright pleasure in her eyes from crucifying the squirrel folds into an innocent, open look. Paulie's eyes are dull. He hangs on the other leg of his rather substantial mother.

"Whass wrong?" Mrs. White asks. "What're you up to?" She jerks her chin at Pal, the wattle of her neck swaying.

Ruthie turns a cherubic face up to her and whispers. She points at me, crushed into the dust, and then at Pal.

Sally fades away into the bushes out of horror or fear as Mrs. White comes over to confront Pal.

"Hi," Pal says sorrowfully. He's heard about the wife of Lijah White, a woman reputed to have taken on all the bad qualities Lijah, himself, got behind him as he cut off Satan in the passing lane. He feels sorry for her. He feels even sorrier because of the cruelty of her children, and he is prepared for her to thank him in some way.

She ignores the friendliness of his greeting and examines the rock-crushed body of the squirrel. As she straightens up, she spits into the dirt, and her forehead, reddened by the exertion of bending over, furrows in what could be mistaken for thought.

"I ain't sure I unnerstan'," she says. She looks at Pal as though he is a box of Twinkies on her New Year's diet.

"Me neither," Pal says, kindly.

"Maybe we oughtta kneel down together and you ask the good Lord to forgive you for what you done here," she says. "Why you wanna go and hurt an itty bitty little crittur like that for?" she asks.

"I didn't . . . ," he begins.

Mrs. White's eyes flash with indignation. She jabs a fat finger at the ground. "You tryin' to tell me that ain'tcher rock?"

Ruthie and Paulie stand arm in arm like a bride and groom and smile.

"I . . . ," he says. "Lady . . . Mrs. White . . . can't you see . . . ?"

Can't she see the nails used to stake me out? Is she incapable of seeing what is right before her? Or is she just unwilling, blinded by the ugliness of the truths she is trying to raise?

"What?" she challenges him.

"Nothing. I'm sorry," he says.

"You sure as shoot oughtta be," Mrs. White replies.

Pal is speechless, even more speechless than his father La Vent was as he stood before the circuit judge refusing remorse for having tried to castrate the mayor of Gilroy.

2.

"I'm really sorry," Pal said.

"So what happened?" Sally clearly was not as pleased as Mary Blue by this turn of events. She made him drive. They headed south through Salinas to Monterey and then wound south again along the coast into Big Sur. Sally sat perched in the passenger's seat looking, without her glasses, a lot like a small, black, bat-winged swallow. The swallow was created to shoot and dart in a circling crowd of sharp shrill cries in the early morning light of harbors and hills. Sally's thoughts are like that. Her feelings come out in words created to dart in apparently different and contradictory directions, each one just missing the other in a pre-programmed close-order drill. She even pronounced her words like a swallow—sharp and quick and moody, the moods shifting as rapidly as the tongue in her mouth.

"I don't know," Pal said.

Her feeling of disappointment was as palpable as the labors of the cheap Chrysler engine lugging up the long incline.

"All you had to do was step down into the baptismal font. Dad-dums would have done the rest."

Once over the incline, the car rocked and swayed almost rhythmically. "I know," Pal said.

Every month the church welcomed new believers, baptizing them in a special Sunday service. The curtains above and behind the altar were drawn open and one by one the new Christians descended hidden concrete on cue, down into a four-foot-deep tank of water. There they stopped to face Pedon, who asked them if they accepted the Lord Jesus Christ into their hearts as their Lord and Savior. As soon as they said yes—and with some of the younger ones, it was hard to tell if they said anything at all—Pedon put an arm around their shoulders, got a good grip on them, placed a handkerchief over their mouths, and pinched their nostrils shut. Saying, "I baptize thee in the name of the Father, the Son, and the Holy Ghost," he laid them backward into the water, submerging them fully to symbolically wash away their sins, and then raised them, dripping, upright.

Pal wondered if anyone else got to the brink of saying yes and realized that like a bystander joins a riot, he was going along with the excitement of the moment, doing something that he really might not want to do because of the thrill of belonging to something larger than himself. He envisioned himself standing in a white robe (what in other contexts is called a hospital gown), the last in line of the three young people who had put their names down to be baptized on the first of the month. Pal was last because Pastor Pedon wanted to warm up with the other two. They were much younger and a good deal smaller, and therefore easier for Pedon to hold as he placed the white handkerchief over their mouths and lay them back into the water. He had to submerse them completely before lifting them back up onto their feet and gently guiding them dripping and saved up the stone steps and out of the tank.

"Poor Dad-dums. He is so disappointed. He spent all morning preparing for you," she said with a twinge of bitterness.

Pedon wore hip-waders underneath his own minister-sized hospital gown, to keep dry. But he had a bad back that came from years of teaching people how to play golf before he became a minister. To lower Pal, who had taken full advantage of his wonder years to grow, below the water, stay balanced, and then raise him up saved and wet could make his back go out without some precedent warming up. Indeed, Pedon had risen early to work out gently on his cross-country ski machine (this was California, after all, where godliness is next to fitness), lift some light weights, and do an hour of slow stretching exercises before downing a muscle relaxer with his morning dose of Metamucil, an extra advantage in his battle against cholesterol and the platelets of Satan that wanted to build up in his arteries and corrode his heart. Even after all that, the idea of Pal's baptism made him grim. When he looked into the mirror and tried to smile in the way he believed John the Baptist smiled knee deep in his rivers of commitment, his smile looked pained and ghoulish.

"I'll bet," Pal replied, trying to sound neutral.

As Pal stood on the top step looking down at Pedon hip-wading in the tank, reaching his left hand up toward Pal to steady him as he descended the five steps in bare feet, Pedon's smile did not look grim but historical. Pal did not know where the idea came from. Pedon's smile looked like Ruthie and Paulie White's, but it came from a time long before Ruthie and Paulie were ever conceived. From a time before Mary Blue's, perhaps, or even before his grandfather's. Whenever the original time, it seemed an absent grin, an accounting grin, as though he, Palimony Blue, already was entered into a ledger that recorded the taking of King Salmon. But rather than a King Salmon, Pal felt a good deal smaller, like a rabbit or a squirrel. He stopped, frozen to the top step. "I don't want to be a *thee*," he thought, as Pedon's smile changed slowly into a frown.

And then he had turned and fled.

"What does that mean, you'll bet?" Sally demanded.

"Nothing. I just meant that knowing your father I believe that he spent a long time preparing for me."

"Didn't sound like it. It sounded sarcastic. You've been sounding sarcastic these days."

When I get the chance to say something, Pal thought. He kept it to himself. That would be sarcastic, though he was tempted to say it, if only to make Sally correct in her evaluation of his attitude. Instead, he pulled to the side of the road as far out of the way of speeding tourists in their recreational vehicles the size of whales as possible and pointed out the blue heron to her. It stood on one leg on a rocky promontory, gazing out over the Pacific Ocean, proud, still, seeming final.

"Wonderful, isn't it?" he asked. "The way he waits until it's time to stop waiting."

"All creatures big and small are proof of God's beneficence," Sally said tersely. She was so sure of things.

"Can I ask you something?" he said.

Sally looked at him out of the corner of her eye, suspiciously.

"How—don't get upset, okay?—how can you be certain that there aren't many gods, many creators? How can you be sure it wasn't Coyote who created Human Beings?"

Sally turned on him. "You're not serious, are you? You aren't actually comparing some stinking animal to God? No way, José. I know there is one God because I've met him in the love of his only begotten son, Jesus Christ, whom he gave to us to wash away our sins."

Jesus as washcloth, Pal thought. "But. . . ."

"But nothing," Sally said vehemently. "I won't sit here and listen to this kind of talk. I won't. So shut up. Shut up, will you? If you're going to speak like the devil, then you can turn this car around and take me home right now. Understand?"

Pal understood. He started the car and edged back onto the winding road, silently wishing the blue heron safe journeys. He continued to drive south toward Big Sur. For several miles Sally was quiet. She pursed her lips and stared out the window, looking away from him. It was a gesture that he recognized, now, her looking away from the source of things that bothered her.

At last she asked gently, her composure regained, "May I ask you if you were sincere when you promised to commit yourself to our Lord Jesus Christ through baptism?"

"I thought I was," Pal said. He was not lying. He wanted to be baptized. In his heart he wanted to belong to something, and Pastor Pedon's church had seemed as good as anything. Putting his name on the baptismal list made so many people happy, not just the Pedons and Whites, but all the congregation overlooked his background and shook his hand to congratulate him on his promise to become one with them in Christ. For the week preceding the baptismal date, he had felt one with them, and the joy he derived from that feeling was great. He could meet one of the congregants downtown and stop and chat about the weather, which was almost always glorious, and feel as though he were greeting a relative, a friend, a brother. He felt that if he knocked on one of their doors hungry or cold or weary, they'd take him in and feed him, wash his feet, give him a place to sleep. But when he stood on the top step of the baptismal tank looking down into the leering grin of Pastor Pedon all that welcome turned to something else, to something like possession. It was as though Pedon was counting Pal among his coup and in counting it was taking hold of and possessing a part of Pal which Pal did not want to give up. A part that some people call soul or spirit. A part Mary Blue called heart.

"You know what I think?"

Yes. But I'm going to hear it anyway, Pal thought.

"I think you're afraid of commitment."

"Probably."

"You are afraid to commit yourself. Not just to Jesus Christ. To God. But to anything."

"Probably," Pal repeated, the emptiness of the repeated word creating a kind of vacuum.

"And," Sally added pointedly, "to anyone. You are afraid of me."

"Maybe," Pal replied, unwilling to argue. It had nothing to do with fear in the sense of feeling scared or lacking in courage. Yet it was a kind of fear. It had a lot to do with sight, with vision, in your heart seeing yourself as a fish to be consumed by a greedy grinning man who would as soon give you twenty-five lashes with a knotted rope as he would try to drown you in a baptismal tank. The fear was of certainty; there was in that man's way of life such certainty. It was that from which Pal had turned and run. And he had run so fast that he left the church without changing into his street clothes, hiding in the bushes behind the Right Reverend Lijah White's double-wide trailer until later when it grew dark and he could sneak home without his clothes through the arroyos and gullies of Gilroy.

"We could work on it together," Sally offered.

Pal knew that he was supposed to answer her gratefully. The best he could muster was silence.

"Well?"

"I don't know," he said.

"You think you really want to go through life uncommitted? I don't believe that. No one wants that. You, of all people, don't want that."

"Maybe not," he said.

Big Sur, as they entered it, seemed bigger and more spectacular than you could say. Like one of those hidden valleys in the Rocky Mountains, where you round a corner and there with its smoke and mist and flashes of light and movement, with its very exhalation, is a valley to describe all valleys: Big Sur, nestled against the Monterey coast of California, was like that. Redwood sequoia and simple pine and spruce. No cedar, true. Cypress, though. And bay, in places, as well as eucalyptus, those tower-high dripping trees that housed a million monarch butterflies as they journeyed, connecting Canada with Peru. Creeks and rivers and sudden meadows with deer that lifted their ears and froze like Simon Says as you passed. The cool bright flicker of jays and redwings in the melting heat of the car as you drove from sunlight to shade to sunlight again.

"You'll join our chess club," Sally was saying. Pal looked at her, realizing he'd not heard a word she'd said for the past several minutes. "If
only I'd pushed my pawns," she said, smiling grimly at the memory, "I
could have been president of the Christian Knights."

"Ah," Pal said.

When he'd met her long ago, he had imagined that her way of
thinking, as well as her enthusiasm for it, was attractive. It seemed honest. Lively and true. At the moment, he wondered if this swallow-like
darting from thought to thought wasn't something that, intriguing in
the right hands, became completely confused in the wrong hands.

"You will like playing chess. And every year we go on a field trip to
Second Mesa in Arizona to play the Hopi kids in chess. There's a Mission of the Rock there. We always win, of course."

"Of course," Pal said.

"They try, those kids. But chess is the kind of game only certain
people can play. There's no denying that."

The kind of people who know the rules, Pal thought. "I wouldn't
try," he said.

"What?"

"You hungry?" he asked. There was a log-built restaurant and gift
shop coming up on the left.

"Famished," Sally said.

He bought her lunch and they ate it at one of the round redwood
tables on a redwood deck that overlooked two gas pumps plugged into
the earth. Across the road, the trees parted slightly, giving them a view
of the ocean in the distance, deep blue with afternoon light reflecting
off the rollers. Sally ate and talked at the same time. Not one dribble of
hamburger juice or tomato or catsup fell from her mouth, even though
it seemed to be going a mile a minute. She didn't even need a napkin.
He was already on his third, tearing it hurriedly like a bingo ticket
from the rectangular napkin dispenser that divided the black pepper
from the white salt, in the hope of catching a spill before it reached his
pants. He felt far away. For a moment, he imagined that he couldn't
hear her. She probably doesn't need deodorant, either, Pal thought.

"So?" Sally said. She shook his arm.

"So what?"

"So there's another baptism next month. You can commit yourself again, then. Come on. Try. You'll feel good for once in your life. Join with us in the fraternity of fellowship."

Pal thought, And wear canary yellow pants.

Seductively, she added, "I'll teach you chess, among other things." She winked.

She actually winked at me, he thought.

"I don't know. I sort of feel out of place. Like food in Ethiopia," he laughed.

"Don't be silly. Everyone is welcome in the fellowship of Christ."

The name of Reverend Colonel Chivington and the words *Sand Creek* abruptly came to mind for Pal. He swallowed them along with the last of his burger, which stuck in his throat for a painful minute. "Well," he said when the pain receded. "I'm sure they are. Still. . . ."

The screen door from the gift shop banged loudly as someone came out onto the deck with their lunch. Pal ducked as though the bang were a gunshot. Then he felt silly. Embarrassed.

"Come on, sweetheart," Sally smiled kindly. "You can be my project. I'll make you my own pet project."

"Don't. Please don't?" Pal said almost in a whisper.

"Why not?" Sally said.

"I don't know. I guess I don't want to disappoint you again. You ready to get going?" he asked.

"Yeah. Sure."

"I've got to go to the toilet," Pal said. "Be right back." He stood up.

"Give me the keys," Sally said. "I'll go unlock the car."

Pal fished in his pocket, pulled out her keys, and set them on the table. "Be right there," he said.

The toilet smelled like a camp urinal. Pal had to hold his breath. He was relieved when he was finished and he walked quickly through the gift shop, panting. When he got outside, the car was gone.

"Sally?" he called.

He looked around the back of the gift shop. On the other side. He looked down the road and up. Then he went to the wooden steps in front of the shop and sat down to imagine what he should do next.

3.

The first ride he got only took him as far as the next campground. He got out at the ranger's kiosk to use the pay telephone to call Mary Blue, collect, and tell her that he was stranded in Big Sur.

"Keep trying," Mary said. "You'll get a ride."

"I will. So I'll see you whenever," he said. "Oh," he added, remembering that this was one of Mary's days to visit La Vent in jail. "How's my father?"

"Doing a lot of reading," Mary replied. She sounded sad, but Pal did not inquire about why. "He's doing good, I guess."

"Good," Pal said. "I'll visit him next week."

"We can talk about that when you get home," Mary said. She hung up.

Pal went back out to the two-lane highway outside the campground, feeling a little hopeless. It was already getting dusky there in the shadow of the trees. The song of a bird—"Bir-dee, bir-dee"—cheered him. Unaware that he was doing it, he began to whisper in sync with the bird, "Bir-dee, bir-dee," turning his face up toward the trees and the sun setting beyond them. "Bir-dee, bir-dee," he sang. He smiled and, rocking lightly from foot to foot as though he were a father comforting a crying baby, he stuck out his thumb.

I let him wait and rock until the rocking was all that mattered to him, until he was absorbed completely and wholeheartedly by the motion, by the delight and calm and importance of swaying back and forth and back. Then and only then was it time to rescue him.

A loud rumbling noise like the low growl of a predatory animal bounced through the forest, silencing the bird that sang to him. It was a sound halfway between thunder and the rapid rolling beat of drums. He looked down the road as a sky-blue Camaro came rumbling up the highway, its glass pack pipes roaring with the threat of power. The Camaro had red, orange, and yellow flames painted onto the hood and encircling the supercharger cowling, with smaller versions of the same flames streaking the side panels as though the wheels were hot, hot, hot. A woman was driving. A dark man was in the passenger's seat.

"Yo," I called out to him. The Camaro eased to a stop fifteen feet in front of him. *"Te quieres llevar a algún lugar?"*

"Sure," Pal said. "I'd love a ride." He walked toward the car. Just as he reached it, the engine roared, the wheels spit gravel and dirt, and the car leapt ahead along the shoulder of the road. Then it stopped again.

"Yo. Come on, amigo. Les get with it, hey?" I called.

Pal tried again. Again the car spurted ahead, leaving Pal annoyed in a cloud of dirt. Again it stopped and I called to him.

"Jus' choking, man. She no good with the clutch, man. She'll turn it off this time."

The engine died. Pal walked up to the car and looked in.

"Hop in," I said. Pal squinted at me. He knew that he'd seen me before, but he couldn't place where we had met. I was older now, since Pryce Packard's birthday party. "You have to climb through the window. The door doesn't work."

Pal climbed through the passenger's window, tumbled headlong into the back, and then with a good bit of twisting and turning in the hard narrow rear seat of the sports car, righted himself. "Thanks," he said. "You going anywhere near Gilroy?"

"I'm stopping at Salinas," I said. "She's going all the way to San Jose," I told him.

Pal looked confused. He frowned.

"Cálmate. Don' vex yourself," I said. "She's giving me a lift, too. Like you, hey?" I spoke loudly as the car took off up the road. "What can you do? There I was jus' hoofing it up the road toward you as fast as I could get my little beaner legs to go when this chingita, here, pulls up and stops and leans across the passenger seat and says, 'Pardon me, but are those dirty Levi's?' and then she just laughs and laughs and offers me a ride. Couldn't pass that up, now, could I, pal?"

Pal remembered. He recognized me. He gasped. "Chingito?" he said.

I turned in the bucket seat and smiled. It was a big smile with big teeth, exaggerated by the darkness of my skin, which had grown darker in the years between the Packard boy's birthday party and now. "How's it hanging?" I asked.

"Chingito. My God. How long has it been? What, years, huh?"

"Too long. But not as long as you think," I said. I laughed. "Just like Henny Penny says."

Pal looked at the woman's face in her rearview mirror. She was wearing dark glasses, but it seemed as though she was smiling behind them.

"Let me introduce you to our chauffeur de jour," I said. "This here is. . . ." I forgot the name she was using.

"Brandy," she said, her voice husky. Strong.

"Brandy," I repeated. "Today, she's going by Brandy. I gotta tell you, man. She's just an accident, my fren. Someone who come along in my hour of need. She's not, if you know what I mean, part of the story. Least she shouldn't be, hey?"

"What story?" Brandy asked.

"His story," I replied. "The one he's living. So," I said, turning back to Pal, "the bitch wanted her daddy to drown you done left you standing at the gas pumps, huh?"

"She was upset," Pal said. "I don't think I'd call her a bitch, though."

"Fine. Call her what you want. Chuss don' call her Amanda."

"Amanda?" Pal asked. I could tell by his brightness that he liked the name. "Who is Amanda?"

"Sorry," I said. I was getting ahead of things. If I got too far ahead, Amanda could end up being just another fake like Sally. "A friend of mine you don't know. But I told her about choo, man. Told her about how you used to buy your mother Corn Nuts and stuff. Fact is, I was telling her once about how you always called your mom collect even on local calls. You know that chica didn't laugh? She understood, man."

"Understood what?" Brandy asked.

"That his mother wants him to call collect."

"How come?"

"Oh, baby, we are thick today, aren't we? 'Cause she wants him to know he don't need no Corn Nuts. Ever."

Brandy pulled up on the shoulder of Highway 101, on the edge of Salinas. I climbed legs first out the open window.

"Hey," Pal said, "let's get together sometime. Shoot some pool, maybe."

"Yeah. Sound good, my man," I replied.

"Give me your number," Pal said. "I'll call."

"Yeah," I said. "I ain't got no phone is the problem."

"Your address then."

"It changes."

"How can I get in touch with you?"

"There are ways, man. There are ways. Ask your mother, man. She knows. Maybe she teach you. See you aroun'."

4.

Pal sat on the curb outside the Blue Note Bar and Lounge, stuck like a cork in the side of the most recent Diggum and Pavum mall. The mall was not completely finished, and most of the stores were empty and not yet open for business. The lights of the blue notes cascading upwards on the vinyl-padded, period-piece door to the lounge were the only lights besides the moon and stars. It gave the broken earth around him, beyond the oiled dirt parking for the Blue Note, an eerie look. The bulldozers and earthmovers had been left, parked and turned off in whatever spot and position they happened to be at quitting time, left helter-skelter like dice tossed down by the thunder. Pal felt strange. Heavy and sad. It was as if he knew that he was sitting on the very spot where the remains of a three-day-old Costano girl had been found wrapped in the arms of her mother's skeleton. Both their skulls were bashed in, and the mother was missing all but the index fingers on both her hands. The others had been cut off by the loving padres, punishment for her having crept across the compound separating men from women to meet her husband, criminally flouting the Católico Mission laws that bade her otherwise.

He pretended to be preoccupied, minding his own business, when Brandy emerged arm in arm with her boyfriend, Michael McCourt, supporting him on seasick legs, almost dragging him into the parking lot.

Pal had shot pool for a couple of hours with Michael, who was pretty good but not as good as he claimed. They played for pitchers of beer and Michael, his red hair increasingly disheveled, drank heavily. When Brandy came round to see if they needed anything, Michael tried to fondle her, forcing Brandy to shirk free of his grip on her hips or waist without spilling the drinks on her tray. The more she told him to stop, the worse he got. Finally, Pal talked Michael into giving up the game and just sitting at a corner table. Michael was furiously drunk. His head lolled. But he managed still to raise it like a memory and peer out through his beady squinting eyes as though staring at a partial eclipse and comment on Brandy's person.

"Nice tits, huh?" McCourt slobbered.

Pal did not reply.

"You oughtta see those tits, my fren. You can bury your head in 'em. Fact, I think I'll get her to show you her tits. Hey!" he shouted. "Branny. Branny, come over here and bend over. Stop giving those suits a free peek and come show my fren here—wass your name?"

"Pal," he whispered. "Maybe you shouldn't shout."

"Why the fuck not?" Michael demanded. "Why not fucking shout, man? She can't hear me, I don't shout. She's busy showing off those magnificent titties she's got to everyone in the Blue Note but us." Michael winked and leaned toward Pal conspiratorially. "Does it for tips. You know how much she makes in a night?"

Pal shook his head. He was embarrassed. He didn't care how much she made. He wanted to get away from this loudmouthed boyfriend of hers. Still, he was more comfortable hearing about her tips than her tits.

"Hunnert dollars. Maybe more," Michael said proudly. "All 'cause of those magnificent tits of hers. Hey! Branny!" he shouted. His head dropped to the table. His mouth fell open and whitish spittle drooled out the corner. He began to snore.

Pal hung his head, hoping that no one would remember his face.

Brandy came over to the table. She looked down at Michael. Then she looked at Pal and gave him a weak, apologetic smile. "Funny," she said—it seemed to Pal that she was speaking to someone sitting in the empty booth behind him. "Even someone as insensitive as him feels it. The more he feels it, the more he drinks to forget he feels it, and the more he drinks, the closer it is to happening. Know what I mean?"

"Yeah," Pal said. "I guess."

Brandy shook her head. She wasn't angry. She wasn't annoyed. She just seemed to him to be very, very sorry. "Well, see you around?" she said.

"Sure," Pal replied.

"Hope you are," Brandy said. She looked back at him over her shoulder and gave him a quick smile as she walked back toward the bar.

Pal had drunk more than he liked in a misguided attempt to keep Michael from drinking too much. His own head felt thick and wiggly. He reached over and raised Michael's head an inch off the table, lifting it by pulling on his hair and then dropping it. Michael's forehead thumped. Michael was gone.

Pal went outside where he sat on the curb in the cool air to clear his head. He was still there, minding his own business, rocking slightly, thinking, when Brandy came out dragging Michael. She had changed out of her uniform of tight, cuffed shorts and a stretch button-up top with a push-up bodice into loose, sensible clothes.

"Got off early," she said, as Pal looked up, questioning. "Figured I'd better get him home."

Pal nodded. He wished she didn't have Michael McCourt. He wished she didn't have any boyfriend at all. But then she wouldn't like him, anyway, so what the heck.

Brandy laughed. "Boss is always willing to let me go before the other girls. Long as I change out of my uniform in full view of the hole he drilled in the wall. He's a real prick, my boss. But he pays well."

Pal looked away. He could feel his eyes turning to doe's eyes as he looked up at her. He admired her strength, her toughness, the way she could laugh at the weakness of others and not make it into anything more than it was. If he didn't know better, he'd say that he liked the look of her face, which seemed, at that moment, inviting. Friendly.

Brandy started to drag Michael over the curb and onto the asphalt.

"You need help?" Pal asked.

She stopped. Laughed. "I need a lot of help," she said. "But not with him. Thanks."

He watched her drag Michael out of the light cast by the neon Blue Note sign. A couple staggered out of the bar arm in arm, the heavy entrance door whooshing pneumatically as the woman cast a glance over her boyfriend's shoulder at Pal. They were followed by three guys with testosterone issues, one of whom commented on Pal's posture in a way that suggested he'd like to beat the crap out of Pal just to prove he could do it. Pal tensed, prepared to fight. The guy's friends weren't interested, and they left him alone. The jazz-blue notes on the padded vinyl door blinked, and he was left in the dim yellow of the security lights over the door. Like a fire hydrant waits for the flames to show themselves in the window of the construction behind it, he continued to sit on the curb as though he was planted there, as though he was connected to something deeper than the surface of the cement and would go on being connected there come rain or shine or the territorial dribble of dogs and drunks. And yet as secure and content as that made him feel, he needed someone else to complete his purpose. He directed his eyes up and away from the individuality of his parking lot presence to the vast laughter of the stars where what he did would matter only if it got connected, and joined with what came before as well as what comes after. He felt as though she—that other someone—was just that moment coming into being far away from the hustle and click of the lounge life that was coming to an end behind him.

Brandy came back into the light, alone. "Hey," she said. "I should've asked. You need a ride somewhere?"

"No," Pal said. "No thanks."

"You're sure?"

"I'm sure. I haven't got far to go."

"Suit yourself," Brandy said.

She disappeared again. Pal heard her car start, back out, and begin to accelerate. She circled around the lot and pulled up in front of Pal. She leaned across the passenger's seat. Pal stood up. The engine idled on growl.

"Say," she said. "Are those dirty Levi's?"

"No," Pal laughed. "No, they're cheap knockoffs."

"Listen," she said. "If you don't mind I could use a hand with him." She jerked her thumb at Michael, who was stretched out in the back seat. He was so still he seemed dead.

"Okay," Pal said. "Long as Mike doesn't mind."

"Mind?" Brandy said, as Pal climbed through the window. "What mind?" She shifted the Camaro into gear and started out of the lot, edging across the dirt exit past the diggers and pavers that looked in the moonlight like the skeletons of dinosaurs.

"He's out of it. And he doesn't even know. He won't know," she added, "unless I tell him sometime when he's sober enough to listen. And even then he won't believe it." She smiled at Pal once again. Her voice was no longer husky but soft as she added, "So who cares if he minds? Certainly not me."

Pal felt shy. He knew he should say something. But what?

"He's not much different than other men. I thought he was, when I met him. Turns out I was wrong." She was genuinely sad. She laughed. "I bet you can't imagine how much I hate men in bars. All secure in their little egos and their stupidity. And don't think it's because I mind them looking at me like I'm a side of beef with a few holes made just for them to penetrate. That's how I see them, too, like blow-up rubber tools that, sober, might just give me a moment's satisfaction. I'd rather they think that just because they tip me for their drinks, they own a piece of me. Long as they don't touch.

"What I hate," she went on, giving Pal a few seconds to absorb that, "is the way these guys with their bulging egos can see through my clothes but they still can't see what I really am."

"What's that?" Pal asked.

"A musician. Songwriter, singer, and jazz flautist. I waitress just to keep body and soul together until I get my first big break. Those losers are living in a bush if they think I'd saddle myself with one of them. They think just stirring the stick shift of their Beemer is enough to get a girl like me off, make me all hot and impatient to get home to my place and rip their Dockers off." She laughed bitterly. "You ever notice how they never want to go to their place? Their faces squinch all up like accountants if you suggest it as they add up the capital costs and gains of infidelity, trying to convince themselves of the low margin of risk if they cheat on their wives and girlfriends with some low-life waitress. Hah! Like I'd want to screw them any more than their wives do. Which is why they're at the Note getting too drunk to get it up instead of at home getting it down, huh?"

"I guess," Pal said. If he was shy at first, he was terrified now that Brandy might think of him the way she seemed to think of most men. "How about Michael?" he asked.

"Mikey? Poor Mikey." She sighed. "He's just so jealous. He can't handle being jealous. So he comes down to work to keep his eye on me and then drinks himself into oblivion. He used to be a good lover, though. These days he's not much more than a sandbag I cart around for traction."

"I think I'd be jealous, too," Pal said. He felt sympathy for Michael. "I mean there's something really awful about knowing other men talk about someone you like."

"Like? Screw, you mean. Michael doesn't like me at all."

"I don't know him," Pal said. "But I do know that I could never sleep with someone I didn't like."

"Really," Brandy said. She pulled up outside an apartment block in downtown Gilroy. "Here we are, Mikey. Wake up, hon, we're home." She turned off the engine and took the keys out of the ignition. Flipping them around with her index finger in the loop of the chain, she said to Pal, "You're kind of cute, you know? In a funny sort of way."

Pal helped her drag Michael out of the car and up the stairs. Brandy went ahead of him to unlock the door. Together they pulled him inside. They laid him across the bed and Brandy began to undress him, beginning with his boots and socks. When she unbuckled his belt, Pal went out to wait in the next room.

"So," she said, standing up close to him as he sat there. Her keys jangled from her finger. She flipped the key ring in circles and said, "You up for a nightcap at my place?"

"I thought this was your place. I thought you and Michael lived together."

"Michael likes to think that. I used to live here. I've got a place on the other side of town now. Over by Devine. Near the park."

"That's a pretty rough neighborhood, isn't it?"

"You need to duck sometimes," Brandy said, laughing. "But I like my neighbors. I get along with Mexicans. And they never ever remind me of the white guys who patronize the Blue Note." She reached down and took his hand and lifted him from the couch.

CHAPTER TEN

I.

"Anything's better than Harry Connick, Jr.," I say, wincing at the idea of Brandy.

Mary Blue raises an empty coffee mug in her hand as though she's going to throw it at me. I duck, though it would not do any good. As her spirit guide, I'm a sitting duck if she should decide to let it fly.

As upset as she is, her face retains a calm, permanent look. Her anger, like her joy, is an emotional frame of mind. It takes a *weyekin* to recognize which it is, given the solid permanence of Mary Blue and the way her immediate concerns, emotions good or bad, are quickly absorbed into the context of generations. Take any emotion, any feeling, any event. Place it in the long term like that and it becomes smaller, less likely to cause one to react the way Mercedes Rota reacted when her future son-in-law, Paquito Morta, was dragged from his job as a shipping clerk and shipped off himself to the jungles of Southeast Asia. Mercedes barely knocked, bursting through Mary's door without waiting for an invitation. She went straight to the kitchen.

Mary Blue's kitchen had always been a place of refuge. Nowadays, with La Vent in jail for shooting the mayor, the kitchen was the soul inside her house, which had become a protective shell. These days, she left her kitchen only out of necessity or to go walking late at night, sneaking into the migrant laborers' camps and leaving turkey-sized foil pans with burritos and enchiladas for people she hardly knew or did not know at all anymore. She kept very much to herself, beading and walking and cooking, cooking, cooking, with no one to eat the food but strangers. When she wasn't doing these things, she cleaned, and then to find her all Mercedes had to do was follow the cord of the vacuum.

Mercedes stood in the center of the room waving her hands, talking loudly, spitting out a rapid-fire mixture of English and Spanish that Mary Blue took to mean that something awful had happened, was happening, or was fated to happen. (The latter was the truth, as it turned out. Any Dreamer who imagined the context of a war in which Mexican, black, and Indian boys were sent out like dogs to find the punji holes, Bouncing Betty mines, and midnight snipers could predict Pablo's future as easily as Chicken Licken's when, years later, John Wayne, who dodged the draft altogether, made himself into a veteran hero who despised protestors as Comsymps, and then went around shouting how the sky was falling.)

With Mercedes, the emotions had to fly out like water from a salad spinner until she was dry enough to speak only one language at a time—either of which Mary Blue would understand.

With Mary Blue, however, strong emotion might only be visible to you either in the tightness of her movements, slightly stiffened like someone in the first stages of arthritis, or in the clear precision of her words as she enunciated each and every syllable, as though to lose one at these moments would be to lose it forever.

Crossing the kitchen to fill her "I ♥ TO BE HUGGED" mug with boiling water, into which she dropped a bag of black tea, she said to me, "You were supposed to walk. Like me. You were supposed to walk until your rhythm matched Pal's need." She set the hot mug on a square of cork on the edge of her beading table. She took up her needle. Her right hand deftly snagged three white beads on the needle's point. She followed it with three blue, and then three more white. "No one said you should take a ride from some *puta* in a muscle car."

"Yeah," I replied, my nerves on edge. "But you know, she offered.

Hey, why walk when you can ride? And in that car. It is some car, let me tell you. I remember this low-rider in L.A. I got a ride in with full pneumatics that could make the car bounce and waggle. Candy-apple red. Metallic flake with tuck and roll? Brandy's Camaro is almost as good as that."

Mary Blue did not even look up as I prattled on. She went on beading—decorating a sun hat today—taking small sips of her tea between stitches.

Fortunately, the phone rang.

"Get that, will you?" she said.

"Sure. Glad to help," I said. "Larue residence," I said into the receiver.

Silence.

I shrugged and was about to hang up when a woman's voice hissed, "Is Attila the Hun home?"

"Who?"

"Sugary Cain there?" the voice said again. It was an angry voice, to be sure.

"Nobody here by that name," I said. I recognized Sally Pedon's voice. But I did not have the energy for her right now. I hung up.

Mary Blue turned and raised her eyebrows.

"Sally," I said. "She been calling a lot?"

"Lately," Mary said. Her anger at me partially abated with the memory of what I'd gone through with Sally.

Mary said, "Her missionizing instinct is powerful. She hates Pal. Calls him any and every name she can think of. But she still wonders if she might not be able to save Pal's soul without saving the man."

The phone rang again.

"Blue-Larue residence."

"Mister Wakee-sha-nameg-wetch in?" Sally asked. "That's Injun for 'Thanks-for-being-a-poophead,'" she said. She giggled, and then slammed her phone down.

"Sally again," I informed Mary.

Mary sighed. She poked her needle into a felt pad she kept for that purpose on her beading table and stood up. Taking a shawl from the back of another chair and throwing it around her shoulders she said, "Come on. Let's walk."

We left the house, passing La Vent's yellow Pontiac, which looked forlorn in the moonlight. Mary Blue's people were always great walkers, able to go long distances without tiring by keeping to an even, steady pace. We headed south at a steady pace, out among scrub and brush, toward the hills that looked like whales sleeping on the night's horizon, huge shadows of fate on a Milky Way bed comprising all the colors in white.

"Where I come from," Mary Blue said, pulling her shawl close around her against the chill of the night air, "we don't believe in what white folks call happiness."

"You're telling me," I said.

"Their *happy* is all in the moment. They're like five-year-olds. They do some small thing. They get some thing they think they want. With my people, with me, the small things like the individual color of a bead may be important, but they only matter when all of them get connected."

"But you're happy," I said. I had to. After all, this was her dream, the world she imagined into possibility. And I was the agent, the segundum mobile, if you will, of that possibility and how it became actuality. If she was not happy, then neither was I.

"As far as happy goes," she said. She stopped walking and gazed up toward the Pleiades.

"You're not happy with La Vent?"

"There's no happy or unhappy with my husband," she answered. "I never expected him to make me happy."

"And now?"

"Now? Now I can see that someone so lost desires only to be found. And he will be found. But he won't find himself in the process." She shook her head. "Come on. Let's keep moving. It's cold." We started up over a ridge, winding around the shrubs and chaparral along a narrow path made by mountain sheep, coyote, and deer.

After several minutes with only the sound of our feet on the path and the brief rush and scurry of an owl hunting nearby, Mary Blue added sadly, "I hoped I could do the finding. With La Vent. I thought I could be his connection, like you are mine. But everything happened too fast. I was too young."

"The wedding? The job?"

"All of it. Mostly the sudden money. The sudden feeling that came with the money that he had a place in the world and that he was appreciated for doing his best to occupy that place. Sudden is no good. It ruins people."

"So what now?"

"What do you mean?"

"Well, what happens to us? To you and me?"

"Palimony," she said. She laughed, her thin substantial body shaking with the eruption of the laugh. "Can you imagine? Palimony. I dreamed it and refused to believe the dream. I let my only son be named Palimony. Ah, well," she sighed. "All we can do, now, is teach him to dream love into his world in a way that doesn't make him needy."

I saw the turn this conversation might take. Criticism of me, of my failure to guide Pal. I kept my mouth shut and waited.

"La Vent is lost to me," Mary said. "Pal is my purpose now."

We turned back for home as we reached the crest of the ridge. The moon was high and bright. I understood that Pal had to be connected, that somehow, some way, I was going to have to help him find the right words, the right path, the full connection not just to Mary Blue but to Mary Blue's great-great-great-great-great-great-grandmother and -grandfather. I was going to have to get him to feel seven generations behind him and see as far as seven generations in front of him. Boy, I had a lot to do. It made me weary just to think about it.

2.

Pal and Brandy moved into a block of HUD apartments constructed out of cardboard and inhabited by noise and violence.

"You're going where?" Mary asked when he told her. "Well, if I can't talk you out of it. Call me, will you. Collect."

The man downstairs nightly abused his wife, at first verbally, screaming epithet-laden insults and threats at her until he had drunk enough liquor and at last his voice was softened by the blows he inflicted on her. The woman next door continually threatened her infant children, swearing she was going to take them out into the countryside and abandon them and let them fend for themselves if they did not stop crying and interfering with the visits of her boyfriends. One night he heard her swear that she would put them in their seat belts and push the car into the reservoir if they didn't stop interfering. She sounded sincere. Pal tossed and turned with nightmare images until he was sick from them and he threw up.

Sleepless from lying there night after night having visions of the two kids, their faces pressed against the auto's glass as water filled their lungs and slowly choked them to death, wondering what he should do, Pal talked Brandy into moving. After only two weeks, they walked out on their lease, losing half a month's rent and the two-month deposit against damage. They moved into a rustic house on Mt. Madonna on the road to Watsonville which another Blue Note waitress named Raylin shared with a Quaker couple, a madman named Carl, who occupied the garage and spent his days collecting rags and newspapers to jam into chinks and keep out the fresh air, and a gentle heavy metal rocker named Mick, who developed the habit of bursting into their bedroom without knocking ("Sorry, thought you said come in"), hoping to see Ray-lin or Brandy and Pal doing something he only imagined in the metallica of his waking dreams.

The house was isolated on a bluff. Beyond the trees below were the winding streets of Gilroy's upper class, miles in the distance. Though they had no near neighbors, the hills around the house were safe—as long as you overlooked Carl and the pair of puma who resented how the incursion of humans lowered property values in the area. The rent was cheap. The owner of the house had bought it during a real estate boom and was now having trouble selling it. As long as the kids took care of the place, he was willing to cut his losses by renting it for less than his mortgage payment and taxes. Even with Brandy and Pal's share being a third, two-sixths of the total, Pal could afford to quit his night job handling sealed red bags of contaminated waste at the local hospital. (The seventh roommate, Carl, seemed to be the Quaker couple's idea of charity. They held the lease, so no one argued with them, at least in part because no one wanted to have to discuss the matter with Carl, or even be near him long enough to ask if he might contribute to the household expenses. And he didn't eat much.)

Pal being at home was a disappointment for Mick, who seemed to lose all hope of finding Ray-lin and Brandy doing things that could fire the sexual imagination of a rocker who had seen it all two or three times over before he had turned thirteen. Every time he burst into the room in the evenings, now, he risked finding Pal reclining on the mattress on the floor, reading or thinking. Sometimes, even, Mick found Pal once again writing words in a journal, a feat Mick could barely imagine for himself.

Pal paid no attention to the formalities of writing English as he'd been forced to do in school. And lately, about all he seemed to write down was names: Advil, Sally, La Vent Larue, Amanda, Brandy, Ray-lin, Carl. Names of people he knew, or of people whom he imagined he knew. One night he even apologized to Mick. Hearing Pal chant "Amanda" with the slow rhythm of sex, poor Mick had burst into the room to find Pal holding his journal and nothing else in his hands.

"Thought you said come in," Mick said. He glanced around the room, wondering where she could have gone. The room lacked a closet. The bookshelves separating Pal's half of the room from Ray-lin's were too low to hide behind. He frowned. His face suddenly sank into a heavy, sad disappointment, like a dog's when his master tells him that he's not going along for this ride.

"Sorry to disappoint you," Pal said, smiling kindly. That made Mick's sadness worse. "So what do you think? You like 'Amanda'?"

"Amanda who?"

"Who is the point," Pal said. "Well, at least it's *Amanda*. The name means 'love.' I guess that's good enough for now, huh?"

Mick's disappointed look turned to annoyance. The way a Klans-
man's wish for power gets taken out on powerless people, he turned on
Pal. "You know something, man? It ain't no fucking wonder you people lost everything."

"Us people?" Pal asked.

"Fucking Indians, man."

"Ah," Pal said. Mick turned and left the room. "Not everything,"
he called after him. Pal closed his eyes and went back to softly chanting.

"Whatever Indians have lost, people like Mick now think they
want," Amanda said. "They turn how into what. Process, the way you
do things properly, into facts. They turn spirit into objects like dream-
catchers and sweat lodges and purchase them. Which means they'll
never get them. Just the shadows of them."

Pal grinned. He closed his journal and lay his head back, and lost
himself in conversation with Amanda.

3.

Schooling had succeeded with Pal and he felt silly, at first, sitting
around nights, dreaming his life away. Even Mick was more produc-
tive, it seemed, and that left only Carl and the Quakers to do less than
he. Yet once he began these first toddling steps toward real dreaming,
he could not stop. He began to change.

At first, he felt angry at himself. Night after night he tried to read,
mulling over the emptiness of his life and waiting for Mick to burst into
the room. His brain dulled with tinnitus, Mick never did quite understand that Ray-lin and Brandy changed out of their cocktail outfits at
work. His entrance into Pal's room was like a late alarm, as Mick tried
to time his entry to the moment just after the two arrived home.

Ignoring Mick, Brandy came in and heaved herself down onto the
mattress and sighed, forcing Pal to put aside his journal or his book and
ask her what was the matter. She would unburden herself about work.
At first, Pal imagined that listening to her without interference or comment would help her to get it all off her chest and out of her mind, sort
of debrief herself as she reentered the normality of her world with him.

But slowly, she began to seem to resent the fact that he was home reading, waiting for her, while she was out making money for them. She
started going into lurid detail of the way men stared at her breasts or
tried to nudge her body with their hands and arms and shoulders and
cop a surreptitious feel. Gradually, the way Brandy talked, these men
became a fraternity that Pal seemed to have joined without volition. He
was like them or they were like him (one can never tell with fraternities
where the likeness begins). Her job, the long hours she had to put in,
the T&A show she had to put on for tips became his fault simply because he was a male.

"So quit," Pal said one night. He was weary of hearing her
complain.

"I need the money," Brandy replied, adding to her stock of accusa-
tions the fact that he was a male, which meant that he was as dense as
Mick or a midnight Appalachian fog.

"I can pay our food and rent," Pal offered.

"Oh, right," Bandy said angrily. "I'm supposed to quit and let some
man support me. You patronizing shit. I can take care of myself."

Pal did not know what to do. He felt frustrated, and he felt sorrowfully inadequate. He kept his mouth shut. He waited. When she
seemed to have calmed down, he tried to put his arms around her to
comfort her. She shrugged him off. "I'm tired," she said. She rolled
away from him, and pretended to go to sleep.

Pal propped his book on his chest and tried to read. His eyes passed
over the same paragraph over and over and over. The words grew
fuzzy and the print ran together, and the confused emotions he felt
seemed to spread out, become thin, and then evaporate in the heat of his
affection for Brandy. Sometimes he pulled out his journal and, turning
to the page that recorded her name, softly chanted the word "Amanda."
He repeated her name enough to disturb Mick's sleep and make him
wonder if he should get up, get dressed, and chance an intrusion into
Brandy's bedroom.

Pal wanted things to be better, happier. But he knew from a childhood of uncaught fish that, if wanting could have been sufficient for

him to imitate the way La Vent's fishing line played out over the deep pools where the big fish lived, he would have been a crack fly fisherman. Instead, he had been a boy hunched up in the boat sucking on the bloody tear in his palm caused by a hook that somehow had embedded itself in his flesh. (And this was the thing, La Vent always thought. You could never quite envision how in hell he had been clumsy enough to manage it. Had his clumsy son reached into the tackle box with his eyes closed and grabbed the first sharp thing that touched his hand, and squeezed *before* ripping his hand up and out of the box?) Even when they tried fishing with waders, and even if the stream or pool wasn't deep enough, he managed to fill the legs of his hip boots with water and stumble and splash, until La Vent could secure his pole, wade over to where he flailed about like a wounded helicopter, and rescue him. Of course with all that . . . what? . . . energy expended, any fish that lived in the county had packed up their gills and swam off elsewhere, hightailing it down the fly-tied highway.

Thus, as much as Pal wanted, he did not know what to do. Dreaming could have helped, but so far I had failed to help him learn. Though now I had reason to be hopeful; with too much time on his hands after work, he began to hang out nights at the Blue Note, thinking his presence might comfort Brandy, if not protect her.

4.

I needed to help Pal envision a context for the here and now, which by connecting him with fourteen generations would make this particular here and now dissolve its own appearance of importance. But my considerations about what to do to help him were complicated by the fact that BrandyWine Gooschurt was not her real name. It was a stage name, like Stitch or Needles, her guitarist and drummer. The fact that her parents, Fitzwilliam Armstrong and Aluicia Espress Doe, had named her Baby Jane after the heroine of a celebrated custody case was reason enough to have changed it. In addition, when she decided to become a musician, she had not wanted to sound either too black or too white. So she settled for the oxymoronic: Heidi Gooschurt. Heidi, the coy little Swiss girl in pigtails and a dirndl who can lead you a merry chase through alpine pastures, her skin so white that it seems, almost, transparent. And Gooschurt, a hard-assed street name, dark-complected and sexy with a viscous emanence. Heidi, however, seemed too moronic even to Stitch (who, in his turn, made Carl look pretty agile). And so she changed it once again to Brandy, to which she added, to ensure people knew her origins, *Wine*: BrandyWine. Despite her commercial transformations, she still didn't make any money playing music.

So she took a fingernail file to the top four buttonholes on her uniform blouse, loosening the stitching so that when she bent to set the bill on a customer's table the blouse could, if she twisted her shoulders in just the right way, pop open to reveal the reasonable cleavage of her breasts and, if she did not straighten up quickly, the aureoles and nipples as well. I have to admit she had nipples that even when they were not hard with desire were something to behold. Those Beemer men in their highwater Dockers would just go nuts with their wallets, ripping out five-dollar bills and trying to toss them at her with drunken nonchalance, an offering to the goddess of hope by which they offended their dates. If they didn't tip large, Brandy followed them to the door and tossed their change at them.

"You call this a tip?" she asked loudly, embarrassing the men in front of their secretaries and neighbors.

She memorized their faces and if they came in again, she refused to serve them.

Observing all this, Pal began to feel angry that Brandy had to sink so low to make money. And it was not a good anger, washed, as it was, with his suspicion that Brandy sort of liked doing it, taking these men for a ride without even getting in their cars, yet enjoying the way their eyes sort of went pop when her blouse pulled open and their dates turned furious faces tight with envy toward the door. Sometimes, on a night she was really having fun, she would rub gently against the man's shoulder or elbow as he fished in his wallet or stuck his hand into his pocket, so when he tried to speak again his mouth was as dry as aluminum and his tongue as thick as sand.

As his anger grew, Pal became blind. He not only suspected that she enjoyed it but that, with the right man, she might just change her act and even pick him up outside, dump her boyfriend, and take him home with her. Now when she complained about that night's customers, he was oh so sympathetic. He encouraged her to complain, while at the same time he began to rack his brains for a way to get her to quit.

"I don't know," Brandy said as they lay there together and listened to Ray-lin groan with some stranger on the far side of the bookcases.

"You could focus on your art," he said. Carl wailed low and long in the garage. Pal tried to recover a childhood memory that made him want to laugh at the idea of art. "You could work on your music. I could pay the bills, but as a loan, until you get going with the band."

"You're sweet," Brandy said. For the moment, he had stepped out of the fraternity of men. "But a band's expensive. How would we pay those bills? We're not Carl, after all." She laughed. She hugged him and kissed his face until soon they were trying noiselessly to imitate Ray-lin and her stranger.

"I'll find a way," Pal said, before Brandy fell into sleep.

It was in a hopeful state of mind, now, that he went to the Blue Note after work. Night after night, he sat at the bar near the waitress station and watched Brandy. But once again, he couldn't help noticing the things she did to increase her tips.

It made her uncomfortable to have him there, and they fought about it. At first she hissed out of the side of her mouth at him as she waited for the bartender to make her drinks. Not too much later, she spoke sharply to him, told him to go home, that she couldn't work with him there.

But still he showed up and still he sat, eavesdropping on the comments men made about her. He'd drink, a slow burn of beer. And if some man made too many comments about his true love or if the comments were too knowing, intimating a knowledge of Brandy that Pal, himself, didn't have, Pal would accost him outside.

One night Advil Johnson came in with a friend of his, a thin, well-dressed, hip, and sort of fay black guy who took to Pal right away. But as they drank together at their table—served by Brandy, who pretended not to know Pal and who seemed to encourage the flirtations of Advil's friend—LaCar began to talk about how he'd known Brandy back when she called herself Heidi. Pal laughed. He did not know that a year ago Heidi had been her name. But as LaCar talked, describing some of the things he did with Heidi and she with him, the verisimilitude of what he said struck Pal. It was like the recognition of art without the pleasure. This recognition felt like a slap in the face to someone who had gotten as drunk as Pal. When LaCar left, Pal followed him outside, jumped him from behind, and began to beat him with a frustration and hurt so overwhelming that, if Advil hadn't rushed out to stop him, he could have sent the poor guy to the hospital.

The fact that Brandy's real name was Baby Jane Doe didn't make things easier for Pal, either. The idea that he was sleeping with Baby Jane while the other men leered at a figment of her imagination should have amused Pal. But it didn't.

He talked to Mary Blue about it. One day, when she came home from visiting La Vent at the county jail she found him pacing up and down the walk to the house, his heels striking the cement like drum mallets. The day was fine, the sky blue and only barely tinged with smog, so Mary walked him the mile and a half to the mercado to buy some tea and tuna fish. Just listening to all of it frustrated her. It frustrated her despite years of her Dreamer's practice at harmony, at the balance that comes from not judging until it's time and even when it became time, usually not judging the person but maybe the results, and not harshly, which came full circle from the balance achieved by not judging, by putting the thing itself in perspective, by connecting it to five hundred years of human activity and thought, by seeing that very little about real human beings really changes. Once you realize that, once you learn to dream, which helps to create that realization, you gain humor—sometimes, outright laughter—but always the humor that is the resilience of survival.

"You have to laugh," Mary said, picking a jar of Best Foods mayonnaise from the shelf and handing it to Pal to put in the basket.

"What do you mean? What's to laugh at?"

"Sometimes nothing. But you have to laugh all the same," Mary replied, calmly. "What kind of tea do you want?"

"A dark one," Pal said to please her. He liked lighter blends, but he knew his mother preferred dark and sometimes smoky blends. Mary Blue smiled and pulled from the shelf a box of Prince of Wales, the tea he called "the Black Prince" because of the deep black coloring of its packaging, and dropped it ceremoniously into his basket. "Maybe I could get another job," he added, humorlessly.

"Maybe you could win bingo big, too," Mary Blue replied. "But if you don't stop this ridiculous fighting, you're going to get killed or arrested. It's one thing to fight real enemies. But these boys at the Blue Note are not your enemy. You are."

"So let them arrest me," he said. Then he gave her a pitiable look. "I have tried, you know. I can't help myself. I get off work and think about going home. I think about Carl being there. Or one of those kung fu Quaker meetings where they do tai chi and testify when the spirit calls. They all look like they're made of dough. Or Mick. I mean the whole house. I don't like going home even if Brandy is there."

"You're not exactly enjoying the Blue Note."

"That's true," he snorted. "I guess if they arrest me, at least I'll get some rest. At least I couldn't go to the bar. Huh?"

Mary Blue knew that the Blue Note wasn't the problem. Neither was Brandy—no more than the slut Ray-lin who shared a bedroom with Brandy and Pal and whom Pal secretly desired. The problem wasn't even his desire, his wanting, misplaced, misenvisioned, and therefore nothing but false. The problem was his lack of context. He was cut off from his history. He had no examples to teach him how to be. Even his parents—Mary, herself, and her failing connecting to La Vent—gave him no example. Not of love. Not of family. So there was his beginning, where he could begin, in love that led to family. Once he had that, if she succeeded, then and only then could he work backwards to connect with his history—his Nez Perce history, which was family because the Nez Perce, the Nu-Mi-Pu, the Human Beings, were nothing if not familial. She needed time to think, to dream how to do this, how to create this possibility and make it come to pass. "Listen," she said. "Why don't you get out of town for a while?"

Chapter Eleven

I.

La Vent came into the visitor's area at county looking peaceful and serene. His lips moved as though in prayer. Until he picked up the communication phone on his side, she did not know that it wasn't prayer, exactly, but the phrases of the jailhouse Christianity he was picking up from the Unitarian chaplain, phrases such as "You shall know a man by his labors"—which was the first complete phrase that she ever heard La Vent Larue utter.

"A woman, too," she replied.

The oxidized look in La Vent's eyes, partly caused by the bullet-proof plastic between their stools, seemed to clear. He looked at her the way a new father looks at the bent and asymmetrical form of his first-born and finds him good and beautiful with such passion that no one dare contradict him or even joke with him about the way babies in general look. It was a kind of love at first sight, different from the way he felt when he met the shy Mary Blue all those years ago, but love nonetheless. This love was chaste, innocent, aphysical, and romantic. La Vent's straight, level eyes narrowed, and his gaze looked through at her as though she were a 3-D puzzle. "Who are you?" he said.

"A friend of Pal's," she replied.

"Pal?" La Vent said absently. "Pal?"

"Your only begotten son," she said. She smiled at the clever way she managed to hide the bitterness she felt toward that son.

They began the longest conversation La Vent had had with anyone lately, and all of it in the swallow-tailed code that only she could follow very easily.

After the guards took La Vent back to his cell, she checked out at the front gate. She felt glad. She felt as though she were doing her duty to God and hoped that He would agree that saving the son must of necessity begin with the father.

2.

On his days off, Pal got out of town. He began hopping freight trains, riding the rails north from Gilroy. He climbed into the beds of pickup trucks or into the caves of boxcars while the train was stopped to change its crew. He rode beyond Mt. Shasta, up into Oregon, and when he made a mistake (it is not always possible to determine just where a freight train is headed), he rode out into the deserts of Utah. He traveled alone, and he went as if he were in a dream that could be re-dreamed when he needed to feel its effects, like the night he awoke in the dark, feeling fingers gently part the pleat in his boxer shorts and slip in to caress his balls, only to feel lips close round his hardening cock and begin to move up and down it, sucking at him. Brandy had never given him a blow job before. Yet he imagined, in the half-sleepy darkness, that it was she doing it, and doing a mighty good job at it at that, before he came and the darkening questions about why she might do this crept into his mind, disturbed his contentment, and made him sit up.

"Umm, that was good," Ray-lin said. "I've wanted to have you in my mouth for what seems like forever. Night after night I've been right over there with just the bookshelf between me and you wishing I was Brandy and Brandy was me."

Imagine the complicated sense of betrayal he felt, he whose mother, despite La Vent's going mad with wanting to emulate Buzz Packard and Bill Diggum, had remained true to the man she had married. Perhaps Pal might be serially monogamous, but monogamous he believed he should be. He loved Brandy. Or he had thought he loved Brandy when they moved in together. Now, he did sometimes have feelings about her that even Carl would be hard-pressed to call "love." He sometimes hated himself; he sometimes hated her more. The two hatreds were as inseparable as the tides, ebbing and flowing, yet always of the same water. Now, he hated himself because he had enjoyed Ray-lin's blow job. Indeed, he had often denied his own desire to be on the other side of the bookcases that divided the room. And now there was no denying it any longer.

He lay awake beside Brandy, listening to the rustle of sheets as Ray-lin turned over in her sleep, or trying to block out the low, stifled groans and moans that came from Ray-lin's side of the room as she masturbated. Sometimes, he hummed to himself, remembering the rides he'd taken on freights, putting himself on those trains and thus far away from this room and the feelings that threatened to cool like Jell-O into something substantial.

He remembered one train heading south out of Medford, Oregon, that turned east at a "Y" junction while he slept. When he awoke, he was in the deserts of Utah, half frozen by the wind whipping through the car. The train slowed briefly on the west side of Ogden and before it could accelerate again, Pal jumped down, spraining his ankle bad.

As if out of the wind, hoboes—five of them in all—gathered around him like shades. Loudly, intending for him to hear and be afraid, they discussed what to do to or with him. They decided that they would let him be if he could prove he wasn't just some kid doing stupid things, but someone who knew what he was doing. They gave him a quiz.

"You tell me," a tall, gaunt hobo said, coming over to where Pal stood, alone, waiting.

He couldn't run. If he did, they'd catch him. He'd seen hoboes move. Like sticky-toed sloths, they seemed indolent and slow until in an instant they saw something they wanted and hopped out of a slow-moving freight, got it, tossed it into the boxcar, and swung like an Olympic gymnast back up into the car—and all in one apparent motion.

It was one thing he admired about hoboes: They seemed so physically contained, like a wound spring. They expended energy only when it was needed, and they seemed able to discern those moments of need almost instinctively. If he ran, they would know he was afraid—and he had the good sense to be very afraid. These were not men who dealt kindly or compassionately with the fearful or the weak.

The gaunt hobo jerked his chin up at Pal. "You got a train going that way." He pointed with his thumb, which curved sharply like an Arabian knife. "You have to get on that train. One way or other. Which end?"

"Which end?" Pal asked, buying time.

"Yeah. Which end of the car you try for?"

Pal figured it was fifty-fifty. "The front," he guessed.

The pack of hoboes hovering nearby seemed to relax. This kid was okay. He knew his rails.

"Wait a minute," a small one said, stepping forward from the pack.

Uh-oh. This one had been standing apart all along, watching, shifting from foot to foot. He worried Pal because of his silence and his size. Small men had a gene that made them small. That same gene, compressed like it was, made them tend to cruelty and meanness.

"Why?" the small hobo demanded. He turned and grinned at his compatriots as if to say "Now we got him."

"Because if you miss, you'll bounce off the car and fall away from the train. Go for the back and you could swing around into the couplings," Pal said slowly.

The other hoboes congratulated him. They patted him on the back and shoulder. They were genuinely happy, relieved of a major worry. They did not want to side with the small hobo and injure this boy. Two of them joyfully went into Ogden, shoplifted some food and bottled water, came back, fed Pal, and then stole a car and took him to the Ogden yards and put him on a train headed west, back to California.

It was an adventure. Even as the train crossed the Sierras, a boxcar, misplaced in the train between two longer cars, rose up through the roof of a snow tunnel like a horse rearing in slow motion before it tumbled a thousand feet into the ravine below. It was a sight. The air brakes set automatically, and as they waited for the railroad crews to bring up engines from Nevada City to remake the train, Pal fell asleep in the cold. A dream of glaciers inching south through the valleys of his grandmothers awakened him, and he realized how stupid it was to let himself go like that and fall asleep. He could have died.

Another trip, he ended up in Portland with a yard detective stalking him in his security car. Suddenly, the detective raced up and flashed on his headlights and leapt out of the car with his pistol drawn and pointed at Pal's chest. By then, fortunately, with all the danger of hopping freight trains, Pal had become self-possessed.

Figuring to deflate the danger by quickly altering the context, Pal raised his right hand in greeting. "Hi," he said loudly, "I was just looking for you."

"You were?" the guard said, letting his gun drop to his side as he considered this new information. He'd expected trouble. He had hoped that Pal would react with fear. He didn't expect this.

Pal opened his eyes and nodded.

Pal answered his questions honestly. He was in the yard because he was looking to hop a freight home. Yes, he knew that technically he was trespassing on Southern Pacific Railroad property. But he wouldn't cause any damage to the trains. Yes, he knew that the yard detective could arrest him, take him downtown, and have him booked by the police. But he hoped he wouldn't.

Pal spoke plainly. The guard started to relax. Eventually, realizing Pal was no threat, he holstered his gun. He explained. Although Pal needed no explanation, he felt the other man's palpable need to talk. To connect with someone, to tell him the whole story. The guard's partner had been stabbed thirty-seven times by hoboes two nights before and was barely hanging on in intensive care. The guard related the whole story, even repeating parts of it twice for emphasis. Because of Pal's very real concern for his buddy, the guard decided to put Pal in the back of his car and drive him to an overpass where he could wait for a train home, hidden by a mound from the switchman's tower. "Show your face," the guard warned him, "and I'll have to bust your ass. Understood?"

Even after trips like these, Pal enjoyed being gone. Indeed, the danger from Ray-lin seemed to him greater than the danger from hoboes and armed guards. The latter could kill the body. The former, given the way he had been raised, could kill something else, an important part of him, something resembling hope.

In one of those wonderful real-life ironies, he was gone so much that Brandy decided that she missed him. The arguments they'd had, the words they had exchanged, which to Pal were permanent (though forgivable), were as nothing, as if they had never been spoken. At night when she came home and he perfunctorily asked her how work was, prepared to force himself to listen and understand, she kept her answers short.

"Okay," she said.

She might sigh, just to be sure he didn't think it was wonderful or what she wanted out of life. But rather than go into it, she would snuggle up to him and begin a long process of making him demonstrate that he still cared for her.

"Sometimes I think you'd rather be on a smelly old train than with me," she said sweetly. She listened with fair contentment as he did his best to say that was untrue.

After a week or two, when she was halfway convinced, she even ventured to say that she had suspected that there were no freight trains but that he had fallen in love with someone else and was spending his nights with her. Pal did not say much in reply. He laughed, as though that was just plain silly. Despite the three or four times Ray-lin had given him blow jobs which he couldn't resist, in his heart he was riding trains in order to be steadfast and true to Brandy. It wasn't true. But still, her not knowing this, her assumption that he was like her, or like other men, closed his heart against her, forced him to articulate (in code, in words hidden in his journal) the fact that he and Brandy came from completely different worlds, different ways of being.

Ironically, in his world one tried as hard as he could to remain true to his words, and he had once said to her he loved her. Thus, the realization that he lived a different way from her made him try to prove otherwise. When one night, after making love, she whispered, "I want to have your baby," he responded that she could, once they were married.

"Married? Why?" she asked.

"To make the baby legitimate. To prove that I won't walk out on you."

Brandy laughed. "Hah. As if marriage is any guarantee."

Double proof of different worlds: Marriage, to him, guaranteed a lot. Just look at what Mary Blue had endured and suffered for La Vent. Only Mary Blue would never in her life call it suffering. It was what you did. There was no other way about it. People who left, cheated, divorced rarely ended up happier or better off. It was not because there was no such thing as happiness, but because happiness took suffering. Happiness required tolerance and allowance. Happiness was something one developed by changing one's self, one's way of seeing the world, one's context—and clearly not something one got by changing (or trying to change) one's husband or wife. People, Mary Blue understood, do not change. Only the contexts in which they live do.

"I'd rather you did something else for me, first," Brandy said before Pal drifted into sleep.

"What's that?"

"Take me on a freight train ride with you."

"Sure."

"You will?"

"I said I would."

"Goody. When?"

3.

The guard at the county jail sat like an old Arab merchant. By now, he expects her. Without a word, she hands him her purse and he opens it briefly to examine the contents as she passes through the metal detector. As silently, he hands her purse back to her and waves at the guard controlling the lockdown door to the visitor's area. The second guard buzzes her inside. He yawns. She is familiar to him, too.

La Vent enters from a different door. He smiles. It is obvious that he's excited, but he controls the physical manifestations of excitement. He places his hands upon the Plexiglas as though on her shoulders, looks into her great gray eyes, and asks, "You will follow me?"

She nods. "As long as you follow Him," she replies. She is deadly serious.

"The path may be a stony one."

She grins. Not as stony as you might think, she says to herself. I'll get that son of yours yet.

"Three days, then?" he says.

"Three days. I'll see you then." She picks up her purse and waves to the guard, who buzzes her out. "Thanks for everything," she says to the guard by the metal detector.

"You're welcome," he says. "He's a model prisoner." He stops, embarrassed. "Will I see you again?" he asks.

"Not on the inside," she replies.

4.

Mary Blue tries her best to dream this:

Pal stands just inside the open door to the boxcar leaning on the iron strap that bisects the opening horizontally. The strap is used to guard cargo like lumber, hold it inside the car with the doors open. To-day, the only cargo is a boy and a girl and a wiry hobo who lurks in the corner, the whites of his eyes enhanced by the contrast with his skin that is dark with dirt and grime. Pal has cleaned a cut on the hobo's hand and covered it with an antibiotic cream from his pack, an act intended to make the hobo unafraid but which has instead made him wary and suspicious.

The train is still, waiting for the green light go-ahead on the last feed to the main line from the yards. Brandy ranges beyond the car, looking for loose tie plates on which to set the five-gallon can with a fire inside. It's winter, and a small fire as the train moves into the mountains between California and Oregon will insulate them from the teeth of the wind biting through the open door when night falls. It will also give off enough light for them to keep their eye on their companion hobo. Even though he has bandaged the hobo's hand—an action Brandy tried to prevent, fearing infection—the hobo remains dangerous, trained to opportunism by experience and, some would say, necessity, like old man Coyote. Pal frowns, wondering if it was his unexpected kindness or Brandy's attempt to stop the kindness that has made the hobo seem more dangerous than he was, like a virus just waiting to strike in the cold and dark.

Neither Pal nor Brandy hears the engines. But suddenly the couplings bang tight with a metallic explosion. The long freight lurches and the long line of cars begins to move. With a swiftness that would surprise someone unfamiliar with riding the rails, the half million tons of train begins to accelerate onto the main line where, as a first-class freight with perishables, mail, and loaded car carriers, nothing will slow it down. Goods are more important in this country than people. Even passenger trains will be pulled aside to clear the tracks in front of it.

Brandy's head jerks up like an elk's on the meadow when the first shots are fired. Slowly, her head swivels toward the train. Her eyes search for the boxcar in which Pal stands still. She spots him, ten cars back and a hundred yards east. Involuntarily, she raises her gloved hand, almost as though waving goodbye. A signal. Then she flings down everything she has gathered, splaying her fingers, flexing them outward like a jazz dancer or a mechanic flicking off oil. She begins to run, lifting her knees high to clear the tumbleweed and hidden junk scattered along the railroad tracks. To Pal, in the moving boxcar, it looks like dance, until Brandy reaches open ground and lowers her knees and begins to sprint toward an imaginary point where the boxcar, constantly grabbing speed into itself, will intersect her path.

The sight of Brandy out there alone, so small, and the intensity of the expression on her face as she runs toward the train, makes Pal feel

like laughing. A joyful laugh, a laugh of expectation, a laugh of gratitude toward this person who is actually going to entrust him with her
life. He spreads his legs for balance, braces himself against the load
strap, takes off his gloves and tosses them deeper into the boxcar. He
closes his eyes for a moment to quell the laughter.

In his mind's eye, he sees Brandy remove the glove from her right
hand, the look on her face open and trusting for one of the first times in
her life. Ten feet from the car her strides lengthen and her toes reach
out to grab the earth like a high jumper's. Five feet from the car, the intersection of their paths almost certain, adjusted for the near constant
acceleration of the train, Brandy leaps, her head back, shoulders strain-
ing, legs working in midair like a broad jumper, her right hand reaching up to grab his right wrist. He, in turn, reaches down and grabs
Brandy's right wrist. Not the hand. The wrist. If each grabs the opposite wrist and one hand slips, there is still the second hand to keep
hold. If each grabs at the other's hand and slips or misses, there is only a
fleeting goodbye as Brandy falls under the boxcar and the trucks cut
her in two.

*Here, Mary Blue pauses. Stops rocking. She thought she was deter-
mined. She tells herself that she wants to go through with it. But a Dreamer
cannot dream someone else's death. That is what she would do, if she could.
But it is against generations of instinct and opposed to any true sense of justice. Brandy is innocent. Mary does not want Brandy to marry Pal, true. But
that is hardly reason to kill her. So she closes her eyes once again.*

Both hands lock on both wrists and, as though they've practiced
this balletic movement before, Brandy tucks her body into a ball, ducks
her head between her shoulders, and Pal draws the cannonball of his
lover up under the load strap and, with amazement and pride, sets
Brandy on her feet. They look at each other proud, confident, like true
friends. Even though in his mind's ear he hears Brandy begin to chide
herself for trusting her life to him, gasping in wonder and disbelief that

he has done what he did, everything is changed. Things will never be the same again.

"Besides that," Mary Blue says. She has interrupted a rather intense Ping-Pong game between me and Tom Yellowtail. "Every time I dreamed it, I knew in my heart that regardless of what names I stuck in, it was Pal out there foraging around, Pal running for the train, and Brandy in the moving boxcar."

"The fact that her name is really Baby Jane Doe didn't help, either," I said.

"It is?" Mary asked, surprised that she did not know this.

"Yep. Brandy is just her stage name. So even if you could have dreamed her death, only her imitation would be dead. Baby Jane would still be very much alive."

Mary sighed. "Ever since La Vent got out of jail and came home I've been dropping beads. Now this. Oh, well. Will you take care of it for me?"

"At your service," I said. "We're tied," I said to Tom Yellowtail.

"The hell we are," he said. He laughed. "You forfeit the game."

5.

I took Mary Blue's vision and began again:

They were still in the rail yards of Medford, Oregon, waiting for a first-class freight. There was snow on the ground at this elevation and they had been waiting most of the day, swinging their arms and banging their shoulders with their fists, trying to keep warm. They waited and they waited. But Brandy refused to ride in a boxcar like a common hobo.

After several hours of waiting in the Medford yards, the blackest person Pal has ever seen cuts out of the pack of hoboes warming themselves around a fire under an overpass about a hundred yards away and saunters up to them and says, "Hey."

"Hey," Pal replies.

I did not look at them directly. My performance this time was one of indirection and did not include looking at them. I let them remain objects in the periphery of my vision while I surveyed the yard and took in everything else happening, especially the movement of yard detectives, closing or opening of switches, and, of course, the makeup and movement of trains.

"Lissen," I say, disturbed that I am speaking like a parody.

They listened.

"Day, ain't it?"

"It is," Pal replies. Brandy hovers behind him.

"Good to have frens." I flick my hand as though tossing him something sharp like a corkscrew or knife. Even he can see the pack of hoboes who, without looking at us, are intently watching this exchange.

"She wants to join you," Pal says, laughing almost merrily. He ignores the intensely bitter look Brandy gives him. She'll make him pay for this betrayal when they get home. "She thought if we were nice about it, if we asked, that we could come down and warm ourselves around the campfire with your friends."

"She ain't too bright, is she?" I ask.

Brandy frowns. Her expression turns dark and more angry. She is going to make Pal pay for me, too. Which will be fine.

"She give good head, that it?"

"She doesn't give head at all," Pal says, a little too quickly.

"Why? Would you mind?" she asks, her jaw clenched.

"Mind? Hey, we coulda sung some songs, too, huh? John Jacob Jingleheimer Smith. Maybe Kum-ba-ya." I darn near look at Pal and wink. But instead, I dart over to a train of hopper cars edging through the yards, bounce up on the ladder of one and take a good look down inside, and then return to them in one movement so swift and fluid and unified that I feel good and bad like a mountain lion.

"Lissen," I say, getting serious. "My frens—over there." I flick my hand again. It is an involuntary action, one I inherited with the body, and one which I found peculiarly annoying. Being black is not easy. "They ask me to come up and say hey."

"Hey then," Pal says.

I toe the dirt, drawing an arc between us. "Yeah. Well, theys also want me to say this." Abruptly, I look Pal straight in the eye. "You can wait all day for a hot shot. Or you can get on that train there and get somewhere, you know?"

"Yeah," Pal says. "Thanks."

I help them pry open the sliding door on a deadhead boxcar. I stand aside and wait while they climb up and in. Brandy protests. The boxcar is dirty. And the stupid train doesn't even have an engine.

"It will," I say to her. "Trust me."

"And where's it going?" She acts like if it isn't a limousine to the Oscars she isn't getting into it.

"Someplace," I say. "Better than no place."

"Someplace. Great. Just where we want to go."

"Listen, Pal," I say, turning to him. "You want to hang around and see what those guys will do if you aren't gone soon, go ahead."

Stopping her before she can begin to give me grief, I add, "And the next time you find yourself wanting to speak, keep it to yourself."

Chapter Twelve

I.

No matter who you invent yourself to be, you can't talk back to a *weyekin*. Not unless he is your very own spirit guide. And if you try, you're doomed to discover the impotence of false or useless words. So, while the image of me as a hobo ate away at Pal, her frustration over not being able to hurt me with words ate away at Brandy, revealing the truth of Baby Jane Doe. Brandy, American made and American raised, just had to talk back to someone. Naturally, she picked Pal.

They fought and argued so much that before long the arguments occurred in their minds. They rarely had to speak. Pal offered up his feelings to her in his mind. Then he imagined her replies, noting the variations and possible replies in his journal, so he could study them later at length.

They made up, and fought again. Again, mostly in his head, with the difference that, gradually, he did not have to imagine himself saying anything at all to be able to know, as though he dreamed it, the acerbity or bitterness or weariness of her response.

Brandy, in her frustration, without much imagination, ultimately failed to understand what was happening. They accused each other silently. And like someone putting his hand into the tackle box and squeezing his fist on fishhooks, the barbs stuck in his palms and made him bleed whenever he tried to rip them out by giving in to her.

The long and short was that they never got married. The dry day came when the twins Beni and Bena Dryl backed their old man's pickup truck into Carl's driveway (for Carl, like a brownstone owner claims the airspace above it, claimed the driveway as a part of his chinked-up garage). They helped Pal load up his things and move, this time up into a four-room cabin behind Boulder Creek. ("You're going where?" Mary Blue asked. "Call collect," she said, this time with a glad inflection.)

Brandy spent the day in bed with Mick and Ray-lin trying out loud things that would make Pal jealous. She failed.

As Pal unpacked his boxes in his new cabin, inspected the pot-bellied wood stove in the bedroom, and wandered outside among the redwoods, he felt alone and somewhat betrayed—by himself, as much as by events. But he did not feel lost.

Tired, yes. And in that state of weariness, even the pages of his journal seemed too much to him and he set it aside. Still, he needed words. "Amanda" was a word he would not now forget, but he needed others to add to it—a last name, for example. It was easy to imagine what Brandy would say. Sally, too, as long as you could imagine her saying what you would never expect. But Amanda. What would Amanda say? And more important, *how* would she say it?

One afternoon, he went into town to buy soap and he ran into me in the drugstore.

"Yo, Pal," I called out as he dug in his jeans pocket for change.

It took him a minute to recognize me. I was darker than he remembered, still having a good deal of the shoe polish left on my skin from the train yards, and my bright tie-dyed T-shirt made me seem even darker by contrast. At last he grinned. "So Mary Blue still cares about all this?" he asked.

"She care, man. Hey. Lookit these," I said. I acted surprised and curious as I picked up a packet of canary yellow Post-its, those squares of paper that you can peel off and stick anywhere—in books, on refrigerators, as messages on your front door for the UPS man.

"I gotta get me some of these," I said. I selected several packets, ranging in size from small two-by-one-inch to three-by-fives that were lined in blue, and stuffed them in my pocket. "What are you gettin'?"

"Soap," he said.

"Soap?"

"Just soap."

We walked toward the cash register at the front of the pharmacy so he could pay for his soap. As we passed the beer, I talked him into a twelve-pack. Near the front was a display of Krylon paints, spray paints in bright colors.

"Hey," I stopped him. "How 'bout we have some fun with these?" I picked up cans of different colors. "Decorate your place, huh?"

He agreed. We waited at the register. An attractive young woman with a white scarf looped loosely around her neck stuck her head in and, without waiting for the clerk's attention, said, "How do you get out of this Hicksville?"

Pal stared at her. The clerk, a middle-aged man with glasses and thinning hair, ignored her characterization of Boulder Creek and politely asked her where she wanted to go.

"Saratoga," she replied, the tone of her voice almost imperious and almost sarcastic, as though just by looking at her he should have known.

The clerk told her where to turn down to Highway 17. "From there I'm sure even you know the way." He smiled at Pal. Pal was not paying any attention.

"I wish I could be like that," he commented as we rode up to his cabin in the Volkswagen van he bought used. "You see how she talks? It's like she doesn't just assume the world will take care of her. It's as though she knows. She is so used to being the center of her world that she never even considers that there might be another way to see it. It's amazing."

I kept my mouth shut. Here was a new danger, a new problem, and it was one that I could only hope would pass, given the brevity of her appearance.

While he began to paint the side of his cabin with Day-Glo Chicano colors, I went in to put away the beer. His four-room cabin was heated by one wood stove in the bedroom. He had to keep the fire in it low if he wanted to sleep through winter nights without a ring of condensation where his neck made contact with his blankets. That left the living room and kitchen—not to mention the bathroom with its rust-pitted tin shower stall—almost as cold as the frig. I snooped around and found his journal and put it away. I left behind my pocketful of Post-its in the drawer of his nightstand beside his bed, like a Gideon Bible.

2.

Like most people, Tara Dunnahowe, once she was a part of Pal's life, never would understand that calling collect was something her Pal was brought up to. Mary insisted on that.

After Pal moved up into the mountains behind Boulder Creek he always called home—by which he meant Mary Blue's house down in Gilroy—collect. The operators—Nakeesha, Miryam, and Tylenowtoo— at first protested in the early goings that the call would be not only cheaper but easier if he placed it direct. Nonetheless, with his usual good humor, he persisted, and the three operators became used to his nightly calls. Frequently, he heard Tyla turn to Keesha or Miryam and say with friendly pleasure in her voice, "It's E.T., again." Miryam might laugh a shy, Quechua laugh that slipped over and sneaked into Tyla's uncovered mouthpiece and down the telephone cables to Pal. Keesha would hiss, "Hush, girl!" afraid they'd all get into trouble.

Mary liked the illusion of a person making the connection between her and her son, rather than some machine. For the whole time La Vent was in jail, her friends had been dropping by to use her telephone and, as she would joke with Mrs. Rodriguez, she couldn't very well treat her own son worse than a Puerto Rican, could she? Many of the Chicanos in Gilroy thought of telephones as a luxury, especially when

Pacific Bell provided phones for free, hung in small glass booths on any corner where six or more people frequently congregated, small glass booths that protected you from the weather while letting you spot what was coming down the road in the shape of a drive-by or truant officer. There was even a case in Mrs. Rodriguez's neighborhood of one of the local gangs taking the phone company to court to force it to install a pay telephone in their clubhouse, as well as to keep it maintained whenever one of the gang's members used the telephone to make his point the way a kid from a better neighborhood might use exclamation marks in a history paper.

"Can you believe it?" Pal exclaimed when he heard about it. "Why didn't we think of that?"

"Because," Mary replied. They weren't the kind of people much given to going to court. It seemed as though every time one of them did, they ended up losing what they came with.

A lot of the time, the public telephones were booked up by half a block of milling girls waiting for calls from their boyfriends or old men waiting to call Forest Lawn. So Mary, partly to fill in the life La Vent had taken with him to jail, invited her friends to come on inside and use hers.

When the phone company sent a man around to sit her down and explain to her that private phones were for private parties, Mary just smiled and told him that every party that used her phone was private. If they wanted, they could even close the door. And she never asked where they were calling since in order to be truly private that was the way it had to be. The man from the phone company eventually gave up and worked out a payment plan so that Mary could have the reasonable expectation of paying off her rather large phone bill in installments, sometime before she died.

The next month or the month thereafter—depending on what festivals or holidays were celebrated in Cozumel, San Juan, or Mexicali—he or another representative from the phone company came back to explain all over again that Mary should not share what she had with her friends and neighbors, and to work out a new and modified payment plan that Mary just might finish paying off in the afterworld.

As La Vent served out his sentence, Mary became a kind of celebrity as the favored customer of Pacific Bell Telephone. People respected her preferred-customer status. They admired the way Pac Bell hand-delivered her bills, as well as her simple generosity. Who was Pal to deny such a person her wish to have him call collect?

Some time later when Tara Dunnahowe pressed her chin against her kneecap, peering down the scope of her legs at her toes while she polished the nails and told Pal that she just did not understand, that Mary was stupid to pay more for telephone service than she had to, Pal patiently tried to explain. He told her in great detail how it wasn't what you paid but what you got for your money—explaining it over and over again in as many different ways as he could imagine until Tara relapsed into her usual fatigued utterances.

"Oh blah!" Tara said.

Pal felt his only recourse to that was to withdraw from the conflict and smile. It was that smile that Tara so affectionately called his shit-eating know-it-all grin. It began to irritate her almost as much as the sound of Pal's voice. The result was that when they made love, the one or two times Tara had the energy and interest, they did it without sound, and Pal held his face still and expressionless in the dim or dark, a preternatural statuette of the god Sex, hinged at his waist.

As for having things, Pal had the example of La Vent's obsession to better himself and his family's lot in life. How, as hard as he worked and as settled as they became, the house was always one room too short and his salary some five hundred dollars too little. And how it all came to naught (though La Vent, gazing at his convert through the bullet-proof glass preparing his arguments for parole, might not agree with the assessment that nothing was what it all came to). But Tara would never be interested in La Vent's odyssey. And so Pal would end up conceding that it was true, Mary did pay an operator a few pennies to connect her with her son.

"But," Pal added. He felt that he had her cornered, and yet he feared that she might not take what he was about to say with good humor and he might end up offending her and her nice parents, "Your mother pays a maid to do her shopping."

"She's a maid," Tara replied.

"Keesha's an operator."

"No, no. You have to pay a maid to keep her."

"Are you saying that my mom ought to pay her operator more?"

"It's not *her* operator."

"Whose is it?"

"Jeez-us!" Tara said. "Can't you get it through your head? You only rent an operator!"

"You own a maid?"

"No, no. I'm not saying that you own a maid. But a maid does lots of other things. Like shop."

"So does an operator."

Tara's shoulders sank, sloping gently in disgust as though the tendons had snapped and she was a puppet without a master. But her face remained bright with hatred.

"And she does it on her own time, right? Which means your mother pays your maid to do other things on your mother's time and not her own. So who's paying too much?"

Tara's habit became to shelter her eyes from the glare, gazing into the palm of her hand. "You don't understand anything, do you?" she'd sigh. "It's like you refuse to see the contradiction."

3.

Pal felt uncomfortable as he waited in the booking room for his father to be released from the county jail. He hardly paid attention to the guard's comment that it had been several days since Larue's niece had been to visit. "I kind of expected your cousin to be the one who picked him up," the guard said.

"Cousin?" Pal said, absently. He was preoccupied with his decision to return to school—community college—partly as a way to maintain his deferment. Handling contaminated waste at the hospital had been considered essential employment, but once he quit that, the noses of his local draft board had begun to twitch as though they smelled something which they couldn't quite place being burned by Sterno or napalm. Mary had agreed that it would be somewhat a contradiction to fight for the very people who had fought against his grandparents. And so he had decided to return to school as a way to avoid what happened to Paquito Morta, who barely stepped off the troop transport before Bouncing Betty bounced up and greeted him with a shower of shrapnel, leaving Maleta Rota engaged and pregnant with a fatherless child.

"Yeah," the guard said. Brown. Gray eyes. About five-four."

Just then La Vent came through the visitor's area.

"Let's go home," La Vent said. He shook Pal's hand slowly, trying to find a place for the kid who said he was his son in the world he now occupied. His voice was muted, watery, and he seemed not sad but amazed, as though he had been struck by lightning and, though he glowed like a holy ghost, was still alive to tell about the experience.

As Pal pulled up in front of Mary Blue's, there was Sally Pedon, standing on the tectonic plates of the earth cracked by heat, handing out tracts to anyone who happened by and sweetly urging them to repent their ways.

"If it isn't Attila the Hun," she said when she saw him.

"Hey, Sally," he said.

"Sister Niedman to you, Mr. Palaver Palmer."

"Niedman?" he asked. "When did you . . . ?"

"I've detached," she said. "But not in the way of Rachna. In the way of Larue."

"Larue? Who? What? Why?" Pal looked at his father, dazed by time and desire.

"After the Whites were killed, the pastor of that deplorable church actually had the gall to ask me to become his organist. Can you believe that?"

Pal had heard on National Public Radio that Paulie and Ruthie White were defending themselves against the charge of drugging and crucifying both their parents behind the house trailer. According to the news reports, the tips of Mrs. White's feet were barely lifted off the ground. Her death was attributed less to the suffocation of crucifixion than to the piercing of her heart with a rust red knitting needle with Ruthie's fingerprints all over it.

But the work of God goes on, despite the misfortunes of the people who minister for Him, and Pedon needed a new organist.

Pal reached out to accept one of her tracts. She refused to give him one. "You're hopeless," she said. "No sense wasting the true way on you."

4.

Sally had come to stay. She was there to greet La Vent when he came home, and she rode in the front seat with him as briefly he took up driving a cab for the Aztlán Cab Company, a fleet of gypsy cabs that went anywhere in the city and even specialized in going places no other cab would go, picking up fares that other cabs passed up. She watched in admiration and approval as he took up hanging out at the old train station, preaching even into the cold hard dusk to the men and women gathered around oil drums to warm their hands at their fires of salvaged wood. She watched, and she learned. She was no dummy. She learned fast. She learned well.

By the time La Vent parked the cab out in front of the house, jacked it up on blocks, and removed the wheels and tires, Sally was doing at least half of the proselytizing. She stood on the rear deck of the yellow Pontiac and harangued passersby on the street—the few there were who were on foot—while La Vent placidly held out pamphlets to Fatty La Beau or the Wasageshiks, who coupled arms and hurried past as though La Vent were offering them a bad memory.

All this, Mary Blue watches from the kitchen window. With her shawl around her shoulders, she continues to rock, continues to bead, continues to cook and deliver the leftovers to the migrant workers in the camps. It is either him or her son. She made the decision what seemed a long time ago; the pattern that was always there is clearly revealed to her now. And even though it hurts her, leaves her alone and missing the young man who once was willing to spend his life waiting in a vinyl booth to give her a ride home in the rain, she does not, cannot, will not try to regret her decision. Children are more important than parents. The children are the way the grandmothers and grandfathers, the great-aunts and great-uncles, survive. The parents can only hope one day to become grandparents and thus, one day, become the proof of survival.

The calm and permanent Mary Blue closes her eyes and rocks above the half-finished broken outline of a horse, its legs repeated in the pattern as though the horse is jumping, paddling the air in an attempt to fly across a stream or ditch. She tries to reconnect the dots of the story. It isn't easy to get the right dots arranged in the right order but it's even harder to put what she knows into words, English or Nez Perce, in such a way as to produce even the bare outlines of a vision that someone else can not only see, but take part in.

She knows what she has to do. She pokes her needles into a black felt pad, rises, and walks slowly and sorrowfully deep into her house to her and La Vent's bedroom where she speaks what sounds like an apology in a language only she understands. She strikes a safety match and holds it to a seashell of sage, which begins to smolder, dipping her face into the smoke as it drifts upward, pulling it toward her face with her hands cupped in the air. Taking a small leather pouch out of her dresser drawer, she kneels on the patterned carpet and begins to rock, back and forth, back and forth, faster at first, and then more and more slowly as her open eyes begin to see beyond the dresser, the smoke, the carpet, and the full-sized bed. If it weren't for the fact that she has already lost that which she would lose of him, she'd feel utterly empty. But La Vent, way back when he hired on to the mayor's way of doing things, lost parts of himself that he will never recover. No matter how powerful his remembering or how strong the acts of his imagination, like sandstone he will wear away until he is no more. Mary believes this. And she knows that because of the yellow butterflies that always inhabit the story, it must be either La Vent or Pal.

Still, she feels sorry that she cannot dream both. It is a matter of power, and one of the stories her grandmother told her was how power came from one source, and one source alone. Try another source—like

Baby Jane Doe changing her name—and the power gets lost. Forever. Using power, giving it up to the dream, is just the opposite side of the coin. If you try to use it to bring into existence more than one context at a time, the contexts will not be full and complete, and the individuals caught in the incomplete contexts will be doomed to meaninglessness.

Her shawl slips from her shoulders. She seems to sleep with visions of a moonstone beach. Long empty of the stones that named it, quartz cast up by the tide and carried off by the handfuls as souvenirs that ended up dry and discarded in black plastic bags and buried in county dumps, on that beach a gray heron perches on his right leg, staring westward. Perhaps it's an illusion of the light spiking the turbinate crest of his head, or the bazaar of once-cheap motels lining the beach's access road. But he seems like a jailhouse guard who expects prisoners to pass him by on parole, as people will pass by the stooped, rigid form of La Vent as he perches on the rear deck of a taxi he has spray-painted canary yellow, a metal-and-glass pulpit.

Only at night, after Sally finally goes home and La Vent goes to sleep in the back seat, do the people come to the cab. They make it a shrine. The dashboard, steering wheel, and rearview mirror become the props for pictures of lost sons and daughters, mothers and fathers, for votive candles in small beaded dimestore jars that illuminate the effigies and images, twinkling off the gilt of frames and the glimmer of beads. Old Mercedes Rota deposits yet another candle, stuck onto the dash with dripped wax, beside the ribbon-draped photograph of her would-have-been son-in-law, Paquito. Fatty La Beau will hang yet another string of beads (each bead capable of saying a different story) from the rearview mirror. Mary feels sad and sorry to see the Wasageshik couple, as young as they are, who will come to mourn their daughter, a fourteen-year-old beauty brought down by stray bullets as she made a run to reach the glass enclosure of a telephone booth. She sees all the ragtag, used-up people in fitless clothing who come to the taxi to make memories of sons and daughters shipped off to battles in Asia, the Middle East, or Los Angeles and who will someday exist—the good people hope—in that future land of her extremely converted husband who

talks not only in his head but in the heart of Mary, as well. On the Day
of the Dead, the front seat becomes a buffet of the favorite dishes of the
ones who have gone away, dishes that let the spirits know that though
gone from this life, they are never forgotten.

A shrine it remains until the morning Pal runs into Emily Marroquin pacing up and down in front of the house, her thin legs marching
her back and forth behind the cab. She is angry. And she is a little
afraid.

"I am bringing this to Roberto," Mrs. Marroquin tells Pal. She
holds up a basket of fruit that she brought to leave beside the photograph of her son, a useless servant who died in a helicopter training accident halfway around the world. In his picture, he is dark and
handsome; his black eyes seem to shine beneath the rigid brim of his
white Marine Corps dress cap.

"So I am bringing this today instead of last week when I planned
because my daughter, you know Elizabeta, she run off last week with
that mechanic of hers and so I had to go after her and bring her back
and then watch her and be sure she goes to school this morning and
cada dia I pray that she'll still be at school when I go to pick her up and
I get here and this *puta* girl from nowhere has gone and moved her
stuff in, righ' in front of Roberto no-the-less."

Sure enough, Sister Niedman has moved the fewness of her stuff
into the cab. She sleeps in the front seat, her legs tucked beneath the
steering wheel, ever as peacefully as La Vent sleeps in the back.

"I'll see what I can do, Mrs. Marroquin," Pal says, patting her
shoulder.

But for the next month, the shrine is closed. The candles burn
down, sputter, and go out. All night long, La Vent's and Sally's voices
whisper back and forth over the seat back as they plan and revise and
polish the morrow's sermonizing and pamphleteering. Together, they
devise new and improved ways to promise the approach of the end of
the world, taking their text from Sierra Club monthlies, transcripts of
talk shows hosted by Rush Limbaugh or Larry King, promotional
pamphlets from telephone companies, or the grace periods of credit

cards, fashioning it all into one senseless but beautiful harangue that few people besides Pal ever stop to admire.

5.

Finding the Post-it notes I left him after I hid his journal, Pal has begun to write on them. It's fun, he discovers, and thinking about what to write next keeps him happily occupied. Today, driving north out of Gilroy, headed home to Boulder Creek, Pal is trying to imagine what Amanda looks like. Love, after all, has to look like someone. Amanda cannot endure too long as an abstract. Sometimes, she has Lolita glasses and deep-fried hair that is stiff from the wind and sun. Someone who likes to be outside. Other times, she has the look of a reader, her eyes almost a colorless black, sloe-eyed and sleepy from hours of scanning the page. He imagines she could be athletic, soft, vibrant, or pensive.

He passes an artichoke field where a sun-ripened man in a Stetson stands in the bed of a pickup truck, a hunting rifle crooked in his elbow, watching men, and women, and children as young as six years of age bend to sever the heads of artichokes and drop them into gunnysacks that they drag along on belts looped over their shoulders. He tries last names for her, out loud. "Amanda Oxheart. Goodheart." He is dissatisfied with the implications of those names, with what they would make him create.

The man in the pickup turns and watches Pal's van—named, affectionately, Old Paint—and Pal recalls that it was about here, just west of Freedom, that a foreman shot a youngster who went to drink from the water trough once too often. Shot to frighten him, to keep the adults in line, more than anything ("You know these people," the foreman had said to the one reporter; the reporter, disgruntled for having to cover a story so small, nodded), and missing his miss, had taken half the kid's skull off with the force of the bullet. Pal weaves Old Paint from lane to lane on the empty highway, just to give the playful foreman a more difficult target. He was, as his boss had said to the papers, "A real bad egg." A real *huevo muerto*. A motherfucker.

"Buencorta," he says. "Amanda Buencorta." Maybe that is it? He'll try it out on a Post-it tonight, write out the name and stick it up on the plate glass of his cabin's living room window. See if it stuck.

He feels happy. Names are like dates. You have to pick one before you can imagine that it means anything. Still, it's risky. Pick the wrong one and no matter how many Post-its you tack onto it as emendations, it won't mean what you want.

Chapter Thirteen

I.

It was my fault, I suppose. Like most young people, Pal thought that once he had the name he could go it alone. Night after night he sat, giving words to people, places, and things, trying to give Amanda not only shape, but background and an attitude as well. It seemed like dreaming. Words create the world—he had learned that much—and without words we are nothing, neither *weyekin* nor human being. Words make things real. But there is a big step that comes before words, precedes the making, a step that is difficult precisely because it is done without words. Indeed, you have to empty yourself of words and make yourself into a round and open receptor—sort of a human sweat lodge or hogan—that awaits what it does not know by naming but only knows by an active and involved waiting, a continuous reshaping of the potential to be. Like a good filmmaker sees the film before he begins to shoot it, the Dreamer sees how it will happen without knowing exactly what it is that will happen.

But Pal was not empty. In fact, he found out that the shyness, the diffidence that he always felt around people, especially women, left him full of words. Besides, he had the examples of Sally, Brandy, the other women he had known (why did he not think of his mother, Mary Blue, or even Mrs. Rota or Emily Marroquin, his mother's good friends?).

And the picture of a large-breasted young woman with a white neck scarf tossed with calculated casualness around her neck asking how to get out of Hicksville just wouldn't go away. Instead of waiting patiently and openly for Amanda to come and give him the words that would make her real, night after night he made her up in words on Post-its, which he pasted up on his living room window and which, for the time being, stuck. He made her different and it took all the energy I had to keep what he made from becoming Amanda. If Amanda had an attitude, it would not be because she was rich and had been raised to expect herself to be the center of activity and thought. Instead of the hot-air balloon of self-esteem, Amanda had to have the kind of confidence that came from overcoming obstacles, not having them removed from her path like slaves sweep stones out of the path of an exotic empress. If Amanda had to have extremely large breasts—and it was possible—she would not wear blouses or sweaters so loose as to hide them in abundant fabric, nor would she walk slumped over, her shoulders hunched. Amanda's breasts, regardless of their size, would make her neither proud nor shy, and they would not account for making her feel different, odd, or even outcast because of a featured accident of fate. Breasts, skin color, nose, height—these are not the same as background or one's way of being in the world, and so empathy for a difference rooted in the former would be misplaced for someone rooted in the latter like Amanda.

One day, on Manresa Beach not too far south of Santa Cruz, he was sitting stiff and still on the gravelly sand trying to imitate the gray heron that stood with one leg raised as though frozen in the midst of trying to scratch an itch, gazing out across the roiling Pacific. In the foreground, sea otters dipped and turned, playing, trying to get the attention of the heron. An Irish setter puppy came barking down the beach, loping with that tongue-lolling, sideways clumsiness and enthusiasm that setters have if they aren't whining, lost outside some stranger's door. The heron did not even turn its head in the puppy's direction but gathered itself together like a wise old woman and, with an air of insouciant leisure, lifted its wings and flew off low, out over the whitecap chop of the receding tide. The puppy, still yapping, followed

the heron out as far as it could and then stood there, proud of its fierceness, until it was knocked from its feet by the rush of an incoming
wave. Having lost the heron, the otters took on the puppy, teasing it,
playing tag with it, swimming in close enough to get it to charge into
the water and then diving and swimming away just out of reach.

Pal hardly noticed the woman who walked past him, dressed in a
thin wraparound skirt, through which you could see the defined
shadows of her legs, and a tank top, until she stopped and whistled for
the puppy. It came loping out of the water, running to Pal instead of to
its owner. It gave Pal a gooey lick on the legs and then shook itself dry,
spraying seawater laced with dogginess all over him.

Pal held up his hands outward in front of his face, laughing and
swearing. The woman sauntered over.

"Maggie," she said. "Come." She looked down at Pal. He looked
up, prepared to be gracious and say it was okay, it was just a puppy, it
was just water, it didn't really smell wet and musty like a basement after a heavy rain, that he had really wanted cooling down—something
along those lines. He was clumsy, like the puppy, so he figured he'd fail
at making her feel that it didn't matter. So he just sat, looking up at her
against the setting sun and grinning like an idiot.

"Heel, Maggie," she ordered the dog. It bounded off to stick its
nose into a swirl of rotting seaweed. "Maggie!" She stamped her foot
imperiously. "I said heel!" The dog ignored her.

"Dogs," Pal said.

She turned. "Pardon me?" she said coolly.

Pal stammered. "I said dogs," he said. "Have a mind of their own.
Don't they?"

She stared at him as though he were a circle of vomit. Then she
asked, "Do you belong here? Are you staying at Pajaro?"

"Pajaro?"

"Dunes," she said. "Pajaro Dunes. It's around the point," she said,
waving her hand southward. "This is part of its private beach."

"Right," he said. He shook himself like the puppy. "Sorry. I was
lost in thought. I wasn't thinking. But sure, yeah, I'm staying there."

"At Pajaro?" she asked in disbelief.

"Yeah. How 'bout you? You visiting Pajaro?"

"Daddy owns Pelican One, Two, and Three," she said. "He always keeps Pelican Three empty so I can come down when I want. I'm not visiting. I'm staying."

"Nice of him," Pal said.

"Are you in one of the condos, then?"

"Yes."

"A renter."

"I'm afraid so. Yes." He succumbed to her way of seeing the world and felt deeply apologetic for being merely a renter and not an owner. "I'm in Sea Otter Two," he said.

She stood, thinking. Maggie came bouncing back up the beach, kicking sand up to announce her arrival. Pal reached out and petted her. "Maggie, here!" the woman ordered. "Heel. Heel, goddamn you!" she shouted. Maggie, tongue drooping nearly to the sand, wobbled over to her and look up hopefully, as though she expected a treat. "Sit," she said, reaching down and pushing Maggie's rear end onto the sand.

"I didn't know there were any Sea Otters," she said to Pal.

"Hmmm," Pal said. "I guess it's like that famous riddle about the trains."

"What's that?"

"There are these two trains. If one leaves San Francisco heading east and the other leaves New York heading west at exactly the same time, how can you be sure that they won't run into each other head-on in a tunnel outside Duluth?"

She frowned, thinking. "I give up. How?"

"There aren't any tunnels in Duluth." He laughed.

She gave him a half-smile. "Whatever made you think of that?"

"Don't you see? We're like those two trains. Neither of us knew the other was leaving the station but here we are, having run into each other even if there aren't any tunnels."

She frowned again. Suddenly, as though she understood, she smiled. "You're kind of cute," she said.

"Thanks."

"Maybe I'll see you around the beach."

"Maybe."

"Come on, Maggie," she said. She patted her thigh and turned to go. Maggie trotted over and gave Pal one last lick, wet and viscous, on the leg, then trotted off down the beach ahead of her. She walked slowly. She stopped, turned. "Listen, do you like movies?"

"Sure," he said.

"I'm going to watch one this evening. If you want to come by. About eight?"

"I'll be there," Pal said, wondering what he'd do between now and eight o'clock.

"Pelican Three. It's at the far end. The last one."

2.

"He is where?" asked Mary Blue. She was not happy with me. Fortunately, she was somewhat distracted. She stood by the kitchen window finishing her first pot of coffee, silently watching Mrs. Marroquin pass back and forth on the sidewalk, waiting to shut the window when Sister Niedman and La Vent rose and began their harangues.

"Place called Pajaro," I replied, snuffling. It had rained at Pajaro Dunes, and I felt as though I had a touch of the flu from hanging around in the intermittent rain. It wasn't getting better with all my running around trying to do Mary's bidding while keeping track of Pal.

"Dunes," Mary said. She set down her coffee mug and picked up her beading. She pulled the needle out from the felt into which she had tucked it the night before. With a deftness unmatched by anyone but a neurosurgeon, she picked up white beads with the tip until she had the exact number that would create a row to be stitched into the background. To look at it, you wouldn't yet be able to tell what the narrative was, even though the project was almost half done. However, you would see from the size of the leather and the detail of the beadwork that it was something real important, from the look of it.

"That's right," I said. Her dexterity was amazing, effortless. "Pajaro Dunes."

"Would you check that?" she said, indicating the oven. She was roasting red and yellow bell peppers. I got up and went over to open the broiler. She could see that their skins were black, the meat of the peppers softened by the roasting. "Turn it off and take them out, will you? Please?" she added.

I took out the pan of peppers and stood beside the sink, peeling the blackened skin from them gingerly as they cooled.

"Thanks," she said. She pulled the needle and thread through and tugged gently to make sure the stitch was tight. "As in sand?" she asked.

"I'd guess so."

"With who?"

"Tara. Tara Dunnahowe." So named because, honestly, I didn't know how.

"Long as you're at it, there are some yellow onions down there. You mind? Two large ones."

I opened the cabinet where she stored onions and peeled them. "How do you want them?"

"Medium," she answered.

I began to dice them up, tears forming in the corners of my eyes.

"So, they let people like us into this place called Pajaro?" she asked in the only words she could use to ask if I didn't think that the kind of people Tara tennised or surfed with weren't sort of different from her only son. How well she remembered La Vent humiliating himself as he tried again and again to do what he called bettering himself.

I chopped the meat of the peppers and scraped the chopped onions into a frying pan with them. Smells began to take over the room as the heat melted the butter in the frying pan and the onions and the peppers began to mingle.

"It's harmless. It's just a bunch of condos on a private beach. Down by Monterey."

"They let people like us into this harmless place?" Mary asked. She could not help but sigh. It was the mayor's son's birthday party all over again.

I nodded.

"Do your best," Mary sighed, beginning to rock with a finality that looked like death.

3.

Pal hung around a strip mall in Watsonville until it was time to return to Pajaro Dunes. The road was little more than an oiled track that ran past artichoke fields out to a spit of sand and earth on which a developer had built maybe fifteen houses and as many condominium units, three condos to a unit, each unit staggered and angled so that one living room or deck did not look directly into another. In front lay the Pacific; behind was a lagoon. From the air, he imagined, it looked like dice tossed down along the near island, although these would probably be pretty expensive dice and, from the boulders he could see along the shoreline, it was a gamble that might not pay off as the sea eroded the promontory and caved the million-dollar houses into the waves.

A redwood swing gate blocked the road beside a security guard's kiosk. There was no answer to the telephone call placed to Pelican Three. Pal waited, hanging around and ignoring the bad attitude of the guard, making him telephone again every fifteen minutes or so. It was turning dark, the hills behind Watsonville gone gold and then red and then purple as the sun set out over the Pacific, when finally the guard raised someone and, not liking it one bit, unlocked the gate and pulled it aside, letting Pal pass through in the army green Volkswagen microbus.

"Thought you'd never get here," Tara said, opening the door when he finally found the right one. "You're late."

They watched two movies. The first was *Pocahontas*, which caused Tara to weep with emotion. Pal felt something, too, but not what she did. The second was *Behind the Green Door*, of which they managed to watch only fifteen or twenty minutes before Tara got up and, sounding as though she was telling her puppy to heel, pulled him into the bedroom where he obediently undressed and climbed in among silken sheets that made him feel slick and cool. When he rolled toward Tara, who lay on her back running her fingers down across her nipples and up along the inside of her thighs, she asked him if he would not mind staying on his side of the bed.

"I'll call you if I need you," she said in a hoarse whisper.

Pal lay back and stared up at their reflection in the mirrored tiles on the ceiling as Tara's hands found their focus and her breathing became more rapid. At last, she gave out a cry that sounded halfway between a baby and a cat, her back arched and her legs jerked slightly, and she went limp.

"Thank you," she whispered before she rolled over and went to sleep. "I don't like to do it all alone."

He lay awake a long time, the image of a hand reaching toward him in a moving boxcar playing over and over with the brutal pumping directness of a triple-X movie. At long last, he fell into a restless sleep just before dawn. When he woke up, Tara was standing beside the bed in brown pantyhose, a white silk half-slip, and sea blue bra, and he reached out and took her arm, playfully intending to pull her back into bed, his dreams having obscured the events and words of the night before.

Tara's stomach became taut with the effort of pulling her wrist free from his grip as he lay among the rumpled covers. Gently, even playfully, but with all the seriousness of her own determination, she said, "Come on, now. Get dressed. I have a date. I don't want to be late."

"Sorry," he said, confused. "You want to go on and I'll lock up when I leave?"

"I'm not leaving," Tara said. "You are."

"Oh," Pal said. He got out of bed and pulled on his clothes. He started for the bathroom.

"Five minutes, okay?"

Pal peed, washed his face. Cupping his hands, he wet his hair and used a brush by the sink to comb out the spikes of hair stiffened by sleeping on them. Grabbing his keys, he said goodbye. Tara stood in the kitchen, making toast in a toaster oven.

"Hey?" she said, taking hold of his elbow. "That was fun last night. Will I see you tonight?"

"Uh, I've got to leave today. Go back to Boulder Creek."

"Oh," Tara said. She looked genuinely disappointed. "Listen," she said, brightening. "I'm free next weekend. Here. Maybe you could come down? I know. We could have a party. No. No, next weekend's too soon. I have to get ready, and people have lives, don't they? We could have the party the weekend after that."

"I guess," Pal said.

"You could even come to it, if you want. I mean, if you help me and all."

"I guess," Pal said again. He wasn't sure he wanted to.

"Do you think you could help me out with it?"

Pal shrugged. "Sure."

"Good," she said, becoming businesslike. "Pick up some nice invitations. Fifty should be enough. I'll give you the addresses and you can fill them out when you come down. Then you can mail them. If they go first class, they should get to people in time. And maybe while you're at the store picking up the invitations you can get me some oysters? Fresh oysters. I mean, as long as you're already there and all."

Pal wondered where she got her ideas of stores and shopping.

"There's a cooler by the front door, if you want to grab it. You can put the oysters in it so they won't spoil if it's hot on the trip down. And," she coyly fingered the buttons on his shirt, "maybe you can come down early. Like Wednesday? We can have some fun together."

"I maybe can get a long weekend off," Pal said.

"Good." As she pushed him out the door, she reminded him, "And whatever you do, don't forget the oysters."

4.

I tried again to make the security guard's attitude so bad the next week that Pal would wake up from this dream of his and ask himself what the hell he was doing and—I could only hope, though not with much expectation of success—tell the guard to *chingate*, turn around, and drive home. But it was going to take something real serious to wake him up from this one.

When security called in to Pelican Number Three, there was no answer. Again, Pal had to wait, but this time a lot longer. Tara showed up three hours later. By then, Pal was sitting on the bench beside the security kiosk in front of the main gate looking as though he had to pee really bad. While she signed him "in," he shifted from foot to foot, made nervous by the look on the security guard's face. She laughed at the way Pal looked. She did not apologize.

"I thought you'd be waiting," he said. "I was worried about the food."

"I got busy," she said. She laughed again. "You look like you're angry."

"I'm not," Pal said. "I'm just. . . . I was just worried. About the food, I mean."

"You know what I like about you?" she said. "You're different. You're almost . . . strange."

Pal accepted that as both apology and a statement that she found him different from the other men she knew. His hurt over having to wait, his worry that the oysters and other surprises he'd brought would spoil in the heat, and his nerves scraped raw by the suspicions of the security guard—all vanished.

She lounged on the sofa in the two-bedroom condo giving him directions as he schlepped in the cooler and bags full of groceries. The way the condos were laid out, to keep automobiles away from the dunes and out of sight of the people on them, made the trip a long and confusing one. If he wasn't careful, he could angle too far left on the maze of wooden walkways and end up going to Anemone One instead of Pelican Three. When he was finished with the groceries, he brought in the heavy paper shopping bag in which he'd put his clothes.

"Mind if I call my mother?" he asked her.

"Your mother?" she said. "You've got to call Mommy and tell her where you are?"

"She knows where I am," Pal replied. "I just want to tell her I got here okay."

"Phone is there," Tara said, pointing. "Dial nine to get an outside line."

"I'll make it collect," Pal said.

"No need. Daddy can pay for you to call your mommy," Tara teased.

He made it collect, anyway.

While she changed clothes, he went into the kitchen. He began to mutter as he unpacked the cooler, storing the perishables in the fridge. "Let this not be angry," he muttered. "Please let this not be angry." He repeated the words, making it into a chant.

Tara emerged from the bedroom wearing a bright paisley two-piece and a linen beach jacket with the diaphaneity of cheesecloth. Against the bright background of the living room windows, her shadow would have been striking and sexy if he had paid attention.

"What?" she asked. "What's wrong?"

"Nothing," he said, muttering again, "Please let this not be," etc.

"Do me a favor while you're here?" Tara said. "Don't mutter. I hate mutterers. My father mutters at my mama, and when he isn't muttering, he's humming. At six A.M. outside my window, he'll hum to the bougainvillea just to annoy me or my sister and wake us up."

"Sorry," Pal said, wondering if he'd ever meet her father or, for that matter, her mother.

"It's okay. Let's take a walk before we satisfy ourselves, okay?" she said. "Then we'll get those oysters shelled."

"Yeah," he said ("Let this not be angry, please let this not be . . ."). "The oysters. Listen, maybe I better run into town for a minute."

"What for?"

"Oh, just get a few things," he said, closing the cooler quickly as she walked toward him.

"What's wrong?" she asked, suspiciously. "You didn't forget the oysters? You dumb shit. You better not have forgotten my oysters."

"I didn't," Pal replied. He closed his eyes and tried to envision the cooler full of ice.

"Good," Tara said. She rolled her neck to loosen the tension that had cropped up at the mere mention of something happening to her oysters. "Good."

Pal lifted the lid of the cooler and looked in, hoping beyond hope that ice would have manifested there, snuggled around the oysters and clams. "We forgot the ice," he said.

"What? Oh, shit, no," Tara said. She pressed her forehead with her thumb and fingers. "No-oo," she moaned. She managed to get a grip on herself, and from beneath her hand she said, "What do you mean 'we'?" she said darkly.

"Ice wasn't on your list," Pal said quietly.

"Goddamn you," Tara hissed. She glared at him. "You mother-fucking idiot. Neither was the cooler, was it?"

Pal had to admit she was right. In that light, he was to blame.

"You dumb fuck," she said. She paced into the living room and back to the kitchen, which divided the entry and dining room from the long, narrow living room.

After several paces, her affectionate nature overcame what could have turned to ugly anger and she laughed and said, "You can just go into Monterey and buy more. You think you can get there and back without getting lost?"

"Sure," Pal said, brightly, relieved that she seemed prepared to forgive him. "No problem. I just head south, right?" He was determined to prove himself to her.

"If you know which way south is," she said. "Take my car. It'll be faster than that wreck of yours. Just try not to wreck it, huh?" she called after him as he took her keys and left.

He drove around Monterey and then wandered from shop to shop along the pier in Monterey. Then, futilely, he drove farther south and then back north of the turnoff for Pajaro searching for fresh oysters and clams. It grew dark out and the bright moon seemed to light up the whitecap waves as though a fluorescence had been turned on beneath the water. One shop owner explained, as he hosed out his seafood shop in rubber boots, chucking the ice into the ocean and washing the bits and pieces of fish and shell over the edge of the pier, that the beautiful phosphorescent glow that illumined the dark ocean was caused by an abundance of microorganisms that made all the shellfish for a hundred miles inedible. Having seen hints of Tara's disappointment already, Pal was reduced to stopping in Watsonville at an all-night grocery to pick up frozen clams and oysters stuffed in cloudy glass jars. It was better than nothing, he told himself.

By the time he got back, Tara was in bed. She left him a note on what looked like a gum wrapper. Cinnamon gum. The note told him she wasn't feeling well and that he could find linen for his bed in the closet outside the bathroom.

He took a walk alone on the beach, all the way up to where the dunes ended in a forested point and barbed-wire fencing. Dodging in among the dunes and high grass to avoid the security guard who cruised the sand on a four-wheeled motorcycle, his long flashlight scanning the beach for interlopers, he sat protected from the warm night breeze and the eerie glow of the red tide.

He sat and rocked slowly in the moonlight. He felt lonely. Words began to come to him, drifting through his mind like acquaintances whose names he'd forgotten. And then names themselves, of Mary, and Sally, BrandyWine and Baby Jane Doe, La Vent and Chingaro. Chingaro. He squeezed his eyes tight and tried to see me, his friend and *weyekin*. He felt inexorably sad, but worse, empty. A backfire, as sharp as the big bang of a freight train's couplings, jolted him.

"Amanda," I whispered.

He heard the word just as the security guard passed on the beach below and swept the dunes with the beam of his flashlight. Pal lay back still, not holding his breath but breathing very slowly, until the motorcycle revved and popped and the guard moved on.

Sitting up, he said her name aloud. "Amanda."

Over and over he said the word. The sound of it was fine and pleasant and as soothing as the gentle ebbing tumble of the night waves.

As he sneaked back down the beach to the condo and to bed, he knew that Amanda would not be angry.

5.

He felt guilty, the next morning, having spent the entire night with Amanda and not once thinking about Tara. Yet the brightness of the sun washing in through the curtains seemed to offer to him all the hope of a Monday after the drear of a foggy Sunday. He was sitting on a bar stool at the kitchen counter thinking how Tara would not like Amanda when Tara emerged from the den of her bedroom, yawning. From the way she stretched, yawned, and then smiled at him almost kindly, the oysters seemed to be forgiven.

"Good morning," he said brightly, hopefully. "Coffee?"

"Is it made like I like it?" she asked.

"It's strong," he said, hoping that was how she liked it.

"Good," she said. "I like things strong."

He padded around and got her a cup of coffee and set it in front of her.

"So did you get the oysters?"

Pal told her about the "red tide." He explained at length what he had learned from the seafood shop owner, followed by additions and supplementations that he had invented as he sat on the lonely dunes and watched those very microorganisms glow in their numerosity.

"Sorry," he said when he was done, both because of the excruciatingly weary look on her face and because of the red tide. "Really."

"God knows," she yawned, "I should've expected something like this from a dumb shit like you. It's okay."

"I really do feel bad about it. I just didn't think . . . I mean, I was so careful to get everything on the list . . . I just. . . ."

"Jeez-us! I said it's okay. Now finish your coffee and get dressed and let's go get some rays."

She was being as sweet as she could about it, really. He understood that her calling him names was just her way of diverting him from feeling bad.

He emptied the heavy paper grocery bag in which he'd packed his clothes and sorted through them. He came out in swim shorts and one of La Vent's old short-sleeved white shirts. "Okay," he said. "Ready when you are."

"What is this?" Tara said, grinning as though he was wearing a joke. She tugged at the collar of his shirt. "You're not gonna wear that on the beach, are you?"

"I was," he said, hesitantly. "Should I wear something else?" He'd gone out and bought new shorts for the trip but in the interest of economy it'd seemed like La Vent's old cotton and polyester office shirts would do if he left them untucked and therefore informal enough for the beach.

"Wait a sec," Tara said. She laughed. "You can't wear *those* on the beach." She disappeared into the walk-in closet in the bedroom and rummaged around. Hangers slid back and forth, then she emerged with two brightly colored Hawaiian shirts. "Here," she said, holding one up for fit like a painter holds up his thumb to change his perspective. "Someone left these here. They should do."

Do they did. He loved them. They were as bright as any dandy's and as soft as any shirt you could wish for, silky on the skin and cool to the sea breezes. They made him feel special, as though he suddenly belonged, and he wore one up and down the beach, morning, noon, and even that night after the football game finally ended. They were a little small, just tight enough to make him conscious of their not being, in every sense of the word, his.

"They're a friend's," Tara said, the word "friend's" pregnant with meaning and staggering on swollen ankles.

"A friend's?"

"Don't worry. He wouldn't mind you wearing them."

"This 'he.' He's been to Pajaro, too?"

"Lots of my friends come to Pajaro," Tara replied, wearily.

Pal let the subject drop and decided to wear the shirts as best he could.

All in all, the day went well. After the close call about the shirts, lying in the sun and roasting slowly seemed to relax Tara, help her forget the flaws in Pal's character. He body-surfed while she sunbathed, and he was good and tired by the time they ate the jars of oysters. They finished off a large bottle of wine and she started on tequila while she turned on Thursday-night football.

By the end of the first quarter, moved by all those men bending over in their stretch pants and a little drunk on her shots of tequila, Tara grabbed Pal by the back of the head, slid down so her head was just propped up enough to see the television, and pulled his face in between her thighs. Obediently, Pal flicked at her with his tongue while she moaned and called out the first names of the Denver Broncos offensive line.

After the third time she did this, however, his jaw ached. He sat massaging it between his hands while she went on rooting for the Broncos, even though from the way the Forty-Niners were scoring, it was obvious her team was going to lose and lose sadly. Her rooting for Denver turned grim and then finally turned cynical.

"I knew it," she'd say with bitter acrimony, as though the insult were personal, when Ronnie Lott knocked down another Elway pass. "Elway's throwing the game. C'mere," she'd say, grabbing Pal's ears.

By halftime, Pal could barely speak. They took a stroll in the light of the red tide along the estuary of the tidal river behind the condos. At the opening of the second half, two more touchdowns were scored immediately by the Forty-Niners—two of the four they scored in the second half.

Later that night as he sat propped up in bed alone, making notes on his Post-its and completely unable to form with his cramped mouth any of the words he wrote down, he decided that the whole thing was kind of funny.

Friday morning found her surly, and Pal barely able to talk. She continued to call him pet names like "dumb shit," but with the oysters forgiven, the affectionate nature of these nicknames started to grate.

"Dmth thit?" His jaw hurt so much that he lisped. His feelings hurt more, though. After the things he'd done.

She disappeared into her bedroom to make a phone call and she re-emerged wearing spandex shorts and a sports halter. "I'm going for a run," she said.

"Where to?" he asked as she rolled back the glass door to the front deck.

"None of your business," she tossed back, and off she went.

"None of my bithneth," Pal muttered. Rather than remain hurt, he decided to surprise her in a way she'd have to acknowledge. He borrowed her car and cheerfully told the security guard, "Be back," waving as he drove quickly down the access road, out through artichoke fields, and toward the isolated highway that ran north to south. Driving all the way back to Santa Cruz, he found some fresh oysters that had been flown in from the East. He got back to Pajaro by four. He opened a bottle of Tara's expensive red wine to let it breathe and began to shuck the oysters into a bowl set in a larger bowl of chipped ice, while he boiled water for pasta in a large pot. He planned to surprise her with candlelight and oysters when she got home hungry for dinner.

Two hours later, he was beginning to worry. He wondered if maybe something bad had happened to her. He added fresh cold water to the pot of simmering water and turned on the air conditioner to clear the humidity that was steaming up the windows.

Three hours later, his skin as cold as his heart, what he felt or feared inadequately measured by the hands of the clock, he went out on the deck to eat alone, watching the other families and couples eating in brightly lit rooms across the dune from Tara's condo. When he was done, he cleaned up, took a brisk walk around the estuary, and then turned in on the sofa to wait.

When Tara came in she smelled like sangria, despite the wad of cinnamon gum she was chewing, combined with a musty smell as though she'd been rolling in seaweed.

"I already ate," Pal said sleepily. "I hope you don't mind."

"I ran into someone," she said.

"Oh? Who?"

"An old friend."

"It's good to have friends," he said. "Do I know her?"

She threw off her clothes and headed for the bathroom and turned on the shower. She turned the pressure high enough to knock grout loose from between the tiles. "Him," she said as he followed her in and sat on the lid of the toilet.

"Oh. Do I know him, then?"

She shut off the water, grabbed her towel, and began vigorously wiping herself dry. "No," she said. "Not really. Well, sort of, I guess. You may have seen him around."

"I guess you had a lot to talk about," Pal commented. "Couldn't you have called, though? Collect, if need be. Let me know? Maybe there wasn't any phone nearby," he added, prepared to forgive her.

Tara swept past him into the kitchen. "Let's get one thing straight," she said. "You, of all people, don't own me. Understand?" Her nose caught the scent and she lifted her nostrils and sniffed. "Do I smell oysters?" she asked, her mood changing.

"Yes," Pal said, his heart sinking. He muttered, "Let this not be angry, please?" under his breath. The old words just weren't working.

Opening the fridge and pawing through the items on the shelves, she stood back and said, "I don't believe it." She stood up and looked at him in the refrigerator's dim light. "You ate them? Tell me you didn't. You fucking ate the oysters?"

"I thought you'd be here for dinner," he said. "I'm sorry." He laughed a little. "You know how it is with Ollie Oyster," he said. " 'Hello, Ollie,' you say, and he says back, 'Hey there,' and gives you the wink, the go-ahead, and you tip up his shell and he slips across the smooth white curve like a lick and caroms off your teeth and just sort of hops down your throat. Next thing you know, though, there's Ollie again, perched on another shell and you say, 'Hello, Ollie,' and he says back, 'Hey there,' and. . . ."

"Blah, blah, blah," Tara said, shooting him a look, a deaf look, a look like Ulysses Grant gazing at Red Cloud who has just finished speaking.

"You kinda lose track," he uttered, hopeless for humor in the face of that look.

"I don't believe you," she said. "Somehow you found some oysters. And then, knowing they're my favorite food, my favorite thing in the whole goddamned world, you ate them up? Who are you? What planet are you from?"

"I said I was sorry," he whispered, later, as he stood in the doorway to her bedroom, feeling lonely and wishing that she was awake. She'd turned her back toward the door and was making noises like she was asleep. "I'll go get some more tomorrow."

He pulled her door shut as quietly as he could. Unable to sleep, he walked, and sat on the deck. Finally, he began doodling, writing on the small pieces of paper that had become his habit. They stuck together along one border. They stuck to the table or the windows, or, as he discovered happily, to the television screen to block out the day-to-day old news.

Chapter Fourteen

I.

He was in Watsonville, wearing one of the Hawaiian shirts with buttons that tugged slightly and pushing a grocery cart along the aisles, browsing through the unit pricing, when I called out down the condiment aisle, "Yo, bro! Where'd you get them cloes?"

"A present," he replied, smiling.

I pushed my cart toward Pal, nodding. "A present, eh?"

"Yeah."

"You mean somebody gave them to you?"

"You got it."

"Gift-wrapped in paper and bows?" I feigned disbelief.

"Well, not exactly. She sort of found them in the closet for me."

"Uh-huh." I winked knowingly and added, "The girl knows cloes, all I can say."

Pal found himself smiling broadly, grateful for my approval. He looked closely at me. "Hey, bro, don't I know you?" he asked.

I shrugged. The two of us stared at each other. The look in my black eyes told Pal that I knew the world in the same way that he knew it. Suddenly, it all came back to him, and he seemed overwhelmed with the sensation that together we knew where art fits into life.

"Chingaro?" he asked, tentatively.

"Palimony!" I said, feigning surprise. "Jesus, Joseph, Holy Mary mother of God, if it ain't the croquet wizard, all growed up. What in the heck are you doing in Taco Villa? Slumming?"

"I'm out at Pajaro."

"Dunes?"

"Yeah."

"Whee-ooo!" I said, shaking my loose fingers floppily, as if they'd been scalded. "We have come up in the world, have we not?"

"It's not mine."

"Ah. Daddy's. I was right. You are slumming. Just in the wrong direction. Listen," I said, "let's go get a beer, eh?"

"I don't know. I've got all this food. It'll spoil if I leave it in the car."

"So put it back. Or leave it here like your girlfriend would do. One of my cousins will put 'em back."

"All of it?" Pal asked. He wondered if Tara had ever been inside a grocery store. "Just how many cousins do you have, anyway?" he asked. He was thinking that half the Mexicanos in California must be cousins of mine. They were.

I grinned. "Come on," I said. "I'll help you."

As we put back the groceries, Pal said, "Tell me. After Big Sur. Where'd you go, man?"

"Peru, man."

"Peru?"

"It was either that or Iraq. Sendero Luminoso ain't any better than Saddam to a Kurd, but at least I speak the language. That way, somebody shouts 'Duck!' I don't start to Moonwalk."

We stood in the parking lot. "I been around other times, too."

"Yeah. I know. Mother. . . ."

I waved away what he was going to say. We were like close friends, and while we might not see the world exactly alike, we saw the world in an alike way. But sentiment, if it went too far and became sentimentalism, would destroy the connection. I went back to Pal's shirt, reaching over and fingering the front of it. "She knows cloes for sure. Can't say she knows size good."

Pal grinned. "It's one of her friends'," he explained. "She's got a lot of friends."

"All kind of the same size. Sort of one size fits all, huh?" I said. "'Cept for you?" I thought a moment. "Say, man, listen. You got time for a few frames. You wanna go to the alley and bowl? I was on my way to meet a friend there, when I got the call to stop in the grocery."

We lost track of time. Pal completely forgot that Tara would be waiting for her G&T and crackers with cheese, and maybe the elusive Oliver Oyster, as he and I tried to catch up on the time that had passed since Mary Blue had dreamed me into his world. I rode along in Tara's sports car, directing him down the coast toward San Simeon, the castle William Randolph Hearst shipped to the States stone by stone and filled with authentic reproductions.

"What you and I are, man," I said, looking out at the white and wooly Swiss cattle with their coats as long as hair, large chests, and long, wavy horns. "Authentic reproductions." I laughed. "The first time I got back from Peru, man, I stopped up at the castle to rest in one of those great big beds that get made up every day by my cousins even though nobody never sleeps in them. Scared the pee outta a night watchman name of Bill when I stepped out from behind a sarcophagus in front of the guest house Patty Hearst's friends tried to blow up and said, 'Hey.' Old Bill was a mixblood like you, and what with his partner catching a nap in the guide's trailer, once he caught his breath and his heart stopped thumping, he gave me my own private tour of that castle.

"I tell you, that Hearst guy was American. He saw stuff, he frigging bought it. Place is filled with junk you couldn't sell at a flea market. But he stayed real homey, too, like he wasn't as rich and powerful as Patty's friends had oughtta blast away at him or his? He had this twenty-foot-long mahogany banquet table with monk's pews lining the walls. Real expensive. So fine that when you carved your sign into them, you did it someplace it wouldn't show, like under the seat. But he had regular catsup and mustard bottles on that table every ten feet or so, like this was just your basic Formica in a migrant's camp. 'Course they were glued down. And the one I broke checkin' it out was filled

with some kind of red goo. Wasn't catsup. That for sure. He even had
his own movie theater and a swimming pool with real gold in the tile.
He must've been a regular porpoise, you know? He didn't have just one
but two pools, man, one outside and one in. Outside one look like a
Greek temple. And you know what? He even got away with keeping
his own whore right there at the castle. Even had special rooms for her
twin kids up in these bell towers. That's something, ain't it? Takes real
cojones to keep a whore right there. She was a starlet, too.

"You know what got me the most, though?"

"No," Pal said. Listening to me go on made him laugh.

"Turn here," I said. I pointed at a graded road that you'd hardly
notice was there. Pal slowed and turned. A hundred yards ahead he
could see a cattle guard between a vee of fence posts that broke the
barbed wire running in either direction.

"The polar bear cage. That guy decided he wanted to own a polar
bear, so he builds this cage made out of white cement that's all smooth,
with caves and waterfalls and pools. And 'cause the bear don't like the
heat much, in the summertime when it gets around a hundred up by
the cage, old man Hearst has a ton of ice a day shipped in and trucked
up the hill just to keep that raggedy bear happy. A ton of ice. You imagine? Shit, I got cousins down in Watsonville cutting 'chokes never even
seen ice. They no like the heat neither, but you don't see no one bringing in ice to cool off the fields, now, do you?"

I laughed. Shook my head. "Polar bears. The world's a funny place,
huh? when the happy stories is all about bears. An' when you gotta
wear borrowed shirts just to go slumming," I added.

The road wound up to a flat depression overlooking the Pacific
Ocean. Disguised as a ranch, the houses and barns were really a radar
station built during the war ostensibly to watch for Japanese planes. Actually, they were a part of an elaborate excuse to seize the nurseries and
homes and property of citizens whose Japanese families had come to the
land of the free fifty-plus years before and to ship them off to intern-
ment camps long enough to make them feel grateful when they were finally released. Since that war, the station had kept a close eye out for

Korean and Vietnamese planes, Russian planes flown by untrained Iraqi pilots, and low-flying Coyotes from Sonora, doing its bit to keep the war effort going despite the lack of a war that would make people feel good. The Holsteins were part of the disguise. If you got up real early, you could sometimes catch a glimpse of a couple of live privates snaking down in camouflage through the wet high-grass to herd the cows up for a quick milking before the dawn's light gave away their purpose, their uniforms, their realities.

"Wouldn't fool an ax handle," Yep said as we passed a bathhouse with a roof that parted like an observatory to expose anti-aircraft guns. Yep—short for Yellow Peril—gave me fives and tens and then hugged me big, a friend from the old neighborhood.

"Milk's pretty fresh, though," he told Pal. He shook his hand and clasped his shoulders with his delicate but powerful hands.

Yep was a funny guy. He was not a very good bowler. Inside the barn that housed squash courts, a gym, a bowling alley, and a fifty-meter pool, we ordered up long-neck beers and went to work in the four lane alley. Pal was not exactly ready for the Pro Bowler's Tour, but at least he kept his ball on the alley. Yep's ball bounced in and out of gutters, jumped into other lanes, and once or twice even bounced off the wall before stuttering down to find some pins to knock over.

Frustrated, but amused, Yep finally screamed, "Ai-yee-ee." Leaving his ball in the rack, he marched double time down his lane, picked up the One pin, and proceeded to beat the other nine pins into submission. He tossed the One pin in after the wounded nine, executed a smart about-face, and marched back up the alley, his face expressionless, where he chalked up a strike on the overhead scoreboard. He turned, the expression on his face challenging me or Pal to protest. We were too busy laughing.

Time passed. We killed it good. Pal felt so good that he did not think once about Tara. It was well past midnight when we wrapped it up and Yep had to follow us down in a vehicle that resembled a heavily armored Mercury station wagon to open the gate at the cattle guard, locking it up after we went through.

Pal dropped me back in Watsonville. "Next time, my man," I said, big with the success of the evening. "This was fun, huh?"

"Yep," Pal said, meaning yep and Yep.

"You take care, slumming. Some nasty shit go on over there in those dunes, hey?"

"Hey," Pal said.

The security guard was clearly unhappy about being awakened before dawn to let Pal drive onto the spit of beach lined with condos. Feeling good, and a little thoughtful, Pal decided to sit out on the deck and wait for the sun to come up.

The cool slant light of the sun was just sliding over the hills when the glass door to Tara's bedroom slid back and a man sneaked out dressed only in spandex bathing trunks. Sliding the door shut ever so quietly, the guy turned and ran into Pal.

"How you doin'?" Pal said.

"I'm . . . uh . . . fine," the guy stammered. He edged up to where Pal sat and then slipped past him quickly, as though he thought Pal was going to stick out his leg suddenly and trip him, or jump up from his chair and try to puree his face.

Pal smiled. He closed his eyes and leaned back. "Take it easy," he said to the guy whose shoulders hunched as he hurried away.

2.

Coming face-to-face with Tara's deceptions sort of spoiled the night he'd had. Pal closed his eyes and leaned back in the chaise longue on the decking outside Tara's door and imagined himself back in Watsonville.

He was in a flower shop, an open-air affair with drop canvas sides run by an old loudmouthed character, name of Van French. He had picked out a bouquet for Amanda and was about to carry it up to the cash register when another bouquet called out, "Hey! Look at me!"

He put the first bouquet back and picked up the second. He was looking at it, admiring the baby carnations and trying to remember if baby carnations were Amanda's favorite? Or was it tiger lilies? One of them reminded her of that woman O'Keefe who painted those over-sized vulvas.

A third bouquet called out, "Not that one, bozo! The cornflowers are wilted in that one!"

He exchanged the second for the third only to hear the second mutter, "Yeah, but the carnations are frayed in that one."

"Nyeh-nyeh-nyeh-nyeh-nyeh," the first bouquet called.

Pal went back and forth and round and round while old man French eyeballed him like a train yard detective, suspiciously thinking that Pal would wait for him to turn his back and then steal the bouquet.

Perhaps cut flowers were not the right thing. Maybe a plant. A hanging plant. Holy Jesus! The hanging plants cost a week's wages. He fingered the hanging spider plants, the ferns and bougainvillea, until old Frenchy began to wish he would just steal a bouquet. He was starting to fear that he was there not to steal a plant but to rob him, and he was just hanging around for the street to empty of witnesses.

Maybe Amanda would rather go out to dinner? When he bought her earrings and gave them to her just for joy, she asked how much he spent and for one reason or another he'd told her the lowest possible price that could resemble the truth, discounting the earrings by forty percent.

"You what!" she said. "You paid how much? That's way too much, Pal. Way too much. I don't want you spending that much on anything for me."

"It is?" he said weakly. He took her to mean that she didn't like them.

So he shook his head at the hanging plants and walked away from the flower stand, determined that he'd remember whether she liked or hated carnations and, next time, buy her flowers.

That morning in that light, Amanda was wearing jean shorts and slipper sandals, a Grateful Dead T-shirt, and Lolita sunglasses shaped like hearts when she waddled out to greet him. She was walking funny, these days, and the way she walked felt to Pal like a premonition. It made him a little nervous.

"Hey," she said. "Where were you? I missed you when I woke up."

Mandy had also taken to napping. She tired easily.

"In the village," he said. It seemed as good a time as any, so he said, "I was by the flower stand. I almost bought you some flowers."

"But you didn't, did you?" Mandy said.

"Well, no."

"Am I supposed to say 'thanks'?"

"Well, no. But I almost did," he said brightly. "Really. At least I think about you."

Mandy shook her head. Her jaw set. She knew he wanted near full marks for the thought. And secretly, she was pleased that he had thought about buying her flowers.

Later, he put his arms around her and said, "You're glad I'm not like other men, aren't you?"

"I'm glad you're you," she replied. "Though it wouldn't upset me if you imitated other men and bought me some flowers now and then."

"Last time I bought you something, you said you didn't like it."

"What? When was that?"

"When I bought you those dangley earrings down in Santa Cruz."

"That was weeks ago, Pal. I said I was sorry for the way it sounded. But I never said I didn't like them. I just said you could've gotten them in San Jose for half the price."

"If you liked them, the price wouldn't have mattered."

"I've worn the stupid things for two weeks straight, for heaven's sake. I still wear them more than any other earrings I have."

"Where are they then?"

"They're in my jewelry case."

"See?"

"I wore them yesterday. I wore them Tuesday. Last weekend, I wore them bowling."

"So I guess it is the thought that counts? 'Cause you're not wearing them now."

Amanda sighed, wondering why she was feeling defensive. "Pal, I said I was sorry."

"Okay," he said. "I guess I'll forgive you."

She tucked her head into his shoulder and sighed.

"Next time I'll buy the flowers," he said, a few minutes later.

She laughed. A short, quick, ironical laugh. She knew that he probably wouldn't. But she also knew this was the best kind of apology for not buying them, and she didn't want him to push her on the earrings. She didn't really care about the flowers. She had other things on her mind. Even though she hadn't seen a doctor, she knew.

"I'm trying," he said. "I'm getting better, aren't I?"

"That you are," Amanda replied. "That you are." She purposely left it unclear whether she meant that he was trying or that he was getting better.

"Sorry," he said, as much to himself as to Amanda, later, as she padded in slippers across the bare wooden floor of the living room to return the book she had finished to the bookshelf. A return to the shelf meant that she liked the book. She finished everything she began out of some combination of guilt, pity, and the sense that at a certain point she has wasted enough time beginning the book. Going ahead and finishing it would waste more, perhaps, yet less than if she put the book down unfinished and then wondered night after night as she tried to begin another book whether that last one ever got any better. Books she didn't like, however, went into a box in the closet to be donated to the county mental hospital, down the road. They did not go back on the shelf.

Through the window, he watched the day go dark, the light on the coast behind the mountains changing to pink and yellow before it turned light blue and then finally clicked black. Dark as it was, listening carefully to the rhythm of his heart, he could see the mountains clearly, along with the stately redwoods that lay claim to Henry Cowell State Park.

"What?" Amanda asked. She ran her finger along the titles, contemplating what she would read next. She pulled a book out, opened it and read the first page, and then closed it and put it back, selecting another.

"Nothing. Just talking to myself."

Mandy went into the kitchen and a few minutes later came out sipping on a glass of warmed milk. She had put on tights against the chill of the midsummer's night air and the horizontal stripes of black and gray made her legs look thicker. The tights originally were black and white striped; Pal, unfortunately, had done the laundry to surprise her.

"Sounded like you said 'Chicago.' " She stood looking at him, balanced back slightly on her heels, her feet splayed out in a vee.

He loved those legs. Their strength. They were not anorexic model's legs but were full and firm with muscles that hid until they were needed, as when she bent at the waist to pick something up from the floor.

"Sorry," he said. "Didn't mean to bother you."

"You didn't bother me," Amanda replied. She took another sip of milk and asked, "Someone you made up?"

"Huh?"

"Were you talking to someone you made up?"

"Sort of," he answered, trying to decide which was more made up, the unimagined that does not feel real, or the imagined real?

"Ah." She turned for the bedroom.

"I won't be long," he said.

"Good." She stopped in the doorway. "What would you say if I said call in sick tomorrow and let's go get oysters in Monterey?"

"Fine," he said without hesitating. "Let's."

"Maybe take a walk on the beach?"

"There's a nice beach at San Simeon," he said. "We can drive inland to Monterey and then down the coast through Big Sur. Spend the day. Maybe we'll see some whales. There should be some around, still."

3.

When he woke up from this dreaming, it was mid-morning already. Tara had banged down a cup of Lapsang tea on the table near his head and gone back into the condo. She reemerged wearing a sleeveless cotton overblouse with bikini panties, carrying a box of zwieback biscuits in one hand and a stack of Post-its in the other. She tossed the Post-its onto the table beside the mug of tea and slouched into a deck chair.

"Been wanting to ask you," she said, her voice muted and lethargic with zwieback. "What the hell are these?" She picked up a couple that were stuck together, peeled them apart, and skimmed over them. "What is all this shit? Just who the fuck is this broad Amanda?"

Pal struggled to find his voice and to control it. He did not want it to begin with hatred or with the things forgotten because of hatred. He knew what it was, now. It was dreaming, and dreaming was an art like Mary Blue's beading, with all the concurrent and concupiscent dangers attendant thereon.

"She is not a broad," he said softly.

"No," Tara laughed. " 'Broad' is probably too nice for her kind." She held up a different group of Post-its. "And then these. Listen to these."

She began to read, flipping from one Post-it to the next, unsticking them as she went. " '1816! 1818! 1825! Loners and drunks pave the way for the inimical William Clark, made governor for the same reason they are all made governor or mayor, senator or president, heroes all like William Clark, the fraternal buddy of Meriwether Lewis who together discovered an already discovered land and opened the way for settlers of a land settled for thousands of years, and then claimed it, made maps of it, which like all their ceremonies of triplicate forms means to them that they own it.' "

Tara raised her eyebrows and gave him a questioning, sarcastic look.

"Chingito's words," Pal said quietly. "Not mine."

"Chingito?"

"A friend."

"Oh, Jesus! I thought you told me you didn't have any friends."

"I did. I guess. Yeah. But he is."

"Hard to believe. I'll say that." She turned her attention back to the Post-its. "These make even less sense. Listen. 'Vigilante. Vigilance. The difference of one tiny little letter but a difference of time that is so far apart that it's like the flip side of a coin. The minute Lewis and Clark

left Mary Blue's father should have planted vigilant guards along the
peaks of the Bitterroot Mountains watching for the missionary vigi-
lantes who would appoint themselves to uphold laws that were not laws
of honesty, family, or courage, but only the laws of greed. But how
should her father, or even Ollokot, have known this? They liked Lewis
and Clark. Lewis liked them. Was it not affection that later made Governor Meriwether Lewis look up from a letter telling him that Chief
Joseph's heart had broken and say to his wife, "I ought to have stayed
home"?'"

"Give me those," Pal said. "Please?"

"When you tell me what all that is," Tara said, holding the Post-its
up and away from him. One broke loose and fluttered, a dying yellow
butterfly-moth, disappearing over the edge of the deck.

"Please?" Pal said. Another Post-it fluttered out of her hand.

"Tell me."

"It's just Mary," Pal said. "It's supplementation. What you would
call a digression." All other people's words. Chingito's. La Vent's.
Mother Mary's. A few of his own. But very few. Things apart in time
overlapping in reality.

Tara laughed. "It makes no sense."

"You have to begin somewhere."

"Okay," she said. She rummaged in the pocket of her overblouse
and pulled out a paper-clipped sheaf of cinnamon chewing gum wrappers, removed the clip, and began going through them. "What about
these?"

"Like I said."

"I never wrote this," she said.

He shrugged. "Somebody did."

"This makes it look like I asked you out."

"Did you ever leave me a note?"

"This makes it sound like I was happy having you follow me and
George around."

"George?"

"One of my friends. He said the two of you met this morning."

"Right." Met? Ran into, was more like it. "Did you ever leave me a note?"

"Yes!" she shouted. "Yes, I left you a goddamned note. But I didn't leave all of these notes."

"But at least one of them is yours?"

"Maybe," she said, shuffling quickly through the stack as though to find the one that was.

"You can't tell which one was?" Could she detect the pride in his voice?

"No, well, maybe this . . . no, maybe . . . , " she stammered.

"The fact is, you can't tell which of those notes is the one left me."

"So?"

"So any one of them could be yours?"

"I guess."

She was defeated, and defeat made her polite. As Pal was making himself some coffee, she came in and gently said, "Listen, we have to go get some food," she said. She picked up the suntan lotion and began smearing more of it around her person. The stench of coconut was unbearable. It made Pal gag.

"Why don't you go get it this time?" he said. "You know where Watsonville is."

"I can't," she said, pleading.

"Why not?"

"Because," she said. "Please go?"

"Because why. Tell me, and I'll go."

"I don't know how to shop," she admitted.

"What do you mean, you don't know how to shop?"

"I never learned. I learned to ride a bike. I learned to swim. I never learned how to shop."

"Who buys your clothes?"

"One of the maids. For special occasions, Mommy has a woman come to the house and she shops for us. And if we're having a party, the caterers do it. I took a chance with our party. I thought you'd know how to do it."

The party! Oh, shit. "All right. I'll go," he said, his attitude suddenly changed.

He had forgotten all about the party. It was next week. What had he done with the invitations? He'd intended to mail them. But he was never near a post office, it seemed, and the invitations must have gotten covered up with other trash like empty Happy Meals from Mickey D's.

"Here," Tara said, regaining her spitefulness. "Take all your strange friends with you." She tossed his Post-its after him.

4.

As he was leaving, the phone rang. He was right by the phone and he picked it up before Tara shouted, "I'll get it."

It was Mary Blue. "It's for me," he called. "Mom?"

"She's gone," Mary Blue said.

"Sally?"

"Sister Niedman. Yes," Mary Blue said quietly.

"Where'd she go?"

"Don't know," Mary said. "Yesterday, when I took him his food, he was sitting on the trunk of the taxi weeping. I didn't see her. I thought she was out collecting telephone company flyers from local Dumpsters. Foraging for more predictions of the end of the world. This morning, he was still there. Still weeping. He hasn't moved. Pal," she said in a tone he'd never heard her use before, "I'm sorry to ask this of you. But bring her back. This isn't a part of his story. Not the way it should be."

"I'll try," he promised.

Chapter Fifteen

1.

Pal drove south to the bridge spanning Lime Kiln Creek and turned in and down to the abandoned campgrounds. He climbed the rock steps carefully, the edge of the footholds eroded by time and weather, and then stood in the sunlight at the edge of the plain. The convent was like the rock steps, eroded. The barn leaned, and the cloisters had lost their roof, except for a few timbers that hung like broken bones into their chambers. He started down through the wild grass. In places, it was as high as his shoulders. There was nothing there. Not for him. Not for anyone.

A dark swift shadow fled across the edge of his vision and he stopped and scanned the sky, shading his eyes from the brightness of the sun. A hawk, its shadow raking the grasses for rodents. As quickly as it had come it had gone, and the hot-crystal sky remained as birdless as it was merciless, the heat held down against the earth by the wild hay and the wild blue of the sky.

Inside the compound, the feeling of emptiness that hovered around him in the heat seem multiplied as though nothing could be more than nothing. The word "absolute" flitted like a mouse through his brain.

The chapel stood ajar like Calvary's tomb. The altar, the hanging tapestries, all were gone, and the pews were rotten and splintered, some of them carved with the initials of other visitors. It had a bad feeling to it, and he longed to be done looking and return to his car. He was not frightened so much as he was saddened by the desolation. But he was determined to find her and take her back if she was there. Mary had asked it of him.

As he stepped into the barn I shook my foot, causing the spurs I was wearing to jangle. He stopped.

"Hello?" he called. "Sally? Sister Niedman? Anyone?"

"Hey," I said, from way up in the darkness. I perched on a crossbeam in the rafters.

"You again," he said. "Isn't it about time you started waiting for me to call?"

"Long past due," I said, adopting a high voice and flicking my pink boa playfully.

"So?"

"So I will. Once what's was is over and what will be begun. I'm perfectly happy to hang around and bug you when I can."

"I don't mind," Pal said. "I kind of like it this way."

"I'm glad." I jumped down from the rafters into a moldy pile of hay. Getting up and dusting myself off, I went over to him and poked him lightly on the chest. "Problem is that until I help you get this right for good, your Amanda's baby is always going to remain a dream."

"Amanda? Baby?"

"You gotta have a baby, man. Otherwise you're like a tetherball hanging from the rope of the past but not connected to no future. Amanda's gotta have it. And you still gotta make her real. Unfortunately, there's this problem of La Vent."

"What's La Vent got to do with Amanda and her having a baby?"

"Law of physics. You take one dream out, you gotta turn one dream in."

"Sounds more like a lending library," he said.

"That'll work," I said. "Anyway, you want that baby, you gotta get rid of La Vent. Don't look so sad," I told him. "I don't mean you actually have to do away with him. He's doing that himself, what with all

his literal fundamentalism. I just mean you gotta get the La Vent out of
you. Stop waiting. Stop doing what everyone else wants you to do."

He looked hang-dog in the shadows of the barn. I wanted to offer
him hope. "By the way, let me give you a little hint. Rachel. Willy, if it's
a boy."

"Rachel?"

"The baby. Her name."

"If I ever have a baby," he said. "I'm not so sure I want one."

I sighed. Ignored him. "It fits her. She'll fit it. I promise."

"Okay," he said reluctantly. He toed the ground with his shoe.
"Can you help me find Sally first?"

"She's gone."

"I know. That's why I'm here."

"No. I mean gone. There's so little there that once she's gone, out of
sight, she's gone. There's no getting her back, no matter what you do or
how you do it. Fox couldn't bring that girl back, let alone Coyote, 'cause
there's nothing to bring."

"What about La Vent?"

"You're too late," I said. "He's gone away, himself, by now."

"Where?"

I held up my wrist and looked at it as though I wore a watch. "He
went through here . . . oh . . . five, ten minutes before you came. On his
way to Teheran."

"Iran?"

I nodded. "Forever," I said.

"But. . . ."

"You did it, Pal," I said.

"Me? What did I do?"

"You dreamed it," I said. "Before you knew how to do it right. Not
me."

"It was you who made me dream it."

"Tsk, tsk," I grinned. "You keep on seeing it," I said. "Meanwhile,
I'll see you when I can."

Pal raced over the mountains. But by the time he reached Mary's house empty-handed several hours later, he found La Vent curled up beside the kitchen table like a lost lamb of Abraham, dead after days of weeping and exposure.

Mary was unpacking and mending the shroud she would bury him in. She seemed to expect Pal to hand her the pink boa to bury with his father.

2.

Palimony Blue was a changed man when he returned to Pajaro Dunes several days later. La Vent had been buried privately and quickly in Nez Perce fashion, with the coffin open over his face and standing upright in the hole in the ground, giving La Vent's soul time to catch up with his Christian spirit, which had crossed the continent and was waiting to board a ship for Teheran. Not given to sudden grief, Mary sent her son back to Pajaro to finish up. Besides, she had been grieving all along for her lost husband and she understood too well her responsibility in the final losing. Pal's story was coming to a crisis point. La Vent's dying could not be allowed to change its direction too much.

When he walked into the condo, Tara had just gotten up and she was trying to fit a slice of toast into the toaster. Each time she did, she waited several minutes, and then pulled the bread out only to discover to her dismay that it was untoasted.

"You have to push the lever down," Pal said, behind her.

She was startled. Then, gathering herself, she demanded, "Just where have you been, dumb shit?"

Until now, the nicknames she called him more and more often had seemed to him affectionate. Nicknames were gestures, distinguishing him from men who were just good friends or men she respected almost too much like her father's business associates. Nicknames that sort of cast a fellow in the right light, making him a special someone, but not so special that affection was completely inappropriate. Nicknames, in Pal's way of thinking, let you say anything and it was okay. Tara could get angry. She could criticize him. She could tell anecdotes in front of him about his foibles and mistakes. But now, with La Vent dead and his heart in an uproar, Pal wondered if maybe the nicknames weren't insults. He wondered if it was only when affection was inappropriate that Tara gave it—to a friend, to the married neighbor at Pajaro named George who sneaked in and out of Tara's bedroom at night like the thief of Baghdad.

"Looks like you had a good night," Pal said, looking around the condo's living room at the empty tequila bottles, the torn condom wrappers, and the tinfoil pans that still held scraps of macaroni and cheese, burritos, and casseroles for two.

Tara frowned. "I'm hungry," she said.

"So fix yourself some food," he replied. He walked right on by her, out the open door to the deck and down onto the beach.

"There isn't any!" she called after him. "You were supposed to get some. Remember, shit brain? That's why you went to town. Almost a week ago. If it weren't for friends, I'd have starved. You hear me?" She stamped her foot petulantly on the deck planking.

The sunlight was still slant but warm as he walked away along the wet sand littered with kelp and driftwood large and small, a sign of both the power and the persistence of the tide. The homeowners had trucked in massive granite boulders and stacked them along the bluff in front of their houses, trying to keep a hold on the sand they owned and stop the night tide from eating its way right under their decks, living rooms, and garages, finally taking their houses plank by plank south to Chingito's Peru. His feet left indentations in the sand that bubbled with the exhalation of mollusks and then filled with seawater and dissolved. His head ached, as much a product of the migrant sun as from all the fun he was having.

He rounded a promontory of dunes topped with fans of sea grass and patches of ice plant. Ahead of him lay a large dark shape on the sand. From a distance it looked as though it had not been tossed up by the early morning tide, but as though it had grown there on the sun-whitening sand. It resembled an overweight sea otter or lion, gray-brown with a high yellow aura, and glistening in the wet morning light.

Up close, it looked like a man in his forties who had gorged himself
on guacamole and prunes. He smelled. But then every death smells.
Some smell with hints of uncertain regret like dill weed; this one
smelled like the soul of surprise, liberal hints of Fontina mixed with the
salty certainty of seaweed, as though he never in the world had expected to become this, turning blue-black beneath the baker's sun and
smelling bad like ripe cheese. As though he had intended to come to be
something else entirely. But the way the body stretched up the sand
with his shoulders in a final shrug proclaimed the vanity of all intention
in the face of death, especially this death, which had been as lonely and
as uncontested and therefore as stupid and sad as unheard thunder rising to a higher place.

Pal poked and prodded the waterlogged flesh with a piece of driftwood. There were scraped patches on his hands and abrasions on his
wrists. He probably had tried to cling to the mussel-encrusted rocks.
His knees and elbows looked raw as though he'd tried to crawl to shore
after he'd been slammed like a sponge to the ocean floor. It made Pal
wonder that the body was that of a man not yet sunk into the funk of
middle age, neither a physical wreck nor a specimen to admire. From
the spindly look of the legs, it had spent the better part of its life leaning
against a lectern or occupying the square space cut out of an office desk,
and it had grown pudgy with the paunch of denial. It was the body of a
man who, not so obviously in decline, wants to prove to you as much as
to himself that, despite statistical probabilities, he isn't, so he goes swimming alone off the tip of the morro and drowns in currents he never
suspected.

Pal imagined him late last evening crawling over the jetty's boulders, climbing with all the caution of his life's profession around to the
seaward side of the point, and, with a now-or-never sigh, diving in with
his hands clasped like a prayer, expecting to swim playfully with the otters and migrating whales before turning in toward shore, reaching the
sand spent but happy that his body had not betrayed him.

Only it had. But then anybody's would, in these currents. An
Olympic swimmer would risk being torn from shore and carried out

beyond the breaking waves and drowned before being indifferently cast up on the beach like so much pollution.

The beach was still fairly deserted, although in another half hour or hour, it would become crowded as condo owners and their guests rushed to walk and jog in the fog of their own individual denials.

Off among the dunes, the apparition of a woman rose, her head and neck veiled like an Arab or a nun, and then vanished as though it'd never been.

A couple in matching outfits jogged their four unleashed surrogate children up the sand, the first of the early morning rush to health. One by one the four dogs trotted over to sniff the dead body. They each lifted their legs and squirted at it, the littlest terrier ducking and dodging the spray of the largest mutt, before trotting on after their masters.

Pal felt as though he should protect the body from these desecrations, but they were gone before he could decide how.

After the dogs came another man bent like the image of Christ lugging his cross up Calvary Street, staggering down the beach beside his wife, who helped him balance a huge burl of driftwood on his shoulder. It must have weighed a hundred and fifty pounds, and the man's thin legs wavered at every step.

The man claimed the corpse as an excuse to pause and rest, dropping the burl to the sand. "He dead?" he panted.

Pal nodded. Someone had to ask the question. And, even more important, someone had to provide the answer. It was as though with the question unexpressed and unreplied to, the dead might continue to exist in some limbonic region where they could neither be alive nor dead.

The man looked worried, his dark eyebrows seeming to grow together over the raccoon eyes of a sun worshipper as he asked, "He from around here?"

"In the end," Pal replied.

Neither of the couple saw the humor of it.

"Makes you wonder, don't it?" the man said. He wanted a conversation. He wanted to let that driftwood burl lie a while longer. "What happened. Why," he said.

"Looks Jewish," his wife butted in, holding her nose and peering closely at the corpse.

"Maybe he just got tired of teaching," Pal said quietly. The scrapes on the corpse's elbows looked like the suede patches of a professor who passes like the memory of a dream through the mind. His right hand clutched a piece of paper or cardboard.

"You knew him?" the driftwood man asked. He gave Pal a nouveau-bureaucratic look, suspicious, secretive, prying.

"Maybe his money belt got wet and drowned him," the wife said, sticking to her own version of the world.

"Honey, I don't think he was wearing a money belt. I can't see where it is if he was, can you?"

"Damn Jews," his wife said. "First they get Hollywood. Now they want our beaches."

"Sweetheart," the man said, rubbing his goatee with his fingers. He was thin, with shoulders so narrow that in conjunction with his slight paunch, his frame resembled a pear. They were both pear-shaped, in fact, except her pear had acid blue eyes and his indifferent brown. Both wore a single earring in the left lobe of their ears. "This man's a friend of his."

She gave Pal a sharp look.

"No," he said. "Not really a friend." He felt bad denying it, and yet the thing was dead and Pal wasn't about to get involved with an explanation, especially not with the lovely Mrs. here, whose world was all paneled and hard. These two would never understand that you can take on the surprised soul of a professor without actually having occupied yourself by making a living as a teacher.

Mrs. Driftwood picked up a stick and moved on sturdy Wurlitzer legs toward the body. "Let's see if he's circumcised," she said.

"Honeybunch," Mr. Driftwood said, his brown eyes tired but determined. "I'm circumcised."

Pal wanted to get out of there. People who hated Jews turned on people like him if they got half the chance and there wasn't a convenient Jew around to hate. Pal had never become what you could call

friends with folks like Mrs. Driftwood. They were never happy with
the answers he had given them on different occasions. They were either
bored by them or too interested in them, as though the answers he gave
confirmed for them something Pal did not want to confirm. Either way,
he gave them no joy. And they always seemed to want him to be guilty
of something, anything. The odd thing was that he always felt as
though he were.

"You're leaving?" Mr. Driftwood looked around, scared, like he
was going to be asked to carry the corpse along with the heavy burl.

"He's all yours."

"We should go, too, Ween. Pick up my coffee table and let's," the
lovely Mrs. ordered her husband.

Sighing, Mr. Driftwood began to wrestle with the burl as Pal disappeared behind the sea grass dunes. He imagined the thrill Tara might feel
when (and if) she found the time to let him tell her about it, if she did not
instantly decide that this body was a history too complicated to tell.

3.

"Goofed on that one," I admitted to him later. We sat out on the
deck drinking coffee and watching whole families lope down the beach
to the end of the spit of sand that was Pajaro Dunes, turn in unison, and
begin jogging back, their leashed cats and dogs panting with the exertion and their owners with happy healthy smiles smeared across their
faces. I had brought him a gift, a porcelain statuette of the Virgin Mary
that I'd picked up along my travels. It had a peel-and-stick base so he
could stick it on the dash of La Vent's cab in memory of Roberto Marroquin or any of our other Catholic friends traveling a world like mine
in search of rest. If he wanted, it could also serve as a television antenna
in a technological marriage of heaven with hell.

"One minute I was swimming along, humping my way through
the whitecaps like Dippy the Dolphin, when all of a sudden this trans-
lucent thing with its elbows all scraped up and bloody starts trying
to take the body back. I wrestled with it, but next thing I knew, I was

surprised by exhaustion and I turned into some black thing the dog dragged ashore."

"Maybe Coyote," Pal said.

"Coyote. Dog. *Hay nada otros* where I am. Not at all."

"Does to me," he protested.

"Yeah. But you don't really matter, do you? That's why I'm still here in one form or another."

"Gee, thanks," he said. "By the way. Speedos aren't really you, if you know what I mean."

"I do," I laughed. "I started off in cut-offs. But strange things can happen, you know?" I heard noises inside the condo. "Listen," I said quickly, "I need you to do me a favor. Soon." I needed a name. Chingito, when all was said and done, belonged to Mary Blue. Like Amanda, if I was going to be his spirit guide and his alone, I needed a name by which I could be called.

"What's that?" he asked in a way that made me think he would do it.

But just then Tara opened the drapes and slid back the glass door to the deck.

Chapter Sixteen

I.

Tara's party turned out to be a little thinner than Tara might have liked. She liked having people snugged up against each other wall-to-wall like carpet. It saved on liquor, for one thing, by slowing progress to and from the wet bar. And it let her take up a central position in the living room and be able to monitor most of the conversations babbling along around her.

Pal had used Chingaro's name and a small bribe to get the custodian at the post office to sort what invitations he could find and get them well into the delivery pipeline. Then he took several rolls of quarters to a pay telephone and called as many people as he could remember, to make sure they were coming. And he knocked on all the doors of all her friends along the beach.

It wasn't eight o'clock yet, but still, Tara was beginning to notice.

"I don't get it," she hissed at Pal, as she squeezed by him on the arm of their history professor. "George isn't here."

"Not yet," Pal said, losing hope, himself. George had not been home; although his wife, a not unattractive woman in her forties, had been. Pal shrugged. What could he do?

He stood in the corner beside the rubber plant, which he had brought indoors to give a rest from the heavy salt of the air outside, washing its leaves with a mild solution of dishsoap and water. From there, he listened to Gip Carnal telling Joe Manifest, another of Tara's good friends, how identity all came down to the card he carried in his wallet. Evidently, Gip taught Indian history and from what he said knew so much that not even an Indian could earn more than a "B" from him. Carnal whipped out his wallet with a flourish as though he were going to give Manifest a large tip. He drew out a blue card sealed in plastic and threw it down on the table.

"It all comes down to this," Carnal shouted. His face turned red with formulated emotion.

"Guy ain't so sure he's real, is he?" I said.

Pal looked up.

Tonight I was a handsome black man all duded up in cowboy drag like it was Halloween, wearing chaps edged in pink braid and spurs that jangled merrily when I walked.

Pal was about to reply when a woman grabbed his arm and pressed the hard nut of her breasts into his arm. She pulled him away from me to tell him in a heavy German accent how modern medicine came either from Indians like him or from witchcraft. She went on and on. And on. Not stopping to breathe. He sort of began to like her. He appreciated her paying attention to him.

"It all comes down to this!" The slap of Gip's card on the table was as sharp as a one-shot derringer.

"We Germans are so guilty," the woman said. "You think it's because of the Jews. Did you know that in the sixteenth century we burned over three thousand witches in the southwest of Germany? Even in the Spanish Inquisition only a dozen of the five thousand women put on trial were ever burned. We, though, are more efficient."

Beneath the guilt there was an echo of pride in German efficiency.

"This is what it's all about! I know! I'm right! I know everything! I don't have to listen to a thing you say!" Gip shouted at Joe.

Tara detached herself from a group by the door and slipped quickly but gracefully toward History and the Indian. You could tell from the expression on her face that Gip was not going to decorate another one of her parties.

Pal smiled. He turned back to the German woman, prepared to say that maybe not all Germans were so efficient, but she had moved on.

She was replaced by a freckle-faced woman in gray suede shorts with flowers on the suspenders and bright orange lipstick.

"Tell me," she said, before he could say anything. "Do you drum?"

"Drum?"

"Janet," she said, introducing herself. "I live in Auk Three. I've been wanting to ask you, are you connected to mother earth and father sky?"

"I guess. I mean, I'm here."

"Drumming is an important aspect of Native American culture. Drumming helps you heal yourself. It lets you put yourself in touch with your own rhythms and lets your soul fly free on the vibrant waves of sound that only you can produce. With a lot of practice, of course. I've been to three weeks of seminars up at Tahoe and I'm just learning to drum right."

I brushed Pal as I passed, heading for the liquor table again. "Ask her if she yodels," I whispered. He grinned and shook his head, his teeth fluorescent against his skin.

"Cretin," Janet huffed. Self-possessed, she said, "So? Do you?"

"I have a drum," he replied. Somewhere in Mary's closet there was the stretched deerhide drum he'd used as a kid when La Vent still took him to dances. He had painted it lovingly with the outline of an elk's head among designs of cheat grass and lightning, a Dreamer's sun and a hunter's moon. "I don't know where it is, exactly."

"You gave it up? You gave up drumming?"

"I guess I did. I don't know." He glanced around the room for the black cowboy in drag. "I didn't really give it up. It just sort of stopped. Once my dad and I stopped going to dances and my father became too busy with his other pursuits. It all seemed, well, you know, nostalgic."

He'd forgotten how long it had been since he'd envisioned Mary taking his drum from the closet, caressing it and singing softly over it before wrapping it up again in a cloth her mother had woven, folding in one side, then the next, and the next. She folded it by quarters and not by opposites, the way you might wrap the skull of your grandfather, before carefully replacing it on its shelf.

"Oh," Janet said. "How sad. How utterly, utterly sad. And you've been out of touch with yourself ever since, I bet?"

"Well. . . ."

He imagined he heard a brief jingle of spurs out on the deck, but when he turned, all he glimpsed was a silver skirt and a pink braid vanishing into the hungry sea roar eating away the sands beneath the houses along the beach.

Janet grabbed his arm and turned him back. "Don't you see that you of all people must drum? It's part of your way of life. It's your history. Drum. You must drum!" she exclaimed. "And keep on drumming until you fill the universe with the sound of the Native American soul. Save us. With the sound. Save us from the discord we've produced on mother earth. Save us from the oil we've put into the ocean out there. Save us. Save—"

"I have trouble saving five bucks," he said.

She looked stricken. She seemed to run out of steam and recede into the quiet tears of an ecological nostalgia.

He was sorry. It was all his father's dying like that. He had not had time to come to terms with it and it made him feel nasty and angry. "Well," he said, "maybe I will."

Tara passed the two of them. Tears of emotion were trickling down Janet's cheek. She beamed at him through them, though, grateful for his sorrow.

"Hi," he said, glad to see Tara. Janet's tears confused him.

"I could use some help," she hissed, "since you're always offering."

"I'd be glad to," he said. "I was just listening to Janet, here, tell me about drumming and my nature and the sound of the universe. It's pretty interesting. But if you need help. . . ."

"Blah-dee-blah blah," Tara said. "Sorry," she said to Janet. "You're

not the only one he makes cry. But you're on your own. Just ignore him
if he gets to be too much." She moved away through the room.

"Janet's not crying because of me," he called after her. "Are you,
Janet?"

Janet, though, was out on the deck leaning up against the black
cowboy, yodeling.

Before Janet disappeared arm in arm together with me in my
flapper-cowboy's costume, I leaned against the railing of the condo deck
and with my arms around her, behind Janet's back, gave Pal two
thumbs up.

Gip sadly slipped his identity back into his wallet and left. The
German woman moved on to heavier guilts. Tara went off to the master bedroom with Joe Manifest where she undressed in front of him as
he knelt on all fours and barked like a dog. Then she ran naked around
the room while Joe crawled about in spurts and darts or slow methodi-
cal stalkings, until finally, her nipples hard with exertion, she let him
catch her and his bark was replaced with the hum of a vibrator.

2.

"Blah blah blah, yourself," he said. He was cleaning up, hand-
washing the champagne glasses and polishing the silver.

"It was your friend Janet who was telling me that I needed to take
up drumming to feel myself and get in touch with my heritage as
though my heritage is some kind of shadow that follows me around just
waiting for me to hug it. I wasn't saying anything. Your friend Janet
was the one who asked me why I didn't take my drum and go to Holly
wood and get a part in a movie so people like her could see what it was
really like to be an Indian. I was only trying to be, as you've asked me to
be so many, many times, sociable. I didn't tell Janet anything I wanted
to tell her. I was being kind and listening to her and you walk up and
do that, say Blah blah, without even giving me any credit, just assuming
it's me going on and on. And so what if I had been? What if I had been

and your friend Janet thought it was interesting? Do you ever stop to think that maybe other people find some of the things I have to say interesting? I'll bet you don't. You never have."

He felt better for getting these things off his chest.

He decided to wait until morning to vacuum because Tara and Joe were asleep. They wouldn't appreciate being awakened.

Tired, he slumped into a wicker chair on the deck overlooking the speargrass rustling among the hillocks of sand in the slight warm breeze. He closed his eyes and began to rock with the image of the moon, divided in half by light and dark, listening to all the voices echoing out of the sea-nudged night as the night and tide ebbed toward dawn. Was it the rustle of chaps, thigh against thigh, or only the speargrass whispering?

"Drum drum drum," a voice whispered.

"There's the sand. There're your hands," an old voice said. "Fight the sand and you may as well have worked in wind."

"Ruff!"

"Raise your HDLs unto the Lord!" a preachy voice said.

"The hands pick up sand and move tenderly above the skin of the earth until what is already there comes out."

"Goo my shirt, please?"

"Bitterness is bad."

"She comes from the Lettuce People."

"She'll make you sad."

"Yeah. Maybe do to her as you did unto. . . ."

"Think about it and what is there in the skin of the earth will be as nothing on the wind."

"It doesn't seem fair," he said. His voice was punctuated by the sea waves nudging the shore.

"Fair?"

"Pooh."

"Yes. Pooh."

"So she comes home smelling stale and used like a barful of men?"

"Why shouldn't she?" he commented. He gave the third voice a different and more sympathetic tone. Compared to the other voices, it was stronger, more resolved, and yet as kind as love.

"Here. You can have fair. Better yet, you can have Buenhuevo."

Out of the shadows, I handed him the word, which he turned like obsidian in his hand, his thumb fitting first this depression and then that. The edges were sharp and cutting with pain, as well as sharp with a secret promise of pleasure.

3.

"Thank God it wasn't Preacheart," she says. "Or Ox. Jesus, where'd you get ideas like that?"

"Sorry," he says.

Mandy pulls into a parking space beside the Bran-Hol-A, a local health food restaurant where you can get anything but what you really want. They're meeting friends of hers for lunch.

"It's okay." She smiles, a broad, forgiving smile that he believes is true. "It doesn't matter all that much."

"I guess," he says with a seriousness that makes her laugh.

"Just if you had kids and they found out. . . ."

He glances at her. Her long brown hair is that day pulled back in a silver comb so it frames her smile. "If I'm ever lucky enough to have kids."

"It could happen," she says. "Sooner than you might imagine."

4.

The next morning, Tara was gone with Joe Manifest. She left him a note telling him to clean up, lock up the condo, and drive her car home. Pal did as he was told, but he left the front and back doors unlocked. Just in case security or a cleaning service locked those, he broke one of the window locks to ensure that it, at least, would be open if ever he or I returned.

He drove slowly up the coast, staying close to the speed limit to keep from being stopped on suspicion of driving a car someone like him couldn't possibly afford. Even driving up Rico Road in Saratoga, he could see the bubble-gum lights of a police cruiser stalking him, until he turned definitively into the Dunnahowe estate.

"George," Mrs. Dunnahowe said, greeting him in the entry hall. "How nice to meet you, finally." She stood holding his hands in hers, lifting his arms lightly as though looking for the telltale patches on his sleeves.

"I have Tara's keys," he said. "To her car."

"And Tara's not here. I'm so sorry. She's in Tahoe for a few days. But please, come in. We're just about to have dinner. Have you eaten? Ash will be glad to meet you at last."

Dinner? It was just past noon. "I don't want to interrupt," he said. "I just came to drop. . . ."

"Interrupt? You, George? Don't be silly. How could you interrupt? It's only dinner. Come-as-you-are. Ash has wanted to meet you. We've heard quite a bit about you."

Indeed, Ash was glad to meet him. As he sat down with Mrs. Dunnahowe at the table, a long reddish rainforest mahogany table that shined so bright in the solarial lunch room he longed for sunglasses, Ash was in his den, locked into the final exciting minutes of a skeet shooting tournament on his satellite TV. Shouts of "Pull" and the blam of shotguns exploding were punctuated by Ash's calling out "Good show" in an imitation British accent that sounded more like Ed Sullivan than an upper-crust Brit. As though they'd expected a guest, an old Chicana maid, no doubt one of Chingaro's *tias*, nudged into the room as silent as fog and plunked a plate in front of him with a quartered head of iceberg lettuce displayed upon it like a crown jewel.

"We eat light, I'm afraid," Mrs. Dunnahowe explained as Corona the maid slipped away, only to return seconds later with a linen napkin and a fork and knife.

"Thank you," Pal said to her.

The old woman stopped as if surprised. Her lips quivered; the spittle dried in the corners of her lips cracked as her face trembled with her attempt to smile. Then she was gone and Pal began to contemplate the wedge of lettuce.

Ash sneaked through the door from the den and slapped him on the shoulder heartily. "Some shoot, eh, boy? A ray-lee gude shew."

Ash sat at the head of the table and smiled dreamily for a second, remembering the truly excellent shots, the thrill of victory and the acceptance of defeat all according to a code Ash admired so much he could never emulate it.

"So, Birch, who have we here?" he asked, smiling down the table at his wife.

"George," Birch Dunnahowe replied. "You know, Tara's friend from the dunes. Awful thing that happened to that man last month, wasn't it? Drowning like that. Just awful. Why he would go swimming like that in the ocean. And at night."

"Georgie!" Ash bellowed. He wanted to slap him on the shoulder again, but he'd already circled the table and taken his wicker seat. He couldn't very well rush back around the table and hit him again. "Or should I call you something else?"

"George is fine," he replied.

Ash nods, thoughtfully. "Georgie-porgie," he said. He held his hand out, palm up, as though waiting for a tip.

"How do you do," he said, reaching across and tentatively slapping Ash's hand, giving him a low five.

"How do I do? Pretty well," Ash said. He swept his extended hand in a possessive arc. "As you can see. Hah hah."

"I didn't mean to interrupt," he said, the silence after Ash's hearty "hah hah" seeming to come quick and loud. He tried to pry a bite of lettuce loose. The lettuce wedge fought back. He pushed the tines of the fork in deeper, twisting until a chunk larger than one bite pulled away and teetered precariously, as though it and the Thousand Island dressing were about to leap into his lap like an affectionate terrier. Stay there, he silently begged the lettuce. Please?

"Don't think twice about it," Ash said, his voice booming around the glass of the solarium. "We have guests all the time. Esperanza always prepares a little extra just in case. Why just last week, I had a man in . . . ," he said, picking up his quartered head of lettuce with his fingers and biting off one end. What happened to the man was lost in the muffle.

Pal wondered if he could get away with doing that. Could he pick up his lettuce with his hands? Or would it be rude, a custom permitted only the lord of the manor?

Birch Dunnahowe gracefully pried layers of her wedge loose and then cut them down to size with the edge of her fork.

He tried to imitate her. He jabbed the tines of his fork into his wedge. A layer did not come loose. In fact, it felt as though he'd stuck the fork into quick-setting glue. No lettuce would come loose. And now the wedge, which had a character all its own, was damned if it was going to give up the grip it had on the fork. He struggled with it, glancing around to see if anyone noticed. Ash was looking at him, expressionless.

"So," he asked, diverting Ash from his war with the lettuce. "How is Tahoe this time of year?"

Ash raised his eyebrows, which had grown together over his nose; it looked like his forehead was crossed by a dark symbol for mountains. "Tahoe? I don't know. We. . . ."

"We always enjoy going up to the lake," Birch interjected.

"Why, yes, we do," he said. "I guess Tahoe is fine?" he said to Birch.

"That's what you always say."

"Ah," he said, lifting his wedge of lettuce and biting off the other end thoughtfully.

Corona returned to place in front of them tall frosted glasses filled with liquids swirling orange and red and blue. A paper umbrella the size of a parachute stuck up from a slice of lime.

"Enjoy," Ash said. He raised his glass to the light and observed the colors swirling slowly like a Lava Lamp.

"Ash made it up," Birch said.

"Call it Diversity on the Rocks," Ash said. "Hah hah. It is on the rocks, too, eh?"

Birch frowned, nodded toward him.

"Oh," Ash said quickly, recovering his skeet shooting composure after his outburst of giddy humor. "So, Georgie boy, what say you about our other little hideaway down at Pajaro Dunes?"

Using his knife like a logger's pike, he held his wedge in place and pulled his fork loose, surreptitiously licking the salad dressing from his fingers while pretending to cough politely. "Great. I love the ocean."

"Looks like you got a little dark," Birch commented. "You should be careful."

"Skin cancer, you know," Ash added. "And you don't want to look like . . . you know."

Indeed he did know. He imagined George down at Pajaro Dunes, wearing loose-fitting Hawaiian shirts as he and Tara strolled peacefully along the beachfront of the condominium. The shirts looked good on George.

An adolescent girl of about fifteen came into the solarium wearing a cotton T-shirt too short for her long body and panties that looked tie-dyed by a crackhead.

He looked down, concentrating on his lettuce.

Ash paid her scant attention. He seemed to think the way she was dressed was all very normal. "So you decided to join us?" he said.

Birch, observing the embarrassment on his face over the sheer colorless all-color of all that exposed skin, tried to put him at ease by asking, "What do you think, George? You like them?"

Them?

"An artist friend of ours made them special. Show George, Shining Oak," she ordered her daughter. Shining Oak obediently exposed her midriff by slowly lifting the hem of her T-shirt up to the white crescent below her breasts and began turning around like lamb in a Lebanese sandwich shop.

"So?" Birch asked.

"Nuh . . . nice," he stammered. A shoal of lettuce broke loose from the iceberg and splashed in his lap. Neither Ash nor Birch seemed to see it happen. They were both admiring their daughter's panties, Ash with a cool possession, Birch with a truly aesthetic appreciation. He managed to sneak the fallen lettuce back onto his plate before Birch could turn and say, "It's so hard to find good art these days, don't you think? As meaningful. As moving. Yes? Like Schnabel. I just love Schnabel."

With his mouth full of lettuce, Thousand Island oozing from the corner of his mouth, the stain in his crotch darkening unseen below the glimmery surface of the table, all he could do was nod.

The meal ended abruptly when Ash declared, "Well, back to the salt mines." He rose and strode back into his den to watch a polo match.

Shining Oak followed Pal to the kitchen, where he surprised Corona and Esperanza (who was older than he could ever imagine) by helping to clear the table, and then outside where she offered to give him a ride home.

"I know a place we could stop on the way," she said as seductively as an adolescent girl in a T-shirt and swirling underpants could, pressing the tips of her breasts against his arm. "You can see what's in my art."

"Thanks," he said, as gently as he could. "But I'm not all that into art."

He walked down the long drive and out through the brick pillars. He was half a mile down the steep road when a jab in his thigh made him reach into his pocket to see what was there and he realized that he still had Tara's car keys. He turned and looked up the hill.

"Fuck it," he said.

For one of the first times in his life he did something mean on purpose. He tossed the chain of keys into the brush beside the road. They could get a locksmith.

"Or they'll just buy a new car," he said.

Taking a deep breath, feeling as though his lungs were full of dates, he kept on walking.

Back down in the flatland where he belonged, when he stuck out his thumb and someone stopped to offer him a ride and asked, "Where to?" he replied, "The nearest train tracks."

5.

Pal sees himself standing there in the intermittent rain watching Tara Dunnahowe descend the steep asphalt path from the once-modern squares of redwood, concrete, and tinted glass that make up the modular wings of a junior college. She's with Joe Manifest. She's dressed expensively, if not entirely tastefully, in a skirt of elasticized cotton suede, a white silk blouse the ruffled lapels of which part just above where a bra would fasten if she were wearing one, and a pale yellow linen jacket, despite the fact that even though it's raining intermittently, it's warm. Her shoes are low, comfortable heels and she carries them in her hand, dangling from her index and middle fingers in a joyful unconcern for the endurance of her patterned stockings and a healthful oblivion to her feet becoming soaked. The rain is warm. But even if it were not, from the bouncing way she descends the path laughing appropriately and periodically at whatever Joe might be saying to her, it's obvious to the casual observer that she would still go without shoes. She's become completely natural. And it's this new natural way she has of enjoying whatever the weatherman serves up that attracts people to her, makes people think that they could be happy just being her pal.

At the bottom of the path, she and Joe pause between the waist-high posts positioned to prevent anything wider than a bicycle from ascending the hill. She asks, "See you when you get back?" or something like that.

"It'll be pretty late on Wednesday. You sure you don't want me just to sleep at home?"

"I don't care what time it is. You come by," she says.

He grins with expectation and replies, "About two-ish?" He considers it a sin to be late, so he never says "two" but adds an "ish" to all his ETAs.

She laughs. They hug each other. She stretches up on tippy-toes to offer him her lips. Her skirt draws tight around her thighs as she stretches.

Pal is embarrassed. He turns away. He glances back toward Tara, who has parted from Joe and is heading his way, unaware of his observing her. Old Paint's hinges groan with the complaint of metal that has lost the ease of its bend and swing to age. She looks up at the noise and pauses, her car keys dangling from her fingers.

He climbs quickly in, settling behind the wheel, and busies himself with the ignition. These days Old Paint takes some goosing to get going. He pumps the accelerator pedal once, twice. He has a vision of the rubber diaphragm of the accelerator pump flexing and shooting gas into the barrel as the choke flange closes to reduce the air and concentrate the fuel for ignition. He can actually see the gas squirt in his imagination. The spark plugs spark. Paint coughs, the engine turns over a couple of times, and stops. He pumps the accelerator twice again, turns the key again, and the cylinders struggle to life. Puffs of blue, wet smoke bounce off the pavement and then rise like signals as he stirs the gearshift lever in search of Reverse.

Pal shakes his head. "I could give you history," he says. "Maybe not the history you want, but. . . ." He realizes he is going on and on. He laughs. When he looks up, she has disappeared, dissolved like a nighttime dream.

CHAPTER SEVENTEEN

I.

A shaft of sunlight makes the dirt beyond the porch of his cabin look paved with yellow. He watches the brown squirrel he calls Stuart gambol about the base of a tree. Every now and then, Stuart the squirrel stops to shake his tail at Pal and chatter before he spirals up around the trunk of a redwood tree.

"La Vent's conversion was hardly the only thing," he says to Stuart. Pal kind of half laughs, like someone who is nervous or shy will do when he states the obvious or the potentially offensive. Stuart stops, raises up on his hindquarters, and frets an edible nut with his front paws.

"In fact," Pal says with a voice that sounds impoverished enough to be bitter, "La Vent's conversion hardly mattered at all. The other things. His trying to be someone he was not. Gradually giving himself away until there was so little left to sustain him and he died. They made it pretty hard."

"What other things?" Amanda asks, the screen door banging behind her. Pal turns to look at her. She has gained some weight. Not in a flabby way. But she is fuller, recently. Already in so short a time her cheeks are rounder and redder. When they take walks or hikes along the beach or into the woods, her toes splay, hardly noticeably, as though she's about to snuggle up to a tree or wrap her knees around a pole.

"Are you using different makeup?" Pal asks her.

"No," she says. "Why?"

2.

Fish Heaven, in Santa Cruz, is nearly empty except for a couple of old farts grizzled by fishing from the end of the Bridge Street pier where the wind grew cold and the sunshine was always hot. They stare at Pal when he enters, their black eyes like Chinese checkers peering out above the silver stipple of their faces, the warning whiteness that measures out the number of their years. Their olive green, neoprene boots are stained by fish guts and bleached by the constant salt spray.

He chooses a table by the windows. The spring day has turned mean and full of bluster, and where the shadowed sea grips the cloudy sky, the horizon is a nasty, gunmetal blue. Pal rubs his hands together, cups them, and blows breath into them to warm them. A bag lady leans into a garbage can and he almost can feel the cold edge of wind as her Persian cap whips at her cheeks. He feels sorry for her. He knew a girl just like this, once, a crazed girl who wore a cap like that even in summer and made him read chapters from a mystery novel she was writing, titled *The Orange Juice Murders*. So it isn't the weather alone that makes him feel for her. Lately, his imagination is getting much stronger. And he can imagine how hard it is to go digging through garbage cans one nickel at a time, as well as the shame she must feel when supermarket clerks look at her like she is a pain in the ass who does nothing but hurt business. And he can also imagine how a little Mad Dog 20/20 would go a long ways toward the illusion of heat on a day like today.

Pal is excited. He feels as though he is waiting for her. Amanda. His own Amanda. For several weeks now the one-inch Post-it with her name on it has been stuck to his living room window. And now the larger three-by-five note demanded by all the syllables in Buenhuevo has taken its rightful place beside it, having been there for five days.

A fat white seagull drifts in on the wind and perches on the round top of the piling outside the window. It cocks its head and peers at him with beady seagull eyes and then lazily lifts its black wings and flaps them. It raises itself as though to leave, coasting a moment on the lift of the wind. Then, deciding that it is too much effort, it settles back onto the piling and peers at Pal some more. In the air again, it shrieks, and its cry momentarily drowns out the arping of the sea lions that live on the crossbraces underneath the pier. The fewer the tourists, the louder the lions, and today, being cold, the only scraps falling among the pilings are the guts kicked off the pier by the men fishing from its railings. The pair of them are in Fish Heaven eating.

"How's it going today?"

Pal turns away from the seagull to the waitress. She wears a lacy spandex top through which he can see the tan of her skin. Her nipples are hard and dark beneath the bright white fabric. Above the aureole of her left breast is a black plastic name tag with "Tammi" embossed on it in white.

"Not bad."

"I'm Tammi," she says. "I'll be your waitress today. Can I get you something to start?"

Made shy by the boldness of her nipples, Pal looks down at the table. "A bowl of paella, please," he says. "And a bottle of your Anchor Steam ale."

"Okey dokey," she says, tossing her shoulders back and turning.

Pal watches her walk the length of the curved cafe counter to the aluminum order wheel hanging in the kitchen's window. She wears short black shorts with cuffs. If it's figure you want, she has it. He sees that the fishermen agree. He laughs. There was a time when, like them, he would've felt desire for her. But today, other than to note the hard work or good fortune that gave her a figure she could clothe like that, he feels nothing at all   no desire, certainly, not even simple lust. In a way, it makes him sad.

He folds a Post-it back and begins writing on a second one underneath when he feels her at his shoulder. She stands there, holding a bottle of ale in her two hands, his glass held to one hand by the pressure from one long middle finger. "Your beer," she says.

"Thanks."

"You a writer?"

"No," he says. He smiles up at her as generously as he can, aware that in Santa Cruz there are a ton of writers. The place was like a lodestone to writers. Especially poets. He is no poet, nor would he want to be.

"Whatcha doing then?"

He considers the possibilities of what he might say. "Nothing much," he replies.

Outside the seagull rises and shrieks. The sky darkens with rain clouds shifting around Lighthouse Point, south.

She stands with her lips pursed. Gently pursed, not in anger, but in hurt.

"Just dreaming," Pal says. He halfway expects her to laugh until he remembers how no one laughs anymore, especially not in Santa Cruz where nothing is funny and everything is serious and if you laugh, people think you either mad or cruel.

The order-up bell rang. "Excuse me," she says. "Your paella."

Pal watches her as she crosses the cafe to the window in which sits his bowl of paella. She is nice. Pleasant. Pretty. Or cute, anyway. Attractive. A failure waiting to happen. She might think she likes him as long as he seems strange or different. Once she realizes that he doesn't change much and he isn't all that much fun, off she'll go with some ridge-bellied Roundhead in a baggy swimsuit. Or she'll begin to suspect that the way they envision the world is different and as slight as that difference might be, he'll still be smiling when she begins to wear a frown.

"The girl with her napping mat," he explains to the seagull who is still out there, perched like the king of protected species.

Somewhere in his carton of fallen Post-its is the record of his first failure at love. It had been with a little girl with blond hair in Gilroy. A sweet white girl, with a round face and big eyes that he colored blue. He called her Marilyn. The truth of her was Marilyn, though her name might have been something else equally "Marilyn." She'd been the only child in kindergarten who had been at all nice to him, for which he had been grateful. The rest of the children of Gilroy had run from him, calling names at him over their shoulders. From the middle-class offspring of Gilroy, the names only made him feel distant and where he did nothing to defend himself, for Marilyn he would have done anything, protected her, defended her against bullies, given up his lunch of tortillas and cheese if she forgot hers. But then she started following him and he couldn't handle it. No longer just nice to him, she brought her chair over next to his when the children circled to sing or hear a story. At nap time she dragged her rush mat over to his so she could lie close to him. She handed him notes that said she liked him and all he could think was that something was terribly wrong with any cute little blond-headed girl who liked him. Why would she? Why should she? He was not likable.

All these years, and nothing has changed, whether she is called Tammi or Marilyn.

"Man, are you ever busy with those," the waitress says, setting his bowl of paella on the table in front of him.

Pal shrugs. The seagull shrieks. The sea lions arp five times. He looks up at her and smiles. Her name badge is gone.

"Well," she says after standing there a moment, "enjoy your paella." She sounds hurt.

He feels bad. He doesn't want to hurt anyone. And it is impolite not to say something to her. So what if she thinks he is odd? Everyone else does. He is used to that. But she is not used to men not being attracted to her.

"Dreaming is an imaginative act. But it's very real," he says. "Like telling stories. The Navajo believe that by articulating something, putting it into words, you actually make it exist. You bring it into being. Dreaming's like that. It makes things exist by imagining them with power. It makes them exist by imagining a world in which they mean a lot."

She frowns. "I have bad dreams," she says.

Pal sighs. "Sorry," he says.

"It's okay. It's not your fault."

He tries to smile at her, but he knows his smile looks more like a grimace.

"I always dream that I'm standing in front of a mirror? And that I'm not there. But I am. But what I am is what someone else sees? Like the mirror is looking over my shoulder in the mirror I'm looking at? It's scary."

"Sounds like it," Pal says.

One of the fishermen holds up a hand to get her attention. The hand is so bent with arthritis that it looks like one of the cypress trees that line the coast, arboreal sprinters whose feet had screeched to a stop at the cliff edge, their bodies and branches flailing.

"Excuse me," Marilyn says.

"Sure." He turns to his paella, shifting his pad of Post-its off beside the salt shaker and Tabasco sauce against the window. He glances out at the seagull, smiles, nods and winks. As though it has been shot, with a shriek the seagull drops down below the pier and out of sight.

"Everything all right?" she asks, coming back after finishing with the fishermen.

"Fine," he says. "Thanks."

She touches him lightly on the shoulder. "I get off at four," she says.

He looks up. She is holding a rush mat in her hands the same way she'd held his bottle of beer.

"Oh," he says. "I'm sorry. I'm waiting for someone."

"But you're eating without her."

"Well," he says. "Yes. She won't be hungry. If she is, we'll get her something." He does not feel like trying to explain to her that his waiting is of a different order than the kind you do while waiting for a bus or a train. That he is waiting for Amanda Buenhuevo. But that he does not necessarily expect her today or tomorrow or even next week. He is waiting by preparing, going through his Post-its, making up new ones, sticking them on his living room window to limit the view out of it, to focus his vision as much as to see which ones stuck.

"I see," Marilyn says, icily. "Here's your check. If you won't be needing anything else."

"Thank you," he says, as she spins on her heels and hurries away. There's a nice guy somewhere just for you, he thinks. Just wait.

He finishes his paella, takes a last sip of his beer, and leaves a generous tip behind by way of apology to Marilyn, as well as to Tammi.

3.

She was picking things up. It was their last night together and tomorrow, she would drive him back to what he called "civilization," but which her father had insisted she learn to call Aztlán when she was growing up in the Salinas Valley. But Joe only laughed at "Aztlán." It wasn't civilized.

It'd been her idea to invite him to the A-frame cabin she'd rented along the shores of Lake Tahoe, an idea she didn't regret, exactly, but an idea that now after it was almost over she would have gladly done without. He was a nice man, so nice that at moments he almost didn't seem quite real. And at first, despite his calling her "Andy," which she hated, she had liked him a lot. She wouldn't have minded "Mandy." But "Andy"? Still, he was smart and serious. Too serious. For example, when he mused over their having met so fortuitously when his brake line began to leak on his way to that convention, he got all tangled up in statistical probabilities. He was all about time and distance and fate. He'd sat on a barstool while she cooked him dinner and posed problems to her, problems such as if you have two trains that leave San Francisco and New York at two-ish in the afternoon and one is traveling at fifty miles per hour and the other at sixty-two, where would they meet?

Her answer, much to his dismay, was quick. "Chicago," she said.

"Chicago," he said. "How do you come up with that?"

"Easy," she replied. "No one with the special soul of someone who likes to ride trains would want either train to stop before it reached

Chicago, now, would she? *Dios mio*," she added, playfully, "do you have any idea what lies between New York and Chicago? And on the other end, what with the Rockies to climb and the momentum down the backside of the mountains, that train couldn't stop in time for Denver, now, could it?"

He shot her a look over the rim of his glass of port. Each night without fail he had one glass of port after dinner, which he insisted on eating at five-thirty-ish every afternoon (or "evening" according to him). His look seemed to say, "Blah, blah, blah." It was a look in which she could foresee him calling her, very late and very drunk, to give her bad news. Bad news always seemed to visit her in the wee hours of the morning, as when her little brother and her sister, along with her parents, had gone down in a plane blown up by terrorists over Lockerbie, Scotland. When someone she liked had to gear himself up to tell her what was on his mind, it had to be bad news. Always. If he had to finish off a whole bottle of port to achieve his determination, it was a safe bet that he'd be telling her that he was leaving her, going away to swim in other waters. When he called her from Morro Bay, on the central coast, his voice grown strange with drink and spoke her name, she could hear his head loll like a jackal weakened by hunger. She didn't even have to ask, "What is it?"

Nor would she regret it. It seemed as though everything she did with him was framed by the A-B-C-D of his thinking. If he wanted to get to E, he always had to go back and begin at A all over again, retracing the steps and then tacking on E with a surgical precision, sort of like tacking on an arm to an amputee. Although had A through D been more interesting, if he could have told it with a little more imagination, she would not have minded. It wasn't the repetition of the what as much as it was how it was repeated. He did it so methodically, between dinner and his port, between his port and the way he hung up his boxer shorts on clip-hangers in the closet even when they were dirty, a ceremony not unlike the one he performed every morning when he tacked up his high school wrestling trunks—he had been a champion flyweight—on the wall of his office, and then took them down in the evening, before he went home to a five-thirty-ish dinner, a prelude to the seven o'clock port. Indeed, to her it seemed as though these few days with him were an interior movement, an adagio trapped inside a sonata, the slow distinct movement leading dreamlike in a sort of emotional dance to a quick and even different finish. It was not an enjoyable dream and by this time the second allegro had ended, the musicians had bowed, and she could hear the technicians sneaking out onto the stage in the dimming lights to collect the music from the stands, as he turned up the volume on a cable news report about famine.

Without thinking, she began stroking his neck, perhaps (I can't be sure from where I am, outside in the spruce tree) wishing it would be otherwise. She gave him a kiss behind the ear.

"Stop it," he said. He jerked away from her, almost spilling his port. "I want to see this."

She stopped. She felt rise in her that confused sort of angry feeling most people call feeling sorry for themselves. She didn't feel sorry for herself, though. After all, she not only came with him to her cabin, she was the one who had the big idea. What annoyed her most was the news report. She hated television, and famine was like one of the nine plots of television, one which got repeated as soon as the station's producer thought he could get away with it. It might be another region or another country, perhaps, but unless the race of the starving kids altered, it would use many of the outtakes from the last report, even some of the same clips or clips that looked the same, starring the same sad lethargic children. Even the response to the report would resemble the last: Everyone would feel bad until tomorrow night.

When the report ended, she reached for the remote and turned off the TV and tried again. He shrugged her hand away once again.

"I've got some work to do," he said. Seeing the dark look on her face, he added, "Don't be upset. Maybe later."

Later, when she got up to go to the bathroom before shutting out the light over the bed she poked her head into the living room of the

A-frame and said, "What do you say on the way home tomorrow we stop and get some. . . ."

"I don't like to stop," he said.

4.

Reluctantly, Pal drove across the boundaries separating their lives to Tara's apartment to comfort and console her. He prepared himself for the way she would say when she answered the door to find her old Pal, and not some unseasonal patch of wind, "Oh. It's you."

"Yep." He felt that he deserved the cold touch of her voice. He had hesitated, after all, and come to provide the comfort she needed a little unwillingly. He'd taken a long time to decide whether or not to bother, another long time to get out of bed and get dressed and get to her home, and an even longer time pacing back and forth beneath the elm tree outside her window, waiting for the lights to go off in her apartment, wondering if he really and truly wanted to knock on her door and subject himself to the old desire that would come from her disguised gratitude.

"Do you know what time it is?" she asked. She took a second look at the helpful, compassionate grin on his face and the way it flickered like a neon light at the mention of time. "No," she said. "I suppose you wouldn't. What do you want?"

"I came to see how you were," he said. "How you really were, and not just the way I thought you were when you last let me get close enough to see the face you had put on for the day."

A flicker of something like doubt crossed her face. Her eyes moved. It was as though she had just seen a shadow disappear behind a barn. Yet she was unsure of what she'd seen or even that she'd seen it, and she wondered what it promised.

"You wanted me to come, didn't you?"

She frowned.

"Can I come in?" he asked cheerfully.

Tara glanced backward over her shoulder into the room he could just see through the chain-restricted crack in the door as if it were crowded and she was checking to see if there was enough space to admit another body. She shrugged, closed the door and slid the chain off, and let it fall open.

"You want some coffee?" She yawned, padding backwards toward the kitchen.

"You've learned how to cook."

"I took lessons from Esperanza," she said.

"Could I ask for tea? If you have it."

"Lapsang?"

"Whatever. Lapsang is fine."

He sat on a new futon sofa patterned with large, white, lily-sized flowers and examined the room, seeking signs of the changes that had occurred in Tara's life since Pajaro. Not much seemed to have changed. Outside of the futon, which was new, there was only a birdcage hanging from a brass stand in the corner. The rubber plant—which stood sentinel to the entry door—had grown, it seemed, and its broad, flat leaves looked shiny and rubbery as though it was glad he was back.

He heard Tara talking to herself in the kitchen, but her voice was too low to make out her words.

"What?" he called out.

There was some rustling and clinking in the kitchen and she emerged animatedly, carrying two steaming mugs.

"You can use that bowl for your tea bag," she said, setting a mug before him.

"Were you talking to me?" he asked.

"Huh? No."

"I thought you said something. In the kitchen."

"I must have been talking to myself," she said. "I do that, these days."

"You should be careful," he said. "Very, very careful. You never know what can happen. La Vent, my father, talked to himself."

She seemed to want to ignore him. She sipped from her mug, the smell of chocolate sifting across to him. She was as nervous as he was, perhaps feeling some of the same things he was feeling.

"So," she said. "It's been a long time."

Instead of pointing out that the reason it had been long was largely her doing, or History's doing anyway, he asked, "Has it?"

She nodded. She looked worried.

"Something worrying you?" he asked. "Anything on your mind you need to tell me?"

She shrugged, tilting her head, a tendon in her neck tightening visibly, momentarily.

"Anything new and exciting in your life?"

"Nothing much," she said. Then she added, "Except maybe that I'm pregnant."

"Ah," he said. He couldn't help smiling. Without stopping to think, he said, "Twins, I'll bet."

"I don't know," she said. "I haven't been to a doctor, yet."

Outside, downstairs, he heard a car pull up and a car door slam. Tara shifted nervously in her seat as though she wanted to go to the window and see who it was. She was pale.

"Why did you ask if it was twins?" she asked.

"Just guessing," he replied. "Though I know a lot more about you than you think."

Footsteps clomped up the stairs inside the building, the loud and inconsiderate homecoming of a late-night drinker. The footsteps paused outside, a key rattled in the lock as though the drunk was struggling to try to get the lock to work, and lo! who should burst into the room panting like a dog but Joe Manifest, himself.

He looked to Tara, raising his eyebrows. She looked frightened, at first, and then—putting the best face on it—acted as though she was glad to see him.

"Joe!" she cried, sloshing her chocolate as she plunked the mug down on an end table and ran to give him a welcoming hug.

Pal imagined that it looked pretty funny to old Joe to find the loved one he took away from another man sitting comfortably at three in the morning, having tea and chocolate with that very man.

"Joe. Joe, Joe, Joe. Thank God," she whispered, her head bent uncomfortably onto his shoulder. He was shorter than she by a head, something he'd never noticed, really, before. "He just barged in. I thought it was you and. . . ."

"Listen, buddy," Mr. History said, stepping up close into his face.

He rose politely to greet him, to do his share to let him know there was nothing going on here before he so rudely arrived.

"I don't know what you think you're doing. . . ."

"Pal," he said. "Palimony. Don't ask," he added in a jovial fashion, meaning that it wasn't the time or the place to go into beginnings.

"I don't care what you want to be," he said. "I just want you out of here."

"Hey, friend, she wanted me to come. You think I like to wake up in the middle of the night and drive all the way over here?"

He paused briefly to realize that he was telling the truth, a truth different from the last time.

"Think again. You may know names and dates, but you don't know shit-all else." Joe's arrogant appropriation of Tara's rights made him angry, otherwise he would not have sworn like that.

"That true?" he demanded of Tara, expecting her to deny it instantly.

She hesitated, looking from him to Pal and back.

"Go on, tell him," Pal said. She knew it was true. Of course, Pal knew she couldn't say she knew it was true, but she didn't expect him to lie, did she?

Tara wavered, again looking from one to the other, comparing the looks on their faces. History's face was open, split like a potato, and his eyes were wide with anger. If it was true, there was hell to pay and he was already adding up the ticket.

"Well?"

She obviously needed help and—can you believe it?—just like that she got it. From him, of all people. He didn't know he was helping. I mean, he didn't figure this out with one of his nostalgias or romantic interpretations of destiny. No, this was a guess, a lucky guess.

"Did you," he began, and then paused for emphasis, the way the sergeant-at-arms pauses as he asks you to swear on the Bible—"Do you [pause] swear [binary pause: they always pause extra with swearing, as though a portion of everything they swear is a baldfaced lie] to tell the whole truth and nothing but the truth [pause] so help you [trinitarian pause] God?"

"Did you te-le-phone him and ask him to come over?"

Bingo.

"No," she said. "No, I did not telephone him," she said. She gave Pal a worried look, afraid that he'd helpfully inquire about what it was she had been thinking roughly an hour or two before he'd arrived and if, indeed, she had not wished out loud for a pal she could talk to.

Pal did not inquire. He was resigned with the same silent resignation the Nez Perce had felt when Lewis and Clark demanded the return of their ponies. The Nez Perce had always known that the ponies were a source of conflict; the Dreamers among them had never doubted but that the ponies would be given back to the indiangivers from east of the Bitterroot Mountains. He knew, as much as they, that when push came to shove, when the truth was a source for conflict, Tara would not admit to her Joe that a telephone was incidental.

Joe was both relieved and vindicated. He swaggered like a quail that believes it has outwitted the dogs. "Listen, buddy," he said, turning again on him.

"Pal," he said.

"Listen, pal, if you don't leave right now and never come back I'm calling the police and I'll let them handle it with you. And this time, we won't refuse to press charges. Not this time. Uh-uh. It won't be like it was before, I promise you."

Promises. He'd promised this, before. Pal looked at him as if to ask, You come and steal my girlfriend, even take her while she's still mine, and then when I don't just disappear, poof! like I'm dead or something, you threaten to call in the cavalry to make me? He was tempted to tell him the truth. But then he would've done an injury to Tara and, well, he wasn't willing to do that, given the nice time they'd been having before he barged in like this.

Joe went to the door and held it open expectantly, hopefully, too, as though he worried he might have to throw him out.

"I'm going," Pal said. He—they, really, since their anger made them a They, a union of the fooling and the fooled—sighed. As he passed out the door, when Little Joe was least expecting it, Pal reached down and tapped him once on the heart. "See you in Tahoe," he said. "Oh. And you might just wonder who gave her those babies."

He looked bitten.

Pal only caught a glimpse of Tara's face before History slammed the door with all the authority he could muster. But it looked happy, ready to exude, much the way it did on the night he had given her a gift-wrapped bag of Corn Nuts.

CHAPTER EIGHTEEN

I.

"You okay?" Amanda asks him.

"Huh?" he says, startled from his dreaming. "Yeah. Sure. Why?"

"You sounded like you were gasping. Like maybe you were sick. As though you were going to throw up or you were having an asthma attack or something."

It's night, late, dark. I can barely see through the window, steamed as it is by the heat emitted in waves by the wood stove in the bedroom, and restricted by the Post-it notes on the window. Lately, he's begun filling Post-its with a speed that could have made his grade school teachers sing his praises. He's even gone out and purchased new, larger pads of them and, combined with the extra-fine pens he's begun to use, he can really crowd those small yellow slips of paper with letters and words.

He was awakened by a weight curled and sleeping on his chest like a large question mark, brought indoors by another image: Tara Dunna-howe standing beside the bed in brown pantyhose, white silk half-slip, and sea blue bra, her stomach taut with the effort of pulling her wrist free from his grip as he lay indolently among the rumpled bedclothes. She was telling him gently, even playfully, but with all the seriousness of her desires to succeed, to come on and let go of her. She did not want to be late. In this case, for a date.

Trying hard not to disturb Amanda, he had slipped out of bed and come into the front room to sit in the ratty armchair culled for his cabin from the streets of Santa Cruz. He stared out the reflective window into the darkness of the woods beyond. The window was like a movie screen for him on which the images play themselves out: He watches Tara finish dressing for school in a skirt with patterned tights. She changes the angora sweater that reveals the utter size of her breasts for a silk blouse that whispers their largesse in the swing and swoosh of the fabric.

Tara dressed, he remembers, with the same equal care as she undressed for lounging around her apartment. But dressed or undressed, Pal can think only of the petals of her skin and the richness of her voice, the seriousness with which she took the world. It was a seriousness that had a lot to do with the size of her breasts. She could, after all, never get away from them. They made her feel like a cyclops with one eye in the middle of her forehead. It was what most women noticed about her first, and quite often what most men wanted to talk about if they dared. He, he remembers, had tried to bury his anxiety between them.

From where I am, the image Pal remembers seems like an imperfect image, suffused with humor and something like resignation, the faint perfume-memory lingering as he watches her finish dressing. An imperfect image for a perfect longing. It was the imperfection that made him feel as though he had done all of it before.

"Sorry," Pal says. "I couldn't sleep."

"You could have turned on the light."

"I didn't want to bother you," he says.

"You wouldn't bother me," Amanda replies. "I sleep better with you in there than out here."

"Sorry. I just needed to think."

Amanda shrugs. She smiles and nods as though she understands or, if she does not, then she's at least willing to accept. Pushing a strand of hair away from her eyes, she goes to the bookshelf in the corner and scans the titles, looking for one she hasn't read or one she might be willing to read again. She consumes books of all kinds—mysteries, novels,

poems, popular histories, even fix-it books from Time-Life. If you were
to bind together the backs of cereal cartons, she'd probably lie in bed
and read it.

Selecting a book on refinishing furniture, she stretches, reaching up
and slipping it off the shelf, and tucks it under her arm. "Be long?" she
asks.

"Nah," Pal says. The images are discrete, and this one of Tara
dressing to pull away from him has just about played itself out. "Long
enough to keep the tent up," he says.

Mandy gives him a slightly confused or wondering look. "Miss
you," she says.

She pauses in the doorway with her back to him, listening to the silence as though it is speech.

"There something else?" he says, breaking the silence. He wouldn't
mind if she stayed. He wouldn't mind at all if she did not leave him
alone with the image of Tara. She's the only one he doesn't mind, and
so when he asks if there's something else, he really is willing to hear it.

"Yes. Well, no. I'll tell you later." Mandy adds softly, "Come back to
bed as soon as you can?"

"In a moment," he promises. She seems to recognize that means that
the show must continue for some time—a minute, an hour, or even all
night, until all the images, all the Post-its, are put in an order that will allow Amanda to emerge from the bedroom and ask, "Are you all right?"

2.

This time I got there early, two days early, to be exact, although two
hours would have been sufficient. I brought along Parker. New as he
was, his training in *weyekin* successes and failures and the consequent
wisdom that comes from failure was already way beyond that of a dork-
head like Chicken Licken—of whom I have begun to tire, if for no
other reason than that the sky has never fallen and thus, since the expectation of future comes out of the experience of the past, we can reasonably expect that it never will. Licken has begun to sound not a little like

those people who predict the end of mother earth. Mother earth will always be there. Even they cannot destroy the earth, but only the people and animal and vegetable life upon it, leaving the planet uninhabited except by arachnids and insects. He often seems to secretly desire the sky to fall because his Chicken's ego needs to be proven right. So Parker and I were there by the roadside when Old Paint gave up the ghost and Palimony Blue began to dance and turn in the dusty mountain light.

It was a wondering Amanda who pulled onto the road's shoulder and waited. This time, she was without a boyfriend. He stumbled up to the passenger window. He was in such a hurried state of anticipation that I was surprised he didn't trip over his left feet and fall on his face in the dirt. He bent over, panting, and gazed into the car.

"Need a lift?" she asked.

The dizziness, the desire to shout, the need to dance—all dissolved. The old fantasy of want for Tara Dunnahowe dissolved, replaced by a new, more real desire. He felt whole in a way he'd never felt before.

That afternoon, Amanda had dark brown hair, drawn back and loosely clipped in back with a rhinestone barrette. She was dressed in a blue cotton skirt and a dark red T-shirt with Greek letters stenciled across her breasts. Her two-dollar sunglasses prevented his seeing the soul of her eyes but not the way of her smile, quick, soft, and warm. She was as happy to find him as he was her.

"Fancy meeting you here," he said. He settled into the passenger's seat, looking away out of shyness from the smile he could feel like a summer's dew on his cheek.

"Took you long enough," she said. She glanced over her left shoulder, pulling back onto the highway.

"Yeah?"

"Yeah. I was beginning to think the whole thing was gonna be about what's-her-name."

"Whozits?"

"Whozits. Whatsits. You know who I mean. Them. Brandy. The stuffy Miss Dunnahowe. The sex without love and love without sex crowd. Hell, the love without love crowd." She laughed.

She glanced in the rearview mirror at the carcass of Old Paint tipping his head as though the hillside were a pillow and he was going to lay down. "You want to stop and call a tow truck?" she asked, gently.

"No thanks. Maybe I'll call one when I get home."

It was a lie. She knew it as well as Pal. He should have felt stupid for saying it. Old Paint was traveling on. Dead. Long before he had slipped on the slick of the fantasies of paying the Plaid family back for making him invisible, he had danced. The dancing had felt good, the dance of dreaming, but also the dance of death. Even now he could hear the bold whispers of Magnesia Jonson, along with the brothers Bena and Beni Dryl, calling to their buddies as they slipped down the hillside shale with wrenches, knives, and snips to strip the hide and hair from Paint before leaving his carcass to be picked over and burned by amateurs. All he could hope was that they would be quick about it. Otherwise, though he felt a deep sadness at the loss of Old Paint, it fit into the cycle of things. Parts to parts. Rust to rust.

"Whatever," she said. "Suit yourself."

He stole a glance at her. Reading the letters stenciled on her shirt, he blurted, "What's 'A-B-Pi'? If you don't mind my asking," he added timidly.

"You didn't dream that I'd be wearing a billboard, did you?" she laughed. "At least it's different, huh?"

"Guess not."

"It's Alpha-Beta-Pi. Store pie. As common as Mrs. Smith's or Sara Lee's." She laughed again at the look on his face.

Like other young men, he had dreamed of an Amanda as direct as this, only to wish, when the dream came true, for a little more indirection and a little less cause for embarrassment.

"What did you think?" she went on. "That I'd belong to some herd of girls who moo over guys with their baseball caps turned backwards? Even you wouldn't make that up." She paused, thinking a moment. "'Course it is true that there's Advil and Magnesia. Birch and Ash. Not to mention the likes of Mr. Patch. Chingito." She touched Pal lightly on the forearm. "Him, I like," she said.

"Me, too," he replied. He shrugged. "Of course he isn't really mine, if you know what I mean. More mother Mary's. A gift from her."

"How's your mom doing?"

"Good," he said.

"Your dad?"

"In Iran by now, I guess."

"He almost kept the bitterness at bay."

"Yeah. Not quite, though. Sally helped, at first."

"Who's Sally?"

"Sally Pedon. Or Sister Niedman. She was given to changing names like you'd change underwear. She kept him company for a while. Kept him from being too lonely. He seemed happy, anyway. Maybe it was that he'd actually converted someone to his way of preaching. I don't know."

"So what happened?"

He sighed. "Someone named Niedman can't stick around forever. She was too needy for La Vent to make her content for very long and then, well, I guess he felt even lonelier after she left than before she moved in. Loneliness can kill you. It killed him, anyway."

"Do tell," she said. She gave him one of those expressionless glances like mother Mary will do when she thinks things that have not yet had a context imagined for them. Things that if you say them sound stupid or prying or arrogant and know-it-all, even if they're true. Especially if they're true.

"Do tell what?" he asked.

"Nothing. It could've happened differently," she said.

"What?"

"The story. It could've come out different. When Sally left, you or your mother could've made it so he wouldn't even notice."

He doubted it. "I hadn't thought of that," he said. "Maybe. But I wasn't there."

He reimagined the glazed, distant look in La Vent's eyes the last time he'd seen him trying to cull the non-Canaanites from the stream of passersby like Joshua outside of Jericho. The way La Vent had not recognized his own son and sometimes, in a very real confusion, even had mistaken Pal for Buzz Packard's kid.

"You may be right," he said.

"So," Amanda asked as they began to overtake the Plaid family, passing them before they could circle back and point at Old Paint and say, "See that, Tartan? They don't even take care of the things they do have. They just go off and leave them beside the road for us to clean up."

Pal stared out the window at a family of four in a dark green Volvo. The children's faces pressed against the window glass, petals on a dark green bough. "What do you think they all eat?" he asked. "What keeps them going?"

Amanda laughed, a wide laugh that caused the Volvo's driver to glance over worriedly, as though Pal and his Amanda might be headed to the same beach he was. "Lettuce," she said. "Great big wedges of iceberg lettuce. Heads of lettuce that Chingito's cousins pee on in the fields and his *hermanas* and *tias* send out unwashed from marbled kitchens. Except," she added, grinning at Pal, "they call it roughage."

Amanda knew without asking where to turn as she drove him up into Boulder Creek to his cabin in the hills. She stopped in town for some food—cheese, crackers, chips and salsa, a tin of instant flavored coffee, and sunflower seeds. "They didn't have Corn Nuts," she explained as he looked through the bag in the pantry-sized room that served as his kitchen.

"Hot water?" he asked.

She opened the tin of coffee, measured out heaping teaspoons of cocoa-colored chemicals, and they shared an international moment.

"A mixblood moment," he laughed, toasting her with his coffee mug.

He went into the bedroom and added logs to the wood stove, the only source of heat in the house. When he returned to the main room, she was standing in front of the picture window, mirrored by the darkness that had fallen outside, reading the stick-up Post-it notes stuck around the window's edges.

"What're these?"

"Memories," he said, quickly adding, "a way of shutting out the view. Although at night when it gets cold, some of the Post-its refuse to stick. Others lose their sticking power and fall off. They do that, I put 'em in that box over there." He pointed at a carton on the floor beside the small bookshelf. A TV sat on the floor between the carton and the shelves. It looked to Amanda as though someone had grabbed the TV by its umbilical and beat it to death against a wall.

"Not many here," she commented, reading the Post-it stuck in the upper left-hand corner of the window. "Parker" was scribbled across it on an angle.

"I'm just beginning," he said, smiling.

She found a Post-it with the name "Amanda Buenhuevo" on it. She frowned. "Who's this?"

"You."

"Me?"

He nodded. "It's the one that stuck."

"Why didn't you just keep a journal?"

"I don't know. I guess whole pages were too daunting. You know, you sit down and try to fill the page. By the time you get to the end of it, what you began with doesn't seem to fit. Or it seems dumb or something. Everything goes left to right, top to bottom, and you get stuck thinking that X comes at the top right or Y shouldn't be in the middle but at the bottom right. That kind of thing. The notes feel freer. They're not, I guess, not in what they say, anyway, but in the way some of them stick and others get wet and the ink of their words runs together, and others go into the box. In the way they go together if you go back and reread them.

"Sorry," he said quickly, realizing that he was babbling. Most women hated the way he went on. For a second, the image of one of them kneeling with a dustpan to sweep up Post-its off the floor gave him a twinge of nostalgia; the memory of her sweeping a lot of them up and throwing them into the garbage without a second's thought made the nostalgia bitter, killed the romance as certainly as if it were a chicken whose neck you snapped.

"For what?" she asked. As a product of his dreaming, she knew what. But she also felt the strange need to fill the seconds of otherwise silent time as she crossed the room, took his cup with the dregs of his mixblood coffee out of his hands and set it on one of the bookshelves, and said, "I take it you won't mind if I stay?"

He shook his head, no.

"Come," she said, tugging at his belt. "We can eat later."

Later, after they'd been to bed and gotten up to eat all the chips and spicy-hot salsa, he lay in bed feeling the salsa go to work on his stomach, blowing him up so good with gas that it was getting hard to breathe. Despite his almost painful need to fart, he marveled over how, after all his failures and all this time, his Amanda felt real enough to hold.

"Promise," Amanda whispered before falling into a sleep as deep as angels, "you'll be here in the morning?"

"It's my house," he said.

"You know what I mean," she replied.

I think he did. She meant imaginatively there with her and not off chasing ghosts of the self-disappeared like La Vent or mirages of vanity like Tara Dunnahowe, or any of the other voices that had to be conflated into singularly generalized voices, in order to give them enough volume to be heard by strangers.

Amanda—his Amanda!—rolled over and went out like a light.

First things first, he thought, slipping out of bed. He came back into the main room where under my watchful eyes he spent the greater part of the night beneath the dim light of a hurricane lamp writing her onto more Post-its, creating a larger place for her and sticking her up on the window, sticking up so many Post-its that even were he to leave on vacation, some would still be there when he returned. Not that he was going on vacation.

Later, he would have to go back and find the beginnings and fill in around this place of hers, a process of dance and dream, of song and saying, which would have daunted even me, had I been able. But for that night, he and I were relieved. And he felt almost giddy with a hap-

piness that made the task seem not only light but possible. He crawled
back into the cold side of the bed and fell asleep in the hope that she
would never, ever pull away from him—even if she were late for the
rest of her life.

3.

A few days later, they showed up walking in what looked like a
commercial dream on the sands of coast above Santa Cruz.

My new *weyekin* apprentice, Parker, was already out there, all
dressed up in his coast guard uniform. "Oh, man," he was saying to the
eye of the whale on the beach, "lookit what you done come to."

His skin was black—don't ask, okay?—and the coast guard cutter,
white with red and blue piping, shining in the tingling light of the
morning, had anchored in as close as it could get to the continental shelf
of beach without endangering itself like the gray whale that had
beached itself in a way Parker, perhaps more than anyone, understood,
and which they were trying to rescue.

A small crowd had formed, growing slowly larger as people were
sucked toward the whale like conventioneers to peanuts at happy hour,
while he and his mates worked at their separate duties. The water cannon on the bow of the ship let loose an arc of seawater. The onlookers
tumbled back in unison and then edged forward as if collectively recognizing the surprising accuracy of the cannon's spray.

"What's wrong with it?" Amanda asked.

Parker tossed a bucket of seawater up into the whale's open, indifferent eyes to keep it from going blind.

There were any number of answers. Sickness from eating fish glow-
ing with strontium 90. An unwanted paint job by the *Exxon Valdez*.
Plain old age. Injury from Japanese gill nets or the high-powered rifles
of the Makah. Whatever, the whale had lost its instinctive sense of direction and purpose and instead of migrating on its true axis, north to south
and south to north, it had turned east against the flow of its history.

"Asian flu," Parker said, finally.

Amanda gave him a slanty sideways look. She wasn't certain whether he was joking or not.

Up close, the look in the whale's eyes seemed beyond the emotions of time and the feeling for the world. There was a chance that if they could get the whale out into deep water again, it might regain its navigational instincts and rejoin its family. Parker's mates, salt-sodden with spray, scrambled about trying to fasten a padded harness around its flukes so the commander could ease the ship backwards and pull the leviathan off the sand as soon as sufficient tide had returned to lift its hugeness so that it would not be injured irrevocably. Someone brought him a pressure canister filled with seawater. He pumped it up and, holding it in one hand like a fire extinguisher, aimed the plastic tip of the thin corded hose at the whale's bleary eyes and squeezed the trigger. The whale was definitely losing it, the sounds coming from its blow-hole sounding at first like an asthmatic's wheeze and finally like a sad sad sigh.

"Oh, man," he muttered. He paused long enough to examine his hands as though they were the cover of a book that hid the contents in the wrong context, the way that in school Pal once had glued a fake cover that declared *The Topic of Cancer* over *Tale of Two Cities* so that he could once again go talk with his old friend the principal. "Oh man, oh man."

His name tag said "Parker Quink." As he rounded the whale to wet the other and equally indifferent nether eye he brushed past Mandy and Pal as though he didn't know him. "Man, oh man, lookit what you gone come to," he said sadly. "Why for?"

His own voice surprised him, filled as it was with compassion. His voice seemed to contain a feeling of compassion that disguised normal feelings of anger, like a mother rocks her baby boy to comfort him, while asking as softly as she can why the hell he thought he could fly by jumping off the roof of the porch. Beneath the softness of the sound were prick points of furied feeling.

The crowd milled closer as though crowding a dying bonfire to roast the last of their marshmallows. A lad in a Mets cap stuck his foot out tentatively and then rendered leviathan a swift kick in the fluke.

Angrily, Parker asked Pal if he was going to help. "You going to get involved?" He held forth his hands. "Took a fuck of a lot for me to get here, you know," he sneered.

Amanda looked confused.

"You don't have to curse. What do you want me to do?" he asked.

"Aha! Yes!" Quink exclaimed, triumphantly throwing his fist into the air like Huey Newton and nodding his buffalo soldier's head up and down. "It's this skin," he whispered, grinning at Pal. "Maybe to start you can keep the folks back. Keep an eye on the kid in the Mets cap. He keeps trying to slice off a hunk of fluke with his Boy Scout knife."

Mandy, with an air of authority, moved the crowd back away from the whale.

Pal moved in close to the urchin in the Mets cap, ready to disarm him if he drew his knife again.

Slowly, the time measured by inches gained and inches seemingly lost, the tide slipped in under the whale and alleviated some of the deadness of its weight. The commander decided it was now or never and while Parker continued to keep the eyes of the whale clear and wet and the harness crew continued to keep the padding moist and pliable and unknotted, the ship eased aft, drawing the whale into the water, much to the disappointment of those in the crowd who'd wanted to see Mr. Death up close and big. Especially our little Mets fan. He nearly wept.

Pal and Quink ended up knee-deep in the surf, hands hanging at their sides as they watched the dinghy alongside the still passive leviathan, the crewmen risking their lives if the beast moved too suddenly, guiding the whale and working the harness. Once it was clear of the continental shelf and floating, the pressure on the harness released by the buoyancy of the water's salt, the white ship accelerated and it, along with the whale, shrank against the horizon.

"There it goes," Parker said. The harness flipped loose and the whale swiftly lifted its fluke to the sky and then disappeared.

"Hope he makes it," Pal said.

Neither of them admitted that nine out of ten whales that lose their way like this, try as they may to stay on course, simply turn in to shore and beach themselves farther south. If Pal knew it, anyway, he didn't let on. Both of them concentrated on imagining that this whale was the one in ten.

When finally Parker threw his arm over Pal's shoulder and they walked back up out of the surf, Amanda seemed worried, nervously shifting her weight on her feet and digging her toes into the sand. "What about you?" she asked, pointing at the ship steaming into the distance.

He grinned. "I'll catch up with 'em," he said. "Don't worry. Say, bro," he said, turning to Pal, "thanks."

He nodded. "You're welcome."

Still surprised by his color, he held up his hands like a child learning to catch a ball or a hobo to a warming fire, turning them over and back, pink black pink black. "Strange, ain't it?" he said. "Black like this."

He nodded. Tried to laugh. You could see the ache in his heart. He was afraid that if he cried out of happiness or sadness, if he even imagined saying the wrong thing, Parker would become stuck in this time, this place, in this color.

"Hey-uh," he said, trying to make him feel better. "Maybe you and me, we'll do something fun together one of these days soon?"

"You name it," Pal said, brightening, although his voice was still weak and hoarse from his nights of wishing. "We could go bowling," he said, at last. "If you're up to it. I'll even let you win."

He grinned. Looking down at his hands, he said, "Guess for sure we'll do some jazz, huh?"

Pal looked Quink in the eyes and smiled and nodded.

"Well," he said, reaching out and slapping him playfully upside the head. "Can't stay. Gotta travel on. Thanks again for getting involved."

"You're welcome," Pal replied.

"Feels good, don't it?"

"I guess. In a way," he said. He became thoughtful, entering that dreamy detachment he'd had ever since the day he was born. "This time." He tried to smile.

Parker Quink turned and started down the beach in the direction opposite to the one Pal and Mandy would take to their car.

Pal called after him, "Hey, Quink!"

Parker held up his hand without turning and kept going. Pal followed him with his eyes as far as he could, and then he was gone.

Pal sat down on the sand, knees tucked up, his chin resting on his arms. He gazed out toward the sun setting over the Pacific. For a long time, he sat there. Mandy sat beside him. She didn't speak. She let him be.

Finally, he said, "Well, we better be going too, don't you think?"

"Mind if I ask what that was all about?" Mandy asked.

"Nothing. Between him and me."

She walked along in silence. Then she said, "Yeah, but is what's between you and him going to be between you and me is the question."

Pal wasn't sure whether she meant between them as a dividing force or between them as a bond.

"Obviously, you know him from somewhere," she said.

"True," Pal replied. "At least I'm beginning to. I know some of his friends better. What I don't know is how it ends," he added. "Though I think I'm beginning to," he said in a whisper. He smiled at her.

"So?" she asked gently.

"So what?"

"What's he about?"

Pal opened the passenger door of her car and waited for her to get in, then circled behind the car and slipped behind the wheel. He started the car, and then hung his hands from the steering wheel, the motor idling, staring out the windshield. "Failure," he said. "I guess what it's about is failure. And love. How it takes the success of failure to make love up in a way you can live with."

Mandy frowned. But she didn't pursue it. She waited.

Later, after they'd consumed most of a pepperoni pizza they'd had delivered, he said, "By the way. Thanks."

"For what?"

"For not pushing." These days, couples seemed to turn each other into archaeological digs, turning up and dusting off the tiniest fragments of their characters and labeling them with pop psychology. It was as though you were supposed to apologize for being who you were, or wish that you'd had a different mother or father or something. But if you wished for that, you wouldn't be who you were and thus you would not be there with them, listening to them weave you into a basket they could put in their living rooms. Mandy seemed willing to let a little mystery live.

Even later still, after she'd asked if he minded if she stayed again and he said that he'd mind if she didn't, and after they sneaked off together into the bedroom for a while, he came back into the main room, tried to fill a Post-it, and gave up in frustration. He was shuffling out a solitary circle dance when Amanda appeared in the doorway to the bedroom wearing one of his T-shirts.

When he turned to look at her, she said, "I just wanted to tell you, I'm real. You know that, right? I'm real. And I'm here. And I plan on staying, if you want."

Chapter Nineteen

I.

She was real, all right, and not unlike any of the other girls or women he had known, she began to criticize his character. Her favorite time was after sex. With her thick brown legs drawn up like two tipis just after they had made love, she would say to him the things she needed to say. She started with the wide world and then eased down into the day-to-day, usually ending with him. Beginning with the way people no longer treated each other with respect or compassion, she could arrive at telling him that she did not appreciate the way he had treated her down at the Bran-Hol-A yesterday or the day before (she never let more than two days pass before she found a time and opportunity for speaking).

"When?" he might ask. "What?"

"When we were with Kitty and Skip?"

"Ah." He smiled and waited. He quickly learned that it was best if he did not protest, or attempt to offer any defense or excuse of his behavior. There was an important difference between the things Amanda said and the things someone else might say. One difference was that where Sally would have begun with Pal and extrapolated to the sins of the world, making Pal the cause of the sin, Amanda began with the error and worked down to Pal, making him not the cause of it, but only a

part of it. Sally isolated Pal. Amanda connected him, even if it was
something to which he did not necessarily want to be connected.
Amanda did not blame him for some failure of her own personal (and
hidden) agenda. Another difference was that there was seldom any rancor in what Amanda said, although there was always emotion in it.
And often, given the energy with which she had just finished pursuing
their mutual satisfaction, he was too content and could do little other
than hear and feel the emotion. But given the joy he felt, he did not
want to do other than hear and feel her emotion, and he lacked the energy or will to counter with his own emotion, unless it was with humor.

In general, her speaking these things prevents rancor from ever
forming. He's learning that he, too, sometimes needs to say things—
although most of the time he finds that the things he thinks he needs to
say seem unimportant or even stupid by the time he finds the right moment to bring them up. Besides, the waiting, the suspension, the looking
for the right moment to bring something up messes all the moments in
between with an awkwardness akin to the faint odor of dog poo on your
shoes. So he writes it down and waits to see what sticks.

"Sorry," he says. He does not ask her what she means. He just says,
"Sorry."

"Try not to do it again?"

"I'll try, okay?"

"Okay."

He won't spend too much time trying to envision what will have
happened down at the Bran-Hol-A over dried-up muffins and thin
clotberry tea, as they lie there side by side in the sand watching the stars
twink on one by one above the susurrus of the Pacific Ocean. Probably,
he will have been mean to her. He may think she is paying a little too
much attention to Skip Laudanum, maybe, or sucking up to Kitty Fishkill a few too many times. He knows himself well enough to expect he's
become snide by trying to become satirical.

Kitty teaches high school English and when she isn't rankling parents by teaching poems like "To Fuck Is to Love Again," she berates the
kids with the feelings of her four failed marriages. When she gets to re-

peating these things at the Bran-Hol-A, her fishhook nose flares its nostrils and her eyes start to waver with the challenge of gooseberry Jell-O. It irritates him the way she sort of includes Amanda by assumption. To Kitty, Amanda is a woman and therefore Amanda agrees with Kitty.

Mandy, though, just lets Kitty talk, even though the assumptions include him in a personal as well as a general way, and despite him wishing as hard as he can for her to reply for him, to defend him at least in the particulars, she won't. Instead, she laughs at what Kitty says about men, tossing him an understanding look that implicitly asks, "What do you care what Kitty thinks?"

He becomes sort of grim, remembering all those times people derided or teased him mercilessly for daring to disagree with them, his cheeks burning with the shame of his own stupidity. Even though he tries to say something funny, the reverberating memory of those failures will cause him to fail. He doesn't sound funny but snide or even cruel, which only confirms Kitty in her convictions.

As if that isn't painful enough, Skip Laudanum sits there smirking, making no bones about the fact that he wants to get into Amanda's art. He even says, as often he has said, that he doesn't see what she sees in him. And since Pal can't see it either, he hacks up the furball of a laugh—and fails to be funny there, as well. If only he could make up one reason for his Amanda to prefer him to the peaceful stupefaction of Skip, it would be easier to be nice to him, get Skip to like him more. They might even be friends, even though not close ones because he could never be direct enough to tell the Skipper how much Amanda dislikes him. Sure, she pretends otherwise, but that is only because he appreciates her elaborately and so she pretends to admire his complicated mental processes and the infinitesimal points of his arguments just like Pal smiles at his witticisms and laughs outright at his jokes.

So, he thinks, as they stroll to her car to drive homeward to watch some nightly news before she suggests they maybe take a walk down the mountain to get coffee, after which she can go to bed to read and he can settle into his chair in the living room, Perhaps I will tell her what I feel tonight. Will have felt, all the nights before. (How many have there been or how many should there be to give you a proper picture? A few? A lot? How much of the illusions of time, in other words, do you need?)

He clears his throat.

Mandy looks at him expectantly.

Maybe, though, he is making up the way Kitty Fishkill or Skipper Laudanum acts? Maybe he is imagining that when Kitty accuses white males of being the cause for all her failures she includes him in the category, like most people who conveniently forget Indians unless you remind them? Maybe he imagines that Kitty's white male also seems to include serial killers and rapists because he would never, in his wildest imaginings, dream of making a woman have sex with him; indeed, Mandy has complained that she can hardly tell when he wants to have sex.

"Unh-unh-uh-uh." He clears the questions from his throat.

"You okay?" Mandy asks.

He nods. Is he making Amanda up to be the way she is, romanticizing her the way Kitty romanticizes him into a killer-rapist? Being a white male is not a pleasant association, and he doesn't want to be associated with them any more than most white males do. To be Kitty's male is like finding a humongous wart on your dick that you kind of pretend isn't really there. When somebody notices, you have to reassure them ("Oh, that. It's just . . . well, it's nothing, really. . . . Yes, it's benign, I promise"). It makes you a great sympathizer, as though sympathizing could ever hide what's on your dick. But it does fool other people with warts. So when Kitty assumes he's just like her great white male—like Skipper Laudanum or the four she's practiced living with happily ever after in sickness and in health—he doesn't see any reason to say anything anymore. He just thinks about the wart Skipper's carrying around between his legs and grins. But while it makes him happy, it also makes him sad, and it confuses the way he behaves.

Probably, these are the things he should tell Amanda.

He will. But right at the moment Manny Mercury, the weatherperson, is telling them that they got nine-tenths of an inch of rain today with a high of sixty-six degrees.

"Felt more like an inch, inch and a half, to me," he blurts. "Look at my jacket. There's at least a foot of rain still on it."

Amanda knows what he's doing, taking issue with the facts, so that if she insists on one truth he can just as easily quibble his way into another. She looks up over the rim of her cup of Vienna Mint coffee and smiles. They're sharing an international moment, even though he refuses to drink the stuff himself because it tastes like toxic waste, which, if you ever make the mistake of allotting a major portion of your evening to reading the label, you realize is what it is.

"Swear it felt more like sixty-eight or -nine," he says. "Only sixty-six, though. Huh!"

"It matters, bozo," Mandy says, still grinning. She knows that this is one of his ways of saying things and it amuses her.

"Why?"

"People like to know."

"Why?"

"They just do, Pal," she says, laughing lightly as though his questions are ticklish, not irritating or annoying.

"They oughtta do the real weather," he says. Imitating Orin Overcast's voice, he says in sonorous, even, Skipper tones, "The average temperature in the financial district today was seventy degrees with a dew point between ten and noon. A slight drop in humidity, with dry winds in the after. Limos hit a record low of sixty-five while public transport remained stifling. I'll have a full report at eleven."

"Thanks, Orin," he says, adopting the fatuous voice of Dilly Schmaltz, the ditsy blond he's invented for the station to hire, to beef up the uglies of its anchor desk. Orin is no Pacino, after all. In fact, he looks a little like George Washington in a possum pelt toupee.

"What do ya have for the weekend?" Dilly giggles suggestively, as though the weekend, if fine, promises to find her performing in a two-piece in a beach party volleyball game.

"Empty," Orin replies, as though Orin, himself, controls the weather. "I'll tell you all about it."

"Goody," Dilly says, grinning at us while her high stiff hair continues to stare at Orin.

Amanda, his Amanda, laughs. She knows this is his way of saying something, and she knows it's just been said. What doesn't matter. She has already forgiven him without going into day-to-day detail or punishment.

That's Amanda.

2.

Mary Blue closes her eyes and rocks above her beadwork, her hands tracing the designs that she has worked into the cradle board, connecting with the swift skill of a blind woman the dots of the story. It is almost done. She feels alone, except for the echo in her heart of voices in the front of the house calling out, "Eat mackerel!" "Repeal the body and save your mind!" "Repent!" "Duck!" Things like that. Voices whose speakers are gone, now, on the journey of the dead. Though there is no one there, the voices are as real as ever, and she misses the speakers.

Her old friend Mercedes drops by to tell her that she should sell the cradle board for a lot of money when she's done. It is beautiful, filled with the curlicues of history, cul-de-sacs of love, and the bright white open hand of the future in which it will all be up to him. To Palimony.

"This looks public?" she says to Mercedes. If her work was appreciated in the glazed eyes of the general public it might mean that it wasn't any good. Even if it was good, it couldn't be long before some guy with unkempt hair-sprayed hair and a hip way of talking would come along with an advance for future work, which was really a way of buying the artist and not the art.

She remembers a painter friend of hers who thought she was so clever to make up an Indian name to sign on paintings she did quickly for money, leaving her time to do her private work. Georgia got so quick and so facile that she began to lose track of what was made up for the public and what was real and private, of what was bad and good. Her inner fear of the public eye overwhelmed her and she turned herself inside out. When Mary found her, she was hunkered down quivering in a corner of her studio, frightened not of the public, but the private eye.

Instead of arguing about it with Mercedes, she asks, "You want some of the Count?"

"*Por favor*," Mercedes says.

Mary sets down her beading and goes to the cupboard. She puts out cereal bowls, spoons, paper napkins. She decants a good half pint of cream into a small pitcher. The Count, as she calls the chocolate-flavored cereal, is really just her excuse for cream. She likes serving food. It's a gift. And it makes her feel less alone. It doesn't even matter what she serves, really, or to whom—if anyone. Although in her way of thinking, cooking, like speaking, is always for someone besides herself. She always makes the same amount of food. If she cooks too much, she takes the warm leftovers down the street to a neighbor's or out to whatever arroyo the growers have hidden the disgrace of the farm laborers' housing in. There is always someone who needs extra food, who can use it to fill a child's or her own stomach, and even produce a fleeting, but nonetheless felt, sense of hope. It is always someone with whom she feels connected afterwards, joined by something more substantial than emotion.

With Mercedes Rota she has shared so much food that they feel like sisters.

3.

"Twins," he says, shaking his head in amused disbelief. "You really did give her twins."

"Dark and confused by time," I tell him. "Me and Parker did it.

They weren't Mr. History's, of course. At least, not exactly. But we did give them names. The boy's name will be Paulie. The girl's is Ruthie. What do you think?"

He takes a bite of the stew meat I have served up for him in a Folgers can.

Pal had been standing beside a warming fire lit with colorful strips of fabric from a Hawaiian shirt that he tore up strip by strip and dropped into the oil drum. He watched the silky pieces of shirt float on the heated air momentarily before they burst into flame and sank, blackening, into the core of fire. From time to time the burning shreds popped, sending threads of sparks floating into the dusky sky beside the empty railroad tracks.

"Hey, yea," I greeted Pal.

"Hey," Pal replied.

"Nice fire. Mind if I use some of it?"

"Go ahead," he said.

He watched carefully as I used a bent coathanger to hang a five-pound Folgers can inside the oil drum. When it was heated properly, I took out two smaller Folgers cans from my knapsack, forked an equal amount of stew into each, and handed one to him.

"Juan Valdez, eh?" he said.

I grinned. "One of my cousins. Only kind tastes good," I said. "Maxwell House do something to stew. Though it's all right for soups. Good?"

He took a taste. The whites of his eyes flashed in the flickering light, surprised. "When did you learn to cook?" he asked.

I grinned again. Waved my hand in an arc to take in half the world around us. "Here and there. I been traveling, as you know. By the way, thanks for the words you give me."

"They all there?"

"More than enough," I said. "A couple that weren't mine." I paused, thinking. "I actually thought about making a little mouse or pet with the extras. You know, keep me company?"

"Yeah?"

"Yeah. Problem was, there wasn't enough to give it legs."

"Sorry," he said.

"No problem. You did good," I assured him. I set down my stew can. "Speaking of traveling," I said. I rummaged around and pulled out a round bundle wrapped carefully in soft white leather. I set it on the ground as gently as a sacred pipe is set before a pipe carrier and with tender respect, pulled back the wrappings leaf by leaf until he could see what it was.

"Got this on one of my travels," I said. "Recognize it?"

"A skull?"

"Yep. Know whose?"

"Not mine."

"Not true," I said. "You look at it closely, it's just like yours. The shape. See these two knobs? Like a valley between front and back?" I held the skull in my right hand and, closing my eyes, felt across the top of his head with my left. "Identical. 'Cause it is your skull, see. Maybe not the one you're wearing, but the one you got yours from.

"Yep-tee-do," I said, whistling through my teeth. "It's yours. Want to know where I got it? From an old man name of Reese in L.A. Reese Hall. He wasn't too happy about my taking it. He paid good money for it. Got it from a midnight archaeologist who took it from Nespelem. Dug it up and smuggled it to California and sold it to this Reese fellow, who used it as a candy dish. Kind of an unusual candy dish, don't you think?" I held it up and turned it slowly in the light, lovingly.

"Want to hold it?"

Pal took the skull gently into his hands. It weighed almost nothing.

"This Reese guy, he claimed that by using it for wrapped candies, and not as an ashtray or bird feeder, he was showing it the kind of respect it deserved. Managed to keep the bone courts from removing it from his possession because the Indian lawyers—remember those guys in La Vent's office with architect's tubes?—couldn't prove beyond a doubt whose skull it was. But I knew. Even without you and Mary Blue having skulls so like it that the resemblance was downright familial, if you know what I mean. I even offered to buy it from this Reese clown so I could return it where it belongs, but he wouldn't hear of it. So I waited till now, when I was traveling and I could just take it."

I grinned at him. "By the way, old Reese thinks the FBI man who took this skull into custody was named Lighters. Lionel Lighters. Seemed kinda fitting to me to use cousin Lionel's name. Family thing, I guess, since it is Mary's father's skull. Your grandfather's."

I carefully removed the skull from Pal's trembling hands and laid it back in the center of the white leather and began to rewrap it.

Three Southern Pacific diesels rumbled past us, shaking the ground as they dragged a long freight train through the yard behind them. I hopped up and dashed over to one of the hopper cars, jumping up on it long enough to look in and then was back at his side as quick as thunder rolls out of lightning.

"Maybe you take one of those chicas you wrote about to visit his bones, his bones'll be there, eh?"

"Doubt any of them would want to go," he said.

I raised my eyebrows at his tone. For a moment I felt myself drift and remember, drift and remember, slipping toward and away from what I'd come to say. "What about this new chiquita you're writing?"

"Amanda?" he said. "My Amanda?"

I nodded.

"Amanda Buenhuevo," he said dreamily.

"She Mexican?" I asked.

"I don't know," he said. "It doesn't matter. She's something."

"Something."

"Yeah."

I guess I knew what he meant. "How long you going to take to write her in completely?"

"What do you mean?"

"She needs more describing, doesn't she? Details. What she looks like. That kind of thing. How does she walk and talk?"

Dropping the last chunk of fabric into the fire, Pal closed his eyes and began to sway in the burst of heat.

"Like a duck," he said. "She walks like a duck. Or like someone trying to avoid stepping on serpentine cracks in the pavement."

"Not enough," I said, rummaging around in my knapsack again. This time I came up with manila envelopes full of sticky little Post-it notes.

"Hey, how did you get those?" he asked, recognizing the envelopes.

"Same way I got Reese's candy dish. I took it."

"Those don't belong to you like the skull does."

"How do you think I knew to give Tara twins?" I asked. I pulled out a group of Post-its I had banded together, took the band off, and flipped through them. "You know, it's strange," I said. "Mary Blue and I always thought you weren't listening. But here's a bunch all about Nez Perce land being stolen by people calling themselves settlers and the Nez Perce who helped them do it. Or these, all about how it's civilized people who let children starve or go to the workhouse or turn sooty tricks on the streets of cities. Or these three with the young La Vent's favorite dates on them: 1816. 1818. 1825."

I handed the batch to him.

He looked at them for a long moment, and then began dropping them one by one into his fire.

"Hey! What are you doing?" I asked.

"Dead lectures," he said. "Names and dates and questions that have to mean what people have already decided they have to mean. Not a single hidden meaning in one of them. Nothing that lets you glimpse the other side of things or look for what's behind or between the words like stories.

"Unless it's twins," he added, grinning as he took both of the manila folders out of my hands and tossed them unceremoniously into the oil drum, turning all his words into ash that rose on the heatedness and then floated away. "My Amanda shall go undetailed," he said. "That way, love is more flexible."

I was stunned, frankly. I dumped out the dregs of our stew and wiped out the cans with a rag before stowing them back in my knapsack. His eyes, as though magnetized with the same charge as my own, watched me sadly, as though he knew this was it, that with the words gone, there was little left to keep me there. His eyes were full of bitterness and joy, hope and despair, full of all things at once like layers of dye swirled together by convection in a pool.

"Well," I said, as a hotshot train of mail and perishable foods pulled into the far end of the yard and began to twist and scree toward us. "Guess I'll be going." I paused. "Hey," I said. "Thanks."

"For what?"

"For staying alive. For not becoming La Vent. Least not yet."

"He's my father."

"True. And everyone ends up like their parents. It's genetics. But the context is different and as long as you hold on to Amanda, your daughter and your son will have a real good chance to be different from La Vent. That's how things change."

"I'm to have a son, now?" he said.

"I didn't tell you? Parker and I worked up so much energy making sure Tara would have twins that we had a lot left over. We gave it to Mandy."

"A girl and a boy."

"Rachel, remember. And Willy. Just not La Vent. Under no circumstances."

"How is La Vent?"

"He's okay. He's in what the Christians call Limbo. Too bad, really. But that's what happens. He keeps himself busy trying to forgive you and Mary Blue for what you did to him. You know, be a real Christian. That's what he'll be doing forever after."

"Being a Christian?"

"Trying to forgive things that need no forgiving. But he can't. It takes a real live human being to forgive. The dead may only be forgiven."

With that I began to walk toward the point at which the hotshot freight would pass us, rising like a figure rises into the distance or into the graying perspective of a painting. He stood there slack-jawed as I swung up onto a piggyback trailer carrier and the train accelerated out of the yard.

EPILOGUE

The night in the mountains is pitch-dark. Like Frog from mud, the moon battles to emerge from a monstrous fog that has overcome the coastal range. Pal sits quietly in his living room, doodling an outline of Frog. He is waiting patiently for Mandy to tell him what she has wanted to tell him for weeks now. It seems to Pal that while it's their story, it is Mandy who must begin it.

Mary Blue leaves him there and goes into the bedroom. Lifting the blankets from Mandy, she reimagines the terrain of Amanda's belly, which used to be fine, almost flat, a small valley ridged by the low bluffs of her rib cage overlooking the soft quicksand of belly just above the snake of her panties. Nowadays, beginning to mound as it is, day by day stretching out farther and farther so the skin has begun to look as though, if it keeps it up, it will go pop! she seems so real that Mary wants to wake her up and tell her all about Sally and Tara, about La Vent, and about all the fathers and mothers before.

For her, for this love, she has made this cradle board, which she now lays beside her on the bed. She has tried, too, to make something of Pal for her. For her alone—in a way no one ever made anything for Tara. But the truth of these things seems but an image of time: There was this, then that, and because of this or that, some other *it* happened.

And she cannot buy the *because*. To buy the *because* seems to her to mean accepting the logic of victims who deny their own fault and even La Vent, who murmured halfway up Calvary Hill to the greatest excuse ever, did not deny his responsibility when in court the judge repeatedly asked him if he hadn't just meant to scare the mayor, not actually shoot him, and La Vent interrupted the muttering movement of his lips that later he would call prayer, looked up at the judge, and replied, "No, your honor. I meant to shoot off his dick," making Advil, Muhmed, Paquito, and Pal laugh at the gentle, almost innocent, self-possessed way in which La Vent said it. (The judge, of course, had to re-create his dignity and authority by threatening them with the very contempt of court that Advil and Muhmed carried with them like a virus.)

So it just was not all this then that. (By It, Mary meant Life—our life, your life, her life with La Vent, and her life without La Vent.) Neither the hunter nor the fisher of men—even La Vent's simulation of the fisher of men—can tabulate the hours by minutes, but must measure their days by Bear or Salmon flickering in the slant of sun. Life is not a matter of she was born, drank coffee, and died. Her life is not a progressive continuum but, like a fisherman, she is. Her life is not horizontal but vertical, and she is at all times her own end: At any moment, you can look down on her like a character in a book, look into the reservoir of all that she was, all that she remembers in beads or all that has been forgotten.

For a long time she worked on the cradle board. Every morning she got up and brewed herself coffee by boiling the grounds until the liquor was thick and black. Then she sat sipping half cups of coffee as the sun sank its fingernails into the coastal mountains and dragged itself up out of the east over Gilroy. Five days a week, just like going to work, she sat at her beading table listening to voices, meditating on the work she did the day before, thanking the sun for its light and warmth, and waiting for the knowledge of what work she wanted to do that day to slip into the frame of her vision.

She started with the blackjack hills of Oklahoma, added Snowbird (cornered in white across from Bear and Badger in their earth colors), Frog's and Salmon's rivers that ran through a valley like the Wallowa Valley of her grandmothers. She stitched on the hoof prints of Lewis and Clark with a cross of black beads bisecting their path and turning it into two paths, one for La Vent and one for her, journeys that merged before two smaller journeys branched out and divided, one running the right edge of the cradle board and the other the left, parallel and shaped the same though divided by their view of the beadwork between.

Because time kept shifting, because *Before* seemed to take up a position in *After* like a swamp one could foresee having to cross, it sometimes was difficult to decide of just what Truth a person like La Vent or Brandy or anyone else was or could be a part, especially if he or she would not hold still long enough to reply, "No. I meant to shoot off his dick." After all (or is it Besides?) when La Vent pulled out his der-ringer or when Tara danced for Pal in her half-slip or pulled away from him in the morning so as not to be late for a date, Amanda—Pal's Amanda—was only beginning to exist. Yet by the time Mandy picked him up hitchhiking the day Old Paint died, the change seemed no greater than the change from the snow-laden gray of winter to the rain-laden gray of spring. Amanda became clearer and more defined slowly, unnoticeably, more revealed, if you will, and yet never fixed or complete—the way real people are and not the way some people want them to be. And now, out of the right border, not far from a yellow car, also with a cross hidden in the yellow, came yet another smaller path of beads.

To her, the beads were like a book, and the people were like voices that through her hands had to speak. Sometimes (with my help, I have to say) the chorus of voices broke down into individual moments ("Loud dull boring voice," Tara sometimes said), words which, like the images in beadwork, until you got too close, you may not have heard or noticed. From the proper distance, by taking just a few steps back or by leaving the house to stand outside in the winds of change or the drizzle of the day-to-day, all the solitary voices became again one large one that was timeless, in which Before and After hardly matter, and in which everything—everything—came down to a matter of love.

Which is to say: Tomorrow they will be Now.

Which is to say: You remember, and you remember Now, and what you remember with love is what is important, not what you've forgotten by hatred, which you can never be sure of.

Which is to say: Though convenient because you can schedule when to get up and tie your shoes, when to salivate, or when it's nearing your time to die, Time does not exist. For Pal, for Mary, Time is always something foreign, brought to them on disease-infested blankets down the barrel of a rifle, and though the People learned about it well by waiting through the endless delays of justice, they knew then—in their hearts and bones—that this Time they were learning about was just the little moments of a timeless greed and an ageless fascination with cruelty. The little voices of death. And only the hungry, the grasping, the greedy, and the diseased live in that time, with those teeny voices. The rest speak according to their season, their voices soft and uncertain and sometimes so integrated into the chorus, seemingly without sound at all.

Which is to say: With love, death gives way to life.

Which is to say: Without dreaming. . . .

About the Author

W. S. Penn is a professor of English and resident writer at Michigan State University where he teaches Narrative Art and Aesthetics (prose) and Literature of the Americas (specializing in Chicano and Native American literature, the oral traditions, and the comic). An urban mixblood Nez Perce, his books include *The Absence of Angels* (novel), *All My Sins Are Relatives* (essays/autobiography), *The Telling of the World: Native American Stories and Art*, *As We Are Now: Mixblood Essays on Race and Identity*, *This Is the World* (stories), and *Feathering Custer* (essays). He has been the recipient of a Resident Artist Fellowship at the Banff Centre for the Arts in Canada, a New York Foundation for the Arts Award, the North American Indian Prose Award, the Stephen Crane Prize for Fiction, a Michigan Arts Council Award, and Writer of the Year (1997) and Editor of the Year (1998) from the Wordcraft Circle of Native Writers and Storytellers. Currently, he is working on a new novel. He lives in East Lansing with his wife, Jennifer, his daughter, Rachel Antonia, and his son, William Anthony.